W9-BDC-810

Outstanding critics and writers

WHEN SHE WAS GOOD

"It's the best book [Roth has] ever written . . . not a false note in the entire novel . . . high, careful tragedy, nasty as life, and Roth emerges as a sort of neo-Dreiser, but a Dreiser who can write!"

—Stanley Elkin, novelist

WHEN SHE WAS GOOD

"Fearfully and wonderfully penetrating . . . And it does its narrative job in so artful-artless a way. A wonder, really!"

—F. W. Dupee, literary critic

WHEN SHE WAS GOOD

"I'm delighted, shook and shaken with [Roth's] novel . . . Lucy is a most terrifying, pitiable heroine, in my imagination a kind of landlocked Joan of Arc."

—R. V. Cassill, novelist
and literary critic

WHEN SHE WAS GOOD

"Seems to me a true book: true to the coarse and banal texture of Lucy's life and true to the fatality of her twisted desires for respectability and control."

—Theodore Solotaroff,
literary critic

hail a great, new bestseller—

WHEN SHE WAS GOOD

"A great book . . . It cuts to the heart of a place, a tight, right American girl and, finally, the reader."

—The Nation

WHEN SHE WAS GOOD

"Remarkably compelling . . . Philip Roth is one of the country's finest, most forcefully intelligent and serious contemporary writers."

—The New York Times

WHEN SHE WAS GOOD

"Compassion mingles with horror in a superb portrayal of a young woman's obsession with moral rectitude."

—Saturday Review

WHEN SHE WAS GOOD

"A powerful study of character and circumstance . . . Brilliantly observed and in the end genuinely moving!

—Book-of-the-Month Club News

Bantam Books by Philip Roth
Ask your bookseller for the books you have missed

GOODBYE, COLUMBUS
LETTING GO
WHEN SHE WAS GOOD
PORTNOY'S COMPLAINT

When She Was Good

Philip Roth

BANTAM BOOKS

TORONTO · NEW YORK · LONDON

A NATIONAL GENERAL COMPANY

WHEN SHE WAS GOOD

*A Bantam Book / published by arrangement with
Random House, Inc.*

PRINTING HISTORY

*Random House edition published June 1967
3 printings through September 1967
Literary Guild of America edition published July 1967*

*Sections of this book have appeared, in slightly
different form, in the* ATLANTIC, HARPER'S,
the SATURDAY EVENING POST, *and* COSMOPOLITAN

Bantam edition published June 1968

2nd printing .... *June 1968*	6th printing .... *June 1969*
3rd printing ...... *August 1968*	7th printing .... *July 1969*
4th printing .... *March 1969*	8th printing ... *September 1969*
5th printing .... *April 1969*	9th printing .... *February 1970*

10th printing

11th printing

12th printing

13th printing

14th printing

To my brother Sandy;
to my friends Alison Bishop, Bob Brustein,
George Elliott, Mary Emma Elliott,
Howard Stein, and Mel Tumin;
and to Ann Mudge:
For words spoken and deeds done

I

1

Not to be rich, not to be famous, not to be mighty, not even to be happy, but to be civilized—that was the dream of his life. What the qualities of such a life were he could not have articulated when he left his father's house, or shack, in the northern woods of the state; his plan was to travel all the way down to Chicago to find out. He knew for sure what he didn't want, and that was to live like a savage. His own father was a fierce and ignorant man—a trapper, then a lumberman, and at the end of his life, a watchman at the iron mines. His mother was a hard-working woman with a slavish nature who could never conceive of wanting anything other than what she had; or if she did, if she was really other than she seemed, she felt it was not prudent to speak of her desires in front of her husband.

One of Willard's strongest boyhood recollections is of the time a full-blooded Chippewa squaw came to their cabin with a root for his sister to chew when Ginny was incandescent with scarlet fever. Willard was seven and Ginny was one and the squaw, as Willard tells it today, was over a hundred. The delirious little girl did not die of the disease, though Willard was later to understand his father to believe it would have been better if she had. In only a few years they were to discover that poor little Ginny could not learn to add two and two, or to recite in their order the days of the week. Whether this was a consequence of the fever or she had been born that way, nobody was ever to know.

Willard never forgot the brutality of that occurrence, which for him lay in the fact that nothing was to be done, for all that what was happening was happening to a one-year-old child. What was happening—this was more his sense of it at the time—was even deeper than his eyes . . . In the process of discovering his personal attractiveness, the seven-year-old had lately discovered that what someone had at first denied him would sometimes be conceded if only he looked into the other's eyes long enough for the honesty and intensity of his desire to be appreciated—for it to be understood that it wasn't just something he wanted but something he *needed*. His success, though meager at home, was considerable at the school in Iron City, where the young lady teacher had taken a great liking to the effervescent, good-humored and bright little boy. The night Ginny lay moaning in her crib Willard did everything he could to catch his father's attention, but the man only continued spooning down his dinner. And when finally he spoke, it was to tell the child to stop shuffling and gaping and to eat his food. But Willard could not swallow a single mouthful. Again he concentrated, again he brought all his emotion up into his eyes, wished with all his heart—and a pure selfless wish too, nothing for himself; never would he wish anything for himself again—and fixed his plea on his mother. But all she did was to turn away and cry.

Later, when his father stepped out of the shack and his mother took the dishes to the tub, he moved across the darkened room to the corner where Ginny lay. He put his hand into the crib. The cheek he touched felt like a sack of hot water. Down by the baby's burning toes he found the root the Indian woman had brought to them that morning. Carefully he wrapped Ginny's fingers around it, but they unbent the moment he let go. He picked up the root and pressed it to her lips. "Here," he said, as though beckoning to an animal to eat from his hand. He was forcing it between her gums when the door opened. "You—let her be, get away," and so, helpless, he went off to his bed, and had, at seven, his first terrifying inkling that there were in the universe forces even more immune to his charm, even more remote from his desires, even more estranged from human need and feeling, than his own father.

Ginny lived with her parents until the end of her mother's life. Then Willard's father, an old hulk of a thing by this time, moved into a room in Iron City, and Ginny was taken to Beckstown, off in the northwestern corner of the state, where the home for the feeble-minded used to be. It was nearly a month before the news of what his father had done reached Willard. Over his own wife's objections, he got into the car that very evening and drove most of the night. At noon the following day he returned home with Ginny—not to Chicago, but to the town of Liberty Center, which is a hundred and fifty miles down the river from Iron City, and as far south as Willard had gotten when at the age of eighteen he had decided to journey out into the civilized world.

Since the war the country town that Liberty Center used to be has given way more and more to the suburb of Winnisaw it will eventually become. But when Willard first came to settle, there was not even a bridge across the Slade River connecting Liberty Center on the east shore to the county seat on the west; to get to Winnisaw, you had to take a ferry ride from the landing, or in deep winter, walk across the ice. Liberty Center was a town of small white houses shaded by big elms and maples, with a bandstand in the middle of Broadway, its main street. Bounded on the west by the pale flow of river, it opens out on the east to dairy country, which in the summer of 1903, when Willard arrived, was so deeply green it reminded him—a joke for the amusement of the young—of a fellow he once saw at a picnic who had eaten a pound of bad potato salad.

Until he came down from the north, "outside of

town" had always meant to him the towering woods
rolling up to Canada, and the weather roaring down,
waves of wind, of hail, of rain and snow. And "town"
meant Iron City, where the logs were brought to be
milled, and the ore to be dumped into boxcars, the
clanging, buzzing, swarming, dusty frontier town to
which he walked each schoolday—or in winter, when
he went off in a raw morning dimness, ran—through
woods aswarm with bear and wolf. So at the sight of
Liberty Center, its quiet beauty, its serene order, its
gentle summery calm, all that had been held in check in
him, all that tenderness of heart that had been for
eighteen years his secret burden, even at times his
shame, came streaming forth. If ever there was a place
where life could be less bleak and harsh and cruel than
the life he had known as a boy, if ever there was a
place where a man did not have to live like a brute,
where he did not have to be reminded at every turn
that something in the world either did not like mankind, or did not even know of its existence, it was here.
Liberty Center! Oh, sweet name! At least for him, for
he was indeed free at last of that terrible tyranny of
cruel men and cruel nature.

He found a room; then he found a job—he took an
examination and scored high enough to become postal
clerk; then he found a wife, a strong-minded and respectable girl from a proper family; and then he had a
child; and then one day—the fulfillment, he discovered, of a very deep desire—he bought a house of his
own, with a front porch and a backyard: downstairs a
parlor, a dining room, a kitchen and a bedroom; upstairs two bedrooms more and the bath. A back
bathroom was built downstairs in 1915, six years after
the birth of his daughter, and following his promotion
to assistant postmaster of the town. In 1962 the side-
walk out front had to be replaced, a whacking expense
for a man now on a government pension, but one that
had to be, for the pavement had buckled in half a
dozen places and become a hazard to passers-by. Indeed, to this very day, when his famous agility, or
jumpiness, has all but disappeared; when several times

in an afternoon he finds himself in a chair which he cannot remember having settled into, awakening from a sleep he cannot remember needing; when at night to undo his laces produces a groan he does not even hear; when in his bed he tries for minutes on end to roll his fingers into a fist, and sometimes must go off to sleep having failed in the attempt; when at the end of each month he looks at the fresh new calendar page and understands that there on the pantry door is the month and the year in which he will most assuredly die, that one of those big black numerals over which his eye is slowly moving is the date upon which he is to disappear forever from the world—he nevertheless continues to attend as quickly as he is able to a weak porch rail, or the dripping of a spigot in the bathroom, or a tack come loose from the runner in the hall—and all this to maintain not only the comfort of those who live with him yet, but the dignity of all too, such as it is.

One afternoon in November of 1954, a week before Thanksgiving, and just at dusk, Willard Carroll drove out to Clark's Hill, parked down by the fence, and on foot climbed the path until he reached the family plot. The wind was growing colder and stronger by the minute, so that by the time he had reached the top of the hill, the bare trees whose limbs had only been clicking together when he left the car were now giving off a deep groaning sound. The sky swirling overhead had a strange light to it, though below, it already appeared to be night. Of the town he was able to discern little more than the black line of the river, and the head lamps of the cars as they moved along Water Street toward the Winnisaw Bridge.

As though this of all places had been his destination, Willard sank down onto the cold block of bench that faced the two stones, raised the collar of his red hunting jacket, pulled on the flaps of his cap, and there, before the graves of his sister Ginny and his granddaughter Lucy, and the rectangles reserved for the rest of them, he waited. It began to snow.

Waiting for what? The stupidity of his behavior

dawned quickly. The bus he had left the house to meet would be pulling up back of Van Harn's store in a few minutes; from it Whitey was going to disembark, suitcase in hand, whether his father-in-law sat here in a freezing cemetery or not. Everything was in readiness for the homecoming, which Willard had himself helped to bring about. So what now? Back out? Change his mind? Let Whitey find himself another sponsor—or sucker? That's right, oh, that's it exactly—let it get dark, let it get cold, and just sit it out in the falling snow . . . And the bus will pull in and the fellow will get off and head into the waiting room, all brimming over with how he has taken someone in once again—only to find that this time no sucker named Willard is waiting in the waiting room.

But at home Berta was preparing a dinner for four; on the way out the kitchen door to the garage, Willard had kissed her on the cheek—"It's going to be all right, Mrs. Carroll," but he might have been talking to himself for all the response he received. As a matter of fact, that's who he *was* talking to. He had backed the car down the driveway and looked up to the second floor, where his daughter Myra was rushing around her room so as to be bathed and dressed when her father and her husband came through the door. But saddest of all, most confusing of all, a little light was on in Lucy's room. Only the week before, Myra had pushed the bed from one end of the room to the other, and taken down the curtains that had hung there all those years, and then gone out and bought a new bedspread, so that at least it no longer looked like the room in which Lucy had slept, or tried to sleep, the last night she had ever spent in the house. Of course, on the subject of how and where Whitey was to spend his nights, what could Willard do but be silent? Secretly it was a relief that Whitey was to be "on trial" in this way—if only it could have been in a bed other than that one.

And over in Winnisaw, Willard's old friend and lodge brother Bud Doremus was expecting Whitey to show up for work at his hardware supply house first thing Monday morning. The arrangements with Bud dated back to the summer, when Willard had agreed to accept his son-in-law once again into his house, if only for a while. "Only for a while" was the guarantee he had made to Berta; because she was right, this just could not be a repetition of 1934, with someone in need coming for a short stay and managing somehow to stretch it out to sixteen years of living off the fat of another fellow's land, which wasn't so fat either. But of course, said Willard, that other fellow did happen to be the father of the man's wife— And just what does that mean, Berta asked, that it is going to be sixteen years again this time too? Because you are certainly still father to his wife; that hasn't changed any. Berta, I don't imagine for one thing that I have got sixteen years left to me, first of all. Well, said she, neither do I, which might be just another reason not even to begin. You mean just let them go off on their own? Before I even know whether the man really is changed over or not? asked Willard. And what if he really has reformed, once and for all? Oh sure, said Berta. Well, sneering at the idea may be your answer, Berta, but it just does not happen to be mine. You mean it does not happen to be Myra's, she said. I am open to opinion from all sides, he said, I will not deny that, why should I? Well then, maybe you ought to be open to mine, Berta said, before we start this tragedy one more time. Berta, he said, till January the first I am giving the man a place to get his bearings in. January the first, she said, but which year? The year two thousand?

Seated alone up in the cemetery, the tree limbs rising in the wind, and the dark of the town seemingly being drawn up into the sky as the first snow descended, Willard was remembering the days of the Depression, and those nights too, when sometimes he awoke in the pitch-black and did not know whether to tremble or be glad that someone in need of him was asleep in every bed of the house. It had been only six months after going off to Beckstown to rescue Ginny from her life among the feeble-minded that he had opened the door to Myra and Whitey and their little three-year-old daughter, Lucy. Oh, he can still remember the tiny, spirited, golden-haired child that Lucy had been—how lively and bright and sweet. He can remember when she was first learning to care for herself, how she used to try to pass what she knew on to her Aunt Ginny, but how Ginny, the poor creature, was barely able to learn to perform the simplest body functions, let alone mastering the niceties of tea parties, or the mystery of rolling two little white socks together to make a ball.

Oh, yes, he can remember it all. Ginny, a fully grown, fully developed woman, looking down with that pale dopey face for Lucy to tell her what to do next—and little Lucy, who was then no bigger than a bird. Behind the happy child, Ginny would go running across the lawn, the toes of her high shoes pointing out, and taking quick little steps to keep up—a strangely beautiful scene, but a melancholy one, too, for it was proof not only of their love for each other, but of the fact that in Ginny's brain so many things were melted together that in real life are separate and distinct. She seemed always to think that Lucy was somehow herself—that is, more Ginny, or the rest of Ginny, or the Ginny people called Lucy. When Lucy ate an ice cream, Ginny's eyes would get all happy and content, as though she were eating it herself. Or if as a punishment Lucy was put to bed early, Ginny, too, would sob and go off to sleep like one doomed . . . a different kind of scene, which would leave the rest of the family subdued and unhappy.

When it was time for Lucy to start school, Ginny started too, only she wasn't supposed to. She would follow Lucy all the way there, and then stand outside the first floor where the kindergarten was and call for the child. At first the teacher changed Lucy's desk in the hope that if Ginny didn't see her she would grow tired, or bored, and go home. But Ginny's voice only grew louder, and as a result Willard had to give her a special talking-to, saying that if she didn't let Lucy alone he was going to have to lock a bad girl whose name was Virginia in her room for the whole day. But the punishment proved toothless, both in the threat and the execution: the moment they let her out of her room to go to the toilet, she was running in her funny duck-like way down the stairs and off to the school. And he couldn't keep her locked up anyway. It wasn't to tie her to a tree in the backyard that he had brought his sister home to live in his house. She was his closest living relative, he told Berta, when she suggested some long kind of leash as a possible solution; she was his baby sister to whom something terrible had happened when she was only a one-year-old child. But Lucy, he was reminded—as if he had to be—was Myra's daughter and his grandchild, and how could she ever learn anything in school if Ginny was going to stand outside the classroom all day long, singing out in her flat foghorn of a voice, "*Loo*—cy . . . *Loo*-cy . . ."?

Finally the day came which made no sense whatsoever. Because Ginny wouldn't stop standing outside a grade-school classroom calling out a harmless name, Willard was driving her back to the state home in Beckstown. The night before, the principal had telephoned the house again, and for all his politeness, indicated that things had gone about as far as they could. It was Willard's contention that it was probably only a matter of a few weeks more before Ginny got the idea, but the principal made it clear to Mr. Carroll. as he had a moment earlier to the little girl's parents, that either Ginny had to be restrained once and for all, or Lucy would have to be kept away from the school, which of course would be in violation of state law.

On the long drive to Beckstown, Willard tried over and over again to somehow make Ginny understand the situation, but no matter how he explained, no matter how many examples he used—look, there's a cow, Ginny, and there's another cow; and there's a tree, and there's another tree—he could not get her to see that Ginny was one person and Lucy was someone else. Around dinnertime they arrived. Taking her by the hand, he led her up the overgrown path to the long one-story wooden building where she was to spend the rest of her days. And why? Because she could not understand the most basic fact of human life, the fact that I am me and you are you.

In the office the director welcomed Ginny back to the Beckstown Vocational School. An attendant piled a towel, a washrag and a blanket into her outstretched arms and steered her to the women's wing. Following the attendant's instructions, she unrolled the mattress and began to make the bed. "But this is what my father did!" thought Willard. "Sent her away!" ... even as the director was saying to him, "That's the way it is, Mr. Carroll. People thinking they can take 'em home, and then coming to bring 'em back. Don't feel bad, sir, it's just what happens."

Among her own kind Ginny lived without incident for three years more; than an epidemic of influenza swept through the home one winter, and before her brother could even be notified of her illness, she was dead.

When Willard drove up to Iron City to tell his father the news, the old man listened, and received what he heard without so much as a sigh; not a single human thing to say; not a tear for this creature of his own flesh and blood, who had lived and died beyond the reaches of human society. To die alone, said Willard, without family, without friends, without a home ... The old man only nodded, as though his heartsick son were reporting an everyday occurrence.

Within the year the old man himself fell over dead with a brain hemorrhage. At the small funeral he arranged for his father up in Iron City, Willard found himself at the graveside suddenly and inexplicably stricken with that sense of things that can descend upon the tender-hearted, even at the death of an enemy— that surely the spirit had been deeper, and the life more tragic, than he had ever imagined.

He brushed the snow off the shoulder of his jacket and stamped away a tingling that was beginning in his right foot. He looked at his watch. "Well, maybe the bus will be late. And if it's not, he can wait. It won't kill him."

He was remembering again: of all things, the Independence Day Fair held in Iron City—that Fourth of July almost sixty years back when he had won eight of the twelve track events and so set a record that stands till today. Willard knows this because he always manages to get hold of an Iron City paper every fifth of July just so as to take a look and see. He can still remember running home through the woods when that glorious day was over, rushing up the dirt road and into the cabin, dropping onto the table all the medals he had been awarded; he remembers how his father hefted each one in his hand, then led him back outside to where some of the neighbors were gathered, and told Willard's mother to give them an "on your mark." In the race that followed, some two hundred yards, the father outdistanced the son by a good twenty feet. "But I've been running all day," thought Willard. "I ran the whole way home—"

"Well, who's the fastest?" one of the bystanders teased the boy as he started back to the cabin.

Inside, his father said, "Next time don't forget."

"I won't," said the child . . .

Well, there was the story. And the moral? What exactly were his memories trying to tell him?

Well, the moral, if there is one, came later, years later. He was sitting in the parlor one evening, across from his young son-in-law, who had stretched himself out with the paper and was about to munch down on an apple and so let the comfortable evening begin, when suddenly Willard couldn't bear the sight of him. Four years of free room and board! Four years of floundering and getting on his feet again! And there he was, on his back, in Willard's parlor, eating Willard's food! Suddenly Willard wanted to pull the apple out of Whitey's hand and tell him to pick up and get out. "The holiday is over! Scat! Go! Where. I don't care!" Instead he decided that it was a good night to give his mementos a look-through.

In the kitchen pantry he found a piece of soft cloth and Berta's silver polish. Then from beneath the wool skirts in his bureau he removed the cigar box full of keepsakes. Settling onto the bed, he opened the box and sorted through. He pushed everything first to one side, then to the other; in the end he laid each item out on the bedspread: photos, newspaper clippings ... The medals were gone.

When he came back into the living room, Whitey had fallen off to sleep. The snow drifts, Willard saw, were floating up to obscure the glass; across the street the houses looked to be going down into the rising white waves. "But it can't be," thought Willard. "It just can't. I am jumping to a rash conclusion. I am——"

During his lunch hour the next day, he decided to take a walk down to the river and back, stopping on the way at Rankin's pawnshop. Ha-haa-ing all the while, as though the whole affair had been a family prank, he recovered the medals.

After dinner that night he invited Whitey to come with him for a brisk walk downtown. What he said to the young fellow, once they were out of sight of the house, was that it was absolutely and positively beyond his understanding how a man could take the belongings of another man, go into a person's private belongings and just *take* something, particularly something of sentimental value: nevertheless, if he could receive from Whitey certain assurances about the future, he would be willing to chalk up this unfortunate incident to a combination of hard times and immature judgment. Pretty damn immature judgment too. But then, no one deserved to be discarded from the human race on the basis of one stupid act——a stupid act you might expect of a ten-year-old, by the way, and not a fellow who was twenty-eight, going to be twenty-nine. However, the medals were back where they belonged, and if he were given an ironclad promise that nothing like this would ever happen again, and furthermore, if Whitey promised to cut out immediately this new business of whiskey drinking, then he would consider the matter closed. Here he was, after all, a fellow who for three years running had been third baseman on the Selkirk High School baseball team; a young man with the build of a prizefighter, good-looking too—Willard said all this right out—and what was his intention, to wreck the healthy body the good Lord had blessed him with? Respect for his body alone ought to make him stop; but if that didn't work, then there was respect for his family, and for his own human soul, damn it. It was up to Whitey entirely: all he had to do was turn over a new leaf, and as far as Willard was concerned, the incident, stupid, mean and silly as it was, beyond human comprehension as it was, would be completely forgotten. Otherwise, there were no two ways about it, something drastic was going to have to be done.

So overcome was he with shame and gratitude that first all the young man could do was take hold of Willard's hand and pump it up and down, all the while with tears glistening in his eyes. Then he set out to explain. It had happened in the fall, when the circus had come to the armory down in Fort Kean. Right off Lucy had started talking a mile a minute about the elephants and the clowns, but when Whitey looked in his pocket he found only pennies, and not too many of them either. So he thought if he borrowed the medals, and then returned them a few weeks later . . . But here Willard remembered just who it was that had taken Lucy down to the circus, and Myra and Whitey and Berta too. None other than himself. When he pointed out this fact, Whitey said yes, yes, he was coming to that; he was, he admitted, saving the most shameful for the last. "I suppose I am just a coward, Willard, but it's just hard to say the worst first." "Say it anyway, boy. Make a clean breast of the whole thing."

Well, confessed Whitey, as they turned off Broadway and started back home, after having borrowed the medals he was so appalled and shocked with himself that instead of using the money as he had intended, he had gone straight over to Earl's Dugout and made himself numb on whiskey, hoping thereby to obliterate the memory of the stupid, vicious thing he had just done. He knew he was confessing to terrible selfishness, followed by plain idiocy, but that was exactly how it had happened; and to tell the truth, it was all as mysterious to him as it was to anyone else. It had been the last week of September, just after old man Tucker had had to lay off half the shop . . . No, no—removing a calendar from his wallet, studying it under the front-porch light as they both stood stamping the snow off their boots—as a matter of fact it was the first week of October, he told Willard, who earlier in the day had had the date fixed for him by the clerk at Rankin's as just two weeks back.

But by this time they were already inside the door. Knitting by the fire was Berta; sitting on the couch, holding Lucy in her lap, was Myra—reading to the child from her poem book before sending her off to sleep. No sooner did Lucy see her Daddy than she slid from her mother's lap and came running to drag him off to the dining room, to play their nightly "yump" game. It had been going on for a year, ever since Whitey's old father had seen the tiny child go leaping from the dining-room window seat down to the rug. "Hey," the big farmer had called out to the others, "Lucy yumped!" That was how he pronounced it, for all that he had been a citizen of this country for forty years. After the old man's death it became Whitey's task to stand admiringly before his daughter, and after each leap, sing out those words she just adored to hear. "Hey, Lucy yumped! Yump again, Lucy-Goosie. Two more yumps and off to bed." "No! Three!" "Three yumps and off to bed!" "No four!" "Come on, yump, yump, and stop complaining, you little yumping goose! Hey, Lucy is about to yump—Lucy is ready to yump— ladies and gentlemen, Lucy has just yumped once again!"

So what could he do? In the face of that scene, what on earth could he possibly do? If after the long deliberation of that afternoon he had decided to consider Whitey's theft forgivable, was he now going to bother to catch his son-in-law in a petty face-saving lie? Only why, why if Whitey felt so depraved after taking the medals, why in hell didn't he put them back? Wasn't that just about the easiest thing for him to do? Now why hadn't he thought to ask him that? Oh, but he was so busy trying to be rough and tough and talking no-nonsense and letting there be no two ways about it, and so on, that the question hadn't even passed through his mind. Hey, you, why didn't you put my medals back if you felt so awful about it?

But by this time Whitey was carrying Lucy up the stairs on his shoulders—"Yump, two, three, four"—and he himself was smiling at Myra, saying yes, yes, the men had had a good bracing walk.

Myra. Myra. Without a doubt she had been the most adorable child a parent could dream of having. Mention a thing girls do, and Myra was doing it while the other little girls were still taking from the bottle. Always she was practicing something feminine: crocheting, music, poetry ... Once at a school program she recited a patriotic poem she had written all by herself, and when it was finished some of the men in the audience had stood up and applauded. And so beautifully behaved was she that when the ladies came to the house for a meeting of the Eastern Star—back when they were still a family of three and Berta had the time to be active—they used to say it was perfectly all right with them if little Myra sat in a chair and watched.

Oh, Myra! A pure delight to behold—always tall and slender, with her soft brown hair, and her skin like silk, and with Willard's gray eyes, which on her were really something; sometimes he imagined that his sister Ginny might have been much like Myra in appearance—fragile, soft-spoken, shy, with the bearing of a princess—if only it hadn't been for the scarlet fever. Back when she was a child the very frailty of his daughter's bones could bring Willard almost to tears with awe, especially in the evening when he sat looking over the top of his paper at her as she practiced her piano lesson. There were times when it seemed to him as though nothing in the world could so make a man want to do good in life as the sight of a daughter's thin little wrists and ankles.

Earl's Dugout of Buddies. If only they had knocked that place down years and years ago! If only it had never even been . . . At Willard's request they had agreed to stop letting Whitey drink himself into a stupor at the Elks, and at Stanley's Tavern too (now under new management—the thought occurred to him as the streetlights went on down in town), but for every human or even semi-human bartender, another (named Earl) was actually *amused* to take the pay check of a husband and a father and cash it for him. And the ironic part was that in that whole so-called Dugout of Buddies there was probably never a man who was one-tenth the worker, or the husband, or the father that Whitey was—that is, when things weren't overwhelming him. Unfortunately, however, circumstances seemed always to conspire against him at just those times, rarely more than a month at a stretch, when he was suffering through a bad siege of what you finally had to call by its rightful name—lack of character. Probably that Friday night he would at worst have weaved up the walk, thrown open the door, made some insane declaration, and dropped into bed with his clothes on—that and no more if circumstances, or fate, or whatever you wanted to call it, hadn't arranged for his first vision upon entering the house to be his wife Myra, soaking those fragile little feet of hers in a pan of water. Then he must have seen Lucy bent over the dining table, and understood (as he could understand, down in that alcoholic fog, if he believed an insult was involved) that she had pushed back the lace luncheon cloth and was doing her homework downstairs so that her mother wouldn't have to face the dragon alone when he returned.

Willard and Berta had gone off to play their Friday rummy. Driving to the Erwins' that night, he agreed that this time they were staying clear through to coffee and cake, like normal people, no matter what. If Willard wanted to go home early, said Berta, that was his business. She herself worked hard all week, and had few pleasures, and she simply would not cut short her night out because her son-in-law had come to prefer drinking whiskey in a musty bar at the end of the day to eating a home-cooked dinner with his family. There was a solution to the problem, and Willard knew very well what it was. But she would tell him one thing—it wasn't giving up the Friday night rummy game and the company of her old friends.

But Myra soaking her feet ... Something told him he shouldn't go off leaving her that way. Not that she was suffering so from the pain, not as she did in later years with her migraines. It was just the *picture* that he didn't like somehow. "You should sit down, Myra. I don't see why you have to stand so much." "I do sit, Daddy. Of course I sit." "Then how come you're having this feet trouble." "It's not trouble." "It's from giving them lessons all afternoon long, Myra, standing over that piano." "Daddy, no one stands over a piano." "Then where did this feet business come from . . . ?" "Daddy, please." What more could he do? He called into the dining room, "Good night, Lucy." When she failed to respond, he walked over to where she sat writing in her notebook and touched her hair. "What's got your tongue, young lady? No good night?" 'Good night," she mumbled, without bothering to look up.

Oh, he knew he ought not to leave. But Berta was already sitting out in the car. No, he just did not like the look of this scene. "You don't want to soak them too long, Myra." "Oh, Daddy, have a nice time," she said, and so at last he went out the door and down to the car to be told that it had taken him five full minutes to say a simple thing like good night.

Well, it was just as he had expected: when Whitey got home, he didn't like the scene either. The first suggestion he had for Myra was that she might at least pull the shades down so that everybody who walked by didn't have to see what a suffering martyr she was. When in her panic she didn't move, he pulled on one to show her how and it came clear off the fixture. She had only taken on all those piano students (seven years earlier, he neglected to add) so as to turn herself into a hag anyway, to cause him, if she could manage it— this, waving the shade in his hand—to start running around with other women, and then have that to cry over as well as her poor crippled toesies. Why she taught piano was the same damn reason she wouldn't go down with him to Florida and let him start a brand-new life down there. Out of disrespect for what he was!

She tried to tell him what she had told her father—that she believed there was no essential connection between her feet and her job—but he would not hear of it. No, she would rather sit up here with her poor toesies, and listen while everybody told her what a no-good rotten s.o.b. she had for a husband, just because he liked to have a drink once in a while.

There was apparently nothing that a man shouldn't say to a woman—even to one he hates, and the fact was that Whitey loved her, adored her, worshiped her—that he didn't say to Myra. Then, as if a torn shade and a broken fixture and all those garbled insults weren't enough for one night, he picked up the dishpan full of warm water and Epsom salts, and for no rational reason in the world, poured it out on the rug.

Most of what happened subsequently Willard learned from a sympathetic lodge brother who was on duty in the squad car that night. Apparently the police tried as best they could to make it look friendly, and not like an out-and-out arrest: they drove up without the siren blowing, parked out of the glow of the street lamp, and stood patiently in the hallway while Whitey worked at buttoning up his jacket. Then they led him down the front steps and along the path to the patrol car so that to the neighbors in the windows it might appear that the three men were just off for one of those bracing strolls, two of them wearing pistols and cartridge belts. They were not so much holding him down as up, and trying to joke him along some too, when Whitey, using all his physical strength, broke from between them. In the first moment no one watching could figure out what he was doing. His body folded once in half, so that for a moment he seemed to be eating the snow; then with a jerk he straightened up, and swaying as if in a wind, heaved an armful of snow toward the house.

The powder fell upon her hair and her face and the shoulders of her sweater; but for all that she was only fifteen, and with her upturned nose and her straight blond hair looked to be no more than ten, she did not so much as flinch; she stood as she was, one loafer on the bottom step and one on the walk, and a finger in her schoolbook—all ready, it seemed, to return to her studies which she had interrupted only to dial the station house. "Stone!" Whitey shouted. "Pure stone!" And here he made his lunge. Willard's lodge brother, frozen till then by the scene—by Lucy, he said, more than by Whitey, whose kind he'd seen before—leaped to his duty. "Nelson, it's your own kid!" Whereupon the drunk, either remembering that he was father to the girl, or hoping to forget that connection for good, evaded the policeman's grasp and went ahead and did apparently all it was he had intended to do in the first place: he pitched himself face-down into the snow.

The following morning Willard sat Lucy down first thing and gave her a talking-to.

"Honey, I know you have been through a lot in the last twenty-four hours. I know you have been through a lot in your whole life that would have been better for you never to have seen. But, Lucy, I have got to ask you something. I have got to make something very clear. Now, I want to ask why, when you saw what was happening here last night—Lucy, look at me—why didn't you phone me out at the Erwins'?"

She shook her head.

"Well, you knew we were out there, didn't you?"

To the floor she nodded.

"And the number is right there in the book. Well, isn't that so, Lucy?"

"I didn't think of it."

"But what you did think of, young lady—*look at me!*"

"I wanted him to *stop!*"

"But calling the jail, Lucy—"

"I called for somebody to make him stop!"

"But why didn't you call *me*? I want you to answer that question."

"Because."

"Because why?"

"Because you can't."

"I *what?*"

"Well," she said, backing away, "you don't . . ."

"Now sit down, now come back here, and listen to me. First thing—that's it, sit!—whether you know it or not, I am not God. I am just me, that's the first thing."

"You don't have to be God."

"No backtalk, you hear me? You are just a schoolchild, and maybe, just maybe, you know, you don't know the whole story of life yet. You may think you do, but I happen to think different, and who I am is your grandfather whose house this is."

"I didn't ask to live here."

"But you do, you see! So quiet! You are never to call the jail again. They are not needed here! Is that clear?"

"The police," she whispered.

"Or the police! Is that clear or not?"

She did not answer.

"We are civilized people in this house and there are some things we do not do, and that is number one. We are not riffraff, and you remember that. We are able to settle our own arguments, and conduct our own affairs, and we don't require the police to do it for us. I happen to be the assistant postmaster of this town, young lady, in case you've forgotten. I happen to be a member in good standing of this community—and so are you."

"And what about my father? Is he in good standing too, whatever that even *means?*"

"I am not talking about him right this minute! I will get to him, all right, and without your help too. Right now I am talking about you and a few things you may not know at fifteen years of age. The way we do it in this house, Lucy, is we talk to a person. We show him the right."

"And if he doesn't know it?"

"Lucy, we do not send him to jail! That's the only point. Is it clear?"

"No!"

"Lucy, I ain't the one who is married to him, Lucy. I don't live in the same room with him, Lucy."

"So *what?*"

"So what I am saying to you is that a lot of things, a great many things, you do not know the slightest thing about."

"I know it's your house. I know you give him a home, no matter what he does to her, or says to her—"

"I give my daughter a home, that's what I do. I give you a home. I am in a situation, Lucy, and I do what I can for the people I happen to love around here."

"Well," she said, beginning to cry, "you're not the only one who does, maybe, you know."

"Oh, I know that, I know that, sweetheart. But, honey, don't you see, they're your parents."

"Then why don't they act like parents!" she cried, rushing out of the room.

Then Berta started in.

"I heard what she said to you, Willard. I heard that tone. It's what *I* get all the time."

"Well, I get it too, Berta. We all get it."

"Then what are you going to do about it? Where will it stop with her? I thought becoming a Catholic at the age of fifteen was going to be the last thing up her sleeve. Running off to a Catholic church, going up to visit nuns for a whole weekend. And now this."

"Berta, I can only say what I can say. I only got so many words, and so many different ways to say them, and after that—"

"After that," said Berta, "a good swat! Whoever in their life heard of such a thing? Making a whole household into a public scandal—"

"Berta, she lost her head. She got scared. *He* made the scandal, the damn idiot, doing what he did."

"Well, any fool could have seen it coming a mile away. Any fool can see the next thing coming too— probably involving the Federal Bureau of Investigation."

"Berta, I'll take care of it. Exaggerating don't help things at all."

"How are you going to start taking care of it, Willard? By going down to the jail and letting him out?"

"I am deciding about that right now, what I'm going to do."

"I want to remind you, Willard, while you are deciding, that Higgles were among the founders of this town. Higgles were amongst the first settlers who built this town from the ground. My grandfather Higgle built the jail, Willard—I am glad he is not alive to see who it was he built it for."

"Oh, I know all that, Berta. I appreciate all that."

"Don't you make light of my pride, Mr. Carroll. I am a person too!"

"Berta, she won't do it again."

"Won't she? Beads and saints and every kind of Catholic gimcrack she has got up in that room of hers. And now this! She's taking over here, as far as I can see."

"Berta, I have explained to you: *she got frightened.*"

"And who isn't when that barbarian goes on the warpath? In the olden days a man like that, they would put him on a rail and run him out of town."

"Well, maybe this ain't the olden days any more," he said.

"Well, more's the pity!"

Lastly Myra. His Myra.

"Myra, I am sitting here debating what to do. And I am really of two minds, I'll tell you that. What has happened here, I never thought I would ever live to see. I have spoken to Lucy. I have gotten her to promise that nothing like this is ever going to happen again."

"She promised?"

"More or less, I would say, yes. And I have just finished talking with your mother. She is at the end of her tether, Myra. I can't say that I blame her. But I believe I have made her see the light. Because her feeling, to put it blunt, is to let him sit in that jail and rot."

Myra closed her eyes, so deep, so deep in purple rings from all her secret weeping.

"But I have calmed her down," he said.

"Yes?"

"More or less, I think so. She is going to accept my judgment of the thing. Myra," he said, "it has been a long twelve-year haul. For everybody living here it has been a long struggle."

"Daddy, we're going to move, so it's over. The struggle is over."

"*What?*"

"We're going to Florida."

"Florida!"

"Where Duane can start fresh—"

"Myra, there ain't a morning of his life he can't start fresh, and right here."

"But here someone else's roof, Daddy, is over his head."

"And how come? Well, what's the answer, Myra? Where is it he is going to get stick-to-it-iveness in Florida that he is not able to have up here? I'd like to know."

"He has relatives in Florida."

"You mean now he's going to go down and live off them?"

"Not live *off* them—"

"And suppose last night had happened in Florida. Or Oklahoma. Or wherever!"

"But it wouldn't!"

"And why not? The nice climate? The beautiful color of the sky?"

"Because he could be on his own. That's all he wants."

"Honey, it's all I want too. It's what we all want. But where is the evidence, Myra, that on his own, with a daughter, with a wife, with all the thousand responsibilities—"

"But he's such a good man." Here she began to sob. "I wake up in the night—oh, Daddy, I wake up, and 'Myra,' he says to me, 'you are the best thing I have,

Myra—Myra, don't hate me.' Oh, if only we could
go—"

In the middle of her very first semester, when Lucy
came home at Thanksgiving time to say that she was
getting married, Whitey sat himself down on the edge
of the sofa in the parlor and just caved in. "But I
wanted her to be a college graduate," he said, lowering
his head into his hands, and the sounds that emerged
from his mouth might have softened in you everything
that had hardened against him, if you didn't have to
wonder if that wasn't why he was making the sounds in
the first place. For the first hour he wept steadily like a
woman, then gaspingly like a child for another, until
even though he wanted you to forgive him, you almost
had to anyway, watching him have to perform that way
within plain view of his own family.

And then the miracle happened. At first he looked to
be sick, or maybe even about to do something to himself. It was actually frightening to see. For days on end
he hardly ate, though he was there at every dinner hour;
in the evening he would sit out on the front porch,
refusing to speak or to come in out of the cold. Once in
the middle of the night Willard heard moving in the
house and came into the kitchen in his robe to see
Whitey looming over a cup of coffee. "What's the trouble, Whitey, can't you sleep?" ". . . don't want to
sleep." "What is it, Whitey? Why are you all dressed?"
Here Whitey turned to the wall, so that all Willard
could see, as his son-in-law's whole big body began to
tremble, was the back of his broad shoulders and his
wide powerful neck. "What is it, Whitey, what is it you
are thinking of doing? Now tell me."

The day after Lucy's wedding Whitey came down to
breakfast wearing a tie with his workshirt, and went off
to the shop that way; at home in the evening he took
out the box of brushes, rags and polish and gave his
shoes a shine that looked to be professional. To Willard
he said, "Want one, while I'm at it?" And so Willard
handed over his shoes and sat there in his stockinged

feet while the incredible happened before his very eyes.

When the weekend came Whitey whitewashed the basement and chopped practically a whole cord of wood; Willard stood at the kitchen window watching him bring down the ax in violent, regular whacks.

So that month passed, and the next, and though eventually he came out of the silent morbid mood and took up a little more his old teasing and kidding ways, there could no longer be any doubt that at long last something had happened to penetrate his heart.

That winter he grew his mustache. Apparently in the first weeks he got the usual jokes from the boys at the shop, but he just kept on with it, and by March you actually forgot how he used to look, and began to believe that the big strapping healthy misdirected boy had, at the age of forty-two, decided to become a man. More and more Willard heard himself calling him, as Berta and Myra always had, by his given name, Duane.

He actually began to behave now as Willard had had every reason to expect he would, given the eager young fellow he had been back in 1930. At that time he was already a first-rate electrician, and a pretty good carpenter too, and he had plans, ambitions, dreams. One of them was to build a house for himself and Myra, if only she would be his bride: a Cape Cod-style house with a fenced-in yard, to be built with his own hands . . . And that wasn't so far-fetched a dream either. At the age of twenty-two he seemed to have the strength and the vigor for it, and the know-how too. The way he figured it, with the exception of the plumbing (and a friend over in Winnisaw had already agreed to install the piping at cost), he could put up a whole two-story house in six months of nights and weekends. He even went ahead and plunked down a one-hundred-dollar deposit on a tract of land up at the north end, a wise move too, for what was only woods then was now Liberty Grove, the fanciest section of the town. He had plunked down a deposit, he had begun to draw up his own building plans, he was halfway into his first year of marriage, when along came national calamity—followed quickly by the birth of a daughter.

As it turned out, Whitey took the Great Depression very personally. It was as though a little baby, ready to try its first step, stands up, smiles, puts out one foot, and one of those huge iron balls such as they used to knock down whole buildings comes swinging out of nowhere and wallops him right between the eyes. In Whitey's case it took nearly ten years for him to get the nerve to stand up and even try walking again. On Monday, December 8, 1941, he took the bus down to Fort Kean to enlist in the United States Coast Guard, and was rejected for heart murmur. The following week he tried the Navy, and then his last choice, the Army. He told them how he had played three years of ball up at the old Selkirk High, but to no avail. He wound up working over in the fire-extinguisher plant in Winnisaw for the duration, and in the evenings was less and less at home and more and more at Earl's Dugout.

But now, here he was on his feet again, informing Myra that when the school year was over she was to call the parents of her students and tell them that she was going out of the piano business. She knew as well as he did that when she had started giving lessons it was only supposed to be temporary anyway. He should never have allowed her to keep it up, even if it did mean extra dollars coming in every week. And he didn't *care* whether she didn't mind occupying herself that way or not. That wasn't the issue. The issue was, he did not require a cushion behind him to catch him if he fell. Because he wasn't falling any longer. That was the whole trouble to begin with: he had gotten himself all those props and cushions to give him a start back into the world, and all they had done was impede his progress by reminding him of the failure he had been, right off the bat. Somehow you start thinking you're a failure, and that there's nothing to do about it, and so the next thing you know there is nothing you *are* doing about it, except failing some more. Drinking, and losing

jobs, and getting jobs, and drinking, and losing them
... It's a vicious cycle, Myra.

Maybe, he said, if he had gone into the Army he
would have come out of that experience a different
person, with some of his confidence back. But instead
he had to walk the streets of Liberty Center all those
years while other men were risking their lives—and
while people in town wondered how a big bruiser like
Whitey Nelson had got out of the fighting and dying,
and pointed a finger at him under their breath for living
off his father-in-law. No, no, Myra, I know what people
gossip, I know what they say—and the worst of it is,
they are probably right. No, heart murmur isn't a person's fault, I know that; no, the Depression isn't a
person's fault either, but this isn't the Depression any
more, you know. Take a look around. This is booming
prosperity. This is a new age, and this time he was not
going to be left behind, not when every Tom, Dick and
Harry you could think of was getting rich and making
the money that was just out there for the asking. So the
first thing, she was to inform those parents that she was
out of the music business as of the end of the school
year. And the next thing was to think about moving
out of her father's house. No, not to Florida. Willard
was probably right about that being so much running
away from the truth. What he had begun to think
about—and he wasn't going to promise right off and be
made a fool of a second time—but what he had begun
to think about was maybe looking into one of these
prefab jobs like the kind the fellow had put up out near
Clark's Hill ...

And here Myra, who had been recounting to her
father all that Duane had said, became teary-eyed, and
Willard patted her back and got all filled up too, and
thought to himself, "Then it has not been in vain," and
the only thing that made him feel unhappy was that it
all seemed to be coming about because little Lucy had
gone ahead and married the wrong person for the
wrong reason.

Spring. Each evening Duane would get up from the

dinner table—slapping at his knees, as though just to rise to his feet was a strengthening experience in itself— and pitting the new self against the old temptations, take a walk all the way down Broadway to the river. At eight on the nose he would be back shining his shoes. Night after night Willard sat across from him in a kitchen chair, watching as though hypnotized, as though his son-in-law was not just another man cleaning his shoes at the end of a hard day, but before Willard's eyes inventing the very idea of the shoe brush and polish. He actually began to think that instead of encouraging the fellow to move out of the house, he ought now to encourage him to stay. It was becoming a genuine pleasure to have him around.

One night in May the two men got to talking serious- ly together before bedtime; the subject was the future. When dawn rose neither could remember who had first suggested that maybe it was really time for Duane to go back to the original plan of his life, which was to be out contracting on his own. With new housing develop- ments going up everywhere, a fellow with his electrical know-how would be swamped with work within a mat- ter of weeks. It was a matter of the necessary capital to begin, and the rest would take care of itself.

Several hours later, a sunny Saturday morning, shaved and in suits, they drove to the bank to inquire about a loan. At seven that evening, after a nap and a good dinner, Duane went off for his constitutional. Meanwhile Willard sat down with a pencil and pad and began to figure up the available money, what the bank said they would loan, plus certain savings of his own ... By eleven he was filling the paper with circles and X's; at midnight he got into the car to make, once again, the old rounds.

He found Whitey in the alleyway back of Chick's Barbershop, along with a strange Negro and a white- wall automobile tire. Whitey had his arms wrapped around the tire; the colored fellow was out cold on the cement. He did all he could to pry Whitey loose from his tire, short of kicking him in the ribs, but it appeared he was having some kind of romance with it. "Now damn it," Willard said, dragging him toward the car, "let go of that thing!" But Whitey staged a sit-down strike on the curb rather than submit to him and his tire being parted. He said he and Cloyd here had run great risks in procuring it, and besides, couldn't Willard see? It was brand-new.

He carried fifty pounds more than Willard, and twenty years less, and so, drunk as he was, it was still nearly half an hour back in Chick's alleyway before Whitey could be detached from what he and his new friend had "borrowed" from God only knew where.

The next morning, for all that he was the color of oatmeal, he came down to breakfast right on time. Wearing a tie. Nevertheless, two weeks passed before mention was made again of bank loans, or personal loans, or the electrical contracting business, and then it was not Willard who brought the matter up. The two were sitting alone in the parlor listening to the White Sox game one Saturday afternoon, when Whitey stood, and glaring at his father-in-law, made his indictment. "So that's the way it is, Willard. One lapse, and a man's whole new life—right down the drain!"

Then in June, while they were all getting ready for bed one night, Myra made a remark to Whitey that did not set very well with him, as it was on the subject of his new life, and hers. Adolph Mertz, who had picked up Gertrude after her lesson that afternoon, had asked if Whitey was still interested in going into electrical contracting; a fellow up in Driscoll Falls was retiring, selling everything he owned at a good price, equipment, truck ... Here Whitey swung at her with his trousers and nearly took her eye out with the buckle of his belt. But he hadn't meant to—he was only warning her not to tease him again about something that wasn't his fault! Why did she go shooting her mouth off about plans that weren't finalized? Didn't she know what the business world was all about? At this stage of the game it was nobody's concern but his—and Willard's, no matter how much her father wanted now to sneak out of the whole thing. As a matter of fact, if it was up to Whitey, he would go back to that bank any day of the week. It was Willard who had withdrawn his support and knocked the confidence out of him about the whole idea, after having encouraged him into it to begin with. Actually, it was living in Willard's house that had undermined his confidence all along, right from the beginning. A grown man being treated like a charity case! Sure, blame it on him—blame it all on him. But who was it who had cried for her Daddy, years back, just because it was a depression and he was out of work, like half the country was, damn it! Who was it that had led them back to her Daddy with his cushy no-risk government job? Who was it that wouldn't leave for the South with her own husband so as to start a new life? Who? *Him?* Sure, always *him!* Only *him!* Nobody but *him!*

And as for striking her—this he said when he came back from the kitchen with an ice pack for her eye—had he ever struck directly at her with the intention of doing her harm? "Never!" he cried, getting back into his clothes. "Never *once!*"

Willard rushed into the hallway as the outraged Whitey started for a second time down the stairs. "Now all of you can just stand around day and night," said Whitey, buttoning his coat, "and talk and laugh and tell stories about what kind of failure I am—because I'm going!" There were tears rolling down his face, and he was clearly so miserable and broken-hearted that for a moment Willard became totally confused, or enlightened. At any rate he saw the truth more clearly than he ever had before in all these fifteen years: *There is nothing the man can do. He is afflicted with himself. Like Ginny.*

But when Whitey passed him the second time—having gone back to the kitchen for one last glass of their precious water, if they didn't mind—he nonetheless let the afflicted fellow proceed out the door, and for good measure, bolted it—and shouted after him, "I don't care what you are! Nobody strikes my daughter! Not in this house! Or outside either!"

Whitey began knocking around two A.M. Willard appeared in the hallway in his robe and slippers and found Myra at the top of the stairs in her nightdress. "I think it's raining," she said.

"Isn't bad feet enough?" Willard shouted up the stairs at her. "Do you want to be blind too?"

Whitey began ringing the bell.

"But what help is it to anything," she said, "for someone to stand out in the rain? And the bad feet have nothing to *do* with him."

"I ain't his father, Myra—I am yours! Let him feel a little rain on him! I just can't worry no more about what help things are doing him or not!"

"But I shouldn't have brought it up. I knew it."

"Myra, will you please stop taking the blame? Do you hear me? Because it is not your doing. It is his!"

Berta came into the hall. "If it is your fault, then you go out and stand in the rain too, young lady."

"Now, Berta—" said Willard.

"That is the solution, Mr. Carroll, whether you like it or not!"

She left her husband and her daughter alone in the hallway. Whitey began to kick against the door.

"Well, that sure takes brains, Myra, doesn't it? To kick a door, that really takes brains, all right."

The two of them stood in the hallway while Whitey continued kicking the door and ringing the bell.

"Sixteen years," said Willard. "Sixteen years of solid this. And listen to him, making an idiot of himself still."

After five minutes more, Whitey stopped.

"Okay," said Willard. "That's more like it. I am not giving in to that kind of behavior, Myra, not now, and not ever either. Now that it is calm I am going to open the door. And us three are going to sit down in the parlor right now, and I don't care if it takes till morning, we are going to get to the bottom of this. Because he will not hit you—or anyone!"

So he opened the door, but Whitey was no longer there.

That was a Wednesday night. On Sunday Lucy came

to town. She wore a dark brown maternity dress of some thick material, from which her face emerged like a smooth little light bulb. Everything about her looked so small, as indeed everything was, except for the belly.

"Well," said Willard cheerfully, "what's on Lucy's mind?"

"Roy's mother told Roy all about it," she replied, standing in the middle of the parlor.

Willard spoke again. "About what, honey?"

"Daddy Will, don't think you're sparing me. You're not."

No one knew what to say.

Finally, Myra: "How is Roy's schooling going now?"

"Mother, look at your eye."

"Lucy," said Willard, and took her by the arm, "maybe your mother doesn't want to talk about it." He sat her down beside him on the sofa. "How about you tell us about you? You're the one with the brand-new life. How's Roy? Is he coming over?"

"Daddy Will," she said, standing up again, "he *blackened* her *eye!*"

"Lucy, we don't feel any better about it than you do. It is not a pleasant thing to look at, and burns me up every time I see it—but fortunately, there was no real physical harm."

"Oh, wonderful."

"Lucy, I am plenty angry, believe me. And he knows it. Word has gotten around to him, all right. He has stayed away three whole days already. Four including now. And from all I understand he is carrying his tail between his legs and is one very ashamed person—"

"But what," said Lucy, "will be the upshot of all this, Daddy Will? What *now?*"

Well, the truth was, he had not quite made up his mind yet on that score. Of course, Berta had made up hers, and told him so every night when they got into their bed. With the lights out he would turn one way, then the other, till his wife, who he had thought was asleep beside him, said, "It does not require squirming, Willard, or thrashing around. He goes, and if she wants to, she goes with him. I believe she is now thirty-nine years old." "Age isn't the question, Berta, and you know it." "Not to you it isn't. You baby her. You watch over her like she was solid gold." "I am not babying anybody. I am trying to use my head. It is *complicated*, Berta." "It is simple, Willard." "Well, it certainly is not, and never was, not by any stretch of imagination. Not with a teen-age high school girl involved, it wasn't. Not when it was a matter of uprooting a whole family—" "But Lucy doesn't live here any longer." "And just suppose they had gone? Then what? You tell me." "I don't know, Willard, what would happen to them then or what will now either. But we two will live a human life for the last years we are on this earth. Without tragedy popping up every other minute." "Well, there are others to consider, Berta." "I wonder when it will be my chance to be one of those others. When I am in the grave, I suppose, if I last that long. The solution, Willard, is simple." "Well, it's not, and it doesn't get that way, either, just by your telling me so fifty times a night. People are just more fragile than you give them credit for sometimes!" "Well, that is their lookout." "I am talking about our own daughter, Berta!" "She is thirty-nine years old, Willard. I believe her husband is over forty, or is supposed to be. They are their own lookout, not mine, and not yours." "Well," he said after a minute, "suppose everybody thought like that. That would sure be some fine world to live in, all right. Everybody saying the other person is not their lookout, even your own child." She did not answer. "Suppose Abraham Lincoln thought that way, Berta." No answer. "Or Jesus Christ. There would never even have *been* a Jesus Christ, if everybody thought that way." "You are not Abraham Lincoln. You are the assistant postmaster in Liberty Center. As for Jesus Christ—" "I didn't say I was comparing myself. I am only making a point to you." "I married Willard Carroll, as I remember it, I did not marry Jesus Christ."

"Oh, *I* know that, Berta—" "Let me tell you, if I had known beforehand that I was agreeing to be Mrs. Jesus Christ—"

So to Lucy's question as to what the upshot would be—"The upshot?" Willard repeated.

To gather his thoughts, he looked away from Lucy's demanding eyes and out the window. And guess who just then came strolling up the front walk? With his hair wet and combed, and his shoes shined, wearing his big man's mustache!

"Well," said Berta, "Mr. Upshot himself."

The doorbell rang. Once.

Willard turned to Myra. "Did you tell him to come? Myra, did you know he was coming?"

"No. No. I swear it."

Whitey rang once again.

". . . It's Sunday," explained Myra when no one moved to open the door.

"And?" demanded Willard.

"Maybe he has something to tell us. Something to say. It's Sunday. He's all alone."

"Mother," cried Lucy, "he hit you. With a belt!"

Now Whitey began to rap on the glass of the front door.

Myra, flustered, said to her daughter, "And is that what Alice Bassart is going around telling people?"

"Isn't that what *happened?*"

"No!" said Myra, covering her blackened eye. "It was an accident—that he didn't even mean. I don't *know* what happened. But it's over!"

"Once, Mother, just once, protect yourself!"

"All I know," Berta was saying, "are you listening to me, Willard? All I know is that it sounds to me as if he is planning to put his fist through that fifteen-dollar glass."

But Willard was saying, "Now first off, I want everyone here to calm down. The fellow has been away three whole days, something that has never happened before—"

"Oh, but I'll bet he's found a warm corner somewhere, Daddy Will—with a barstool in it."

"I know he hasn't!" said Myra.

"Where was he then, Mother, the Salvation Army?"

"Now, Lucy, now wait a minute," said Willard. "This is nothing to shout about. As far as we know he has not missed a day of work. As for his nights, he has been sleeping at the Bill Bryants', on their sofa—"

"Oh, you *people!*" Lucy cried, and was out of the room and into the front hallway. The rapping at the glass stopped. For a moment there was not a sound; but then the bolt snapped shut, and Lucy shouted, "Never! Do you understand that? Never!"

"No," moaned Myra. "No."

Lucy came back into the room.

Myra said, ". . . What—what did you do?"

"Mother, the man is beyond hope! Beyond everything!"

"A-men," said Berta.

"Oh, you!" said Lucy, turning on her grandmother. "You don't even know what I'm saying!"

"Willard!" said Berta sharply.

"Lucy!" said Willard.

"Oh *no,*" cried Myra, for in the meantime she had rushed past them into the hallway. "Duane!"

But he was already running down the street. By the time Myra had unlocked the door and rushed out on the porch, he had turned a corner and was out of sight. Gone.

Till now. Lucy had locked him out, and Whitey had watched her do it to him; through the glass he had seen his pregnant eighteen-year-old daughter driving shut the bolt against his entering. And had never dared return after that. Until now, with nearly five years gone and Lucy dead . . . He must be waiting down in that station twenty minutes already. Unless he had become impatient, and decided to go back where he came from; unless he had decided that maybe this time he ought to disappear for good.

—The pain shot down Willard's right leg, from the hip to the toe, that sharp sizzling line of pain. Cancer!

Bone Cancer! There—again! Yesterday too he had felt it, searing down his calf and into his foot. And the day before. Yes, they would take him to the doctor, X-ray him, put him to bed, tell him lies, give him painkillers, and one day when it got too excruciating, ship him off to the hospital and watch him waste away ... But the pain settled in now, like something bubbling over a low flame. No, it was not cancer of the bone. It was only his sciatica.

But what did he expect sitting outside like this? The shoulders of his jacket were covered with snow; so were the toes of his boots. The first sheen of winter glowed on the paths and stones of the cemetery. The wind was down now. It was a cold, black night ... and he was thinking, yes sir, he would have to pay attention to that sciatica, no more treating it like a joke. The smart thing was probably to take to a wheelchair for a month or so, so as to get the pressure off the sciatic nerve itself. That was Dr. Eglund's advice two years ago, and maybe it wasn't such a silly idea as it had seemed. A nice long rest. Throw an afghan over his knees, settle down into a nice sunny corner with the paper and the radio and his pipe, and whatever happened in the house, let it just roll right by him. Just concentrate on getting that sciatic nerve licked once and for all. Surely that is a right you have at seventy years of age, to wheel yourself off into another room ...

Or he could pretend not to hear everything; let on that he was getting a little deaf. Who'd know the difference? Yes, that might well be a way of solving the whole thing, without bringing a wheelchair into the bargain. Just look blank, shrug your shoulders and walk away. In the months to come he could pretend every once in a while to be slipping some with his faculties. Yes sir, just have to make their way without him. Welcome to use his house for a while, that was fine with him, but beyond that—well, he just wasn't all there in the head, you know. Maybe to make his point so that it stuck, he ought to, on purpose to be sure, and knowing exactlly what he was doing all the while, and not in Berta's direction of course, do as his sad old friend John Erwin had begun unfortunately to do, and wet the bed.

"But why? Why should I be senile? Why be off my head when that is not the case!" He jumped to his feet. "Why be getting pneumonia and worrying myself sick—when all I did was good!" The fear of death, horrible, hateful death, caused him to bring his lids tight down over his eyes. "Good!" he cried. "Unto others!" And down the hill he went, shedding snow from his jacket and his cap, while his old, aching legs carried him as fast as they could out of the graveyard.

Not until he was past the cemetery road and under the street lamps of South Water Street did Willard's heartbeat begin to resume something resembling at natural rhythm. Just because winter was beginning again did not mean that he was never going to see the spring. He was not only going to live till then, he was alive *right now*. And so was everybody shopping and driving in cars; problems or not, they are alive! Alive! We are all alive! Oh, what had he been doing in a cemetery? At this hour, in this weather! Come on, enough gloomy, morbid, unnecessary, last-minute thinking. There was plenty more to think about, and not all of it bad either. Just think how Whitey will laugh when he hears how in the middle of the night, as though in judgment of itself, the building that used to house Earl's Dugout caved right in, roof first, and had to be demolished. And so what if Stanley's is under new management? Whitey had as much disdain of a low-down saloon as anybody when he was being himself—and that was a good deal more often than it might appear, too, when you were purposely setting out to remember the low points in his life. You could do that with anybody, think only about their low points ... And wait till he sees the new shopping center, wait till he takes his first walk down Broadway—sure, they could do that together, and Willard could point out to him how the Elks had been remodeled—

"Oh hell, the fellow is nearly fifty—what else can I even *do?*" He was speaking aloud now, as he drove on into town. "There is a job waiting for him over in Winnisaw. That has all been arranged, and with his say-so, with his wanting it, with his *asking* for it. As for the moving in, that is absolutely temporary. Believe me, I am too old for that other stuff. What we are planning is January the first . . . Oh, look," he cried to the dead, "I am not God in heaven! I did not make the world! I cannot predict the future! Damn it anyway, he is her husband—that she loves, whether we like it or not!"

Instead of parking at the back of Van Harn's, he pulled up in front so as to take the long way to the waiting room, so as to have just another thirty seconds of reflection. He entered the store, slamming his wet cap against his knee. "And most likely," he thought, "most likely won't be there anyway." Without coming into the waiting room, he set himself to peer inside. "Most likely I have set up there for no good reason at all. In the end he probably did not even have it in him to come back."

And there was Whitey, sitting on a bench, looking down at his shoes. His hair was now quite gray; so was the mustache. He crossed and recrossed his legs, so that Willard saw the undersides of his shoes, pale and smooth. A little suitcase, also new, sat beside him on the floor.

"So," said Willard to himself, "he did it. Actually got on a bus and came. After all that has happened, after all the misery he has caused, he has had the nerve to get on a bus and then get off it and to wait here half an hour, expecting to be picked up . . . Oh, you idiot!" he thought, and unseen yet, glared at his middle-aged son-in-law, his new shoes, his new suitcase—oh, sure, new man too! "You dumb cluck! You scheming, lying, thieving ignoramus! You weak, washed-out lushhead, sucking the life's blood from every human heart there is! You no-good low-life weakling! So what if you can't help it! So what if you don't mean it—"

"—Duane," said Willard, stepping forward, "how you doing, Duane?"

II

1

When young Roy Bassart came out of the service in the summer of 1948, he didn't know what to do with his future, so he sat around for six months listening to people talk about it. He would drop his long skinny frame into a big club chair in his uncle's living room and instantly slide half out of it, so that his Army shoes and Army socks and khaki trousers were all obstacles to cross over if you wanted to go by, as his cousin Eleanor and her friend Lucy often did when he was visiting. He would sit there absolutely motionless, his thumbs hooked around the beltless loops of his trousers and his chin tipped down onto his long tubular chest, and when asked if he was listening to what was being said to him, he would nod his head without even raising his glance from his shirt buttons. Or sometimes, with his bright, fair face, with those blue eyes as clear as day, he would look up at whoever was advising him or questioning him, and see them through a frame that he made with his fingers.

In the Army, Roy had developed an interest in drawing, and profiles were his specialty. He was excellent on noses (the bigger the better), good on ears, good on hair, good on certain kinds of chins, and had bought a manual to teach himself the secret of drawing a mouth, which was his weak point. He had even begun to think that he ought to go ahead and try to become a professional artist. He realized it was no easy row to hoe, but maybe the time had come in life for him to tackle something hard instead of settling for the easiest thing at hand.

It was his plan to become a professional artist that he had announced upon his return to Liberty Center late in August; he had barely set down his duffel bag in the living room when the first argument began.

You would have thought he was a kid returning home from Camp Gitche Gumee instead of the Aleutian Islands. If he had forgotten in the time away what life had been like for him during his last year of high school, it did not take Lloyd and Alice Bassart more than half an hour to refresh his recollection. The argument, which went on for days, consisted for the most part of his parents saying they had had experiences he hadn't, and Roy saying that now he had had experiences they hadn't. After all, it just might be, he said, that his opinion counted for something—particularly since what they were discussing was his career.

To make a point, in fact, he spent the whole of his third day home copying a girl's profile off a matchbook cover. He worked it over and over and over, taking just a quick break for lunch, and only after an entire afternoon behind the locked door of his bedroom did he believe he had gotten it right. He addressed three different envelopes after dinner, until he was satisfied with the lettering, and then sent the picture off to the art school, which was in Kansas City, Missouri—walking all the way downtown to the post office to be sure that it made the evening mail. When a return letter announced that Mr. Roy Basket had won a five-hundred-dollar correspondence course for only forty-nine fifty, he tended to agree with his Uncle Julian that it was some kind of clip joint, and did not pursue the matter any further.

Just the same, he had proved the point he had set out to prove, and right off. When he had been called up by the draft board for his two years' service, his father had said that he hoped a little military discipline would do something toward maturing his son. He himself seemed willing to admit bungling the job. Well, the way things turned out, Roy had matured, and plenty, too. But it wasn't discipline that had done it; it was, to put it bluntly, being away from them. In high school he may have been willing to slide through with C's and C-minuses, when with a little application of his intelligence (*Alice Bassart*: Which you have, Roy, in abundance), he could easily have had straight B's—probably even A's, if he had wanted them. But the point he wished to make was that he was no longer that C student, and no longer would be treated like him either. If he put his mind to a job he could do it, and do it well. The only problem now was which job it was going to be. At the age of twenty, nobody had to tell him that it was high time to begin thinking about becoming a man. Because he was thinking about it, and plenty, don't worry.

He continued to work on his own out of the art manual, in exasperation moving on to the neck and the shoulders, after four days of going from bad to worse with the mouth. Though he by no means relinquished his first choice of being a professional artist, he was willing to meet his family halfway and at least listen to whatever suggestions they might have. He had to admit being tempted by Uncle Julian's suggestion that he come to work for him and learn the laundromat business from the ground up. What was particularly appealing about the idea was that the people in the towns along the river would see him driving around in Julian's pickup truck and think of him as some punk kid; and the ladies who managed the laundromats would think of him as the boss's nephew, and suppose his life was just a bed of roses—when in actuality his real work would only begin at night, after everyone was asleep, and behind his bedroom door he stayed awake till dawn, perfecting his talent.

What wasn't too appealing was the idea of using family as a crutch, and right at the outset. He couldn't bear the thought of hearing for the rest of his life, "Of course, it was Julian gave him his start . . ." But of more significance was the damage that accepting something like this could do to his individuality. Not only would he never really respect himself if he just stepped into a job and rose solely on the basis of personal privilege, but how would he ever realize his own potential if he was going to be treated like one of those rich kids who were just coddled up the ladder of success their whole life long?

And there was Julian to consider. He said he was altogether serious about the offer, provided Roy really wanted to work the long hard hours he would demand of him. Well, the long hard hours didn't bother him. A really vicious mess sergeant had once, just out of meanness, kept him on KP for seventeen consecutive hours scrubbing pots and pans, and after that experience Roy realized he could do just about anything. So once he had made up his mind about the direction his life was going to take, he had every intention—to throw Julian's language right back at him—of working his balls into the ground.

But what if he went in with Julian, started taking a salary, and then decided to go off in September to the Art Institute in Chicago; or even to art school in New York, which was by no means impossible? He was giving his parents' objection every consideration (whether they appreciated that or not), but if he finally did decide in favor of professional artist as a career, wouldn't he have wasted not only his time, but Julian's as well? Probably to his uncle, whose affection he valued, he would wind up seeming ungrateful—and maybe that would even be sort of true. Ingratitude was something he had to guard against in himself. Though he was sure his classmates at school and his buddies in the service thought of him as easy-going and generous— his first sergeant used to sometimes call him Steppin' Fetchit—he had been told he had a tendency to be selfish. Not that everybody didn't have one, of course, but certain people had a way of exaggerating things all out of proportion, and he just didn't feel like giving an ounce of support to a suspicion about him which it was

actually unfair for anybody (particularly a person's own
father) to hold in the first place.

Moreover, what he had a real taste for, following the
monotony and tedium of the preceding months, was
adventure, and you couldn't really expect that the laundromat business would be packed with thrills, or even
particularly interesting, to be frank about it. As for the
security angle, money really didn't matter that much to
him. He now had two thousand dollars in savings and
separation pay, plus the G.I. Bill, and anyway he had
no ambition to be a millionaire. That's why, when his
father told him that artists wind up living in garrets,
Roy was able to say, "What's so wrong with that? What
do you think a garret is? It's an attic. My own room
used to be the attic, you know," a fact Mr. Bassart
couldn't easily dispute.

What he had a taste for was adventure, something to
test himself against, some way to discover just how
much of an individual he really was. And if it wasn't the
life of an artist, maybe it was some kind of a job in a
foreign country, where to the natives he would be a
stranger to be judged only by what he did and said, and
not by what they knew about him from before . . . But
saying such things was often only another way of saying you wanted to be a child again. Aunt Irene made
that point, and he was willing to admit to himself that
she could be right. He was always willing to listen to
what ideas his Aunt Irene had, because (1) she usually
said what she had to say in private and wasn't just
talking to impress people (a tendency of Uncle Julian's); (2) she didn't butt in, or raise her voice, when
you argued back or disagreed (his father's courteous
approach); and (3) she didn't ever respond with sheer
hysterics to some idea or other he had most likely
thrown out just to hear how it sounded (as his mother
had a habit of doing).

His mother and his Aunt Irene were sisters, but two
people couldn't have been more different in terms of
calmness. For example, when he said that maybe what
he ought to do was leave Liberty Center with a pack on

his back and see what the rest of the country had to offer, before making any major choice he would later be stuck with, Aunt Irene registered some interest in the idea. All his mother could do was push the old panic button, as they used to say in the service. Instantly she started to tell him that he had just returned from two years away (which of course he didn't know), and to tell him that he ought to make up his mind to go to the state university (and use that intelligence of his "as God meant you to use it, Roy") and then finally to accuse him of not listening to a word she said.

But he was listening, all right; even sunk down in that big chair, he took in all her objections, more or less. Those she had raised previously a hundred times or more he felt he had the right to tune out on, but he got the drift of her remarks, more or less. She wanted him to be a good little boy and do what he was told; she wanted him to be just like everybody else. And really, right there—in his mother's words and tone— was reason enough for him to be out of town by nightfall. Maybe that's what he ought to do, just shove off and not look back—once he had made up his mind what part of the country he ought to see first. There was always a sack for him in Seattle, Washington, where his best Army buddy, Willoughby, lived (and Willoughby's kid sister, whom Roy was supposed to be fixed up with). Another good buddy, Hendricks, lived in Texas; his father owned a ranch, where Roy could probably work for his grub if he ever ran short of loot. And then there was Boston. It was supposed to be beautiful in Boston. It was the most historic city in America. "I might just try Boston," he thought, even as his mother went gaily on losing her senses. "Yes sir, I might just pick up and head East."

But to be honest, he could use a few more months of easy living before starting in roughing it again, if that's what he finally decided it was best for him to do. He had spent sixteen months in that black hole of Calcutta (as they called it), eight to five every day in that scintillating motor-pool office—and then those nights. If he ever saw another ping-pong ball in his *life* . . . and the weather! It made Liberty Center seem like a jungle in South America. Wind and snow and that big gray sky that was about as inspiring to look at as a washed blackboard. And that mud. And that chow! And that narrow, soggy, undersized son-of-a-bitching (really) excuse for a bed! Actually he *owed* it to himself not to go anywhere until he had caught up on all the rest he had probably lost on that g. d. bed—and gotten one or two of his taste buds back to functioning too. After an experience like that he surely couldn't say he minded having breakfast served to him in a nice bright kitchen every morning, and having a room of his own again where everything didn't have to be squared away with a plumb bob, or taking as long as he wanted (or just *needed*) in the john, with the door closed and nobody else doing his business at either elbow. It felt *all* right, he could tell you, to eat a breakfast that wasn't all dishwater and cardboard, and then to settle down in the living room with the *Leader,* and read it at your leisure, without somebody pulling the sports page right up out of your hands.

As for his mother chattering away at him nonstop from the kitchen, he wasn't so stupid that he couldn't understand that why she was concerned for him was because he happened to be her son. She loved him. Simple. Sometimes when he finished with the paper he would come into the kitchen where she was working, and no matter what silly thing she was saying, put his arms around her and tell her what a good kid she was. Sometimes he'd even dance a few steps with her, singing some popular song into her ear. It didn't cost him anything, and as far as she was concerned, it was seventh heaven.

She really meant well, his mother, even if some of her pampering ways were a little embarrassing at this stage of the game. Like sending him that package of toilet-seat liners. That's what he had received at mail call one day: a hundred large white tissues, each in the shape of a doughnut, which she had seen advertised in a medical magazine at the doctor's office, and which he was supposed to sit on—in the Army. At first he actually thought of showing them to his first sergeant, who had been wounded in the back at Anzio during World War II. But thinking that Sergeant Hickey might misunderstand, and instead of making fun of his mother, make fun of him, he had strolled around back of the mess hall late that night and furtively dumped them into a can of frozen garbage, careful first to remove and destroy the card she had enclosed. It read, "Roy, please use these. Not everyone is from a clean home."

Which was a perfect case of her meaning well, but not having the slightest idea that he was a grownup whom you couldn't *do* things like that to any more. Nevertheless, there had been times up in Adak when he missed her, and even missed his father, and felt about them as he had in those years before they had started misunderstanding every word that came out of his mouth. He would forget about all the things they said he did wrong, and all the things he said they did wrong, and think that actually he was a pretty lucky guy to have behind him a family so concerned for his well-being. There was a guy in his barracks who had been brought up in Boys Town, Nebraska, and though Roy had a lot of respect for him, he always had to feel sorry for all that he had missed, not having a family of his own. His name was Kurtz, and even though he had the kind of bad skin Roy didn't exactly like to have to look at at mealtime, he often found himself inviting him to come to visit in Liberty Center (after they all got sprung from this prison) and taste his Mom's cooking. Kurtz said he sure wouldn't mind. Nor would any of them have minded, for that matter: one of the big events in the barracks was the arrival of what came to be known as "Mother Bassart's goodies." When Roy wrote and told his mother that she was the second most popular pinup girl in the barracks, after Jane Russell, she began to send two boxes of cookies in each package, one for Roy to keep for himself, and another for the boys who were his friends.

As for Miss Jane Russell, her latest film had been banned by a court order from the movie house in Winnisaw, a fact which Alice Bassart hoped Roy would take to heart. *That* Roy read to Sergeant Hickey, and they both got a good laugh out of it.

In the months, then, after his discharge, Roy made it his business first to catch up on his sleep, and second to catch up on his food. Every morning about quarter to ten—well after his father had disappeared for the day— he would come down in khakis and a T-shirt to a breakfast of two kinds of juice, two eggs, four slices of bacon, four slices of toast, a mound of Bing cherry preserves, a mound of marmalade, and coffee—which, just to shock his mother, who never had seen him take anything at breakfast but milk, he called "hot joe" or "hot java." Some mornings he downed a whole pot of hot joe, and he could see that actually she didn't know whether to be scandalized by what he was drinking or thrilled by the amount. She liked to do her duty by him when it came to food, and since it didn't cost him anything, he let her.

"And you know what else I drink, Alice?" he'd say, smacking his gut with his palm as he rose from the table. It didn't make the same noise as when Sergeant Hickey, who weighed two twenty-five, did it, but it was a good sound just the same.

"Roy," she'd say, "don't be smart. Are you drinking whiskey?"

"Oh, just a few snorts now and then, Alice."

"*Roy*—"

Which was where—if he saw she was really taking it all in—he might come up, put his arms around her and say, "You're a good kid, Alice, but don't believe everything you hear." And then he'd give her a big, loud kiss on the forehead, sure it would instantly brighten not only her mood, but the whole morning of housework and shopping. And he was right—it usually did. After all was said and done, he and Alice had a good relationship.

Then a look at the paper from cover to cover; then back into the kitchen for a quick glass of milk. Standing beside the refrigerator, he would drink it down in two long gulps, then close his eyes while the steely sensation of the cold cut him right through the bridge of the nose; then from the breadbox a handful of Hydrox cookies, one of his oldest passions; then "I'm going, Mom!" over the noise of the vacuum cleaner . . .

In his first months back he took long walks all over town, and almost always wound up by the high school. It was hard to believe that only two years before, he had been one of those kids whose heads he would see turned down over their books, suffering. But it was almost as hard to believe that he wasn't one of them too. One morning, just for the heck of it, he walked all the way up to the main door, right there by the flag-pole, and listened to the voice of his old math teacher "Criss" Cross, that sweetheart, droning through the open window of 104. Never again in Roy's entire life— *never*—would he have to walk up to the board and stand there with the chalk in his hand while old "Criss" gave him a problem to do in front of the entire class. To his surprise, the revelation made him very sad. And he had hated algebra. He had barely passed. When he had come home with a D his father had practically hit the ceiling . . . Boy, the things you can miss, he thought, if you're a little crazy in the head, and strolled on, down through the ravine and out to the river, where he sat in the sun by the landing, separating Hydrox cookies, eating first the bare half, then the half to which the filling had adhered, and thinking, "Twenty. Twenty years old. Twenty-year-old Roy Bassart." He watched the flow of the river and thought that the water was like time itself. Somebody ought to write a poem about that, he thought, and then he thought, "Why not me?"

> The water is like time itself,
> Running . . . running . . .
> The water is like time itself,
> Flowing . . . flowing . . .

Sometimes even before noon he was overtaken with hunger, and he would stop off downtown at Dale's Dairy Bar for a grilled cheese and bacon and tomato, and a glass of milk. At the PX in Adak they wouldn't make a grilled cheese and bacon and tomato sandwich. Don't ask why, he once said to Uncle Julian. They just wouldn't do it. They had the cheese and the bacon and the tomato and the bread, but they just wouldn't put it all together on the grill, even if you told them how. You could talk yourself red in the face to the guy behind the counter, but he simply wouldn't *do* it. Well, that's the old chicken s—t Army, as he told Julian.

Afternoons he would often drop by the public library, where his old steady, Bev Collison, used to work after school. With his drawing pad in his lap, he would look through magazines for scenes to copy out. He had lost interest in the human head, and decided that rather than drive himself crazy trying to get a mouth to look like something that opened and closed, he would specialize in landscapes. He looked through hundreds of *Holiday* magazines—without much inspiration—though he did get to read about a lot of places and national customs of which he was totally ignorant, so it wasn't time wasted—except when he fell asleep because the library as usual was so damn stuffy, and you actually had to make a requisition to get them to open a window and let some air in the place. Just like the Army. The most simple-minded thing, and you had to go around all day getting somebody's permission to do it. Oh, brother, was it good to be free. With a whole life ahead of him. A whole future, in which he could be and do anything he wanted.

During the fall he would usually walk back out to the high school late in the afternoon to watch the football team practice, and stay on until it was practically dark, moving up and down the sidelines with the plays. Close in like that he could hear the rough canvasy *slap!* as the linemen came together—a sound he especially liked—and actually see those amazing granite legs of Tug Sigerson, which were said never to stop churning, even at the bottom of a pile-up. They would pull ten guys off him and there would be old Tug, still going for the extra inch, the inch that by the end of a game really could be the difference between victory and defeat. Or suddenly he would have to go scattering back with the little crowd of spectators, as one of the halfbacks came galloping straight at them, spraying chunks of dirt so high and so far that on his way home Roy sometimes found a little clump of the playing field in his hair. "Boy," he'd think, breaking the earth in his fingers, "that kid was *movin'*."

The guy you especially wanted to watch up close, just for the beauty of it, was the big left end, Wild Bill Elliott. Wild Bill had spent three years faking the opposition out of their pants, and was the highest-scoring end at Liberty Center since the days of Bud Brunn himself. In about one second flat he would fake the defense right, left, then *cut* left, buttonhook, take a Bobby Rackstraw bullet right in the belly, then—with just a *shoulder*—fake right again, only to turn and zoom straight down the center of the field—until Gardner Dorsey, the head coach, blew his whistle, and Bill came loping on back in that pigeon-toed way he had, tossing a long underhand spiral toward the line of scrimmage, and calling out, "Heads up, baby." Whereupon one of the onlookers beside Roy would say, "Ol' Bill would have gone all the way that time," or Roy might even say it himself.

From over on the baseball field he would hear the band being put through their paces for Saturday's game. "Attention, please, band. *Ba-and!*" he could hear Mr. Valerio calling through his megaphone . . . and really, it is about as good a feeling as he can ever remember having, hearing the band start up with the alma mater—

> We're driving *hard*
> For Li-ber-*ty*,
> We're going to *win*,
> A vic-to-*ry*

—and seeing the first team (three consecutive years undefeated—twenty-four straight) rise up out of the huddle, clapping their hands, and the second team digging in, and Bobby Rackstraw, the spidery quarterback, up on his toes piping out the signals—"Hut *one* hut *two*"—and then, just as the ball is snapped, looking up to see a faint white moon in the deepening sky over the high school.

For the hour of the day, for the time of his life, for this America where it is all peacefully and naturally happening, he feels an emotion at once so piercing and so buoyant it can only be described as love.

One of the stars of the football team in the fall following Roy's discharge from the Army was Joe "The Toe" Whetstone. He was a fleet-footed halfback (he'd done the hundred in 9.9) and the greatest place-kicker in the history of the high school—some said, the history of the state. Since the summer Joe had been dating Roy's kid cousin Ellie, and on Saturday nights, while Julian and Roy were having a talk together, or a beer, Joe would come around to pick up Ellie and take her to what had become a weekly event for the Liberty Center Stallions, the victory party. He would sit with the two of them in the TV room while "The Princess Sowerby," as Julian called her, decided what dress to wear. At first Roy didn't have too much to say to Joe. He had never really traveled with the athletes in high school, or with any gang, if he could help it; you lost your identity in a gang, and Roy considered himself a little too much of an individualist for that. Not a loner, but an individualist, and there's a big difference.

But Joe Whetstone turned out to be nothing like Roy had imagined. You might have thought that with his reputation, and being so good-looking, he would turn out to be another one of those swell-headed wise guys (like Wild Bill Elliott, who was big for spitting through his teeth into the aisle at the movies in Winnisaw, or so Roy had heard). But Joe was respectful and polite to the Sowerbys—and to Roy too. It took a while, but slowly Roy began to understand that the reason Joe sat there in his coat, nodding his head at whatever Roy might say, and himself saying hardly anything at all, was not because he was looking down his nose at him, but because he was actually looking up. Joe might be the greatest high school place-kicker in the history of the state, but Roy had just come back from sixteen months in the Aleutian Islands, across the Bering Sea from Russia itself. And Joe knew it. One Saturday night when Ellie came bounding down the stairs, Joe jumped to his feet, and Roy realized that the famous Joe "The Toe," with six different scholarship offers already in his hip pocket, was really nothing more than what Ellie was—a seventeen-year-old kid. And Roy was twenty, Roy was an ex-G.I. . . .

Very shortly Roy began to hear himself on Saturday nights saying things like "They sure gave you the rush act today, Joe," or "How's Bart's ankle?" or "How bad's the rib going to be on the Guardello kid?" Some nights now it was Ellie who had to do the waiting while the three men finished up discussing whether Dorsey ought to have converted Sigerson from a tackle in the first place; or whether Bobby (Rackstraw) was going to be too slight for college ball, bullet arm or no bullet arm; or whether Wild Bill ought to go to Michigan (which had the big name) or to Kansas State, where at least he could be sure he was going to be with a coach who liked to move the old ball in the air.

Those afternoons Roy went over to watch football practice he would almost always end up moseying over to the wooden bleachers back of the goal post so as to watch head-on as Joe placed his fifty through the uprights.

"How you doin', Joe?"

"Oh, hi, Roy."

"How's the old toe?"

"Oh, holding up, I guess."

"That a boy."

It was also down at this end of the field that the cheerleaders practiced. After Joe had finished up—"So long, Roy"; "See you, kiddo"—Roy would button his field jacket, turn up the collar, lean back on his elbows, stretch his legs down across three rows of wooden stands, and with a little smile on his face, hang around a few minutes more watching the cheerleaders go through their oh-so-important repertoire of tricks.

"Give me an L—"

"L," Roy would say, in a soft mocking voice, not caring whether they heard or not.

"Give me an I—
Give me a B—"

Throughout his four years of high school Roy had had a secret crush on Ginger Donnelly, who had become head cheerleader when they were juniors. Whenever he saw her in the halls he would begin to perspire along his upper lip, just as he did in class when suddenly he found himself called upon to answer a question he hadn't even heard the teacher ask. And the fact was that he and Ginger had never exchanged a word, and probably never would. However, she was built, as the saying goes, like a brick s. house, a fact Roy couldn't seem to ignore, not that he always tried. In bed at night he would begin to think about the way she had of leaning back from the waist to do the Liberty Center locomotive, and he would get an erection; at the games themselves, after a touchdown, Ginger would do cartwheels the length of the field, and everybody would be screaming and cheering, and Roy would be sitting there with an erection. And it was ridiculous, because she wasn't that kind of girl at all. Nobody had ever even kissed her, supposedly, and besides, she was a Catholic, and Catholic girls wouldn't even let you put your arm around them in the movies until you were married, or at least engaged. Or so went one story. Another was that all you had to do was *tell* them that you were going to marry them, right after graduation, and they "spread," as the saying goes, on the very first date.

Even where Ginger was concerned there had been stories. Almost every guy in Liberty Center would tell you that you couldn't get near her with a ten-foot pole, and a lot of the girls said she was actually thinking about becoming a nun. But then this fellow named Mufflin, who was about twenty-five and used to hang around the high school smoking with kids, said that his friends over in Winnisaw told him that at a party across the river one night, back in Ginger's freshman year (before she'd gotten so snooty), she had practically taken on the whole Winnisaw football team. The reason nobody knew about it was because the truth was immediately suppressed by the Catholic priest, who threatened to have all those involved thrown in jail for rape if even one of them opened his mouth.

It was a typical Mufflin story, and yet some guys actually believed it—though Roy wasn't one.

Roy's usual taste in girls ran to the ones who were a little more serious and sedate about things—Bev Collison, for instance, who had more or less been his private property during senior year, and was now a junior in elementary ed at the University of Minnesota (where Roy thought he might decide to go at the last minute, if everything else fell through). Bev was one of the few girls around who didn't live her life as though she were in a perpetual popularity contest; she would just as soon leave the showing off to the show-offs, and didn't go in for giggling and whispering and wasting whole evenings on the phone. She'd had a straight B average, worked after school at the library, and still had time for extracurricular activities (Spanish Club, Citizenship Club, *The Liberty Bell* advertising manager) and a social life. She had her two feet on the ground (even his parents agreed—bravo!) and he had always respected her a lot. Actually, it was because of this respect that he had never tried to make her go all the way.

Still, it was the hottest and heaviest he had ever gone at it with anyone. In the beginning they used to kiss standing up in her front hallway (for as long as an hour at a stretch, but all the time in their coats). Then one Saturday after a school dance Bev agreed to let him into the living room; she took off her own coat and hung it up, but refused to let Roy remove his, saying he had to go in two minutes because her parents' bedroom was directly over the sofa, toward which Roy was to stop trying to push her. It was several weeks more before he was finally able to convince her that he ought really to be allowed out of his coat, if only as a health measure; and even then she didn't consent, so much as give up the fight, after Roy had already sort of slipped it half onto the floor, necking with her all the while so she wouldn't know. And then one night after a long bitter struggle, she suddenly began sobbing. Roy's first thought was that he ought to get up and go home before Mr. Collison came down the stairs; but he patted her a lot on the back and said everything was all right, and that he was really sorry, he hadn't actually meant it; and so Bev asked, sounding relieved, hadn't he really? and though he didn't know exactly what they were talking about, he said, "Of course not, never, no," and so from then on, to his immense surprise, she was willing to let him put his hand wherever he wanted above the belt so long as it was outside her clothes. There followed a bad month during which Bev got so angry with him that they very nearly broke up; meanwhile Roy was pushing and pulling and pleading and apologizing, all to no avail—until one night, fighting him off, Bev (inadvertently, she tearfully contended later) sank a fingernail so deep into his wrist that she drew blood. Afterward she felt so rotten about it that she let him put his hand inside her blouse, though not inside her slip. It so excited Roy that Bev had to whisper, "Roy! My family—stop snorting like that!" Then one night in Bev's dark living room they turned on the radio, very, very low, and of all things, on "Rendezvous Highlights" they were playing the music from the movie *State Fair,* which had recently been revived over in Winnisaw. It was their movie, and "It Might As Well Be Spring" was their song—Roy had gotten Bev to agree. In fact, Roy's mother said that he looked a little like Dick Haymes, though, as Bev commented, least of all when he tried to sing like him. Nevertheless, in the middle of "It's A Grand Night For Singing" Bev just fell backward on the sofa with her eyes closed *and her arms behind her neck.* He wondered for a moment if it was really what she wanted, decided it must be, decided it *had* to be, and so, taking the chance of his life, drove his hand down between her slip and her brassiere. Unfortunately, in the newness and excitement of what she was letting him do, he caught the buckle of his watchband on the ribbing of her best sweater. When Bev saw what had happened she was heartsick, and then scared, and so they had to stop everything while she worked to pick up the stitch with a bobby pin, before her mother saw it in the morning and wanted an explanation. Then on the Saturday before graduation it happened; in the pitch-black living room he got two fingers down onto her nipple. Bare. And the next thing he knew she was off visiting her married sister in Superior, and he was in the Army.

As soon as he was shipped to the Aleutians—even before the first shock of the place had worn off—he had written Bev asking her to get the University of Minnesota to send him an application form. When it arrived, he began to spend a little time each evening filling it out, but shortly thereafter it became evident to him that letters from Bev herself had just stopped coming. Fortunately by this time he was more adjusted to the bleakness of his surroundings than he had been on that first terrible night, and so was able to admit to himself that it had been pretty stupid to think of choosing a university because a girl he once knew happened to be a student there. And absolutely idiotic is what it would have been if after being discharged he had gone ahead and showed up in Minneapolis, to find that this girl had picked up with somebody new, neglecting however to tell him anything about it.

So the application remained only partially completed, though it was still somewhere among "his papers," all of which he planned to go through as soon as he could have two or three uninterrupted days so as to do the job right.

The cheerleader Roy was sort of interested in was named Mary Littlefield, though everybody called her "Monkey," he soon discovered. She was small and had dark bangs, and for a short girl she had a terrific figure (which you really couldn't say was the case with Beverly Collison, whom in his bitterness Roy had come to characterize, and not unjustly, as "flat as a board"). Monkey Littlefield was only a junior, which Roy figured was probably too young for him now; and if it turned out that she didn't have a brain in her head, then it was just going to be curtains for little Monkey, even before the first date. What he was in the market for this time was somebody with a little maturity in her attitudes. But Monkey Littlefield did have this terrific figure, with these really terrifically developed muscles in her legs, and that she was a big-shot cheerleader didn't faze him as it had with Ginger Donnelly two years before. What was a cheerleader, anyway, but a girl who was an extrovert? Moreover, Monkey lived up in The Grove, and so she knew who Roy was: Ellie Sowerby's cousin and a good friend of Joe Whetstone's. He imagined that she knew he was an ex-G.I. simply because of his clothes.

When she and her cohorts started in practicing their cartwheels, Roy would lace his fingers together behind his neck, cross one ankle over the other, and just have to shake his head; "Oh, brother," he would think, "they ought to know what it's like up in the Aleutians."

By then it would be nearly dark. The team would begin drifting off the field, their silver helmets swinging at their sides as they headed for the locker room. The cheerleaders would pick up their coats and schoolbooks from where they lay in piles on the first row of bleachers, and Roy would raise himself up to his full six feet three inches, stretch his arms way out and yawn so that anybody watching would just think of him as being more or less easygoing and unruffled. Then, taking one long leap to the ground, he'd plunge his hands down into his pockets and start off toward home, maybe kicking high out with one foot, as though practicing his punt . . . and thinking that if he had a car of his own there would probably be nothing at all to saying to Monkey Littlefield, "I'm going up to my cousin's, if you want a lift."

Buying a car was something he had begun to give a lot of thought to recently, and not as a luxury item either. His father might not like the idea now any more than he had in high school, but the money Roy had saved in the service was his own, and he could spend it just as he liked. The family car had to be asked for days in advance and had to be back in the garage at a specific time every night; only with a car of his own would he ever be truly independent. With a car of his own he might just give this Littlefield a run for her money—once he had made sure that she wasn't just an extrovert and nothing else . . . And if she was? Should that stop him? Something about the muscles in her legs told Roy that Monkey Littlefield either had gone all the way already, or would, for an older guy who knew how to play his cards right.

. . . Up in the Aleutians it seemed that almost every guy in the barracks had gotten some girl to go all the way, except Roy. Since it didn't hurt anyone, and wasn't so much a lie as an exaggeration, he had intimated that he himself had gone all the way pretty regularly with this girl from the University of Minnesota. One night after lights out, Lingelbach, who really had the gift of gab, was saying that the trouble with most girls in the U.S.A. was that they thought sex was something obscene, when it was probably the most beautiful experience, physical or spiritual, that a person could ever have. And because it was dark, and he was lonely—and angry too—Roy had said yeah, that was why he had finally dumped this girl from the University of Minnesota, she thought sex was something to be ashamed of.

"And you know something," came a southern voice from the end of the barracks, "in later life those are the ones wind up being the worst whores."

Then Cuzka, from Los Angeles, whom Roy couldn't stand, began to shoot his fat mouth off. To hear him talk, he knew every sex secret there ever was. All you have to do to make a girl spread her chops, said Cuzka, is to tell her you love her. You just keep saying it over and over and finally ("I don't care who they are, I don't care if they're Maria Montez") they can't resist. Tell them you love them and tell them to trust you.

How do you think Errol Flynn does it? asked Cuzka, who acted most of the time as though he had a direct pipeline to Hollywood. Just keep saying, "Trust me, baby, trust me," and meanwhile start unzipping the old fly. Then Cuzka began to tell how his brother, a mechanic in San Diego, had once banged this fifty-year-old whore with no teeth, and soon Roy felt pretty lousy about saying what he had out loud. Skinny and scared as Bev had been, she was really a good kid. How could she help it if her parents were strict? The next day he was able partially to console himself over his betrayal by remembering that he hadn't actually mentioned her name.

Lloyd Bassart had come to the conclusion that Roy ought to apprentice himself to a printer over in Winnisaw. His father liked to say the word "apprentice" just about as much as Roy hated to hear him say it. The knowledge of this aversion in his son didn't stop him, however: Roy ought to apprentice himself to a printer over in Winnisaw; he knew his way around a print shop, and it was an honorable trade in which a man could make a decent living. He was sure that the Bigelow brothers could find a place for Roy—and not because he was Lloyd Bassart's boy but because of the skills the young man actually possessed. Artists starve, as anyone knows, unless they happen to be Rembrandt, which he didn't think Roy was. As for enrolling in college, given Roy's grades in high school, his father could not imagine him suddenly distinguishing himself at an institution of higher learning by his scholarly or intellectual abilities. Though Alice Bassart pointed out that stranger things had happened, her husband did not seem to believe they would in this instance.

Lloyd Bassart was the printing teacher at the high school—not to mention the right arm of the principal, Donald "Bud" Brunn, the one-time all-American end from the University of Wisconsin. When the new consolidated high school had been built in Liberty Center in 1930, people still had a picture in their minds of Don Brunn making those sensational end-zone catches over his shoulder during his four years in the Big Ten. What catching a football over your shoulder had to do with organizing a curriculum or estimating a budget was something that would remain incomprehensible to Alice Bassart unto the day she died, but nevertheless, on the basis of that skill, Don, who had been teaching civics and coaching athletics down in a high school in Fort Kean, was offered the position in his old home-town. Being no fool, at least where his own interests were involved, he accepted. And so for eighteen years—eighteen solid years of midstream, as Alice expressed it whenever her anger caused her to become slightly inco-herent—Don had been the principal (at least he sat in the principal's office) and Lloyd had been what Alice Bassart called "the unofficial unsung hero." Don wouldn't so much as hire a new janitor without letting Lloyd take a look at him first, and yet Don got the salary of a principal, and was some kind of household god to parents in the community, while Lloyd, as far as the general public was concerned, was nobody.

When Alice got off on this subject, Lloyd often found it necessary to quote what he said were the words of a man far wiser than either of them, the poet Bobbie Burns:

> "My worthy friend, ne'er grudge an' carp,
> Tho' Fortune use you hard an' sharp."

He agreed that Don was a grinning nincompoop, but that was one of the facts of life he had learned to accept long ago. After this much time you certainly couldn't go around all day hoping and praying that the fellow might see the light and resign; if he could see that much light there might not be any cause for him to resign. Nor could you wait for him to slip on a banana peel; for one thing, Don was a healthy ox, destined to outlive them all, and for another, such an idea was beneath Alice even to think, let alone to say aloud. Either you could make your way through life with the bitter taste of envy always in your mouth, or you could remember that there are people in this world far worse off than yourself, and be thankful that you are who you are, and have what you have, and so on.

Could Roy help it if he felt more like spending his evenings at Uncle Julian's than at home? Not that he considered Julian perfect by any means, but at least his uncle believed in having something of a good time in life, and all his ideas weren't about two centuries old. "Wake up!" Roy wanted to shout into his father's ear. "It's 1948!" But that Julian knew what year it was you could see right off, even in something like his clothes. Whereas the big magazine in Roy's house was *Hygeia,* Julian took *Esquire* every month, and followed their clothing tips from top to toe. He was maybe a little too loud with his color combinations, at least for Roy's taste, but you had to admit he was right in the current style, whatever it happened to be. Even his opinion of Mr. Harry S Truman ("half asshole and half Red") didn't keep him from having a collection of Harry Truman sport shirts that could knock your eye out ... At any rate, to appear in a public place without a tie wasn't something Julian considered a scandal, nor did he act as though life on this planet was coming to an end if Roy showed up at the house with his shirttail accidentally hanging out. That Roy wasn't going to get all worked up over things that were only "externals" was something Uncle Julian seemed capable of understanding. "Well," he'd say, opening the door to his nephew in the evenings, "look who's here, Irene—Joe Slob." But smiling; not like Roy's father, whom all through the Army his son had remembered most vividly as he used to see him coming out of Mr. Brunn's office—gray hair combed slick, mouth shut, tall and straight as an arrow—and wearing that damn gray denim apron, like the town cobbler.

After he had come home from World War II, Julian had sat down to figure out what people needed that would be cheap and helpful to them and profitable to himself: he had come up with the idea of the laundromat. So simple, and yet within a year the quarters and half dollars that the ladies in the towns along the river dropped into the washers and driers of the El-ene

Laundromatic Company left Julian twenty thousand dollars to himself.

Now, Roy had no particular desire to follow in the footsteps of a businessman; it was not only personal considerations that caused him to hesitate before Julian's offer to teach him the business; there was a matter of principle involved. Roy didn't know if he still believed the way he used to in free enterprise, at least as practiced in this country.

During his last few months up in the Aleutians, Roy had listened from his sack when some of the college graduates in his barracks had their serious discussions at night about world affairs. He himself didn't say much then and there, but often on the following day he would find occasion, while sitting around the motor-pool office where he was supply clerk, to talk over some of the things he had heard with Sergeant Hickey. To be sure, he didn't swallow everything this Lingelbach said that was critical of America. Sergeant Hickey was perfectly right: anybody could make destructive criticisms, anybody could just go ahead and start knocking things left and right all day long; to Sergeant Hickey's way of thinking, if you didn't have something constructive to say, then maybe you shouldn't say anything at all, especially if you happened to be wearing the uniform and eating the chow and drawing the pay check of the country you thought was so terrible and awful. Roy agreed that Sergeant Hickey was perfectly right: there were some guys in the world who would never be satisfied, even if you fed them all day long with a silver spoon, but still you had to give this guy from Boston (not Lingelbach, who was an outright loner and odd-ball, but Bellwood) a lot of credit for his arguments about the way they did things in Sweden. Roy agreed right down the line with Sergeant Hickey and his Uncle Julian about Communism, but as Bellwood said, Socialism was as different from Communism as day from night. And Sweden wasn't even *that* socialistic.

What had made Roy begin to wonder if after his discharge a person like himself might not be happy living in a place like Sweden was (1) they had a high standard of living, and it was a real democracy with the Four Freedoms; but (2) they weren't money-mad, Bellwood said, the way people in America were (which wasn't a criticism, it was a fact); and (3) they didn't believe in war, which Roy didn't believe in either.

Actually, if he hadn't just returned from sixteen months in the Aleutians, he might have gone off and gotten himself a job as a deckhand aboard a freighter bound for Sweden, and once there, found some kind of good, honest work, and not in Stockholm either, but in some fishing village such as he had seen photographs of in *Holiday*. He might even have settled down there and married a Swedish girl, and had Swedish children, and never have returned to the United States again. Wouldn't that be something? To think, if that was what he wanted, he could pick up and do it, and without explaining himself to anyone ... However, for the time being he'd really had his fill of the sun coming up at ten A.M. and going down practically at noon, and the rest of what should be day being night. Probably that's what got to the Swedes themselves—because something did. Sergeant Hickey, who saw all the magazines before they were put in the day room, came into the office one morning and announced that in the new issue of *Look* it said that more people jump off of buildings in Sweden than in any out-and-out capitalistic country in the world. When Roy later brought this up with Bellwood, he didn't really have much to say in Sweden's defense, except to start quibbling over percentages. Apparently there was a heck of a lot of gloom over there that Bellwood hadn't mentioned, and very frankly, for all Roy's willingness to sympathize with their form of government so long as it was a democracy with free elections, by and large he would prefer at the end of a day's work to spend his leisure time with people who knew how to relax and take it easy. Moderation in all things, that was his motto.

Consequently, he found that he would just as soon spend his evenings at the Sowerbys' as hang around at home, where he either had to keep the radio at a whisper because his father was upstairs writing some report for Mr. Brunn, or else his father was downstairs and they were discussing something called Roy's Future as though it were a body he had found on the front lawn: now look here, Roy, what do you intend to do with it?

As for Lloyd Bassart's disapproval of Roy's nightly social call over to the Sowerbys' (and of his brother-in-law Julian as an influence and confidant), he disguised his real objections by saying that he didn't feel Roy should make himself a permanent fixture in another family's house simply because they had a television set. Roy said why should his father mind if the Sowerbys themselves didn't? Uncle Julian was interested in what the postwar Army was like, and in what the younger generation was thinking, and so he liked to talk to Roy. What was so wrong with that?

However, the "talks" between Julian and Roy consisted, as frequently as not, of Julian's pulling Roy's leg. Julian got a kick out of kidding Roy, and Roy got sort of a kick out of being kidded, since it really put them on a buddy relationship. Of course, sometimes Julian went too far with his kidding, particularly the night Roy had said he really didn't think he could ever be satisfied as a human being unless he was doing something creative. As it happened, he was only repeating something he had once heard Bellwood say, but it applied equally as well to him, even though he hadn't thought it up personally. Uncle Julian, however, chose deliberately to miss the point, and said it sounded to him as though what Roy needed was a good piece. Roy had laughed it off and tried to act nonchalant, even though his Aunt Irene was in the dining room, where she could hear every word they said.

Julian's sense of humor wasn't always up Roy's alley. It was one thing if you were in the barracks, or the motor-pool office, to say f. this and f. that, and another when there were women around. Where Uncle Julian's language was concerned, Roy felt his father had his strongest case. And then sometimes Julian got his goat with his opinions on art, which were totally uninformed. It wasn't the security angle he wanted Roy to think about before going off to some la-dee-da art school; it was the sissy angle. "Since when did you become a lollipop, Roy? Is that what you were doing up there in the North Pole, turning pansy on the taxpayers' money?"

But by and large the kidding was good-natured, and the arguments they had didn't last very long. Though Uncle Julian was just a couple of inches over five feet, he had been an infantry officer during the war, and had nearly had his left ball shot off more times than he could count. And even though he said it just that way, regardless of the age or sex of anyone listening, you had to admire him, because it was the pure truth. The guy who had called out "Nuts!" to the enemy had gotten all the publicity at the time, but apparently Julian had been known throughout the 36th Division as "Up Yours" Sowerby; more than once that was the message he had shouted back to the Germans, when another man would have withdrawn or even surrendered. He had risen to the rank of major and been awarded a Silver Star; even Lloyd Bassart took his hat off to him on that score, and had invited him to address the student body of the high school when he returned from the war. Roy remembered it yet: Uncle Julian had used hell and damn twelve times in the first five minutes (according to a count kept by Lloyd Bassart), but fortunately thereafter simmered down, and when he was finished, the students had risen to their feet and sung "As the Caissons Go Rolling Along" in his honor.

Julian called Roy "you long drink of water," and "you big lug," and "Slats," and "Joe Slob," and hardly ever just Roy. Sometimes his nephew had no sooner stepped into the foyer than Julian had his fists up and was dancing back into the living room, saying, "Come on, come on, Slugger—try and land one." Roy, who had learned in gym class how to throw a one-two punch (though he had not yet had occasion to use it in the outside world), would come after Julian, openhanded, leading with his right, while Uncle Julian would bob and weave, cuffing aside the *one* before Roy could deliver the *two*. Roy would circle and circle, looking in vain for his opening, and then—it never failed to happen—Julian would cock back his right arm, cry "Ya!" and even as Roy was ducking his chin behind his fists and hiding his belly back of his elbows (just as he had been taught in high school), Julian would already be swinging one leg around sideways to give his nephew a quick soft boot in the behind with the toe of his bedroom slipper. "Okay, Slim," he'd say, "sit down, take a load off your mind."

But the best thing about Julian wasn't his happy-go-lucky manner: it was that his experience in the Army made him appreciate how hard it was for an ex-G.I. to adjust back to civilian life at the drop of a hat. Roy's father had been too young for World War I and too old for World War II, and so the whole business of being a veteran was just one more aspect of modern life that he couldn't get into his head. That a person's values might have changed after two years of military service didn't seem to mean anything to him. That a person might actually *benefit* from a breather in which he got a chance to talk over some of what he had learned, to digest it, didn't strike him as anything but a waste of precious time. He really made Roy's blood boil.

Julian, on the other hand, was willing to listen. Oh, he made plenty of suggestions too, but there was a little difference between somebody making a *suggestion* and somebody giving you an *order*. So all through that fall and into the winter, Julian listened, and then one evening in March, while he and Roy were smoking cigars and watching the Milton Berle Show, Roy suddenly began during the commercial to say that he was starting to think that maybe his father was right, that all this valuable time was just slipping through his fingers, like water itself.

"For crying out loud," Julian said, "what are you, a hundred?"

"But that isn't the point, Uncle Julian."

"Come on, get off your own back, will you?"

"But my life—"

"Life? You're twenty years old. You're a twenty-year-old kid. Twenty, Long John—and it won't last forever. For Christ's sake, live it up a little, have a good time, get off your own back. I can't stand hearing it any more."

And so the next day Roy finally did it; he hitched over to Winnisaw and bought a two-tone, second-hand 1946 Hudson.

2

◦━◦━◦━◦━◦━◦━◦━◦━◦━◦━◦━◦━◦━◦━◦━◦

From between the curtains in her bedroom, Ellie Sowerby and her friend Lucy watched him begin to take it apart and put it together again. Every once in a while he would stop and sit up on the fender, with his knees to his chest, swinging a Coke bottle back and forth in front of his eyes. "The war hero is thinking about his future," Eleanor would say, and the very idea caused her to snort out loud. Roy, however, appeared to pay no attention to either of them, even when Eleanor rapped on the window and ducked away. As the weather grew warmer, he would sometimes be seen slouched down in the back of the Hudson, his legs thrown up over the front seat, reading a book he had taken out of the library. Ellie would call out the window, "Roy, where in Sweden are you going to live?" To which his answer would generally be a loud slam of the rear door of the car. "Roy's reading all about Sweden. Half the farmers around here came running from there. He wants to *go* there."

"Really?" asked Lucy. She did not take offense, because her own grandfather who had been a farmer had come from Norway.

"Well, I hope he goes somewhere," Ellie said. "My father's worried he's liable to decide to move in with us. He practically lives here as it is." Then, out the window, "Roy, your mother phoned to say she's selling your bed."

But by this time he was under the car, the soles of his shoes all that was visible from the second floor. The only time that he appeared to experience the girls as alive was down in the living room, when he wouldn't move his legs so much as half an inch, and the two had to step over him to get out through the French doors to the back lawn. Generally he acted as though teams had been chosen, himself and his Uncle Julian on one, and the two girls and Mrs. Sowerby on the other.

But if there were such sides, Lucy Nelson had no sense that Irene Sowerby was on hers. Though Mrs. Sowerby was polite and hospitable to her face, Lucy was almost certain that behind her back the woman disapproved of who and what she was. The very first time Ellie had brought her home, Mrs. Sowerby had called Lucy "dear" right off the bat; and a week later Ellie was no longer her friend. She disappeared from her life as unexpectedly as she had come into it, and the person responsible was Irene Sowerby, Lucy was sure. Because of what she knew about Lucy's family, or because of whatever she had heard about Lucy herself, Mrs. Sowerby had decided that she was not the kind of girl she wanted Ellie bringing home in the afternoons.

That was in September of senior year. In February (as if four months of conduct not quite becoming so refined a young lady hadn't intervened) Ellie slid a note, all cheery and intimate, into Lucy's locker, and after school they were walking together up to The Grove. Of course Lucy should have left her own note in return: "No, thank you. You may be insensitive to the feelings of others but you are not going to be insensitive to mine and get away with it. I am not nothing, Ellie, whether your mother thinks so or not." Or perhaps she should not have given Ellie the courtesy of any reply, and just let her show up at the flagpole at three-thirty to find no Lucy waiting breathlessly to be her idea of a "friend."

She felt bitter toward Eleanor, not only because she

had picked her up so enthusiastically and dropped her so suddenly, but because Ellie's instantaneous display of affection had caused Lucy to make a decision she wouldn't otherwise have made, and which later she was to regret. But that was not really Eleanor's fault as much as it was her own (or so she seemed willing to believe as she reread the note scrawled across the blue stationery monogrammed EES at the top). The reason she should have nothing to do with Ellie Sowerby was because she was Ellie's superior in every way imaginable, except for looks, which she didn't care that much about; and money, which meant nothing; and clothes; and boys. But just as she had known Ellie to be her inferior, and had gone off with her when invited back for a second afternoon in September, so in the last week of February she followed along once again.

Where else was there to go? Home? As of February 28 she had only two hundred more days to live in that house with those people (times twenty-four is four thousand eight hundred hours—sixteen hundred of them in bed, however) and then she would be down in the new Fort Kean branch of the women's state college. She had applied for one of the fifteen full honors scholarships available to in-state students, and though Daddy Will said that to have received anything at all was an honor, she had been awarded only what the letter of congratulation called "A Living Aid Scholarship," covering the yearly dorm bill of one hundred and eighty dollars. She would be graduating twenty-ninth in a class of one hundred and seventeen, and now she wished that she had worked and slaved for A's in those courses like Latin and physics, where she had felt it a real victory to get even a B-minus. Not that financial difficulties were going to prevent her going off to school. Over the years her mother had somehow managed to save two thousand dollars for Lucy's education; this, plus Lucy's own eleven hundred dollars in savings, plus the Living Aid Scholarship, would see her through four years, provided she continued to work full time at the Dairy Bar in the summers and was careful about spending on extras. What disappointed her was that she had wanted to go off completely independent of them; as of September, 1949, she had hoped to have to rely upon them for nothing more for the rest of her life. The previous summer she had settled upon Fort Kean State College because it was the least expensive good school she could find, and the one where she had her strongest chance to get financial assistance; she had declined to apply anywhere else, even after her mother had revealed the existence of her secret "college fund."

Why Lucy detested taking the money was not only because it would continue to bind her to home, but because she knew how it had been paid out to her mother, and she knew why too. Almost into the fifth grade she had thought it made her rather special to be the daughter of Mrs. Nelson, the piano teacher; then, all at once, the kids waiting on the porch in warm weather or sitting on their coats in the hallway in winter, were her own classmates—and that fact caused her to be filled with a kind of dread. No matter how fast she ran home from school, no matter how silently she tried to make it into the house, there would always be some child already at the piano, invariably a boy, who invariably would turn his head away from his lesson in time to catch sight of his classmate, Lucy Nelson, scooting up the stairs to her room.

At school she came to be known not as the kid whose mother gives the piano lessons but the kid whose father hangs around Earl's Dugout—of that she was sure, though the division she now sensed between herself and her schoolmates was such that it did not permit her to ask what they actually thought, or to learn what it was they really did say behind her back. She pretended, of course, that hers was a normal household, even after she had begun to realize it was not—even after her mother's pupils went back out into town to spread the story of what Lucy Nelson's family was really like.

Of course, when she was small, she was nearly able to believe it when she told her friends that it was actually her grandparents who lived with them in their house, and not the other way around. Right off she told new friends that why she couldn't bring anyone home in the afternoon was because her grandmother, whom she loved dearly, had to take her nap then. And she had new friends often. There was a period when every girl her age who moved to town heard from Lucy about her grandmother's nap. But then a new girl named Mary Beckley (whose family moved on again the following year) began to giggle at the story, and Lucy knew that somebody had already cornered Mary Beckley and told her Lucy's secrets. This so angered Lucy that tears came popping out of her eyes, and that so frightened Mary that she swore on her life that she'd giggled only because her baby sister took naps too . . .

Only, Lucy didn't believe her. And from then on she refused ever to tell a lie again, to anyone about anything; from then on she brought no one to her home, and did not offer explanations for her behavior either. So, from the age of ten, though she had no friend who was her confidante, nobody she cared about ever saw her mother taking from her students the little envelopes of money (and saying, "Thank you very much," so very, very sweetly), or what was far worse, the dread of dreads, saw her father coming through the front door and falling down drunk in the hall.

Not even Kitty Egan, whom she discovered in her second year of high school, and who for four months was as intimate a companion as Lucy had ever had. Kitty didn't go to Liberty Center High, but to the parish school of St. Mary's. Lucy had just started working four nights a week at the Dairy Bar, and she met Kitty because of the scandal: Kitty's older sister, Babs, who was only seventeen, had run away from home. She hadn't even waited until Friday, when the girls at the Dairy Bar were paid, but had taken flight after work on a rainy Tuesday night, probably still in her waitress uniform. Her accomplice was an eighteen-year-old boy who swept up at the packing company and came from Selkirk. A post card addressed to "The Slaves at Dale's Dairy Bar" and mailed from Aurora, Illinois, had arrived in town at the end of the week.

"Headed for West Virginia. Keep up the good work, KIDS." And signed, "Mrs Homer 'Babs' Cook."

Kitty was sent around to the Dairy Bar by her father to pick up Babs' wages for Monday and Tuesday. She was a tall, skinny girl whose most striking feature was the absence of any complexion; she had no more coloring than the inside of a potato, even when she came in out of the cold. At first she seemed as unlike Babs as she could be, until Lucy learned that Babs had dyed her hair black so as to look like Linda Darnell (it had originally been orange like Kitty's); as for her skin, Babs caked it in so much mud, Kitty said, you would never know that actually she was part anemic.

The family had always had their troubles with Babs. The only satisfaction she gave them was to wear crucifix earrings in her pierced ears and a cross around her neck, and *that,* Kitty said, was only to draw attention to the space between her breasts—which was the only real thing there anyway, the space. The breasts were things like toilet paper or her brother Francis' socks that she stuffed into her brassiere. Babs wasn't five minutes away from St. Mary's—a dark brick building just by the Winnisaw Bridge—when she would duck into some alleyway to cover herself with pancake make-up, from the roots of her dyed hair to the tops of her homemade breasts, all the while puffing a Lucky Strike cigarette. Kitty told Lucy about the terrible thing she had once found in her sister's purse—"Then I found this terrible thing once in her purse"—and when Babs discovered that Kitty had flushed it down the toilet, she screamed and yelled and struck her in the face. Kitty never told anyone—except the priest—for fear that her parents would severely punish her older sister, who, she said, needed mercy and forgiveness and love. Babs was a sinner and knew not what she was doing, and Kitty loved her, and every morning and every night she prayed for her sister living down there in West Virginia with a boy who Kitty believed was not even her husband.

There were three more children at home, all younger than Kitty, and she prayed for them too, especially for

Francis Jr., who was soon to have an operation for his "mastoidistis." The Egans lived out near the Maurer Dairy Farm, where Mr. Egan worked, in a house that was nothing more than a dilapidated old shack. There were nails poking out of the timbers, and flypaper dangling, though it was already fall, and every unpainted two-by-four seemed to have its decoration of exposed wire. Lucy, upon entering, was afraid to move for fear of brushing up against something that would cause her to feel even more nausea and more despair than came from simply seeing the place where Kitty had to eat and sleep and do her homework.

And when Kitty said that in the afternoons her mother had to take a nap, Lucy was afraid to ask why, knowing that behind such a lie there could only be some dreadful truth she did not want to hear; she wanted only to get outside into the air, and so, thinking that the door nearest her led to the yard, she pushed against it. In a tiny room, asleep on a double bed, lay a pale woman in a long gray cotton slip, wearing on her left foot—in bed!—a crippled person's shoe. Then she was introduced to Francis Jr., who instantly showed her the spot where he appeared to have been whacked with a stick behind the ear. And Joseph, aged eight, whom Kitty had to take into the house to change out of his overalls, which were—"as usual," Kitty said—soaking wet. And tiny Bing—named for the singer—who just dragged his sleeping blanket around and around the backyard, crying for someone named Fay, who Kitty said didn't even exist. And then Mr. Egan appeared, whom Lucy might even have liked for his big lumbering stride and his blazing green eyes had not Kitty earlier pointed to something hanging from a nail in the rear of an open shed, which she whispered was a cat-o'-nine-tails. In all, it was the most wretched and unhappy family Lucy had ever seen, heard of, or imagined; if possible, it was worse even than her own.

She and Kitty began to meet regularly after school. Lucy, standing in the park across the street from St. Mary's, would watch the Catholic kids rushing out the side doors and imagine them all going back to houses just like Kitty Egan's, even though the old Snyders, who were Catholics and lived three doors down on Franklin Street, owned a house almost exactly like her Daddy Will's.

Lucy told Kitty her secret. They walked down to the south end of Water Street, and from a safe distance she pointed out the door to Earl's Dugout of Buddies. Kitty whispered, "Is he there now?"

"No. He's working. At least he is supposed to be. He goes there at night."

"Every single night?"

"Almost."

"Are there women?"

"No. Whiskey."

"Are you sure there are no women?"

"Well, no," Lucy said. "Oh, it's awful. It's horrible. I hate it!"

It didn't take very long for Kitty to tell Lucy about Saint Teresa of Lisieux, the Little Flower—Saint Teresa, who once said, "It is for us to console Our Lord, not for him to be consoling us . . ." Kitty had a little book with a blue cover called *The Story of a Soul,* in which Saint Teresa herself had written down all the wonderful things she had ever thought or said. Even though the weather had begun to turn and the days to grow dim by late afternoon, the two girls would sit on a bench in the little park across from St. Mary's, huddled close together in their coats, while Kitty read to Lucy passages that she said would change her whole life, and get her into heaven for all eternity.

In the beginning Lucy could not seem to get the hang of it. She listened attentively, sometimes with her eyes closed so as to concentrate better, but soon it began to seem that not being a Catholic, she was fated never to understand whatever it was that so inspired Kitty. She herself was Lutheran on one side and Presbyterian on the other, and the latter had been her church, back when her mother had been able to get her to go. A kind of melancholy about her spiritual stupidity slowly settled upon her, until one day, despising both herself and her narrow Protestant background, she looked over Kitty's shoulder at a page of the mysterious book, and discovered that it wasn't hard to understand at all. It was only that in reading aloud, Kitty—who suddenly seemed to her so hopelessly, so disgustingly, ignorant—substituted "a" for "the" and "he" for "she" and "what" for "when," and left out entirely those words she couldn't pronounce, or changed them into others.

Still, Kitty loved Saint Teresa as Lucy had never loved anything, at least that she could remember; and so, gradually, when she began to get the drift of Saint Teresa's meaning, and saw again and again how it flooded Kitty with joy to pronounce aloud those very words, nearly all of which Saint Teresa herself had written, she began to wonder if perhaps she shouldn't forgive Kitty Egan her reading problem and try to love Saint Teresa too.

It was Kitty who brought her to meet Father Damrosch. She began to take instruction from him for an hour after school two days a week, and to spend still other hours in the church, lighting endless candles to Saint Teresa, after whose life she and Kitty were going to model their own. At her first retreat she was given a black veil to keep by Sister Angelica of the Passion, a dark little woman with shiny skin and rimless spectacles and hair beneath her nose that so resembled a man's mustache that Lucy said nothing of it for fear of offending Kitty, who adored Sister Angelica and didn't even seem to notice the long black hairs. Kitty had told Sister Angelica about Lucy in a letter, and so the sister knew all about Lucy's father, for whom she had already prayed at Kitty's request. Sister Angelica was also praying for Babs in West Virginia. In vain, however, did they all wait for news from the vanished sinner. It was as though she had stepped directly from that restaurant in Aurora, Illinois, into Hell itself.

Kitty and Lucy would read aloud to each other their favorite passages from Saint Teresa, who had left this fallen world at twenty-four, a gruesome death of weakness, cold, coughing and blood. " '. . . to become a saint one must suffer the great deal,' " Kitty read, " 'always seek when is best, and forgot oneselfish . . .' "

They both chose what Sister Angelica called "Saint Teresa's little way of spiritual childhood." Teresa's only care, said Sister Angelica to Lucy, was that no person should ever be distressed or even inconvenienced by what she was enduring; "daily she sought opportunities for humiliating herself" (Sister Angelica read this to Lucy from a book, so it was not just something she was making up)—"for instance, by allowing herself to be unjustly rebuked. She forced herself to appear serene, and always courteous, and to let no word of complaint escape her, to exercise charity in secret, and to make self-denial the rule of her life." The doctor who attended Teresa in her final illness had said, "Never have I seen anybody suffer so intensely with such an expression of supernatural joy." And her last words, in the slow agony of her dying, were, "My God, I love Thee."

So Lucy dedicated herself to a life of submission, humility, silence and suffering; until the night her father pulled down the shade and up-ended the pan of water in which her mother was soaking her beautiful, frail feet. After calling upon Saint Teresa of Lisieux and Our Lord—and getting no reply—she called the police.

Father Damrosch did not choose to call upon her himself when she (who usually attended at least two) failed to show up at a single Mass that Sunday, nor when she did not appear the following week for her instruction. Instead he apparently arranged for Kitty to be excused early from school one day so as to meet Lucy outside the high school, which recessed each afternoon thirty minutes before St. Mary's. Kitty said that Father Damrosch knew about Lucy's father spending the night in jail. Kitty said that this was only another reason for her to hurry and be converted. She was sure that if Lucy asked, Father Damrosch would see her an extra hour a week, and rush the conversion along so that she could be taking her first Communion within a month. "Jesus will forgive you, Lucy," Kitty said, whereupon Lucy turned in anger and said that she did not see that she had anything for which to be forgiven. Kitty begged and begged, and finally when Lucy told her, "Stop following me! You don't know anything!" Kitty began to weep and said she was going to write Sister Angelica so that she too would pray for Lucy to embrace the teachings of the Church before it was too late.

She feared for a while that she would run into Father Damrosch downtown. He was a big burly man, with a mop of black hair, who liked to kick the soccer ball around with the Catholic boys after school. His voice and his looks made girls who were even Protestant swoon openly in the street. He and Lucy had had such serious discussions, during which she had tried so hard to believe the things he said. "This life is not our real life," and she had tried with all her might to believe him ... How had he found out so quickly what had happened? How did everybody know? At school, kids she hardly recognized had begun to say, "Hi," as though it had been discovered she were dying of some dread disease and everybody had been told to be nice in the few weeks remaining to her. And after school a group of hideous boys who hung out smoking back of the billboard shouted after her, "Hey, Gang Busters!" and then imitated a machine gun firing. After they had kept at it for a whole week, she picked up a stone one afternoon, turned suddenly around, and threw it so hard that it left a dark mark where it struck against the billboard. But the boys only continued to jeer at her from where they had fled into a vacant lot.

At home she continued to insist upon eating by herself in the kitchen, rather than with *him,* whom her grandfather had gone down and taken out of jail the very next morning. If the phone beside the table rang while she sat looking angrily at her food, she prayed that it would be Father Damrosch. What would her grandmother do when the priest announced himself? But he never did. She even thought of going directly to him—not to ask his help or his advice, but because she recognized one of the boys who called her "Gang Busters" from seeing him at nine o'clock Mass with his family every Sunday. However, she would let Father Damrosch know right off, she had nothing to be forgiven for and nothing to confess. Who was Kitty Egan even to suggest such a thing? A homely, backward girl from an illiterate family, whose clothes smelled like fried potatoes and who couldn't read a sentence from a book without getting it all balled up! Who was she to tell Lucy *anything*? And as for Saint Teresa, that Little Flower, the truth was, Lucy couldn't stand her suffering little guts.

She gathered together her black veil, her rosary, her catechism, her copy of *Story of a Soul* and all the pamphlets she had accumulated at the retreat and from the vestibule at St. Mary's, and put them into a brown paper bag. What prevented her from simply dropping the items separately into the bottom of her wastebasket was the knowledge that her grandmother would see them there, and think that it was because of her objections to "all that Catholic hocus-pocus" that Lucy was giving up going into the Church. She did not wish her to have the satisfaction. What she decided to do about her religion, or about anything relating to her personal life, was the business of nobody in that house, least of all that snoop.

She carried the paper bag with her to work that night, intending to drop it into a garbage can along the way, or toss it into a lot. But a rosary? a veil? a crucifix? Suppose the bag was found and brought to Father Damrosch? What would he think then? Perhaps the only reason he had refrained from calling her so far was because he felt it improper to interfere in a family already so strongly opposed to conversion; or perhaps he believed it improper to meddle in a private matter before his assistance had been asked for; or perhaps he had sensed all along that Lucy only half believed the things he told her and so would be immune to anything further he might have to say; or perhaps he had never really been that interested in her to begin with, thought of her as just another kid, and if she came to him, would only resume stuffing her full of catechism so as finally to stuff her into the confessional, where, like stupid Kitty Egan, she could ask forgiveness for sins that were not really her own and say prayers for people that did them absolutely no good. He would try to teach her to learn to love to suffer. But she hated suffering as much as she hated those who made her suffer, and she always would.

After work she hurried out Broadway toward the river. At St. Mary's she entered without genuflecting, placed the bag on the last bench, and ran. Outside, there was only one light on in the rectory ... Was Father Damrosch standing behind one of the dark windows, looking down at her? She gave him a moment to call for her to come inside. And tell her what? This life is a prelude to the next? She didn't believe it. There is no next life. This is what there is, Father Damrosch. This! Now! And they are not going to ruin it for me! I will not let them! I am their superior in every single way! People can call me all the names they want—I don't care! I have nothing to confess, because I am right and they are wrong and I will not be destroyed!

One night two weeks later Father Damrosch came into Dale's Dairy Bar for a black and white ice cream soda. Dale popped immediately out from the back to say hello, and to serve the priest personally, saying all the while what a great honor it was. He refused to take Father Damrosch's money, but the father insisted, and when he left, one of the waitresses said to Lucy, "He's absolutely *gorgeous*." But Lucy only continued carefully refilling the sugar bowls.

The very next term Lucy took the music appreciation course, where she was prevailed upon by the teacher, Mr. Valerio, to become interested in the snare drum; so for the next year and a half the problem of what to do after school was solved by band. Either they were practicing in the auditorium, or on the field, or on Saturdays were off and away to a football game. There were always kids dashing in and out of the bandroom, or shoving from behind onto the bus, or jamming together, epaulet to epaulet, in the band section, to stay

warm while the game itself—which Lucy hated—wore
interminably on. As a result, she was hardly ever alone
around school to be pointed out as the kid who had
done this or that terrible thing. Sometimes as she was
rushing up out of the school basement with her drum,
she would see Arthur Mufflin slinking around the basketball courts, or perched on his motorcycle, smoking.
He had been thrown out of Winnisaw High years ago,
and was some kind of hero to the boys who used to call
her "Gang Busters" and "J. Edgar Hoover." But if he
himself had any smart remarks to make she didn't wait
to hear them. She would just start in practicing the
marching cadence and continue all the way to the field,
beating it out so loud that whether he called to her or not,
she didn't even know.

But then, altogether unexpectedly, at the very start
of her senior year, band was over. She had cut practice
twice in two weeks to go up with Ellie Sowerby to The
Grove; to Mr. Valerio she explained (her first lie in
years) that her grandmother was ill and needed her—
and he had swallowed it. So there was no tension
between them at all; she was still his "dream girl." Nor
had the thrill gone out of marching up the field at the
start of the afternoon, guiding her line, "Left ... left
... left, right, left," and drumming out the muffled
cadence till they reached the midfield stripe and
launched into the National Anthem. It was the moment
of the week she had come to live for, but not because
of anything so ridiculous as school spirit—or even love
of country, which she supposed she had, though no
more than an ordinary person. It wasn't the flag, snap-
ping in the breeze, that gave her the gooseflesh so much
as the sight of everybody in the stands rising as it
moved down the field. She saw from the corner of her
eye the arms sweep up, the hats swept off, and felt the
drum thump-thumping softly against the guard on her
leg, and the warmth of the sun fell on her hair where it
poked out from under her black and silver hat with the
yellow plume and oh, it was truly glorious—until that
third Saturday in September, when they turned at the
midfield stripe to face the stands (where everyone was

silently standing facing them) and she tightened her hold on the smooth sticks, and Mr. Valerio climbed onto the folding chair that had been brought out to the field for him, and he looked down at them—"Band," he whispered, smiling, "good afternoon"—and then in the moment before he raised his baton, she realized (for no good reason at all) that in the entire Liberty Center Consolidated High School Marching Band, there were only four girls: Eva Petersen, who played the clarinet and had a wall-eye; the harp-bell player, Marilynne Elliott, whose brother was a big hero, but who herself stammered; and the new French-horn player of whom Mr. Valerio was so proud, poor Leola Krapp, who had that name and was only fourteen and already weighed two hundred pounds—"stripped," the boys said. And Lucy.

On Monday she told Mr. Valerio that working in Dale's Dairy Bar at night and having band practice in the afternoons wasn't giving her time enough to study. "But we finish by four-thirty." "Still," she said, looking away. "But you managed last year, Lucy. And on the honor roll." "I know. I'm really sorry, Mr. Valerio." "Well, Lucy," he said, "you and Bobby Witty are my mainstays. I don't really know what to say. The big games are just coming up." "I know, Mr. Valerio, but I think I have to. I think I better. College is coming up too, you know. And so I really have to knuckle down and make an all-out effort—for my scholarship. And I have to make the money at the Dairy Bar. If I could quit that, of course, then I could have this ... but I just can't." "Well," he said, lowering the lids of his big black eyes, "I don't know what's going to happen to the rhythm in that drum section. I hate even to think about it." "I think Bobby can carry them, Mr. Valerio," she said, feebly. "Well," he sighed, "I'm not Fritz Reiner. I suppose this is what they mean by a high school band." "I'm really sorry, Mr. Valerio." "It's just I don't often get a person, boy or girl, who is serious about the snare drum the way you are. Most of them, if you'll pardon my language, just beat the damn thing to death. You *listen*. You've been my dream girl, Lucy." "Thank you, Mr. Valerio. I really appreciate that. That means a lot to me. I sincerely mean that." Then she laid on his desk the box in which she had folded up her uniform. The silver hat with the black peak and the gold plume she carried in her hand. "I'm really sorry, Mr. Valerio." He took the hat and put it on his desk. "My drums," she said, weakening by the moment, "are in bandroom."

Mr. Valerio sat there flicking the plume on her hat with one finger. Oh, he was such a nice man. He was a bachelor with a slight limp who had come to them all the way from a music school in Indianapolis, Indiana, and his whole life was band. He was so patient, and so dedicated; he was either smiling or sad, but never angry, never mean, and now she was letting him down, and for a selfish, stupid, unimportant reason. "Well, so long, Mr. Valerio. Oh, I'll stop by and say hello, and see how things are going—don't worry about that."

Suddenly he took a very deep breath and stood up. He seemed to have collected himself. He took one of her hands in his two and shook it, trying to look happy. "Well, it was good having you aboard, Dream Girl."

The tears rolled down her cheeks; she wanted to kiss him. Why was she doing this? Band was her second home. Her first home.

"But," Mr. Valerio was saying, "I suppose we are all going to survive." He clapped her on the shoulder. "You take care now, Lucy."

"Oh, you take care, Mr. Valerio!"

A little girl with braids was sitting in the swing on the porch when Lucy came running up the front stairs. "Hi!" the child said. Whoever was already at the piano stopped in the middle of a bar as she slammed the door and took the stairs, two at a time.

As she turned the key in the bedroom door she heard the piano start up again downstairs. Instantly she pulled out her desk chair, stood up on it, and looked at her legs in the mirror over the dresser. They had hardly any shape; she was just too short and too skinny. But what could she do about that? She had been five one and a half now for two years, and as for weight, she didn't like to eat, at least not at home. Besides, if she got any heavier her legs would just get round, like sausages—that's what happened to short girls.

She climbed down off the chair. She looked at herself straight on in the mirror. Her face was so square—and boring. The word "pug" had been invented to describe her nose. Eva Petersen had tried to give her that as a nickname in the band, but Lucy had told her to cut it out, which she did instantly, what with her own wall-eye. A pug nose wasn't that bad, actually, except that where hers turned up at the end it was too thick. And so was her jaw, for a girl at any rate. Her hair was a kind of yellowish-white, and she knew that bangs didn't help all that squareness any, but when she lifted them up (as she did now), her forehead was so bony. Well, at least her eyes were nice—or would have been had they belonged to someone else, though that was the trouble: they *did* belong to someone else. Sometimes she used to look at the mirror in the bandroom, and with her hat on she would be terrified by the resemblance she bore to her father—particularly those two round blue stains beneath the steep pale brow.

She had freckles too, but no pimples—her only physical blessing.

She stepped backward so as to see all of herself again. All she ever wore was that plaid skirt with the big safety pin in front, and her gray sweater with the sleeves pushed up, and her ratty loafers. She had three other skirts, but they were even older. And she didn't care about clothes. Why should she? Oh, why had she quit band?

She clutched at the back of her blouse so that it pulled tight across her front. Her breasts had started growing when she was eleven; then to her relief, a year later, they had just stopped. But weren't they going to start again? She did know an exercise that supposedly could enlarge them. The health teacher, Miss Fichter, had demonstrated it to them in class. It was out of *American Posture Monthly,* a magazine with a picture on the cover of little twin boys in white briefs, standing on their heads and smiling. There was nothing there to cause giggling, as far as Miss Fichter could see, and that went for the exercise as well, whose purpose was all-around health and attractiveness. If only they got into the habit of exercising their muscles when they were young, they would always be proud of themselves physically. Too many teen-age girls in this school *slouch,* said Miss Fichter, and she said it as though she really meant *lie* or *steal.*

You did the exercise with your hands out in front of your chest: first you pushed the right fist into the open left palm, and then the left fist into the open right palm. You did this twenty-five times, each time chanting in rhythm, as Miss Fichter did, "I must, I must, I must respect my bust."

In front of her mirror, behind the locked door, and without the words, Lucy gave it a try. How long before it began to work? "Da *dum,*" she said, "da *dum* ... da-*dum,* da-*dum,* da-*dum.*"

Oh, how she would miss band! How she would miss Mr. Valerio! But she simply couldn't march any more with those girls—they were freaks. And she wasn't! And nobody was going to say she was either! From now on it would just be her and Eleanor Sowerby together. In Ellie's room was a bed with a white organdy canopy and a dressing table with a mirror top, where they would do their homework on the afternoons when it rained; on nice afternoons, they would sit out in the back, reading together in the sun, or just walk around The Grove, doing nothing except looking at lawns and gabbing. If by the time they got back it was dark, most likely the Sowerbys would invite her to join them for supper. On Sundays they would ask her to come with them to church, and stay on afterward for dinner. Mrs. Sowerby was so soft-spoken and attentive, she had called her "dear" the very afternoon they were intro- duced—to which Lucy had nearly, idiotically, respond- ed with a curtsy. And Mr. Sowerby had come noisily into the house at five—"Pappy Yokum's home!" he'd called, and then had given his wife a loud wet kiss right on the mouth, even though she was a plump woman with gray hair who, Ellie said, had to wear rubber stockings to keep her veins in. It was Ellie's current joke to call him Pappy Yokum, and his to call her Daisy Mae, and silly as this struck her, Lucy had nonetheless found herself very much in awe of what appeared at last to be a happy family.

So she quit band. And Ellie dumped her. "Oh, hi there," Ellie would say as they passed in the corridors, and then just keep walking. For a week Lucy was able to tell herself that Ellie was only waiting for her to return the invitation. But how could she invite her home if she didn't even get a chance to talk to her? And even if she was able to, did she want to? One day, after two solid weeks of being ignored, she saw Ellie sitting in the cafeteria at the same table with some of the shallowest and silliest girls in the entire school, and so she thought to herself, well, if *those* are the kind of girls she really prefers, et cetera, et cetera.

Then in late February she found the note slipped down through the air vents into her locker.

Hi, Stranger!

I've been accepted at Northwestern (big deal) so the pressure is off, and I can relax now. Meet me at the flagpole at three-thirty (please please).

Your fellow suffering senior,
Ellie
LCCHS, Class of '49
Northwestern '53 (!)

This time Lucy was far less impressionable. Thinking back to September, to the sheer idiocy of quitting band so as to be Ellie Sowerby's friend—well, it was as though she had been ten years old. She had really gone against every principle she had. It had been weak and stupid and childish, and though in the interim she had despised Ellie, and plenty, she had despised herself no less. For one thing, it was a matter of absolute indifference to her who lived in The Grove—that was the truth. Nothing used to infuriate her more than to take a drive with her family on Sunday (back when she was young enough to have to go where they wanted her to) and have her mother point out the house up in The Grove that her father had once almost bought. As if where you lived or how much money you had was what was important, and not the kind of human being you were. The Sowerbys had a full-time maid, and a $30,000 house, and enough money to send a daughter off to a place like Northwestern for four years, but the fact remained that Lucy Nelson was still more of a person than their own daughter would ever be.

To Ellie the biggest thing in life was clothes. Outside of Marshall's store in Winnisaw, Lucy had never seen so many skirts in one place as Ellie had hanging in her big wall-length closet with the sliding doors. Some afternoons, when it rained and they studied together in Ellie's room (exactly as she had imagined they would), she looked up to discover the closet doors ajar; whole minutes often passed before she was looking down into her book again, trying to find her place. When the weather began to turn warm and by three o'clock it was suddenly too hot for the coat that Lucy had worn to school that morning, Ellie would tell her just to pull any old sweater out of the bureau drawer and wear it for the rest of the afternoon. Only there weren't any old sweaters in there.

One afternoon the sweater she put on turned out to be one hundred percent cashmere. She didn't realize this until out on the lawn, she took a quick look at the label and went breathless at what she had done. By this time, however, Ellie was calling for her to help pound in the croquet wickets, and Mrs. Sowerby had already seen her pass through the living room. And she had already seen the look of disapproval move across Mrs. Sowerby's face, at the first glimpse of the sagging plaid skirt coming down the stairs topped by Ellie's lemon-colored sweater. "Have a good game," Mrs. Sowerby had said, but that, Lucy realized too late, wasn't at all what she had been thinking. To go back upstairs, however, to change the cashmere for cotton, or even lamb's wool, would be to admit that she was indeed guilty of choosing it deliberately, when in actuality she had taken it in all innocence. Upon lifting it from the overstuffed drawer she had not thought *cashmere,* she had only thought *how soft.* It had nothing to do with being covetous and she would not give credence to any such suspicion by traipsing all the way past Mrs. Sowerby a second time. She had no intention of ever being made to feel inferior again, not by Ellie, and not by any member of her family . . . and that was the reason she gave herself for keeping the soft lemon-colored sweater on her back until the very minute that she changed back into her heavy winter coat and left for home.

Shortly thereafter Ellie trimmed her bangs for her. Lucy kept saying, "Not too much. Really. My forehead, Ellie."

"What a difference!" Ellie said when they looked at the results in the bathroom mirror. "I can *see* you now."

"You took too much off."

"I didn't. Look at your eyes."

"What's wrong with them?"

"They look great. They're really a great color if you could ever see them."

"Yes?"

"Hey, what about wearing it up? Let's see what it looks like up."

"My head's too square."

"Let's just see, Lucy."

"Don't cut anything."

"I won't, jerk. I just want to *see.*"

So, too, Ellie just wanted to see what Lucy's plaid skirt would look like if they let down the hem three inches to give it "The New Look."

It seemed so silly to be allowing this to happen to her, so incredible that it *was* happening. She didn't even respect Ellie, so where did she get off treating Lucy like her stooge? And she didn't respect Ellie's parents that much any more either. What was Mrs. Sowerby but a social snob? As for Mr. Sowerby—well, she hadn't figured him out yet. Daddy Will liked to crack corny jokes, and her father used to think he was being funny when she was small and he called her "Goosie," but Mr. Sowerby was almost always joking, and was almost always loud. Whenever he was down in the living room, Lucy took her time going between Ellie's bedroom and the bathroom at the end of the hall. "Pike this," he'd call to his wife in the kitchen. "Just pike this!" And then at the top of his voice he would read from the newspaper something that Harry Truman had done which just infuriated him. Once he called, "Irene, come here, Irene," and when she came into the living room, he put a hand on her behind and said (softly now, but Lucy, frozen in the upper hallway, could hear by holding her breath), "How's the health, tootsie?" How could she approve of the way he talked to Mrs. Sowerby, or the kind of language he used? She certainly didn't believe that Mrs. Sowerby did, what with all her airs. She had the distinct feeling that all this hugging and kissing was something Mrs. Sowerby simply had to endure. It almost made Lucy feel sorry for her.

On the other hand, Mr. Sowerby *was* Liberty Center's outstanding war hero. On his return to town the Mayor had actually led a motorcade down to the train station to meet him. Lucy had only been a freshman when he came to the high school to talk, but she remembered that his speech had left a sobering impression on the people in the community who had thought the worst was now over. His topic had been, "How to Make This World a Better Place to Live In"—or, as some of the boys referred to it afterward, "How the Hell to Make This God Damn World a Helluva Better Place to Live In—Damn It!" It was mostly about remaining vigilant in the coming years against what Mr. Sowerby called the threat of atheistical Communism. The very next day there had been an editorial on the front page of the Winnisaw *Leader* calling upon Major Sowerby to run for Congress in the 1946 elections. Ellie said that he had decided not to only because her mother didn't feel it would have been right to take Ellie out of her school once again, if they had had to move to Washington, D. C. Because of the war she had already had to attend schools in North Carolina and

Georgia (which, said Ellie, accounted for her sometimes falling into a southern accent without even realizing it). Ellie loved to tell how the Governor had spoken to her father on the phone, and how her father had said he didn't want the Governor to think he was putting responsibility to family above responsibility to country, and so on and so forth. The conversation came out different each time Ellie reported it; once it even occurred at the Governor's "mansion." Only the tone in which the story was told remained the same: smug.

Of course Lucy appreciated Ellie's generosity with her possessions, and it was hard to say she wasn't good-natured, but one thing that was unforgivable was being condescended to. The day that Ellie began to fuss with her clothes she got so furious that she wanted to leave right then and there; and she would have too, were it not that Ellie had already unstitched the hem and was busy pinning up a new one, and she herself was in her slip and blouse, sitting at Ellie's dressing table and looking out between the curtains at Ellie's cousin, the Army veteran, working on his Hudson.

Roy. She had never called him that, or anything. And he did not appear even to *know* her name, or even to associate her with the girl who worked behind the counter at Dale's Dairy Bar. Between September, when she had caught her first glimpse of him at Eleanor's, and February, when grace had fallen upon her a second time, she had observed him many times as he sat at the counter of the Dairy Bar; sometimes she had seen him headed down Broadway carrying his sketch pad. During those months without band and without Ellie, when she used to hole herself up every afternoon in the public library, there was a period of a few weeks when he always seemed to be coming out of the library just as she was going in. He was friendly with Dale, and once she'd seen him talking seriously with Miss Bruckner, the librarian. So it wasn't shyness that explained his solitude; he just seemed to prefer to be alone—which was one of the things that had begun to make her think that he might be an interesting person. Also she knew who his father was—Mr. Bassart, who introduced the speakers at assembly programs, and was known to be one of the strictest though one of the fairest teachers in the entire school. And she knew he had recently returned from serving two years in the Army, overseas.

Ellie always made fun of him. "He thinks he looks like Dick Haymes. Do you think he does?"

"I don't know."

"If he wasn't my cousin I suppose I'd think he was cute. But I *know* him," she would add ominously. Then, out the window: "Roy, sing like Dick Haymes. Come on, Lucy never heard your imitations. Do Vaughan Monroe, Roy. You really look more like him anyway, now that you're so *mature*. Sing 'Ballerina,' Roy. Sing, 'There, I've Said It Again.' Oh, please, Roy, please, we beg of you on bended knee."

Lucy would go scarlet, and Roy would make a sour face, or say something like, "Act your age, will you?" or, "Really, Ellie, when are you going to grow up?"

Roy was going to be twenty-one. What he was doing the times she saw him meandering slowly down Broadway, whacking his sketch pad against his thigh, or on the evenings when he sat at the Dairy Bar counter, rattling the ice round and round at the bottom of his Coke, or on the weekends he spent sunk down into the club chair talking with his Uncle Julian, was trying to decide just what to do with his life. He was at a genuine turning point: that was the expression she had heard him using one Saturday. And it had stayed with her.

What was Roy going to become? An artist? A businessman? Or was he going to ship out, and really give Sweden a chance? Or would he do something completely bizarre and unpredictable? Once she heard him remind his uncle that he didn't only have the G.I. Bill, he had a G.I. home loan too. If he wanted to, he could actually go off and buy a house of his own, and then live in it. His Uncle Julian laughed, but Roy said, "Poo-poo my ideas all you want, kiddo, but it's true. I don't have to be anybody's slave, not if I don't want to be."

From the bed where she was sitting hemming Lucy's skirt, Ellie said, "What are you looking at?"

Lucy dropped the edge of the curtain.

"Not Roy, I hope," Ellie said.

"I was just looking outside, Ellie," she said coldly.

"Because don't waste your breath on that one," said Ellie, biting the thread. "You know who he likes?"

"Who?"

"Monkey Littlefield."

To Lucy's astonishment her heart made some sort of erratic movement.

"Roy's major interest these days is s-e-x. Well, he's picked the right girl, all right."

"Who?"

"Littlefield."

". . . Does he take her out?"

"He's still deciding whether to lower himself or not. Or so he says. He said to me. 'Is she a kid, or has she got a brain in her head? Otherwise I don't want to waste my time.' I said, 'Don't worry, Roy. She's no kid.' So he said, 'What is that supposed to mean?' And I said, 'I know why you like her, Roy.' And he got all red in the face. I mean, everybody knows her reputation. But Roy pretended he didn't."

Lucy pretended by her expression that she did.

Ellie went on. "I said, 'It isn't her personality that makes her popular, Roy.' So he said, 'Well, that's all I asked, Ellie, whether she even had a personality or not.' 'Well, ask Bill Elliott about her personality, Roy, if you haven't already.' So he said, 'I didn't even know she went out with him.' 'Not any more, Roy. Even *he* doesn't respect her any more. I'll leave the rest to your imagination,' I said, and then you know what he said? 'Go play with your jacks, Ellie.' He tells my father all his big sex exploits in the Army, and Daddy lets him, which he shouldn't, either. You know when they start laughing down there together?"

"No. I don't think so."

"Well, they do. And what do you think they're laughing about?"

"Sex?"

"He's got it on the brain. Roy, I mean," Ellie added.

By April the elastic at the top of Roy's Army socks had begun to unravel. Every time the two girls stepped over him—"Excuse us, cousin, will you, *please?*" said Eleanor—Lucy saw, between the shrunken, fading khaki trousers and the drooping socks, the white and slender part of his leg. At the beginning of the month, a week of hot, wonderful, summery weather swept across the Middle West, pushing into bloom almost overnight the forsythia in the Sowerby garden; one afternoon, just as she stepped to Ellie's bedroom window to take a quick look outside—at the new flowers—Roy began pulling his T-shirt off over his head. In only a matter of seconds she had turned back to Ellie, who was searching a drawer for an old pair of shorts for Lucy to wear, but the sight of his long smooth cylindrical upper half stretching down over the open hood of his car remained in her mind all afternoon.

Near the end of the month, when Roy bought the camera and began to get the photography magazines, he came to Eleanor and said that he wanted to do some studies in black and white down by the landing. He needed a girl to sit under the tree he'd picked out. It might just as well be Ellie.

Ellie's color rose; she had auburn hair that shone, and hazel eyes that changed sometimes to cat-gray, and in repose she was not only one of the prettiest girls Lucy had ever seen, but also looked altogether poised and intelligent. She could easily have passed for nineteen or twenty, and she knew it.

"Look, Roy," she said, dropping into her southern accent, "why don't you-all get Monkey Littlefield? Probably she'll even do cheesecake fo' ya'. A la Jane Russell—yo' favorite actress."

"Look," he said, making his sour face, "I don't even know that Littlefield kid. And I've never even seen a Jane Russell movie in my life, actually."

"Oh, I'm *shoo*-wa of that. You only had her little ol' pinup all over your walls in the Army, but you never *seen* her in a movie."

"Look, Ellie, who are you supposed to be, *Gone With the Wind?* I want to do this study. So say either yes or no. I haven't got all day."

Ellie said she'd think about it, and then went up and changed into her new white linen dress, all the while telling Lucy about the kind of letters her Aunt Alice had gotten while Roy was in the Army. S-e-x, to his own family.

They drove off to the river. Lucy came along for the ride. That was how Roy had extended the invitation, when she said that she'd better go home. "You can come for the ride, if you want. I don't charge anything"—all the while using a little pressure gauge he had bought to check the air in a front tire that he said looked to him to be low.

He posed his subject (because that's all she was, and he hoped she could understand what that meant) by the big oak near the old pier. Ellie kept wanting to look off in profile toward Winnisaw, but Roy wanted her looking straight up into the tree. Every few shots or so he came over and yanked on one of the branches so as to get the shadows to fall in the right places.

Ellie said she would like to know what he meant by "the right places."

"I'm talking technically, Eleanor. Will you shut up?"

"Well, it's hard to know these days, Roy, when you say 'the right places.' Considering where your mind is."

"Oh, look at the branches, *please?* The whole idea, Ellie, is The Marvel of Spring. So look up, and not at me."

"I hear you at night, Roy."

"Hear me *what?*"

"Laughing. And I know what you're laughing about too."

"Okay, what?"

"Guess."

At the end of the afternoon Ellie said, "Why don't you take some of my friend?"

He sighed deeply. "Oh—okay. One." He turned all

around. "Well, where'd she disappear to? I haven't got all day."

Ellie pointed to the bank of the river where the black pilings jutted out into the water.

"Hey," Roy called, "want your picture taken? I've got to leave, so if you want it, let's go."

Lucy looked up. "No," she said.

"Lucy, come on," Eleanor called. "He needs one of a blonde."

Roy had to slap his own forehead. "Who said that?" he wanted to know.

"She *likes* you," Ellie whispered.

"Now who told you that, Eleanor? Who told you something like that?"

Lucy stood at attention under the tree, looking straight at the hole in the camera, and he took a picture. One. She noticed that he did not refer to the light meter first.

When the picture was developed, he showed it to her. She was heading down the Sowerby drive for home when he came out of the house behind her. "Hey."

Despite herself, she turned. He trotted down the drive in a kind of loping, pigeon-toed run.

"Here," he said. "You want it?"

She had hardly taken the picture from his hand when he added, "Otherwise I'm going to throw it away. It's not too hot."

Glaring at him she said, "Just who do you think you're talking to, you!" and thrust the photograph at his chest and walked angrily home.

That evening he appeared at Dale's Dairy Bar, where she worked on Mondays, Tuesdays and Wednesdays from seven to ten, and on Fridays and Saturdays from seven to eleven-thirty. He sat where she had to take his order: a grilled cheese with bacon and tomato.

When she put down the sandwich in front of him, he said, "Hey, about this afternoon"—he took a bite out of the sandwich—"I'm sorry." She went on about her business.

When finally she came back to ask if he would care for anything more, he said it again, as sincerely as he could, and this time without a mouthful of food.

"Pay the cashier," she answered, giving him his check.

"I know that."

She had been watching him, however, for months; he was always so busy thinking about himself that he usually left the money on the counter. "You never *do* it," she answered sharply, and started away, realizing that she had said the wrong thing.

Sure enough, he followed her down the counter. What a smile. From ear to ear. "Don't I?"

"Pay the cashier, please."

"What time do you get off work?"

"Never."

"Look, I really am sorry. I meant the picture was no good. Technically."

"Pay the cashier, please."

"Look, I'm really genuinely sorry. Look ... I don't lie," he said when she did not respond. "I don't have to," he said, hitching up his trousers.

He was parked outside at closing time. She refused to accept a lift home. She did not even acknowledge the offer.

"Hey," he said, driving slowly along beside her, "I'm only trying to be nice." She turned off Broadway, up Franklin, and the car turned with her.

After proceeding in this way for another block, he said, "Well, no kidding, what's wrong with trying to be nice?"

"Look, you," she said, and her heart was beating as though some terrible catastrophe had just occurred, "look, you," she said again, "leave me alone!" And from then on, he was unable to.

He took hundreds of pictures of her. Once they spent a whole afternoon driving around the countryside in search of the right barn for her to stand in front of. He wanted one with a falling roof and a gloomy air, and all they could find were big red ones freshly painted. Once he made her stand in front of a white cement wall by the high school, in the full noon light, so that her bangs looked like white straw, and her blue eyes like the eyes in a statue, and the bones of her square serious face appeared to be stone beneath her skin. He entitled the photograph "Angel."

He began a whole series of black and white studies of Lucy's head, which he called "Aspects of an Angel." At first he had to tell her to stop frowning, or glaring, or fidgeting, and to stop saying "This is ridiculous" every two minutes; but after a while, as her embarrassment diminished, he did not have to tell her to stop doing anything. He told her practically every day that she had fantastic planes in her face, and that she was a far better subject than someone like Ellie, who was all glamour and no substance. He said girls like Ellie were a dime a dozen—just look at the magazines. *Her* face had character in it. Every afternoon he picked her up at school at three-thirty, and they went off on one of their photographic expeditions. And at night he was parked outside the Dairy Bar, waiting to drive her home.

At least that was where he drove her the first week. When he asked one night about coming inside awhile, she said absolutely no. To her relief, he did not ask again, once she had consented to drive with him out beyond The Grove to the wooded bluff that overlooked the river, which was called Picnic Paradise by the Winnisaw County Park Commission and Passion Paradise by the high school kids. There Roy would turn off the lights, flip on the radio, and try with all his might to get her to go all the way.

"Roy, I want to leave now. Really."

"Why?"

"I want to go home, please."

"I sort of love you, you know that."

"Don't say that. You don't."

"Angel," he said, touching her face.

"Stop. You almost put your finger in my eye."

" 'You sigh, the song begins,' " he sang along with the radio, " 'you speak and I hear violins, it's maaaa-gic.' "

"Roy, I'm not going to do anything. So let's go now."

"I'm not asking you to do anything. I'm only asking you to trust me. Just trust me," he said, trying once again to put his fingers between the buttons of her uniform.

"Roy, you're going to tear something."

"I'm not. Not if you don't fight. Just trust me."

"I don't know what that means. You say that, and when I do, then you only start going further. I don't want that, Roy."

But he was singing into her ear.

> "Without a golden wand,
> Or mystic charms,
> Fantastic things begin,
> When I am in your . . . *arms!*

"Oh, Lucy," he said.

"Not there," she cried, for on *arms* he had sunk an elbow into her lap, as though by accident.

"Oh, don't fight me, don't fight me, Lucy," he whispered, digging round and round, "trust me!"

"Oh, stop! No!"

"But I'm outside your clothes—it's only an elbow!"

"Take me home!"

Three weeks passed. She said that if that was all he was interested in each and every night, she did not think they should see each other ever again. He said that it wasn't all he was interested in, but he was a grown man and he hadn't thought she was going to turn out to be just another kid who didn't know what life was all about. He hadn't thought she was going to turn out to be like Ellie, a professional virgin—a c.t., if she knew what that was. She didn't, and he said he had too much respect for her to tell her. The whole point was that he wouldn't even have started up in the first place with a girl he couldn't respect; nor would he have invited her out in the car if he didn't think she was mature enough to handle some ordinary premarital petting. She said petting was one thing and what he wanted was something else. He said he would even settle for petting if she would just relax; she said that as soon as she started to relax, he stopped settling. She said she wasn't Monkey Littlefield; he said well then, maybe that was just too bad for her; and she said well then, go back to her if that's what you're really after; and he said maybe I will. And so the next afternoon when she came out of school the car wasn't there. Ellie wasn't waiting for her either; she had stopped weeks ago, once Roy got involved with Lucy on his "Aspects of an Angel" series. Lucy didn't know what to do with herself. Again, nowhere to go.

That night she was walking home from the Dairy Bar when a car pulled up alongside her. "Hey, girlie, want a lift?"

She did not look around.

"Hey, Lucy." He blew the horn and pulled over to the curb. "Hey, it's me. Hop in," he said, throwing open the door. "Hi, Angel."

She glared at him. "Where were you this afternoon, Roy?"

"Around."

"I'm asking a question, Roy. I waited for you."

"Oh, come on, forget it—get in."

"Don't tell me what to do, Roy," she said. "I'm not Monkey Littlefield."

"Gee, I thought you were."

"And just what is that supposed to mean?"

"Nothing, nothing. It's a joke!"

"Is that where you were this afternoon? With her?"

"I was pining for you. Well, come on, I'll drive you home."

"Not until you apologize for this afternoon."

"But what did I do?"

"You broke an engagement, that's all."

"But we had a fight," he said. "Remember?"

"Well, if we had a fight, why are you here now? Roy, I won't be treated—"

"Okay, okay, I'm sorry."

"Are you? Or are you just saying it?"

"Yes! No! Oh, get in the car, will you?"

"But you do apologize then," she said.

"*Yes!*"

She got into the car . . . "Where do you think you're driving, Roy?"

"I'm just driving. It's early."

"I want to go directly home."

"You'll get home. Did you ever *not* get home?"

"Turn around, Roy. Please, let's not start this again."

"Maybe I want to talk to you. Maybe I have some more apologizing to do."

"Roy, you're not funny. I want to go home. Now stop this."

Just past The Grove he pulled onto the dirt road, instantly turning down his headlights (the unwritten code of Passion Paradise) until he came to a clearing where no other car was parked.

He flipped the parking lights off now, and the radio on, and tuned in "Rendezvous Highlights." Doris Day was singing "It's Magic."

"Boy, either it's coincidence or it's just our song," he said, trying to pull her head toward him. " 'Without a golden wand, or mystic charms'—" he sang. She resisted his gentle tug on the back of the neck, so he bent his face toward her closed mouth and wide-open eyes. "Angel," he said.

"You sound like a movie when you say that. Don't."

"Oh, brother," he said, "you can really destroy a mood."

"Well, I'm sorry. I expected to be driven home."

"I'll take you home! You can at least move over for the time being," he said. "Well, will you move over, *please?* So I don't get a steering wheel in my chest, *do you mind?*"

She began to shift to her right, but before she knew it he had her pinned up against the door and was kissing her face. "Angel," he whispered. "Oh, Angel. You smell like the Dairy Bar."

"Well, I happen to work there. I'm sorry."

"But I *like* it," and then before she could speak again, he pressed his mouth on hers. He did not fall away until the record was over, then with a sigh. He waited to hear what the next song would be.

"Don't fight me, Lucy," he whispered, stroking her hair. "Don't; it's not worth it," and along with Margaret Whiting he began to sing " 'There's a tree in the meadow, with a stream drifting by'—" and to move his hand up under her slip. "Don't," he said, when she began to struggle. "Trust me. I just want to touch your knee."

"I don't believe that, Roy. That's ridiculous."

"I swear. I won't go any higher. Come on, Lucy. What's a knee?"

> I will always remember
> The love in your eye—
> The day you carved upon that tree,
> I love you till I die.

They continued kissing. "See?" he said, after several minutes had passed. "Did I move it? Well, did I?"

"No."

"Didn't I say you could trust me?"

"Yes," she said, "but don't put your tongue on my teeth, please."

"Why not? What's it hurting?"

"Roy, you're just licking my teeth, what's the sense to it?"

"There's a lot of sense to it! It's passion!"

"Well, I don't *want* any."

"*Okay*," he said, "okay. Calm down. I'm sorry. I thought you liked it."

"There's nothing even to like, Roy—"

"*Okay!*"

> There was a boy,
> A very strange, enchanted boy.
> They say he wandered very far,
> Very far, over land and sea.

"I love this," Roy said. "It's just out. The guy who wrote it is supposed to live just like that."

"What is it?"

" 'Nature Boy.' Just what the guy who wrote it actually is. It's really got a great message. Listen to the words."

> This he said to me:
> "The greatest thing you'll ever learn,
> Is just to love, and be loved in return."

"Lucy," Roy whispered, "let's sit in the back."

"No. Positively no."

"Oh, hell, you don't have any respect for a mood—do you know that?"

"But we don't *sit* in the back, Roy. We tried to, but you really want to lie *down* in the back."

"Because the back doesn't have a steering wheel, Lucy, and it's more comfortable—and it's plenty clean too, because I cleaned it out myself this afternoon."

"Well, I'm not going back there—"

"Well, I am! And if you want to sit up here alone, go right ahead!"

"Oh, Roy—"

But he was out of the car and into the back seat, where he promptly stretched out, his head against one door and his feet through the open window opposite. "That's right, I'm lying down. Why shouldn't I? It's my car."

"I want to go home. You said you'd take me home. This is ridiculous."

"To you, sure. Boy, no wonder you and Ellie are friends. You're a real team." He mumbled something she couldn't understand.

"I'd like to know what you said just then, Roy."

"I said two c.t.'s, that's what."

"And what are they?"

"Oh," he moaned, "forget it."

"Roy," she said, turning on her knees, now in real anger, "we went through this last week."

"Right! Right! We sat in the back. And did anything terrible happen?"

"Because I wouldn't let it," she said.

"So then don't let it this time," he said. "Look, Lucy," and he sat up and tried to take hold of her head, which she pulled away. "I respect what you want, you know that. But all you want to do," he said, slumping backward, "is to get your picture taken, and get driven home at night, and what the other person feels . . . well, I happen to *feel* something! Oh, forget the whole mess, really."

"Oh, Roy," and she opened the front door and got out of the car, as she had on that awful night the week before. Roy threw open the back door so violently that it careened on its hinges.

"Get in," he whispered.

In the back he told her how much he could love her. He was pulling at her uniform buttons.

"Everybody says things like that when they want what you want, Roy. Stop. Please stop. I don't want to do this. Honestly. Please."

"But it's the *truth*," he said, and his hand, which had touched down familiarly on her knee, went like a shot up her leg.

"No, *no*—"

"Yes!" he cried triumphantly. "*Please!*"

And then he began to say trust me to her, over and over, and please, please, and she did not see how she could stop him from doing what he was doing to her without reaching up and sinking her teeth into his throat, which was directly over her face. He kept saying please and she kept saying please, and she could hardly breathe or move, he was over her with all his weight, and saying now don't fight me, I could love you, Angel, Angel, trust me, and suddenly into her mind came the name, Babs Egan.

"Roy—!"

"But I love you. Actually now I do."

"But what are you doing!"

"I'm not doing anything, oh, my Angel, my Angel—"

"But you will."

"No, no, my Angel, I won't."

"But you're doing it *now!* Stop! Roy, *stop* that!" she screamed.

"Oh, damn it," he said, and sat up, and allowed her to pull her legs out from under him.

She looked out the window at her side; the glass had fogged over. She was afraid to look over at him. She didn't know whether his trousers were just down, or completely off. She could hardly speak. "Are you crazy?"

"What do you mean, crazy? I'm a human being! I'm a man!"

"You can't do something like that—by force! That's what I mean! And I don't want to do it anyway. Roy, get back in front. Dress yourself. Take me home. Now!"

"But you just wanted to. You were all ready to."

"You had my arms pinned. You had me trapped! I didn't want anything! And you weren't even going to— to be careful! Are you absolutely *insane?* I'm not doing that!"

"But I would use something!"

She was astonished. "You would?"

"I tried to get some today."

"You *did?* You mean you were planning this all day long?"

"No! No! Well, I didn't get them—did I? Well, did I?"

"But you tried. You were thinking about it and planning it all day—"

"But it didn't *work!*"

"Please, I don't understand you—and I don't want to. Take me home. Put your trousers on, *please*."

"They're on. They were always on. Darn it, you don't even know what I went through today. All you know is your own way, that's all. Boy, you are another Ellie— another c.t.!"

"Which is *what!*"

"I don't use that kind of language in front of girls, Lucy! I respect you! Doesn't that mean anything to you at all? You know where I was this afternoon? I'll tell you where, and I'm not ashamed either—because it happened to involve respect for you. Whether you know it or not."

And then, while she pulled her slip down and rearranged her skirt, he told his story. For almost an hour he had waited outside Forester's for Mrs. Forester to go upstairs and leave her goofy old husband alone at the counter. But once Roy got inside, it turned out that Mrs. Forester had only gone back into the storeroom, and she was up by the register ready to wait on him before he could even turn around and walk out.

"So what could I do? I bought a pack of Blackjack Gum. And a tin of Anacin. Well, what else was I supposed to do? In every store in town my father's name is a household word. Every place I go it's 'Hi, Roy, how's G.I. Joe?' And people see me with *you,* Lucy. I mean, they know we're going together, you know. So who would they think it was for? Don't you think I think about that? There's your reputation to consider too, don't you think? There are a lot of things I happen to think about, Lucy, that maybe don't cross your mind, sitting in school all day."

Somehow he had confused her. What really did she want him to do? To have bought one of those things? He certainly wasn't going to use it on her. She wasn't going to let him *plan* what he was going to do to her hours in advance, and then act as though the whole thing was the passion of the moment. She wasn't going to be used or tricked, or be treated like some street tramp either.

"But you were overseas," she was saying.

"The Aleutians! The Aleutian Islands, Lucy—across the Bering Sea from the U.S.S.R.! Do you know what the motto is up there? 'A woman behind every tree'— *but there are no trees.* Get it? What do you think I did up there? I made out order forms all day. I played eighteen thousand ping-pong games. What's the *matter* with you!" he said, sinking in disgust into the seat. "Overseas," he said sourly. "*You* think I was up in some harem."

". . . But what about with someone else?"

"I never did it with anyone else! I've never done it in my entire life, all the way!"

"Well," she said softly. "I didn't know that."

"Well, it's the awful truth. I'm twenty years old, almost twenty-one, but that doesn't mean I go around doing it with every girl I see. I have to *like* the person, first of all. You listen to stupid Ellie, but Ellie doesn't know what she's talking about. The reason, Lucy, I don't take Monkey Littlefield out is because I don't happen to respect her. If you want the truth. And I don't like her. And I don't even know her! Oh, forget it. Let's just go, let's just call it quits. If you're going to listen to every story about me you hear, if you can't see the kind of person I am, Lucy, then pardon my language, but the hell with it."

He liked her. He actually did like her. He said people knew that they were going together. She hadn't realized. She was going with Roy Bassart, who was twenty and had been in the service. And people knew it.

"—over in Winnisaw," she was saying. Oh, why was she going on and on with this subject?

"Sure, I suppose they have them over in Winnisaw, they probably give them out on the streets in Winnisaw."

"Well, you could have driven over, that's all I mean."

"But why should I? Even going into Forester's on Broadway is going too far, as far as you're concerned. So what's the sense? Who am I kidding? Myself? I spent a whole afternoon hanging around outside waiting for that old hag to disappear, and it wouldn't have made any difference anyway. You'd only hate me worse. Right? So where does that leave me? Well, what is it you want to say, Lucy? That you'd say yes, if I had something?"

"No!"

"Okay, now we know where we stand! Fine!" He

threw open the back door on his side. "Let's go home! I can't take any more of this, really. I happen to be a man and I happen to have certain physical needs, as well as emotional needs, you know, and I don't have to take this from any high school kid. All we do is discuss every move I make, step by step. Is that romantic to you? Is that your idea of a man-woman relationship? Well, it's not mine. Sex is one of the highest experiences anybody can have, man or woman, physical or mental. But you're just another one of those typical American girls who thinks it's obscene. Well, let's go, Typical American Girl. I'm really a good-natured, easygoing guy, Lucy, so it really takes something to get me in a state like this—but I'm in it, all right, so let's go!"

She didn't move. He was really and truly angry, not like somebody who was trying to deceive you or trick you.

"Well, what's the matter now?" he asked. "Well, what did I do wrong now?"

"I just want you to know, Roy," she said, "that it isn't that I don't like you."

He made the sour face. "No?"

"No."

"Well, you sure do hide it."

"I don't," she said.

"You do!"

". . . But what if you don't like me? Really? How can I know you're telling the truth?"

"I told you, *I don't lie!*"

When she didn't respond, he came closer to her.

"You say love," Lucy said. "But you don't mean love."

"I get carried away, Lucy. That's not a lie. I get carried away, by the mood. I like music, so it affects me. So that's not a 'lie.' "

What had he just said? She couldn't even understand . . .

He climbed back into the car. He put his hand on her hair. "And what's wrong with getting carried away by the mood anyway?"

"But when the mood leaves you?" she asked. She felt

as though she weren't there, as though this were all
happening a long time ago. "Tomorrow, Roy?"

"Oh, Lucy," he said, and began kissing her again.
"Oh, Angel."

"And what about Monkey Littlefield?"

"I told you, I told you, I don't even know her—oh,
Angel, *please,*" he said, sliding her down against the
new slipcovers he himself had installed. "It's you, it's
you, it's you and only you—"

"But tomorrow—"

"I'll see you tomorrow, I promise, and the next day,
and the next—"

"Roy, I *can't*—oh stop—"

"But I'm not."

"But you are!"

"Angel," he moaned into her ear.

"Roy, no, please."

"It's okay," he whispered, "it's all right—"

"Oh, it's not!"

"But it is, oh, it is, I swear," he said, and then he
assured her that he would use a technique he had heard
about up in the Aleutians, called interruption. "Just
trust me," he pleaded, "trust me, trust me," and, alas,
she wanted to so badly, she did.

A week before Lucy's graduation the news arrived:
Roy had been accepted at the Britannia School of
Photography and Design, which had been established,
according to the catalogue and brochure, in 1910. They
were delighted to enroll him for the September session,
they said, and returned with the letter of acceptance the
dozen studies of Lucy he had enclosed with his application.

At the little impromptu party he gave that evening in
Roy's honor—Ellie and Joe, Roy and Lucy, Mr. and
Mrs. Bassart—Uncle Julian said they all owed a debt
of gratitude to Lucy Nelson for being so photogenic.
She deserved a prize too, so he gave her a kiss. He was
still somebody whom she hadn't made up her mind she
actually approved of, and when she saw his lips coming her way she had a bad moment in which she

almost pulled away. It wasn't just Mr. Sowerby's behavior with his wife, or his language, that caused her to
be slightly repulsed; nor the fact that someone five foot
five and smelling of cigars wasn't particularly her idea
of attractive. It was that during the last month there
had been several occasions when she thought she had
caught him looking too long at her legs. Could Roy be
telling his uncle what they were doing? She just
couldn't believe it; he might know they parked up at
Passion Paradise, but so did Ellie and Joe Whetstone,
and all they did was neck. At least that's what Ellie
said—and surely what her parents believed. No, nobody knew anything at all, and Mr. Sowerby was probably only looking at the floor, or at nothing, those times
she thought he was looking at her legs. After all she
was just eighteen, and he was Eleanor's father, and her
legs had no shape, or so she thought, and it was ridiculous to imagine, as she had when she had found herself
alone with him in the house one Saturday afternoon,
that he was going to follow her up to Ellie's room and
try to do something to her. She was getting sex on the
brain, too. She and Roy really had to stop what they
had begun, she just knew it. He liked it so much he was
dragging her up there every night, and maybe she liked
it too, but liking it wasn't the issue . . . What was, then?
That's what Roy asked, whenever she started saying,
"No, no, not tonight." But why not tonight, if last night?

Anyway, when Mr. Sowerby kissed her it was loud
and on the cheek, and everyone was laughing, and
Mrs. Sowerby was right there watching, trying to laugh
too. It was as unlike Lucy as anything could be—in a
way it was one of the strangest things she had ever
done—but in the confusion that came of being told in
public that she was attractive, in the excitement that
came of being so much a part of this celebration, of this
family, of this house, she shrugged her shoulders,
turned bright red and kissed Uncle Julian back. Roy applauded. "Bravo!" he cried, and Mrs. Sowerby stopped
trying to laugh.

Well, too bad for her. There really was very little
Lucy could do that met with Mrs. Sowerby's approval.

She was a dowdy, snobbish woman who even seemed to hold against Lucy the fact that it was she who had finally had the strongest influence in deciding what Roy should become. Which was certainly none of Mrs. Sowerby's business—even though that did appear to be the case: why Roy had decided to go to photography school in Fort Kean, where Britannia was located, seemed to have less to do with the quality of the training he would receive there—or with whatever natural talent he had for taking pictures, to be frank—than with the fact that Lucy happened to be going down to school in Fort Kean too.

That Roy had been guided in his decision by such a consideration was hardly a fact that displeased Lucy. On the other hand, it was one more refutation of that idea she had formed of him before they had met: that he was a serious young man who had choices before him of real magnitude and gravity. No, he wasn't exactly turning out to be entirely as she had imagined him back then—not that that was all to his discredit, however. For one thing, he really wasn't as rude and ill-mannered as he had first appeared. And he wasn't indifferent to others' feelings; least of all to hers. Once the showing off had stopped, once he was no longer as frightened of her (she realized) as she had been of him, he was altogether sweet and considerate. In his amiability he even reminded her a little of Mr. Valerio, which was certainly a compliment.

Nor was he superior in his attitudes, which was something she had just assumed would be the case, given his age and experience. He never tried to boss her around—except for sex; and even there she knew that when she decided enough was enough (probably that very night), there was nothing he would be able to do to force her to resume. There was nothing he could have done to force her to start, either, only why hadn't she realized that at the time? The worst that could have happened was that he would never have seen her again. And would that have been a tragedy? Truthfully, there were a lot of important ways in which she was discovering that she didn't like Roy that much. At times it even seemed as though it were she who was two and a half years older than Roy, not the other way around. She simply couldn't bear him when he sang those songs into her ear, first of all. He was so childish sometimes, even if he was now twenty-one and old enough to vote, as he kept saying to everyone. Sometimes the things he said were nothing less than stupid. In the car, for instance, he kept telling her that he loved her ... But was that stupid? What if it was true? Or what if he was only saying it for fear that if he didn't she wouldn't let him go all the way any more? Oh, she knew, she knew, she knew—they should never have started up in the car. It wasn't right if you weren't married, and it was even worse with someone you never could marry, either. *We must stop!* But somehow it made no more sense to stop now that they had begun than it had made to start in the first place. What she should really stop was the whole stupid thing!

Yes, she was very, very confused—even on that wonderful, cheery night at the Sowerbys', which began with Uncle Julian (as Roy had encouraged her to call him) kissing her as though she were another member of the family, and ended with his bringing out of the refrigerator a real bottle of French champagne, exploding cork and all ... Oh, how could she possibly believe the suspicion, growing larger in her every day, that he probably wasn't going to have one of any consequence at all, when they all stood around him with glasses raised, and said in unison, "To Roy's future!"

After graduation she began her summer schedule at the Dairy Bar: from ten to six, every day but Wednesday and Sunday. Midway through July she and Roy drove down to Fort Kean one Wednesday to look for a place for him to live in September. After inspecting each rooming house he came back to where Lucy sat in the parked car, and said he didn't think the place was right, at least for him; either the room smelled funny, or the landlady looked suspicious, or the bed was too short, something he had had enough of for sixteen months in the Aleutians. In the one place that was ideal—one huge room with a bed in it that used to be the landlady's husband's (who'd been six foot *five*), where the toilet was spotless, and the roomer guaranteed a shelf of his own in the refrigerator—there was no private entrance.

Well, said Lucy, there had to be.

At four that afternoon they had the worst argument they had ever had with each other, and far and away the worst Roy had ever had with anyone, his father included. To what was still the best all-around deal, all she could do was vehemently shake her head and say no, there had to be a private entrance if he expected ever to see her again. Suddenly, crying out, "Well, I don't care—it's me who has to live here!" he wheeled the Hudson around and drove back to the house with the long bed.

When he got back to the car he took a road map from the glove compartment and on its face carefully drew a rectangle. "This is my room," he said, managing not to look at her. It was on the first floor, a corner room with two tall windows on either side; all four let out onto a wide porch surrounded by shrubs. They were as good as four private entrances. At night a person could just step in and out of the windows exactly as though they were doors . . . Well, what did she want to say? Was she really planning on never speaking to him again, or did she have an opinion to express?

"I expressed my opinion," she said. "It didn't mean anything to you."

"It did."

"But you went ahead and rented the room anyway."

"Because I wanted to, yes!"

"I have nothing further to say, Roy."

"Lucy, it's a room! It's only a room! Why are you doing this?"

"You did it, Roy. Not me."

"*Did what?*"

"Acted like a child, again."

Before starting back to Liberty Center, Roy drove around to the Fort Kean College for Women. He pulled the car to the curb so Lucy could take another look at her new home. The college was across Pendleton Park from the main business section of Fort Kean. It had been built as a boys' preparatory school in the 1890's; in the thirties the school went under, and the property had been unused until the war, when it was occupied by the Army Signal Corps. After V-J Day the site had been purchased by the state, barracks and all, for its expanding educational program. It was certainly not the ivy-covered college campus one saw in the movies, or read about in books; the barracks that the Army had thrown up, long faded yellow buildings, were used as classrooms, and the administration building and dormitory was an old square fortress-like structure of gray stone that stood almost directly onto the street and resembled the County Courthouse in Winnisaw. At the sight of it, however, Lucy thought, "Only fifty-nine days more."

"Which is your room?" asked Roy, looking out the car window.

She did not answer.

The school was across from a row of stores, one of which was called "The Old Campus Coffee Shop." Roy said, "Hey, want a Coke in the Old Campus Coffee Shop?"

No answer.

"Oh, Angel, I do care what you think. You know that. What you think is important to me. But I have to live somewhere, don't I? Well, Lucy, just be reasonable—don't I? That's not being a kid, or a child, or whatever you said."

"Yes, Roy," she finally said, "you have to live somewhere."

"Don't be sarcastic, Lucy, really. Sometimes you're just too sarcastic, when I'm only asking for a simple answer. I've got to get my eight hours' sleep if I expect to get the most out of classes. Well, *don't* I? So I *need* the long bed. Well, is that a stupid statement too?"

She thought, *Everything you say is a stupid statement!* "No," she said, for he had taken her hand, and really seemed to be in pain.

"So then how can you be angry? Lucy, come on, what's the sense of fighting? Let's have a Coke, okay? Then we'll start home. Come on, say the fight is over. Why ruin the day? Look, am I forgiven for my terrible sin, or are you going to keep this silly thing up forever?"

He actually appeared to be near tears. She saw that there was no point in arguing with him any further. For in that instant she made up her mind—if only she had made it up earlier in the day, she could have saved them both the misery of a fight: she would never set foot in that room of his so long as he lived, no matter how many windows it had, or even doors. It was really as simple as that.

"Okay," she said, "let's have a Coke."

"That's my girl," said Roy, kissing her on the nose, "that's my old angel girl."

From that afternoon on she knew for sure that Roy wasn't for her. That very night she would not drive up with him to Passion Paradise. When instantly he grew sulky and morose, and seemed about ready to break into tears again, she told him it was because she was not well. It happened to be the truth, but then at home with a thick black crayon she circled on her calendar the day she would make it altogether clear their romance was over (at the same time x-ing out another day of her life in Liberty Center: fifty-eight to go).

It looked as though the bad news could not be broken to Roy until Sunday: the following night there were already plans to drive up to the Selkirk Fair with Ellie and Joe, with whom they doubled at least once a week now that Lucy was working only during the day; and on Friday evening Roy expected her to go over to Winnisaw with him to see *A Date with Judy;* then on Saturday there was the barbecue at the Sowerbys'. It was a barbecue for the Sowerbys' adult friends, and when Roy's uncle had invited "the long drink of water" to come and to bring "Blondie" with him, it had delighted Lucy (secretly) no less than Roy. She was coming to like Mr. Sowerby more all the time, and to admire certain of his qualities. As Roy said, he really didn't give a hoot about people's opinions; he did and said whatever he wanted, whenever he wanted. She still thought he was a little coarse with his language, but she didn't object, corny though it was, when he called her "Blondie," which seemed to have become his nickname for her, or even when he put his arm around her waist one evening and said (in a joshing way, of course, and winking at Roy), "You just tell me, Blondie, when you get tired of looking up at this big lug and want to look down at a little one."

She would have circled Friday then instead of Sunday, had it not been for the Sowerbys' Saturday night barbecue, at which her presence had specifically been requested by the host himself. That was awfully hard to turn down. She supposed she could wait until Sunday without losing anything—gaining three nights more away from home, in fact. Surely any diversion, even if it involved Roy, was better than sitting up in her hot room, listening to her family rocking downstairs on the porch; or lying awake in the dark bedroom, unable to sleep until she heard her father's footsteps coming up the stairs and she had determined (solely for the record) whether he was actually going off to bed sober.

What had always made summer particularly awful was that with all the doors and windows open, her sense of the presence of those whom she could hardly abide was painfully, horribly acute. Just to hear someone she hated *yawn* could drive her to distraction if she happened to be in an angry mood. Now, however, she was out every night until twelve-thirty, by which time they were usually asleep (not that it was any pleasure hearing someone you hated snore, if it made you start thinking about them). On the hottest nights, rather than being locked up with her family, she and Roy would sit on one of the benches down by the river, catching what breeze there was and staring off into the black stillness of water under the Winnisaw Bridge. She would think about college and Fort Kean—*away, away*—and often Roy would begin to sing to her, in a voice that really wasn't that bad, or so she was willing to admit in the pleasure of contemplating the future that would soon be hers. He sang like Vaughan Monroe, and like Dick Haymes; he could do Nat "King" Cole singing "Nature Boy," and Mel Blanc doing "Woody Woodpecker," and Ray Bolger (whom he thought he resembled in build) doing "Once in Love with Amy." After they saw *The Jolson Story* he did for her his imitation of the incomparable Al Jolson. That was how Roy introduced himself as hand in hand they sat down by the river on those close nights during what was to be the last summer of Lucy's arduous and unhappy youth. "Ladies and gentlemen, if you will, the incomparable, the one and only, Al Jolson.

> "Oh, how we danced,
>   On the night we were wed,
>   We danced and we danced—"

Fifty-eight days. Fifty-seven. Fifty-six.

At the Sowerby barbecue on Saturday night she got into a long, serious discussion with Roy's father—their first real talk—in which she heard herself assuring Mr. Bassart that he really shouldn't have anxiety or doubt any longer about Roy's future. Mr. Bassart said that he still could not figure where the interest in photography had suddenly come from. His experience with young people had long ago convinced him not to bank too heavily on sudden enthusiasms, since they had a habit of disappearing under strain. He was, he admitted, relieved that the months wasted wading around in what he called "a swamp of half-baked ideas" had come to an end, but now what concerned him was whether Roy had really chosen something he was going to be able to stick with when the going got rough. What did Lucy think? Oh, said Lucy, his heart was really in photography, she was sure of it.

"What makes you so sure?" asked Mr. Bassart in his flat voice.

She thought quickly and said that photography wasn't such an astonishing interest for Roy to have, when you thought that really it was a wonderful way of combining his present interest in drawing with his old interest in printing.

Mr. Bassart reflected upon what she had said.

So did she, reddening. "I think that's true, in a manner of speaking, Mr. Bassart."

"It's clever," he said without smiling, "but whether it's true is something I'll have to think about. What about your own plans? What are your own personal educational goals?"

Perspiring away under the brand-new peasant blouse that she had purchased for the party, she told him . . . Develop a logical mind . . . self-discipline . . . increase her general fund of knowledge . . . learn more about the world we live in . . . learn more about herself . . .

It was difficult to tell when to stop (exactly as it had been in the scholarship application), but when Mr. Bassart finally said, during a paragraph break, "Those are all good goals," she believed she had won approval enough for the time being, and shut up.

And—she later realized—he had asked not a single question about her background. He did not appear to be any more interested in the subject than Julian Sowerby; men like that judged you not on family history, but on the kind of person you were. Only Mrs. Bassart (who seemed to have fallen instantly under her sister's influence) and Irene Sowerby seemed to hold against her things she wasn't even responsible for. The others, to their credit, weren't interested in gossip and ancient history—Roy included.

Since the beginning of summer Roy had taken to picking her up at the house after dinner each night. She was always ready when he arrived, giving him little encouragement, she hoped, to linger and make conversation. On the one occasion when he seemed to be trying to draw her into revealing something, she answered so sharply that he had never brought up the subject again. It was after his first meeting with her family, all of whom were gathered in the living room after dinner. The young man arrived, was quickly introduced and led by Lucy straight back out the door.

Driving over to the movie, Roy said, "Wow, your mother's a real looker, you know that?"

"Yes."

"You know who she reminds me of?"

"No."

"Jennifer Jones." No answer. "Listen, did you see *Song of Bernadette?*"

She had, with Kitty Egan, three times; but her conversion was her own business too. It hadn't even taken place.

"Of course, your mother's older than Jennifer Jones ..." Roy said. "And your grandfather is Mr. Carroll from the post office. Now, I didn't even know that. Ellie never mentioned it."

"He's retired," she said. Why on earth had she given in when he said it was time he was introduced to her "folks"?

They were crossing the Winnisaw Bridge. "Well, your father seems like a nice guy."

"I don't talk about him, Roy! I never want to talk about him!"

"Gee, sure, okay," he said, raising one hand over his chest. "Just making conversation."

"Well, don't."

"Well, okay, I won't."

"That subject does not interest me *at all.*"

"Okay, okay," he said, smiling, "you're the boss," and after a silent minute during which she contemplated asking him to pull the car over to the side so that she could get out, he switched on the radio and began to sing.

From then on, neither Bassart nor Sowerby asked any question about her home life. Ellie couldn't have cared less, and so it was only in the company of Irene Sowerby, or Roy's mother, that Lucy became unduly conscious of what ordinarily she was able, after all these years of practice, to drive clear out of her mind. Of late she hardly ever had cause (outside the house) to think of herself as the kid who had done this or the kid whose father had done that. To the many people she met socially at the Sowerbys' for the first time on that Saturday night—among them, the principal, Mr. Brunn and his wife—she was, very simply, Roy Bassart's girl.

"So," said Mr. Brunn, "this is the young lady I hear is keeping our old alum in line these days."

"Oh, it's a matter of opinion, Mr. Brunn, who's keeping who in line," said Roy.

"And are you off to school in September, dear?" asked Mrs. Brunn. Dear. Just like Mrs. Sowerby.

"Yes," said Lucy. "Fort Kean College for Women."

"They've got themselves quite a little setup down there," said Mr. Brunn. "Very nice. Very nice."

"Lucy graduated twenty-ninth in the senior class this year, Mr. Brunn, before she tells you herself."

"Oh, I recognized Lucy—I knew she was up there. Good luck to you, Lucy. Keep up our reputation. We've sent them some fine girls down there and I'm sure you're going to turn out to be no exception."

"Thank you, Mr. Brunn. I'll try my best."

"Well, that'll do it, I'm sure. See you, Roy; see you, Lucy."

So, later that night, up in Passion Paradise, what could she do? It wasn't till Sunday that she was to tell him that she'd had enough, and it was still only Saturday night. And when she told him, what would happen? "I'm not going to be able to see you again. Ever." "*What?*" "Because we don't really have any business together, Roy." "But ... what do you mean? Haven't these months meant anything at all? Look, why else am I going to Fort Kean to school—who inspired me to go there, except you?" "Well, you'll just have to go for a better reason than that." "What better reason is there but love!" "But it's not love—it's just sex." "It's *what?*" "Sex!" "Not to me ... Look, is that what it is to you? Because to me ... Oh, *no*," he'd weep, "this is terrible ..." And then—she just knew it—he wouldn't go to Fort Kean at all. If she broke off with him now, he would give up Britannia, give up all his plans, probably in the end give up photography too, despite what she had said to his father in his defense. And then he *would* be right back in his swamp of ideas ... But that was his affair, not hers ... Or was it? He was so good

to her, so kind to her, sweeter to her than anybody had
ever been before in her life, and day in and day out
too. How could she turn around now and be so heartless and cruel? Especially when it was only a matter of
a few more weeks. It might even mean his whole
career. Because he depended on her—he listened to
her—he loved her. *Roy loves me.*

At least that's what he said.

"I love you, Angel," he said at the door. He kissed
her nose. "You made a real hit tonight."

"On who?"

"Mr. Brunn, for one. Everybody." He kissed her yet
again. "Me," he said. "Look, sleep tight." From the
bottom of the steps he whispered, *"Au revoir."*

She was very, very confused. Ten months ago she
was still in the band, marching behind Leola Krapp,
and now she was going steady! Going all the way
practically every night!

She circled six days in July and ten in August, and
then on September first she took her crayon and circled
four times around the day after Labor Day. She had
started out to circle Labor Day itself, until she remembered that she and Roy and Ellie and Joe Whetstone
were to go off canoeing on the river, an event that had
been planned by Roy weeks before. If only everything
weren't planned so far in advance! If only he didn't
need her so, depend on her so, love her so! *But did
he?*

When they arrived on Labor Day morning at the
Sowerbys', Roy's Aunt Irene came outside to say that
Ellie had been sick in the night and was still sleeping.
She suggested that the three young people had better go
off by themselves for the day. But even as she spoke, a
very sad and wan-looking Ellie appeared in the upstairs
hall window, wearing her bathrobe. She waved.
"Hi."

"Ellie," said Mrs. Sowerby, "I suggested to the others
that they'd better go off without you today, dear."

"Oh, no."

"Eleanor, if you're not well, you surely cannot go
canoeing."

"Your mother's right," said Joe.

"But I want to go," Ellie called down in a weak voice.

"It wouldn't be safe, El," said Joe. "Really."

"Joe is right, Eleanor," said Mrs. Sowerby.

"But I *planned* to go," said Ellie, and suddenly she drew down the shade, as though she was about to weep.

It was decided that the three young people should come inside while Ellie washed and dressed and had a little breakfast of tea and toast; then if she really did seem to have recovered, perhaps the youngsters could go ahead with their plans. Ellie's troubles had begun the previous evening while Mrs. Sowerby had been away at an informal meeting of the officers of The Quilt Society. In Mrs. Sowerby's absence, Ellie and her father had sat around the TV set, eating three pounds of cherries, followed by a quart of vanilla fudge ice cream, topped off with half a chocolate nut cake left over from dinner.

Julian Sowerby, feeling fine, claimed Ellie's upset stomach had nothing to do with a little dish of ice cream and a piece of cake; Ellie simply had the heebie-jeebies about going away to school in two weeks. Roy said that maybe Ellie had inherited her father's good looks (everyone laughed, Julian loudest of all) but that perhaps she hadn't been so fortunate as to inherit his cast-iron stomach.

"That's probably true, Mr. Sowerby" was Joe's comment. Joe assured Mrs. Sowerby that if she let Ellie come along, he would be sure to see that she didn't touch anything sweet. Mrs. Bassart had prepared an immense picnic basket for them, but Roy said that he and Joe would take care of Ellie's portion without too much trouble.

In a few minutes Ellie came down the stairs in white shorts, white polo shirt and white sandals. Her tan—nurtured daily on the back lawn and down by the landing—looked dazzling, as did her hair, which over the summer had taken on a coppery sheen. But this morning her face looked small and worn, and her

"Hullo" was hardly audible as she went off to the kitchen to try to put a little food into her long, shapely body . . . Her body. Her long and shapely body! Lucy's understanding of Ellie's condition was instantaneous. *My God, it's happened. To Ellie Sowerby.*

Julian Sowerby drove off with his clubs to the Winnisaw Golf Club, and the young people consented to forgo the canoeing and take Mrs. Sowerby's advice and find a nice shady spot up at the picnic grounds to have their outing. But even hidden away under a tree the temperature rose steadily; about one o'clock Ellie began to feel woozy, and so they drove back to the Sowerbys' in Roy's car. The house was very quiet. The shades were drawn in the front bedroom, where apparently Mrs. Sowerby was taking a nap; and the family car was still gone, a fact that caused Ellie some consternation. Apparently she had expected to find her father already home.

"Do you want me to wake your mother, El?" asked Joe.

"No, no. I'm all right."

Joe and Roy decided to go out to the backyard and listen to the Sox double-header on the Sowerby portable. Ellie asked Lucy to come up with her to her room. Once there she locked the door, threw herself onto her bed, and beneath the white organdy canopy, began to cry.

Lucy watched her friend weeping her heart out. On the lawn below she saw the person responsible pick up a croquet mallet and begin to knock a ball around through the wickets. In two days Joe was to report for freshman football practice at the University of Alabama. Partly it was Ellie's recollection of life in the South during the early years of the war that seemed to have influenced Joe to accept the Alabama scholarship. Joe was to leave for school the very next day—but would he still go? Or would Ellie now go with him?

Roy had organized the day's outing, and had his mother prepare the lunch as his own farewell party to Joe Whetstone, whom he had come to consider his closest buddy. Lucy herself had always thought of Joe as one big blah. Sure, he was a great athlete, she supposed, and you had to admit he was handsome and rugged-looking, if you liked that type, but he had not a single opinion of his own on any subject. Whatever you said, Joe agreed with. There were times when she felt like reciting the Declaration of Independence just to watch his head go up and down and to hear him say, after every famous sentence, "You bet, that sure is true, that sure does make a lot of sense, boy, that's just what my Mom says . . ." The temptation to reveal him for the imbecile that he was came over her most strongly when Roy was purposely acting for Joe's benefit, telling some funny story about what had happened to him up in the Aleutians, or discussing some college football team he and Joe called "The Crimson Tide" and which normally he didn't seem to be interested in at all. But she had never given in to the temptation; she hadn't even told Ellie her real opinion of Joe Whetstone. And now it was too late. Now Joe had gotten Ellie into trouble, the worst kind of trouble there could possibly be for a girl. And Joe didn't even appear to know it.

Roy called to Joe. "Appling's up. Two on. No score."

"*Go,* Luke," said Joe, knocking the wooden ball clear through a wicket at the other end of the lawn. "Hey, Joe, the Arm," he said.

"Oh, boy," Roy said sourly, "swing and a miss. Strike one."

"Come *on,* Lukey babe," said Joe, posing with his mallet like a batter all coiled up to swing. "Hey," said Joe, "Stan the Man," and he changed his batting stance and swung at an imaginary ball. "Gooing, going—"

"Foul!" said Roy.

"Shucks," said Joe, "pulled it too hard."

"Shhh," said Roy, looking quickly up at the house as Joe fell to the lawn laughing.

. . . What about college now? What about the Sowerbys? What about Ellie's future, if she had to marry Joe

Whetstone? And what if he already knew and didn't care? Maybe he wanted to marry Ellie, but she was crying because she didn't want to marry him!

"I have—I have to tell somebody," Ellie said, turning to Lucy and clutching the pillow to her chest.

"What?" said Lucy softly. "Tell what, Ellie?"

Ellie pushed her head back into the pillow and again began to weep. She had done a stupid thing. A terrible, stupid thing. Her whole life would never be the same.

". . . Why? What is it?"

She had listened in on someone else's telephone conversation. "And it's not the first time, either," said Ellie, sobbing.

Then she's not pregnant.

Down below Roy said, "Base hit!"

"Go, Sox," said Joe. "Pour it on, baby."

"And the run scores," cried Roy. "And another! Two nothing!"

Petulantly Lucy said, "What do you mean? Ellie, I can't understand you."

"I listened in on someone else's telephone conversation . . . and it was awful."

"Whose?"

"Oh, Lucy, I don't want my mother to know. Never!"

"Know *what?*"

"Is the door locked?" asked Ellie.

"You locked it," said Lucy impatiently.

"Then . . . Sit over here. On the bed. I don't want to shout. Oh, I don't know what to do. This is so awful . . . I've been trying to tell you for so long. I needed somebody's advice that I could talk it over with . . . But I just couldn't. And I shouldn't. Oh, but I just have to—but, Lucy, you have to promise me. You can't repeat it to anyone. Not even Roy. *Especially* not Roy."

"Ellie, I don't even understand what you're—"

"My father!" said Ellie. "Lucy, don't tell ever—do you promise? You have to promise me, Lucy. Please, so I can tell you."

"I promise."

"My father has women!" Ellie burst out. "On the side!"

Lucy received these words with equanimity: it was as though a truth she had known in her heart all along had finally been confessed by Eleanor.

"And that's not all," said Ellie. "Lucy . . . he gives them money."

"Are you sure?"

"*Yes.*"

"How do you know he does?"

"That's what I heard on the phone." She closed her eyes. "Actual money," she said, and the tears rolled off her cheeks onto her white polo shirt.

Just then they heard the door to Mrs. Sowerby's room open, down the hall.

"Dear, are you in there?" she asked.

"Yes. Lucy too. We're only talking, Mother."

"Are you all right?"

"It got too hot, Mother," said Ellie, frantically wiping her eyes. "But I'm fine. I promise. It was practically a hundred, though. And buggy. And crowded. All kinds of people from Winnisaw."

For a moment they heard nothing; then the sound of Mrs. Sowerby descending the stairs. Neither of them spoke until the screen door opened down below and Joe was saying, "Sox are out in front, Mrs. Sowerby, four to nothing."

"Sure," said Roy, "she's the right one to tell, all right. Hey, Aunt Irene, tell Joe which team Luke Appling plays for. No, no, tell him what a bunt is. Come on, give him your great definition of a bunt."

Roy and Joe could be heard down on the back lawn, teasing Mrs. Sowerby about sports, and Mrs. Sowerby could be heard obligingly making them laugh . . . while upstairs Eleanor began to tell Lucy the whole story.

It had begun about a year ago, on a summer night when she and her father had been home alone. It was after eleven and she was in bed, when suddenly she remembered she had forgotten to tell Judy Rollins not to say anything to anyone about something Ellie had told her, and so she reached over and picked up her bedside telephone. Of course, the instant she heard her father talking on the downstairs line she knew she should hang up. Only, the voice on the other end she recognized as belonging to nobody but Mrs. Mayerhofer, the manager of Daddy's laundromat in Selkirk, about whom he was always complaining to her mother. Mrs. Mayerhofer was, as he put it, a little slow on the pickup; there actually wasn't a single thing that he didn't have to explain to her ten times before she got it right. He kept her on almost solely out of pity— abandoned by her husband, she had an infant child to support—and because, unlike her predecessor, the illustrious Mrs. Jarvis, it didn't appear that Mrs. Mayerhofer was going to steal him deaf, dumb and blind.

On the phone her father was saying that he just couldn't get up to Selkirk until the end of the week because he was so tied up right here in Liberty Center, and Mrs. Mayerhofer said that she didn't think she could wait until the end of the week, and Ellie still remembered thinking, "Boy, what a moron," until she heard her father laugh and say that in the meantime then she was just going to have to make do with the old hot-water bottle. Mrs. Mayerhofer laughed, and Ellie said it was as though her bones and her blood and everything inside her had turned to stone. She pushed the receiver down into her pillow and held it there for what seemed like ages; when at last she raised it to her ear again, the line was free—and so she called Rollins. What else could she do?

This was just before she and Lucy had first gotten to know each other, Ellie said. Actually, she had been dying back then to tell Lucy what she had overheard, only she'd felt so ashamed and embarrassed—and very shortly so uncertain as to whether what she had heard meant what she had taken it to mean—that she decided to stop seeing Lucy entirely for the time being, rather than risk ruining their friendship and making a terrible fool of herself and her family.

For the moment Ellie's words confused Lucy, and not simply because of the disordered way in which her friend offered her explanation. She had to work out in her head the significance of all that Ellie had just said—that is, the significance to herself.

She would lie awake, Ellie was saying, just lie awake after that for hours on end, in dread of ever overhearing such a conversation again . . . and then silently lift the phone off the receiver. It was a nightmare; she didn't want to catch him, and she couldn't stop trying to. Then that winter her father came home one evening and said that Mrs. Mayerhofer ("my mental giant" was his expression) had flown the coop; just disappeared from her apartment in Selkirk—baby, baggage and all. The very next day he drove up to interview and hire somebody else for the job. The woman selected was named Edna Spatz.

And that was all that had happened. She never heard him with Mrs. Mayerhofer on the phone a second time, nor was there any reason for her to suspect Edna Spatz. Yet every time her father went off to the Selkirk store, Ellie knew it was to carry on behind her mother's back—even though she knew too that Edna Spatz had a husband in Selkirk and two small children. This was about the time she and Lucy had started seeing each other again, and on more occasions than she could even count, Ellie had wanted to blurt out to her the whole horrible story about Mrs. Mayerhofer. Only Mrs. Mayerhofer was so terribly dumb and uneducated. So he couldn't with her, he simply couldn't. He simply wouldn't even want to.

Or so she had gotten herself to believe, until last night. She had been on the stairs when the phone rang, and so she raced up to her room thinking that it was Joe, who had said he would call around nine. In the meantime her father had picked up the downstairs phone; "It's okay, Princess," he had called up to her, "it's just for me." She had called back, "Okay, Daddy," and gone ahead into her room, closed the door, and without any knowledge that she was even going to do it, gently lifted the phone off the hook. At first she couldn't even hear the words being spoken. It was as though she had a heart beating in her head, and another in her throat, and the rest of her simply didn't exist. On the other end a woman was speaking. Whether it was Edna Spatz, she didn't know. She had come to imagine Mrs. Spatz as no less a dimwit than Mrs. Mayerhofer, and the trouble with the voice on the other end was that it sounded smart . . . and young. The woman was saying that if she couldn't cover her check she didn't know what would happen to her. Her father said this was something he would have to take care of later—*and not by telephone.* He was whispering into the phone, but he was angry. The woman began to cry. She said that the agency had threatened to take her to court. She called him Julian, Julian, and she wept. She said she was sorry, she knew she shouldn't call, she had dialed and hung up half a dozen times over the weekend, but who else did she have to turn to but Julian, Julian?

It was at that point that Ellie felt she could not bear to hear another word. The woman sounded so unhappy—and so young! So she buried the phone in the pillow again, and just sat there, not knowing what to do. Only a minute or so later her father called up the stairs to her. She replaced the phone as quietly as she could and came quickly down to him, chattering gaily all the while. She knew he was watching her every expression to see whether she had been listening, but Ellie was sure that she had not given herself away in anything she had said or done. She kept talking about Joe this and Joe that, and instantly sat next to him on the couch when invited to—"Keep me company, Daisy Mae"—and even let him hold her hand while the two of them watched TV together and ate all those cherries. That's why she had consumed so much junk; she was afraid to stop for fear he would think something was bothering her. And all the time they were sitting on the couch she had the most absurd thought: that she had an older sister, whom she knew nothing about, and that it was she who had been on the phone asking her father to send money. Of course she was only making up the idea of a sister, and knew it—and so then she began to think that maybe she was making up the whole incident.

"Lucy, I'm so confused—and miserable! Because I just don't know. Do you think it's true?"

"What's true?"

"What I heard."

"Well, you heard it, didn't you?"

"I don't know. Yes! But who is it? Who could it possibly be? And my poor mother," she said, weeping profusely once again, "she doesn't even know. Nobody knows. Nobody but you and me—and him . . . and her!"

All the youngsters were invited to stay for supper on the Sowerby lawn: roast beef sandwiches, corn on the cob, apple pie and ice cream—except for Ellie, who had consommé, half of which she left in the bowl. Mr. Sowerby offered each of the boys a bottle of beer, against Mrs. Sowerby's better judgment. "Come on, they'll all be in college in a week. Roy here is responsible for us winning the war against the North Pole. A little beer'll do him good, put some hair on his chest."

Joe took a sip and laid the glass aside; Roy drank his right out of the bottle. Then he opened the top button of his shirt and looked inside. "Nothing," he said.

They sat out on the lawn till long after dark. Ellie was stretched out in a beach chair with an afghan thrown over her, and just her head sticking out. It looked very, very small. Roy sat on the grass, holding his beer bottle in one hand; his head swung back against Lucy's legs whenever he took a swig from the bottle. Joe Whetstone was stretched out on his stomach, his chin resting on his two fists. He was looking up at the sky, and every once in a while he said, "Boy, oh, boy. Look at them all."

Roy said he'd known a guy in the service who believed in the stars. Joe said, "No kidding."

"Absolutely," said Roy, "to some people it's practically a religion in itself."

"No kidding," said Joe. "I wonder how many there really are."

Julian Sowerby asked how his Princess was.

"Better," she answered after a moment.

"I believe you were just missing home," said Julian Sowerby, "before you even went away from it."

"Boy, I'll bet that can happen," said Joe.

"Sure, sure. Homesick, plus all that vanilla fudge ice cream with, I understand from reliable sources, a little butterscotch sauce, *and* walnuts—"

"*Roy!*" cried Ellie weakly.

Roy and Joe laughed.

"Roy, don't tease her," said Mrs. Sowerby.

"Sorry, Ellie-o," said Roy.

Julian lit a cigar. "How about it, Joe?"

"Oh, no, sir," Joe said. "Got to stay in shape."

"Won't affect your toe, boy," Julian said.

"No, thank you just the same, Mr. Sowerby. Didn't mean to waste the beer either."

"Take it off my taxes," said Julian, to Joe's amusement. "How about you, General?" he asked Roy.

"Sure," said Roy, "if it's a good one. Toss."

Julian threw a cigar his way. "Fourteen-fifty a box, it ain't what I could call a stinkweed, wise guy."

The smoke from Roy's cigar rose around his head. "Not too bad," he said, holding it off at arm's length and muffling a cough.

"A real pro," said Uncle Julian.

Ordinarily Lucy couldn't stand to watch Roy smoke a cigar or drink a beer; he really cared very little for either. But this evening there were matters more grave to brood upon than Roy's showing off for his uncle. There was the uncle himself, whose secret had finally been revealed; there was Ellie, who knew the secret; there was Mrs. Sowerby, who did not; and there was herself. All these months she had been believing that Ellie was indifferent to her past, and suddenly it was clear that nothing but that past had caused Ellie to befriend her in September, and to resume that "friendship" again in February. It was a startling discovery. All this time, so stupidly, so innocently, so dreamily, she had been thinking that to Ellie Sowerby she was not the kid whose father hung out at Earl's Dugout, not the kid who had gained notoriety by calling the police to come take him away, when that was precisely who she was. All she was. It had caused her much pain that afternoon to understand that all of her attraction for Ellie lay in that past which she herself wanted never to think about again so long as she lived.

And it had made her angry too. Her temptation earlier in the afternoon had been to rise in indignation and tell Ellie exactly what she thought of her. "You mean that's what I am to you, Ellie? That's why you wanted me to be a friend? To my face, you actually have the nerve to admit that when you dropped me, it was because you believed you didn't *need* me any more? And what exactly did you think I was going to do for you, anyway, in return for letting me wear your precious sweater?"

On and on and on, but in her head only. At first she restrained her anger so as to hear the story of Julian Sowerby's deception to its conclusion, but even before Ellie had finished, she began to understand Eleanor's attraction to her as something else entirely. Ellie actually *admired* her. Her courage. Her pride. Her strength. Wasn't that a deeper way, a truer way, to see it? Ellie Sowerby, with all her clothes, and boys, and beauty, and money, had turned for help and advice—to her.

Well, what should Ellie do, then? *What?* Her mind began to examine the possibilities.

"Hey, what happened to Blondie tonight?" Julian was asking. "Cat got Cutie-Pie's tongue?"

"Oh, no."

"Thinking about college, aren't you, Lucy?" said Mrs. Sowerby.

"Yes."

"It's going to be a wonderful experience for all of you," said Irene Sowerby. "These will be the four most beautiful years of your life."

"That's what my Mom says too, Mrs. Sowerby," said Joe.

"Yes, it's going to do all of you a world of good," said Mrs. Sowerby, "to be away from home."

Poor Mrs. Sowerby. Poor woman. How mortifying. How wrong. How unjust ... It was the first time that her heart had opened fully to Ellie's mother. She saw at last that she was something more than her own potential enemy. To understand that Mrs. Sowerby suffered was somehow to understand that she existed, had a life, had motives and reasons having nothing to do with frustrating and opposing Lucy Nelson. The fact was that she had never opposed her. The decision Ellie had made to stop seeing Lucy back in September had, by her own admission, nothing at all to do with any instructions she had received from her mother. Only now could Lucy see that during these past months Mrs. Sowerby had never been anything but kind to her. Her ways might be somewhat old-fashioned and her manner a little remote, but was that so bad? What harm had she ever done Lucy? My God, it wasn't Mrs. Sowerby who had been small-minded, it had been Lucy herself! She should be ashamed of herself for her suspicions. Even when she had appeared wearing one of Ellie's cashmere sweaters, Mrs. Sowerby's exasperation probably had to do entirely with Eleanor's barely disguised condescension, and nothing to do with disapproval of Lucy for being covetous of her daughter's clothes. She was a patient, gentle and sympathetic person—look at her treatment not only of Lucy, but of Roy. She alone, of his entire family, seemed to take his problems and dilemmas seriously; she alone accorded him genuine respect. Who had the dignity, the self-possession of Mrs. Sowerby? She could think of no one.

And was this the reward to be paid that dignity? Was this how Julian Sowerby chose to express his respect and gratitude to a woman of such refinement and generosity? Because she happened to have to wear special elasticized stockings; because in her middle age she was tending toward heaviness; because her hair had begun to turn to gray, was that sufficient cause for such a person to be deceived, disgraced, discarded by a philandering loud-mouthed little pig of a man? Blondie! Cutie-Pie! What a person! What a disgusting cheat of a person!

Yet in her heart she had always known. That was the amazing part.

What should Ellie do? Tell her mother? Tell her Uncle Lloyd? Or should she speak directly to her father, so as to spare her mother from ever knowing? Yes, go to him; and if he promises to end his associations with his women, promises never to resume with them again . . . Or perhaps first she ought to find out who the woman was. And then go to *her*. Yes, and tell her that she must break off relations with her father instantly, or risk exposure—even incarceration, if it turned out (as it might) that she was a prostitute who sold her services to men like Julian Sowerby. Or perhaps Ellie should keep her secret, bide her time, wait for the phone to ring again—and then lift the extension and instead of burying the truth in her pillow, instead of simply sitting like a ninny enduring his treachery, put an end to it once and for all: "This is Eleanor Sowerby. I am Julian Sowerby's daughter. I should like to know your name, please."

All at once, air colder and fresher than any they had felt in months seemed to descend on the Sowerbys and their young guests.

"Wow," said Joe softly. In his excitement he sat straight up. "It's fall. It's really fall."

"Hey, let's get this Princess in the house," said Julian Sowerby. He stood and stretched, so that his cigar went waving over his head like some signal.

"Good idea," said Joe. He and Roy told Mrs. Sowerby that since it was the maid's night off, the two of them would carry in all the dirty dishes. They made a big fuss about not letting her touch anything, and shooed her directly into the house.

Mr. Sowerby began to fold up the chairs, and Roy began to whistle "Autumn Leaves" as he went around collecting the silverware. Joe, piling plates, was saying to him, "Do you realize, Big Roy-boy, that tomorrow at this time—"

Suddenly Ellie was at Lucy's side, whispering into her ear.

"What?" said Lucy.

". . . forget everything."

"What do you mean?"

"I mean—*never mind!*"

"But . . . didn't it really happen?"

"Hey, my two colleens," Julian called, using an Irish accent. "Enough giggling now and into the house with you."

They started quickly across the lawn. Ellie shivered, pulled the afghan up over her hair, and started to run for the open door.

Lucy hissed, "But, Ellie, what are you going to do?"

Ellie stopped. "I'll—I'll—"

"What?"

"Oh, I'll just go to Northwestern."

"But," whispered Lucy, taking hold of her arm, "your mother?"

But now Roy and Joe rushed up from behind— "Coming through! Hot stuff! Watch it, ladies!"—and anything further she said would have been overheard. And then Julian Sowerby suddenly had each of them by the arm, and, laughing, ran them into the house.

The next day Joe left for Alabama, and then Ellie herself became desperately busy with shopping and packing, and was almost perpetually in the company of her mother—who still seemed to be innocent of what was happening behind her back. The few times they were together for more than a minute, Lucy hardly had a chance to open her mouth, before Ellie said, "Shhh, later," or "Lucy, I think never mind, really," and finally, "Look, I was all wrong."

"You *were?*"

"I misunderstood, I'm sure, yes."

"But—"

"*Please,* let me just get to college!"

By the time they parted they seemed hardly even to be friends any longer, if they ever had been. Ellie and her family drove off to Evanston on the second weekend in September, and on the Monday following, on a day that Lucy had encircled with five black rings on her calendar, she and Roy drove down with a carful of luggage to begin their schooling in Fort Kean.

3

She passed out twice in the second week of November, first in a booth in The Old Campus Cofeee Shop, and the afternoon following, upon rising from her seat at the end of English class. At the student health center, a barracks building that had been converted into the infirmary, she told the doctor that she believed she might be suffering from anemia. Her skin had always been on the pale side, and in winter the tips of her toes and fingers went white and icy when it got very cold.

After the examination she dressed and sat in a chair the doctor had pulled back for her in his office. He said that he did not believe the problem was with the circulation in her extremities. Looking out the window, he asked if she had been having any trouble lately with her periods. She said no, then she said yes, and then, clutching her coat and her books in her arms, she rushed out the door. In the narrow corridor she felt herself spinning, but this time the sensation lasted only a second.

As soon as she pulled shut the door of the phone booth in the coffee shop she realized that Roy would be in class. His landlady, Mrs. Blodgett, answered, and Lucy hung up without even speaking. She thought of dialing the school and having him called to a phone;

but what would she say to him? The strange sensation she began to have—as the first wave of confusion gave way to a second, even more severe—was that it did not have anything to do with him anyway. She found herself thinking like a child who does not know the facts of life, who thinks that pregnancy is something that a woman does to herself, or that simply happens to her if she wishes hard enough.

In her room she looked at all the ridiculous markings on her calendar. Just the previous Saturday, after Roy had driven her back to the dormitory from the movies, she had drawn a thick black ring around Thanksgiving Day. Suddenly she felt dreadful; she went and stood with her mouth open over the toilet, but all she could cough up were some brownish strands of liquid. The dread remained.

That evening she did not answer when the on-duty girl rapped on the door to her room and said that a Roy was on the phone.

At eight in the morning, the other girls drifting down to the dining hall or running off to class, Lucy rushed back to the infirmary. She had to wait on a bench in the corridor until ten, when the doctor finally arrived.

"I was here yesterday," she said. "Lucy Nelson."

"Come in. Sit down."

Before she began to speak he came around to the door and pushed it shut all the way. When he returned to his desk, she told him that she did not want a baby.

He pushed his chair back a little and crossed one leg over the other. That was all he did.

"Doctor, I'm a freshman. A first-semester freshman."

He said nothing.

"I've been working for years to go to college. At night. In a soda fountain. Up in Liberty Center. That's where I'm from ... And summers too—three whole summers. And I have a Living Aid Scholarship. If I hadn't gotten in here I might not even have been able to go to school at all—because of money." But she did not want to plead poverty, or even helplessness. What he had to know was that she was not weak, she was strong, she had undergone many hardships, and much suffering—she wasn't just another eighteen-year-old girl. It wasn't merely that she needed his help; she *deserved* it. "This is my first real experience away from home, Doctor. I've been waiting for it all my life. Saving for it. It's all I've had to look forward to for years."

He continued to listen.

"Doctor, I'm not promiscuous, I swear it. I'm just eighteen! You've got to believe me!"

Until then the doctor had sat there with his glasses pushed up on his forehead. Now he adjusted the spectacles down onto the bridge of his nose.

"I don't know what to do," she said, trying to regain her self-control.

His face remained immobile. He had soft gray hair and kind eyes, but he only scratched the side of his nose.

"I don't know what to do," she said again. "I really don't."

He crossed his arms. He rocked a little in his chair.

"Doctor, I never had a boy friend before. He was my first one. That's the truth—it really is."

The doctor swung the chair around and looked out the window, toward "The Bastille," as the girls called the main building. He had pushed his glasses up again, and now he began rubbing at his eyes. Maybe he had been out on an emergency all night and was tired. Maybe he was thinking of what to say. Maybe he wasn't even listening. He came out to the school four mornings a week for two hours, so what did he care? He had a practice of his own to worry about; this was just so much extra cash. Maybe he was only letting time pass before he sent her away to deal with her own mess.

He turned back to her. "And where is the young man?" he asked.

"... Here."

"Speak up, Lucy. Where?"

She felt herself becoming meek. Or was it protective? "In Fort Kean."

"And now that he's had his fun, that's it, I suppose."

"What?" she whispered.

He was rubbing at his temples with the tips of his fingers. He *was* thinking. He was going to help! "Don't you girls know what they're up to?" he asked in a soft and unhappy voice. "Can't you imagine what they'll be like when something like this happens? A bright and pretty little girl like you, Lucy. What were you thinking about?"

Her eyes welled with tears at the sound of her name. It might have been the first time she had ever heard it spoken. *I'm Lucy. I'm bright. I'm pretty.* Oh, her life was just beginning! So very much had happened to her in the last year alone—in the last month. Already there was a girl on her floor who knew a boy she wanted to fix Lucy up with. Only there had never once been an opportunity to meet him, what with Roy coming around every single night, if only to stop off and say hello. She was away from home at long long last—and starting to be pretty! Why, why had she gotten involved with him to begin with? Because he called her Angel? Because he took those pictures? Because he sang all those stupid songs into her ear? That big goon hadn't the faintest idea what she was all about. All summer long he'd acted as though she were some kind of girl she wasn't—as though she were some sort of Monkey Littlefield. And she had let him. She had let him have his stupid way! And now this! Only, *this* was what happened to farm girls, to girls who didn't study, who quit school, who ran away from home. To Babs Egan, but not to her. Hadn't enough happened to her already?

"Doctor, I don't *know* what I was thinking about." She began to cry, despite herself. "All I mean is, lately I don't even know what I'm doing sometimes." She covered her face with her fingers.

"And what about the boy?"

"The boy?" she said helplessly, rubbing her tears away.

"What does he plan to do about all this? Run off to the South Seas?"

"Oh no," she moaned, sadder than ever, "no, he'd marry me tomorrow," and an instant too late she realized that she had said the wrong thing. It was the truth, but it was the wrong thing to have said.

"But you don't want to." The doctor was speaking to her.

She looked up from her lap, partly. "I didn't say that."

"I have to have it straight, Lucy. Just as it is. He wants to, but you don't want to."

She rose from her seat. "But I'm not even here three whole months! I'm a first-semester freshman!"

He was moving his glasses up again. He had such a big, wrinkled, friendly face—you just knew he had a family he loved, and a nice house, and a calm and pleasant life. "If the young man wants to marry you—"

"What of it? What if he does?"

"Well, I think that's something that must at least be taken into consideration. Don't you?"

Blankly she said, "I don't understand." And she didn't.

"His feelings are something that have to be taken into consideration. His love for you."

Dumbly she sat there shaking her head. He didn't love her. He just sang those stupid songs into her ear.

"—what he wants," the doctor was saying, "what he expects, too."

"But he doesn't *know* what he wants."

"You say he wants to marry you."

"Oh, that isn't what I mean. He says things, but he doesn't even know what! Doctor—please, you're right, I don't want to marry him. I don't want to lie to you. I hate liars and I don't lie, and that's the truth! Please, hundreds and hundreds of girls do what I did. And they do it with all different people!"

"Perhaps they shouldn't."

"But I'm not bad!" She couldn't help herself, it was the truth: "I'm good!"

"Please, you must calm down. I didn't say that you were bad. I'm sure you're not. You mustn't jump at everything I say before I finish saying it."

"I'm sorry. It's a habit. I'm terribly sorry."

"They shouldn't," he began again, "because most of them aren't old enough to pay the price if they lose. If they get into trouble."

"But—"

"But," his voice rose over hers, "they're old enough to want the love. I know."

The tears moved again into her eyes. "You do understand. Because that's what happened to me, just what you said. That's exactly it."

"Lucy, listen to me—"

"I am, Doctor. Because that *is* what happened—"

"Lucy, you're not alone in this."

At first she thought he meant that there were other girls in school in the same fix—perhaps even in the infirmary rooms along the corridor beyond his office.

"There is a young man," the doctor said.

"But—"

"Listen to me, Lucy. There is a young man, and there is your family. Have you spoken to your family about this yet?"

She looked into her plaid skirt, where her fingers were clutched at the big safety pin.

"You do have a family?"

"Yes. I suppose."

"I think you have to forget your embarrassment and take this problem to your family."

"I can't."

"Why not?"

"I have a terrible family."

"Lucy, you're not the first eighteen-year-old girl to think her family is terrible. Surely you've discovered that since you've been at school."

"But my family *is* terrible. I don't think it—it's true!"

He said nothing.

"I ignore them. I have nothing to do with them. They're inferior, Doctor," she added when he still didn't seem to believe her.

"In what way?"

"My father drinks." She looked him straight in the eye. "He's a drunkard."

"I see," he said. "And your mother?"

Helplessly she was weeping again. "She's too good for him."

"That doesn't sound inferior," the doctor said quietly.

"Yes, but she should have left him years and years ago, if she had any sense. Any self-respect. She should have found a man who would be good to her and respect her." Like you, she thought. If you had met my mother, if she had married you . . . She heard herself saying, "Some people think, someone said once, she looks like Jennifer Jones. The actress."

He handed her a tissue and she blew her nose. She mustn't ask to be pitied; she mustn't whimper; she mustn't fall to pieces. That's what her mother would do.

"Lucy, I think you should go home. Today. Maybe she understands more than you imagine. Maybe she won't be angry. I would think from what you say that she wouldn't be."

She did not respond. He was trying to get out of it. That's exactly what he was beginning to do.

"You seem to love her. Probably she loves you too."

"But she can't help, Doctor. Love has nothing to do with it. Love is what's *wrong* with her. She's so weak. She's so insipid!"

"My dear, because you're upset now—"

"But, Doctor, *they can't help!* Only you can help," she said, standing. "You must!"

He shook his head. "But I can't, I'm afraid."

"But you have to!"

"I'm terribly sorry."

Could he mean it? Could he understand the situation

as he did, and then turn around and say he wasn't going to help? "But this isn't *fair!*" she cried.

The doctor nodded his head. "It isn't."

"So then what are you going to *do* about it? Sit there pushing your glasses up and down? Sit there being wise to me? Call me 'my dear'!" Instantly she sat back down in her chair. "Oh, I'm sorry. I didn't mean that. But why are you . . . ? I mean, you see what happened. You understand." She felt now that she had to plead with him, to convince him that he was right. "You *do* understand, Doctor. Please, you're an intelligent person!"

"But there are limits. On all of us. People may want things, that doesn't mean that we can give them."

"Please," she said angrily, "don't tell me what I know in that tone. I am not a child."

A moment passed. He stood.

"But what's going to happen to me? If you don't help . . ."

He came around to the side of his desk.

"Don't you care?" she asked. "What about my whole life!"

For the first time she sensed his impatience. Then he spoke. "You cannot expect me, young lady, to save your life."

She rose; she faced him where he was standing at the door. "Please do not lecture me in that superior tone! I refuse to be lectured to by a perfect stranger who doesn't know the first thing about all I have had to put up with in my life. I am not just another eighteen-year-old girl, and I won't take your lectures!"

"And what will you take instead?" he said sourly.

"What?"

"I'm asking what you expect, Lucy. You're interesting," he said, "in your expectations. You're perfectly right—you are not just another eighteen-year-old girl." He opened the door.

"But what about my life? How can you be so cruel to me!"

"I hope you come upon someone you can listen to" was his answer.

"Well, I won't," she said in a low, fierce tone.

"That would be too bad."

"Oh," she said, buttoning her coat, "oh, I hope—I hope you're happy, Doctor, when you go home to your nice house. I hope you're happy with all your wisdom and your glasses and your doctor's degree—and being a coward!"

"Goodbye," he said, blinking only once. "Good luck."

"Oh, I won't rely on luck, Doctor. Or on people either."

"On what, then?"

"Myself!" she said, and marched through the open door.

"Good luck," he said softly as she brushed by him, and then shut the door behind her.

"You coward," she moaned as she went rushing off to the coffee shop; "you weakling," she wept as she carried the phone book into the booth at the back of the store; "you selfish, heartless, cruel—" as she drew her finger down the list of physicians in the yellow pages of the directory, imagining them one after another saying to her, "You cannot expect me, young lady, to save your life," and seeing herself dragging from one office to another, humiliated, ignored and abused.

On Thanksgiving Day they all sat down to the turkey and she told her family that she and Roy Bassart had decided to get married. "What?" her father said. She repeated herself. "Why?" he demanded to know, and slammed down the carving instruments.

"Because we want to."

Within five minutes the only one still at the table was her grandmother. She alone ate right through to the mince pie while overhead various members of her family, in various ways, tried to get Lucy to unlock her door. Berta, however, said she was sick and tired of disorder and tragedy, and refused to allow every single pleasant moment to be destroyed by one person or another, year in and year out.

Roy phoned at four in the afternoon. She came out

of her bedroom to take the call, but would not speak until the kitchen was cleared of adults. Roy said that he couldn't get away to see her before nine. But what had they said when he told them? Nothing. He hadn't told them yet.

At nine-thirty he telephoned from the Sowerbys', saying that he had decided to wait until he was back in his own house, alone with his parents, before he broke the news. "Well, when will that be, Roy?" "I don't know exactly. Well, how can I know exactly? Later." But he was the one who had wanted to call them a week ago from Fort Kean; he was the one, she said, who had thought there was nothing that wrong with having to get married, so long as you were a couple who was going to marry anyway, probably, sooner or later. He was the one—

"Here," he said, "Ellie wants to talk to you."

"Roy!"

"Hi," Ellie said. "Hi, Lucy. Sorry about not writing."

"Hello, Eleanor."

"It's just been work, work, work. You can imagine. I'm going crazy in this science course. Hey, we're all rolling on the floor listening to Roy's adventures in that Britannia school. What a place! And I'm actually drinking. Hey, come over."

"I have to stay home."

"I hope it's not hard feelings, or anything, about not writing . . . Is it?"

"No."

"Well, I'll see you tomorrow. Have I got things to tell you. I've met somebody *marvelous*," Ellie whispered. "I almost sent you his picture. I mean, he's perfect."

At midnight she came out of her bedroom to call Roy at his home. "Did you tell them?"

"Listen, what are you doing? Everybody's sleeping."

"Didn't you *tell* them?"

"It was too late."

"But I told mine!"

"Look, my father's shouting down the stairs asking who it is."

"Well, tell him!"

"Will you please stop instructing me on what to do every minute?" he said. "I'll do it when I'm—" Suddenly he hung up.

She dialed again. Mr. Bassart picked up the phone. "Just who is this?" he asked.

She didn't breathe.

"Look, no pranks at this hour, whoever you are. If it's one of you boys in my fifth-period class, don't think I'm not going to find out who."

In the morning she telephoned again.

"I was going to call *you*," Roy said.

"Roy, when are you going to tell them?"

"It's only eight in the morning. We haven't had breakfast, even. My Aunt Irene's coming over."

"Then you *did* tell them."

"Who said that?"

"That's why your aunt's coming to your house!"

"How can you say that? How do you know that's even true?"

"Roy, what are you hiding from me?"

"*Nothing.* Can't you just let things settle for a few hours? My God."

"Why is your aunt coming over at eight o'clock in the morning? Who even called her?"

"Oh, look, okay," he said suddenly, "if you have to know—"

"I do! Know what!"

"Well, my father wants me to wait till June."

"Then you did tell them!"

". . . When we came home."

"Then why didn't you say that last night!"

"Because it just so happened that I wanted to give you good news, Lucy, not bad. I was trying to spare you, Lucy, *but you won't stop pushing me against my own timetable!*"

"Timetable? Roy, what are you talking about? How can we wait until June!"

"But he doesn't *know* about that!"

"And don't you tell him either, Roy!"

"I have to hang up. She's here."

At noon he called to say that he wasn't driving back to Fort Kean until Monday, so perhaps she had better plan to take the bus down on Sunday night.

"I'm calling from a booth, Lucy. I'm on my way to Mr. Brunn's to pick up something for my father. I have to hurry—"

"Roy, please explain instantly what this means."

"I'm trying to take care of some things and iron them out, all *right? Do you mind?*"

"Roy! You can't do this! I have to see you, right now!"

"I'm hanging up, Lucy."

"No!"

"Well, I am. I'm sorry. So get ready."

"If you hang up, I'm coming over to your house this minute. Hello? Do you hear me?"

But the line had been disconnected.

She called Eleanor's house.

"Ellie, it's Lucy. I have to talk to you."

"Why?"

"Oh, not you too?"

". . . Me too, what?"

"Ellie, you had to talk to me once—now I have to talk to you. I have to know what's going on, Ellie. I'll come right over."

"Now? Lucy, you better not—right now, I mean."

"Is anybody home?"

"No. But they're all—going crazy."

"Why?"

"Well, Roy says you want to marry him."

"He wants to marry *me!* Didn't he say that?"

"Well, yes . . . Well, sort of. He says he's thinking about it . . . But Lucy, they think you're making him— Uh-oh, somebody's pulling into the driveway. Everybody's been driving back and forth all morning . . . Lucy?"

"Yes."

". . . Are you?"

"What?"

"Well, making him."

"No!"

"Then—why?"

"Because we want to!"

"You do?"

"Yes!"

"But—"

"But what, Eleanor!"

"Well . . . you're so young. We all are. I mean, it's a surprise. I guess I just don't know what I mean, really."

"Because you're a dope, Ellie! Because you're a stupid, insipid, self-centered, selfish dope!"

In the early evening she took a bus back to Fort Kean. The doors to The Bastille were chained shut, and she had to walk all around the cold campus before she found the watchman. He led her over to the Buildings and Grounds Office in Barracks Number Three, sat her down in a chair, and took out his spectacles to look for her name in the student directory.

And all those names printed in the register made her think: *Run away*. Who would ever find her?

In her room she beat her fists on the pillow, on the headboard, on the wall. It was awful. It was horrible. Every other college girl in America was home right now, having a good time with her friends and her family. Yet her mother had begged, her grandfather had begged, even her father had asked her to stay. They said that it was just that they were stunned by the news. Wouldn't she agree, they reasoned through the door, that it was a little unexpected? They would try to get used to it, if only she wouldn't run off like this on a holiday weekend. They were shocked at first, and had maybe lost their heads. It was, after all, only the first semester of that college life she had been dreaming about for so long. But probably she knew what she was doing, if her mind was made up the way it sounded that it was. So wouldn't she stay through Monday?

When she was fifteen years old and on her own decided on Catholic as her religious preference, had they stood in her way? No, she had insisted that it was what she wanted, and they had decided to let her go ahead. And later, when she had changed her mind, and turned back to Presbyterian again, well, that too had been her own decision, made on her own, without interference from any person in the family. And the same with the snare drum. Another decision made on her own, that they had honored and respected, until finally she decided to give that up too.

Of course they weren't meaning to draw any comparison between taking up the snare drum and taking a husband for life; but their attitude had been that if she preferred beating the drums to resuming piano (which, they reminded her, she had dropped at ten, her own decision once again), or beginning something like accordion, which had been Daddy Will's compromise suggestion, they had no choice but to let her have her way. Their house was not a dictatorship; it was a democracy, in which every person had his ideas—and was respected for them too. "I may not believe what you say," said Daddy Will through the door, "but I will fight for your right to say it." So wouldn't she reconsider and not rush off now to some lonely, empty school? Why didn't she stay and talk it over? After all, Grandma had been baking all week, and for her. "For Thanksgiving," said Lucy. "Well, honey, that's not much different, when you think about it. It's your first big weekend home from college, there isn't one of us doesn't realize . . . Lucy? Are you listening to me?"

But what about her father acting as though the whole thing was a monumental tragedy? Since when did anything having to do with her sacrifices, her suffering, bring tears to his eyes? She could not bear the pretense. And who said she was quitting college? He kept wandering around the house, crying, "I wanted her to go to college," but who had said she wasn't? All she had said was that she was getting married to Roy . . . Or did they know why without her explaining further? Were they content to accept what she told them, simply to avoid the humiliation of confronting the truth? She picked up her French grammar and threw it clear across the room. "They don't even *know*," she said aloud, "and still they're letting me do it!"

If only they'd say *no*. NO, LUCY, YOU CANNOT. NO, LUCY, WE FORBID IT. But it seemed that none of them had the conviction any longer, or the endurance, to go against a choice of hers. In order to survive, she had set her will against theirs long ago—it was the battle of her adolescence, but it was over now. And she had won. She could do whatever in the world she wanted—even marry someone she secretly despised.

When Roy returned to Fort Kean on Monday evening, and switched on the light in his room, he found Lucy sitting in a chair by the window.

"What are you doing here?" he cried, dropping his suitcase. "The shades are up!"

"Then pull them down, Roy."

Instantly he did. "How did you get inside?"

"How do I always get inside, Roy? On all fours."

"Is she home?"

"Who?"

"My landlady!" he whispered, and without another word, slipped out the door and into the hallway. She heard him whistling his way up the stairs and into the bathroom. *You sigh, the song begins, you speak and I hear* . . . Overhead she even heard him flush the toilet. Then he was sliding into the room again. "She's out," he said, shutting the door. "We better turn off the lights."

"So you won't have to look at me?"

"So she doesn't *find* you here, if she comes home. Well, she just might come home. Well, what's the matter with you?"

She rose and clutched her stomach. "Take a guess!"

"*Shhhh.*"

"But she's out."

"But she'll be back! We *always* have the lights out, Lucy."

"But I want to talk to you, and face to face, not on a phone, Roy, where you can—"

"Well, I'm sorry, but the lights are going off. So get ready."

"But are we getting married or aren't we? Tell me, so I know what to do next, or where to go, or God knows what."

"Well, at least let me take my coat off, will you, please?"

"Roy, yes or no."

"Well, how can I give you a yes or no answer when it's not a yes or no question?"

"But that's exactly what it *is*."

"Will you calm down? I've been driving for two hours."

While he was hanging his coat in the closet, she came up behind him and stood on her toes. "*Yes or no, Roy!*" up toward his ear, which was still a foot above her.

He ducked away from her. "Now, first, I'm turning the lights off. Just to be safe. Well, look, Lucy, I agreed when I rented here not to have girls in my room."

"But you had me, Roy, and plenty."

"But *she* doesn't know about it! Oh, darn it. Here go the lights," and without pausing to hear an objection, he turned them off.

"Okay, now you don't have to look at me, Roy. Tell me what happened over your long Thanksgiving holiday. While I was down here in an empty dormitory all by myself for two whole days."

"First off, I didn't tell you to go back to any empty dorm. Second, I'm going to sit down, if you don't mind. And why don't you sit, too?"

"I'll stand, thank you."

"In the dark?"

"Yes!"

"Shhhh!"

"Begin," she said.

"Well, let me get settled . . . Okay."

"What?"

"I've got them to come around part way."

"Continue."

"Oh, sit *down*, will you?"

"What's the difference? You can't see me."

"I do too see you! Hanging over me. Sit down, *please*."

She had been waiting for over an hour. It wasn't sitting she wanted, it was sleep. She lowered herself onto the edge of the bed and closed her eyes. *Go to Mr. Valerio. Run away.* But neither idea made sense. If she should see anyone, it was Father Damrosch. But what would he do? That was precisely his trouble: he couldn't *do* anything. He was about as much help as Saint Teresa, or Jesus Christ. He looked so strong, and listened to everything she said, and said such beautiful things himself ... but it wasn't beautiful things she needed to hear. Something had to be *done*.

"First off," he was saying, "don't think it was easy for me. It was hell, actually."

"What was?"

"Pretending you weren't pregnant, Lucy, when everybody kept asking me over and over again *why?*"

"And did you tell them?"

"No."

"Are you sure?"

"Yes! *Shhhhh!*"

"You're the one who's shouting."

"Well, you make me."

"You might be shouting because you're lying, Roy."

"I did not tell them, Lucy! Will you stop accusing? Actually, I keep wondering why I don't. Why can't I just speak the simple truth? If we're going to be married anyway."

"Are we?"

"Well, we would be ... if I told them, I mean."

"You mean if you don't, we're *not?*"

"Well, that's the point. That's what's so confused. I mean, they had so many arguments for why we should at least wait until June."

"And?"

"And, well, they're all good arguments. I mean, it's just hard to argue against a good argument, that's all."

"So you said you'd wait."

"I said I'd *think* about it."

"But how *can* we?"

"Look, I had to get out of the house, didn't I? I've missed a whole day of school already."

"You have a car, you can drive—"

"*But I couldn't leave it the way it was!* Don't you understand anything!"

"Why couldn't you? Why didn't you?"

"Why should they all be furious at me, Lucy, and so confused about everything? I'm not doing anything wrong. The opposite, in fact, the very opposite! Why don't we just tell *the truth?* I don't have to lie to my parents, you know."

"I don't have to lie to mine either, Roy, if that's what you mean."

"But you are."

"Because I want to!"

"*Why?*"

"Oh, why won't you be a man about this! Why are you acting this way!"

"But you're the one who's hiding the simple fact that would make them all understand the whole thing!"

"Roy, do you honestly believe they will all love and adore me when they hear that I'm going to have a baby?"

"They'd *understand* is all I'm saying."

"But only two people have to understand—you and me."

"Well, maybe that's all you think . . . with your family."

"And what's wrong with my family that isn't with yours, Roy? Look, you, if you don't want to marry me," she said, "because someone has begun to tell you that I'm not good enough for you, well, believe me, you don't have to."

A moment passed. And another.

"But I do want to," he said at last.

"Roy, I think you really don't." She buried her head in her hands. "That's the truth, isn't it? 'Trust me, trust me'—and that's the real truth."

"Well ... no ... Well, you certainly haven't been acting these last few days like the kind of person someone would like living in the same house with particularly. I'll tell you that ... Suddenly you're so—"

"So what? Lower class?"

"No," he said. "No. Cold."

"Oh, am I?"

"Well, sort of, recently, yes, as a matter of fact."

"And what else am I?"

"Well, all kidding aside, Lucy, you're just acting so angry."

"You might be a little angry too, if you had agreed beforehand with someone—"

"But I don't mean normal angry!"

"What?"

"Well—practically crazy!"

"You honestly think because I'm angry I'm *insane?*"

"I didn't say *I* did. I didn't say insane."

"Who did say it then?"

"No one."

"Who?"

"*No one!*"

"Maybe," she said after a moment, "you *make* me insane, Roy Bassart."

"Then why do you want to marry me so much?"

"I *don't* want to!"

"Oh, then don't do me the favor, you know."

"I don't think I will," she said. "Because that's really what it would be."

"Oh, sure. And what will you do instead? Marry somebody else?"

"Do you know something, you? I've been getting rid of you since July, Roy. Since the day you took this room because it had a long bed in it, you—you baby!"

"Well, you sure are a slow worker, I'll say that for you."

"I'm not slow! I have sympathy for you! I felt *sorry* for you."

"Oh, sure."

"I was afraid you'd give up photography if I hurt your little feelings. But I was going to do it, Roy—on Thanksgiving Day of all days, and I would have, too, if I didn't have to marry you instead."

"Oh, don't feel you have to, you know."

"I thought when you collapsed, at least you'd be in Liberty Center, where you could go eat your Hydrox cookies."

"Well, don't worry about my crying, if I can put in my two cents. I don't cry that easy, for one thing. And as for Hydrox cookies, that's irrelevant to anything. I don't even know what it's supposed to mean, in fact. Besides," he said, "if you wanted to drop somebody, don't worry, you'd drop him. You wouldn't bother too much about their crying either."

"No?"

". . . Because you don't have emotions like other people."

"Don't I? And who said that?"

"Lucy? Are you crying?"

"Oh, no. I don't have emotions like other people. I'm a piece of pure stone."

"You *are* crying." He came over to the bed, where she was stretched out, her face still in her hands. "Don't. Please, I didn't mean it. Really."

"Roy," she said, "who said I was insane to you? Who said I didn't have emotions?"

"Ordinary emotions. Nobody."

"Who was it, Roy? Your Uncle Julian?"

"No. Nobody."

"And you believed him."

"I didn't. He didn't say it!"

"But I could tell you about him too! Tell you plenty. The way your Uncle Julian looks at me! How he kissed me at your party!"

"This summer, you mean? But that was a joke. You kissed him back. Lucy, what are you even saying?"

"I'm saying that you're blind! You're blind to how awful people are! How rotten and hateful they are! They tell you I'm lower class and don't have ordinary emotions, and you believe them!"

"I don't."

"And all on the basis of what? Why, Roy? Say it!"

"Say *what?*"

"My father! But I didn't put him in jail, Roy!"

"I didn't say you did."

"He put himself there! That was years ago, and it's over, and I am not beneath you or them, or anyone!"

The door opened; the light went on over their heads.

In the doorway stood the widow from whom Roy rented his room: Mrs. Blodgett, a thin, nervous and alert woman with a little coin-slot mouth and a great capacity for expressing disapproval by merely reducing the thing in size. She did not speak right off; she did not have to.

"Well, just how did you get in here?" Roy asked, as though he were the one who was outraged. He had moved instantly between Lucy and the landlady. "Well, how, Mrs. Blodgett?"

"With a key, Mr. Bassart. How did *she* is a better question. Stand up, you hussy."

"Roy," whispered Lucy. But he continued to hide her behind him.

"I said get up from that bed," said Mrs. Blodgett. "And get out."

But Roy was intent upon making his point. "You're not supposed to use a key in another person's door, for one thing, you know."

"Don't tell me the things I'm not supposed to do, Mr. Bassart. I thought *you* were an Army veteran, or so you said."

"But—"

"But what, sir? But you don't know the rules of this house, is that what you're going to have the gall to tell me?"

"You don't under*stand*," said Roy.

"Understand what?"

"Well, if you'd calm down, I'll tell you."

"You just tell me, whether I'm calmed down or not, which I happen to be anyway. I've had others like you, Mr. Bassart. One in 1937, and another right on his heels in 1938. They look all right, but the looks is about the whole of it. Underneath they're all the same." Her mouth became invisible. "Crooked," she said.

"But this is different," said Roy. "She's my fiancée."

"Who is? You just let her out, so I can see her."

"Roy," Lucy pleaded. *"Move."*

At last he did, smiling all the while. "This is Mrs. Blodgett, my landlady, who I mentioned to you. Mrs. Blodgett"—he rubbed his hands together, as though he had been awaiting this pleasure for a long time—"this is my fiancée. Lucy."

"Lucy what?"

Lucy stood, her skirt finally covering her knees.

"Why were the lights off and all that shouting?" asked Mrs. Blodgett.

"Shouting?" said Roy, looking around. "We were listening to music. You know I love music, Mrs. Blodgett."

Mrs. Blodgett looked at him in such a way as to openly admit to skepticism.

"The radio," he said. "We just turned it off. That was the noise, I guess. We just drove down from home. We were resting. Our eyes. That's how come the lights were dim."

"Off," said the tiny mouth, disappearing.

"Anyway," said Roy, "there's my suitcase. We did just get back."

"Who gave you permission, young man, to bring girls into my house against the rules? This is a dwelling place. I told you that when you first arrived, did I not?"

"Well, as I said, we just drove down. And I thought since she was my fiancée, you wouldn't mind if we rested." He smiled. "Against the rules." No answer. "Since we're getting married."

"When?"

"Christmas," he announced.

"Is that so?"

Lucy was the one being asked.

"It's the truth, Mrs. Blodgett," said Roy. "That's why we came down late from home. Making plans," he said with another big smile; then he turned somber and penitent. "I may have broken a rule about bringing Lucy in here, and if I did, I'm sorry."

"There are no ifs about it," said Mrs. Blodgett. "Not that I can see."

"Well then, I'm sorry then."

"Lucy what?" asked the landlady. "What's your last name, you?"

"Nelson."

"And where are you from?"

"The women's college."

"And is this true? Are you marrying him, or are you just some girl?"

"I'm marrying him."

Roy raised his hands. "See?"

"Well," said Mrs. Blodgett, "she could be lying. That's not unheard of."

"Does she look like a liar?" asked Roy, putting his hands in his pockets and shuffling over toward Lucy. "With this face? Come on, Mrs. Blodgett," he said winningly. "She's the girl next door. Actually, she practically is, you know."

The landlady did not smile back. "I had a boy in 1945 who had a fiancée. But *he* came to me, Mr. Bassart—"

"Yes?"

"—and told me his plans. And then brought the young lady around on a Sunday to be properly introduced."

"A Sunday. Well, that's a good idea, all right."

"Let me finish, please. We then arranged that she might come here to visit until ten in the evening. I did not even have to make it clear that the door to the room was to be left open. He understood that much."

"I see," said Roy with considerable interest.

"Miss Nelson, I am not a close-minded person, but where I have my rules I am strict. This happens to be my dwelling place, and not some fly-by-night person's hotel. Without rules it would go to rack and ruin inside of a month. Maybe you'll understand how that happens when you're older. I certainly hope you do, for your sake."

"Oh, we understand now," said Roy.

"Don't ever try to trick me again, Mr. Bassart."

"Oh, now that I know the ten o'clock setup—"

"And I know your name, young lady. Lucy Nelson. S-o-n or s-e-n?"

"S-o-n."

"And I know the dean over at your school. Miss Pardee, correct? Dean of Students."

"Yes."

"Then don't you ever try to trick me either."

She started for the door.

"So then," said Roy, following her, "at least we're all squared away, anyway."

When Mrs. Blodgett turned to show him what she thought of that last remark, Roy smiled. "I mean, we're all forgiven and everything, right? I know innocence of the law is no—"

"You are not innocent, Mr. Bassart. My back was turned. You are guilty as sin."

"Well, I suppose in a manner of speaking . . ." And he shrugged. "Now the rules, Mrs. Blodgett—just so I'm sure I've got them straight."

"So long, sir, as the door is left open—"

"Oh, absolutely, wide open."

"So long as she is out of here at ten o'clock—"

"Oh, out she'll be," said Roy, laughing.

"So long as there is no shouting—"

"That was music, Mrs. Blodgett, really—"

"And so long, Mr. Bassart, as there is a marriage, Christmas Day."

For a moment he looked dumfounded. Marriage? "Oh, sure. Good day, don't you think? Christmas?"

Mrs. Blodgett went out, leaving the door ajar.

"Bye," said Roy, and waited until he heard the door

to the back parlor being closed before he fell into a chair. "Wow."

"Then we *are* getting married," said Lucy.

"Shhhhh!"—rising up out of the chair. "Will you— *yes*," he said all at once, for the parlor door had opened, and Mrs. Blodgett was headed back to the stairs. "Mom and Dad feel—oh, hi, Mrs. Blodgett." He tipped an imaginary hat. "Have a nice sleep now."

"It is nine forty-eight, Mr. Bassart."

Roy looked at his watch. "Right you are, Mrs. Blodgett. Thanks for reminding me. Just finishing up talking over our plans. Night, now."

She started up the stairs, her anger not much abated, it seemed.

"Roy—" Lucy began, but in two steps he was at her side; one hand he pressed to the back of her head, the other to her mouth.

"So," he said loudly, "Mom and Dad felt that for the most part your suggestion—"

Her eyes stared wildly at him, until the bedroom door could be heard closing overhead. He took his wet hand from her lips.

"Don't you ever—ever—" she said, so enraged that she could hardly speak, "do that again!"

"Oh, golly," he said, and threw himself backward onto his bed. "I'm actually going off my *rocker* with you! What do you expect, when she was on the *stairs*, Lucy?"

"I expect—!"

"Shhhhh!" He shot up on the bed. "We're getting married!" he whispered hoarsely. "*So shut up.*"

She was suddenly and completely baffled. She was getting married. "When?"

"Christmas! *Okay?* Now will you *stop?*"

"And your family?"

"Well, what about them?"

"You have to tell them."

"I will, I will. But just lay *off* for a while."

"Roy . . . it has to be now."

"*Now?*" he said.

"Yes!"

"But my mother is in bed, *and quiet down!*" After a moment he said, "Well, she is. I'm not lying. She goes to bed at nine and gets up at five-thirty. Don't ask me why. That's how she does it, Lucy, and how she's always done it, and there's nothing I can do to change her at this stage of the game. Well, that's the truth. And furthermore, Lucy, I have had it for tonight, really."

"But you must make this official. You just can't keep me living this way. It's a nightmare!"

"But I'll make it official when I think it should be!"

"Roy, suppose she calls Dean Pardee! I don't want to be thrown out of school! I don't need that in my one life, too."

"Well," he said, smacking the sides of his head, "I don't want to be thrown out either, you know. Why else do you think I told her what I did?"

"Then it is a lie and you don't mean it *again!*"

"It's not! I *do!* I always have!"

"Roy Bassart, call your parents, or I'll do something!"

He jumped out of the bed. "No!"

"Keep your hands away from my mouth, Roy!"

"Don't scream, for God's sakes! That's *stupid!*"

"But I am pregnant with a human baby!" she cried. "I'm going to have your baby, Roy! And you won't even do your duty!"

"I will! I am!"

"*When?*"

"Now! Okay? *Now!* But don't scream, Lucy, don't throw a stupid fit!"

"Then call!"

"But," he said, "what I told Mrs. Blodgett—I had to."

"Roy!"

"*Okay,*" and he ran from the room.

In a few minutes he returned, paler than she had ever seen him. Where the hair was clipped short at his neck, she could see his white skin. "I did it," he said.

And she believed him. Even his wrists and hands were white.

"I did it," he mumbled. "And I told you, didn't I? I told you she'd be sleeping. I told you he'd have to wake her up and get her out of bed. Well, didn't I? *I wasn't lying!* And I wouldn't be thrown out of school. Why did I say *that!* I'd only be thrown out of this room— and what difference does that make anyway? Nobody else cares about my self-respect anyway, so why should I worry about it? *He* doesn't worry about it! *She* doesn't worry about it! And you—you were going to *scream!* My self-respect, oh, the heck with that, all you want to do is scream and confuse people. That's your way, Lucy—to confuse people. Everybody's way. Confuse Roy—why not? Who's he, anyway? But that's over! Because I'm not confused, Lucy, and from here on out that's the way things are going to be. We're getting married, you hear me—on Christmas Day. And if that doesn't suit people, then the day after—but that's it!"

The door opened upstairs. "Mr. Bassart, there is that shouting again! That is not music, that is clear shouting, and it will not be tolerated!"

Roy stuck his head out into the hallway. "No, no, just saying good night to Lucy here, Mrs. Blodgett— finishing up the old wedding plans."

"Say it then! Don't shout it! This is a dwelling place!" She slammed her door shut.

Lucy was crying.

"*Now* what are the tears for?" he asked. "Huh? *Now* what hundred thousand things did I do wrong? Really, you know, maybe I've had just about enough com- plaining and criticizing of me, you know—from you included, too. So maybe you ought to stop, you know. Maybe you ought to have a little consideration for all I've been through, *and just stop, damn it!*"

"Oh," she said, "I'll stop, Roy. Until you change your mind again—!"

"Oh, brother, I'll make that bargain. *Gladly.*"

Whereupon, to his surprise, she threw open the win- dow, and out of anger, or spite, or habit left the room as she had entered it. Roy rushed into the hallway to the front door. Noisily he opened it—"Good night," he called. "Good night, Lucy"—and noisily he closed it, so that upstairs Mrs. Blodgett would continue to believe that everything was really on the up-and-up, even if a little too loud.

Tuesday, Aunt Irene for lunch at the Hotel Thomas Kean.

Wednesday, his mother and father for dinner at The Song of Norway.

Thursday, Uncle Julian, a drink in the taproom of the Kean, lasting from five in the afternoon until nine in the evening.

At nine-thirty Roy dropped into a sofa in the downstairs living room of The Bastille. The corner in which Lucy had chosen to wait for him was the darkest in the room.

"And I haven't eaten," he said. "I haven't even eaten!"

"I have some crackers in my room," she whispered.

"They're not going to treat me like this," he said, glaring down his legs at the tips of his Army shoes. "I won't sit by and listen to threats, I'll tell you that."

". . . Do you want me to get the crackers?"

"That isn't the point, Lucy! The point is, pushing me around! Thinking he could make me sit there! Just *make* me, you know? Well, I don't need them that bad, I'll tell you that. And I don't want them either, not if they're going to take this kind of attitude. What an attitude to take—to me! To somebody they're supposed to care about!"

He got up and walked to the window. Looking out at the quiet street, he banged a fist into his palm. "Boy!" she heard him say.

She remained curled up on the sofa, her legs back under her skirt. It was a posture she had seen the other girls take while talking to their boy friends in the dormitory living room. If the house mother came into the living room, it would seem as though nothing unusual were going on. So far no one in the dorm knew anything; no one was going to, either. In her two and a half months at school Roy hadn't left her alone enough to make any close friends, and even those few girls she had begun to be friendly with on the floor, she had drawn away from now.

"Look," said Roy, coming back to the sofa, "I've got the G.I. Bill, haven't I?"

"Yes."

"And I've got savings still, right? Other guys played cards, other guys shot crap—but I didn't. I was waiting to get out. So I saved! Purposely. And they should know that! I told them, in fact—but they don't even *listen*. And if worst ever came to worst, I'd sell the Hudson, too, even with all the work I put in it. Do you believe me, Lucy? Because it's true!"

"Yes."

Was this Roy? Was this Lucy? Was this them together?

"But they think money is everything. Do you know what he is, my Uncle Julian? Maybe I'm just finding out—but *he's* a materialist. And what a vocabulary! It's worse than you even think it is. What respect for somebody else!"

"What did he say? Roy, what kind of threats?"

"Oh, who cares. *Money* threats. And my father—him too. You know, by and large, whether he knew it or not, I used to respect him. But do you think he has any emotional respect for me, either? He's trying to treat me like I'm in his printing class again. But I just got out of serving my time in the Army. Sixteen months in the Aleutian Islands—the backside of the whole goddamn world. But my uncle says—you know what he says? 'But the war was over, buster, in 1945. Don't act like you fought it.' See, *he* fought it. He won a medal. And what's that have to do with anything anyway? Nothing! Oh—up his."

"Roy," warned Lucy, as some senior girls came into the living room.

"Well," he said, plopping down next to her, "they're always telling me I should speak up for myself, right? 'Make a decision and stick to it, Roy.' Isn't that all I heard since the day I got home? Isn't my Uncle Julian always shooting off about how you have to be a go-getter in this world? That's his big defense of capitalism, you know. It makes a man out of you, instead of just hanging around waiting for things to come your way. But what does he know about Socialism anyway? You think the man has ever read a book about it in his life? He thinks Socialism is Communism, and what you say doesn't make any difference at all. None! Well, I'm young. And I've got my health. And I sure don't care one way or the other about ever being in the El-ene washing-machine business, I'll tell you that much. Big threat that is. I'm going to photography school anyway. And you know something else? He doesn't know right from wrong. That's the real pay-off. That in this country, where people are still struggling, or unemployed, or don't have the ordinary necessities that they give the people in just about any Scandinavian country you can name—that a man like that, without the slightest code of decency, can just bully his way, and the hell with right and wrong or somebody's feelings. Well, I'm through being somebody he can toss his favors to. Let him keep his big fourteen-dollar cigars. Up his, Lucy—really."

The next morning, when the alarm rang at six-thirty, she went off to the bathroom to stick a finger down her throat before the other girls started coming in to brush their teeth. This made her feel herself again, provided she skipped breakfast afterward, and avoided the corridor back of the dining hall, and forced soda crackers down herself from time to time during the morning. Then she could get through the day's classes pretending that she was the same girl in the same body, and in the same way too—alone.

But what about last night? And the night before that? The fainting spells had stopped two weeks back, and the nausea she could starve to death every morning, but now that Roy's body seemed to be inhabited by some new person, the truth came in upon her as it never had before: *a new person was inhabiting hers as well.*

She was stunned. Her predicament was *real*. It was no plot she had invented to bring them all to their senses. It was no scheme to force them to treat her like flesh and blood, like a human being, like a girl. And it was not going to disappear either, just because somebody besides herself was at long last taking it seriously. It was real! Something was happening which she was helpless to stop! Something was growing inside her body, and without her permission!

And I don't want to marry him.

The sun wasn't even above the trees as she ran across Pendleton Park to downtown Fort Kean.

She had to wait an hour in the station for the first bus to the north. Her books were in her lap; she had some idea that she could study on the way up and be back for her two-thirty, but then she had not yet a clear idea of why she was suddenly rushing up to Liberty Center, or what would happen there. On the bench in the empty station she tried to calm herself by reading the English assignment she had planned to do in her free hour before lunch, and during lunch, which she didn't eat anyway. "Here you will have a chance to examine, and then practice, several skills used in writing effective sentences. The skills presented are those—"

She didn't want to marry him! He was the last person in the world she would ever want to marry!

She began gagging only a little way beyond Fort Kean. When he heard the sounds of her distress, the driver pulled to the side of the road. She dropped out the back door and threw her soiled handkerchief into a puddle. Aboard again, she sat in the rear corner praying that she would not be ill, or faint, or begin to sob. She must not think of food; she must not even think of the crackers she had forgotten in her flight from the dorm; she must not think of what she was going to say, or to whom.

What *was* she going to say?

"Here you will have a chance to examine, and then practice, several skills used in writing effective sentences. The skills presented are those used by writers of the models in the Description Section—" Years ago there was a farm girl at L.C. High who took so large a dose of castor oil to try to make the baby come out that she blew a hole in her stomach. She contracted a terrible case of peritonitis, and lost the baby, but afterward, because she had come so close to dying, everyone forgave her, and kids who hadn't even noticed her before— "Here you will have a chance to examine, and then practice, several skills used in writing—" Curt Bonham, the basketball star. He had been a year ahead of her. In March of his last term he and a friend had tried to walk home across the river one night while the ice was breaking up, and Curt had drowned. His whole class voted unanimously to dedicate the yearbook to him, and his graduation photograph appeared all by itself on the opening page of *The Liberty Bell*. And beneath the black-bordered picture was written—

Smart lad, to slip betimes away
From fields where glory does not stay . . .
ELLIOT CURTIS BONHAM
1930—1948

"What is it?" her mother asked when she came through the front door. "Lucy, what are you doing here? What's the matter?"

"I got here by bus, Mother. That's how people get from Fort Kean to Liberty Center. Bus."

"But what is it? Lucy, you're so pale."

"Is anyone else home?" she asked.

Her mother shook her head. She had come running from the kitchen, carrying a small bowl in her hand; now she had it thrust up to her chest. "Dear, your coloring—"

"Where is everyone?"

"Daddy Will took Grandma over to the market in Winnisaw."

"And he went to work? Your husband?"

"Lucy, what is it? Why aren't you in school?"

"I'm getting married Christmas Day," she said, moving into the parlor.

Sadly her mother spoke. "We heard. We know."

"How did you hear?"

"Lucy, weren't you going to tell us?"

"We only decided Monday night."

"But, dear," said her mother, "today is Friday."

"How did you hear, Mother?"

". . . Lloyd Bassart spoke to Daddy."

"Daddy Will?"

"To your father."

"Oh? And what came of that, may I ask?"

"Well, he took your side. Well, that's what came of it. Lucy, I'm answering your question. He took your side and without a moment's hesitation. Despite our not having been properly told by our own daughter, the day of her own wedding—"

"What did he say, Mother? Exactly."

"He told Mr. Bassart he couldn't speak for Roy, of course . . . He told Mr. Bassart we feel you are mature enough to know your own mind."

"Well—maybe I'm not!"

"Lucy, you can't think everything he does is wrong just because he does it. He *believes* in you."

"Tell him not to, then!"

"Dear—"

"I'm going to have a baby, Mother! So please tell him not to!"

"Lucy—you are?"

"Of course I am! I'm going to have a baby and I hate Roy and I never want to marry him or see him again!"

She ran off to the kitchen just in time to be sick in the sink.

She was put to bed in her room. "Here you will have a chance . . ." The book slid off the bed onto the floor. What was there to do now but wait?

The mail fell through the slot in the hallway and onto the welcome mat. The vacuum cleaner started up. The car pulled into the driveway. She heard her grandmother's voice down on the front porch. She slept.

Her mother brought her tea and toast. "I told Grandma it was the grippe," she whispered to her daughter. "Is that all right?"

Would her grandmother believe that she had come home because of the grippe? Where was Daddy Will? What had she told him?

"He didn't even come inside, Lucy. He'll be back this afternoon."

"Does he know I'm home?"

"Not yet."

Home. But why not? For years they had complained that she acted contemptuous of everything they said or did; for years they complained that she refused to let them give her a single word of advice; she lived among them like a stranger, like an enemy even, unfriendly, uncommunicative, nearly unapproachable. Well, could they say she was behaving like their enemy today? She had come home. So what were they going to do?

Alone, she drank some of the tea. She sank back into the pillow her mother had fluffed up for her and drew one finger lightly round and round her lips. Lemon. It smelled so nice. Forget everything else. Just wait. Time will pass. Eventually something will have to be done.

She fell asleep with her face on her fingers.

Her grandmother came up the stairs carrying a wet mustard plaster. The patient let her nightgown be unbuttoned. "That'll loosen it up," said Grandma Berta, pressing it down. "The two important things, rest and heat. Plenty of heat. Much as you can possibly stand," and she piled two blankets more onto the patient.

Lucy closed her eyes. Why hadn't she done this at the start? Just gotten into bed and left it all to them. Wasn't that what they were always wanting to be, her family?

She was awakened by the piano. The students had begun to arrive for their lessons. She thought, *"But I don't have the grippe!"* But then she drove the thought, and the panic that accompanied it, right from her mind.

It must have begun snowing while she was asleep. She pulled a blanket off the bed, wrapped it around her, and at the window, put her mouth on the cold glass and watched the cars sliding down the street. The window began to grow warm where her mouth was pressed against it. Breathing in and out, she could make the circle of steam on the glass expand and contract. She watched the snow fall.

What would happen when her grandmother found out what really was wrong with her? And her grandfather, when he got home? And her father!

She had forgotten to tell her mother not to tell him. Maybe she wouldn't. But then would anything happen?

She scuffed with her slippers across the old worn rug and got back into her bed. She thought about picking up her English book from the floor to work a little on those sentences; instead she got way down under the blankets and with her faintly lemony fingers under her nose, slept for the sixth or seventh time.

Beyond the window it was dark, though from where she sat propped up in the bed the snow could be seen floating down through the light of the street lamp across the street. Her father knocked on her door. He asked if he could come in.

". . . It's not locked" was her response.

"Well," he said, stepping into the room, "so this is how the rich spend their days. Not bad."

She could tell that his words had been prepared. She did not look up from the blanket, but began to smooth it out with her hand. "I have the grippe."

"Smells to me," he said, "like you've been eating hot dogs."

She did not smile or speak.

"I tell you what it smells like. Smells like Comiskey Park, down in Chicago."

"Mustard plaster," she finally said.

"Well," he said, giving the door a push so that it closed, "that's one of your grandmother's real pleasures in life. That's one," he said, lowering his voice, "and the other is . . . No, I think that about covers it."

She only shrugged, as though she had no opinions on people's habits, one way or the other. Was he clowning because he knew, or because he didn't know? She saw from the corner of her eye that the pale hairs on the back of his hands were wet. He had washed before coming into her room.

The smell of dinner cooking down below caused her to begin to feel ill.

"Mind if I sit at the foot here?" he said.

"If you want to."

She mustn't be sick, not again. She mustn't arouse in him a single suspicion. No, she did not want him to know, ever!

"Let's see," he was saying. "Do I want to or don't I want to? I want to."

She yawned as he sat.

"Well," he said, "nice and cozy up here."

She stared straight ahead into the snowy evening.

"Winter's coming in with a rush this time," he said.

She glanced quickly over at him. "I suppose."

By looking instantly out the window, she was able to collect herself; she could not remember the last time she had looked directly into his eyes.

"Did I ever tell you," he said, "about the time I sprained my ankle when I was working over at McConnell's? It swelled way up and I came home, and your grandmother just lit up all over. Hot compresses, she said. So I sat down in the kitchen and rolled up my trouser leg. You should have seen her boiling up the water on the stove. Somehow it reminded me of all those cannibals over in Africa. She can't see how it can be good for you unless it hurts or smells bad."

Suppose she just blurted out the truth, to him?

"A lot of people like that," he said ... "So," and gave her foot a squeeze where it stuck up at the end of the bed, "how's school going, Goosie?"

"All right."

"I hear you're learning French. Parlez-vous?"

"French is one of my subjects, yes."

"And, let's see ... what else? You and me haven't had a good conversation in a long time now, have we?"

She did not answer.

"Oh, and how's Roy doing?"

Instantly she said, "Fine."

Her father took his hand off her foot at last. "Well," he said, "we heard, you know, about the wedding."

"Where's Daddy Will?" she asked.

"I'm talking to you right now, Lucy. What do you want him for while I'm talking to you?"

"I didn't say I wanted him. I only asked where he was."

"Out," her father said.

"Isn't he even going to have dinner?"

"He went out!" He rose from the bed. "I don't ask where he goes, or when he eats. How do I know where he is? He's out!" And he left the room.

In a matter of seconds her mother appeared.

"What happened now?"

"I asked where Daddy Will is, that's all," Lucy answered. "What's wrong with that?"

"But is Daddy Will your father or is your father your father?"

"*But you told him!*" she burst out.

"Lucy, your voice," said her mother, shutting the door.

"But you did. You told him! And I didn't say you should!"

"Lucy, you came home, dear; you said——"

"I don't want him to know! It's not his business!"

"Now stop, Lucy—unless you want others to know too."

"But I don't care who knows! I'm not ashamed! And don't start crying, Mother!"

"Then let him talk to you, *please*. He wants to."

"Oh, does he?"

"Lucy, you have to listen to him. You have to give him a chance."

She turned and hid her face in the pillow. "I didn't want him to *know*, Mother."

Her mother sat on the bed, and put her hand to the girl's hair.

"And," said Lucy, moving back, "what was he going to say, anyway? Why didn't he just say it out, if he had anything to say?"

"Because," her mother pleaded, "you didn't give him the chance."

"Well, I'm giving *you* a chance, Mother." There was a silence. "Tell me!"

"Lucy . . . dear . . . what would you think . . . What would you say—what would you think, I mean—of going for a visit—"

"Oh, no."

"Please let me finish. Of going to visit your father's cousin Vera. In Florida."

"And is that his idea of what to do with me?"

"Lucy, till this is over. For the little while it will take."

"Nine months is no little while, Mother—"

"But it would be warm there, it would be pleasant—"

"Oh," she said, beginning to cry into the pillow, "very pleasant. Why doesn't he ship me off to a home for wayward girls, wouldn't that be even easier?"

"Don't say that. He doesn't want to send you anywhere, you know that."

"He wishes I'd never been born, Mother. He thinks I'm why everything is so wrong with *him.*"

"That's not *so.*"

"Then," she said, sobbing, "he'd have one less responsibility to feel guilty about. If he even felt guilty to begin with."

"But he does, terribly." ·

"Well, he should!" she said. "He is!"

Some twenty minutes after her mother had run from the room, Daddy Will knocked. He was wearing his lumber jacket and held his cap in his hands. The brim was dark where the snow had dampened it.

"Hey. I hear somebody's been asking for me."

"Hullo."

"You sound like death warmed over, my friend. You ought to be outside and feel that wind. Then you'd really appreciate being sick in bed."

She did not answer.

"Stomach settle down?" he asked.

"Yes."

He pulled a chair over to the side of the bed. "How's about another mustard plaster? Berta called me at the Erwins' and on the way home I stopped and bought a whole fresh packet. So just say when."

She turned and looked at the wall.

"What is it, Lucy? Maybe you want Dr. Eglund. That's what I told Myra . . ." He pulled the chair right up close. "Lucy, I never saw anything like the change in him this time," he said softly. "Not a drop—not a single solitary drop, honey. He is taking this whole decision of yours right in his stride. You set a date and it was just fine with him. Fine with all of us—whatever you think is going to make you and Roy happy."

"I want my mother."

"Don't you feel good again? Maybe the doctor—"

"I want my mother! My mother—and not him!"

She was still looking at the wall when her door was opened.

"Myra," her father said, "sit over there. Sit, I said."

"Yes."

"All right, Lucy. Turn over." He was standing by the side of the bed. "Roll over, I said."

"Lucy," her mother begged, "look at us, please."

"I don't have to see that his shoes are shined and his jaw is set and what a new man he is. I don't have to see his tie, or him!"

"Lucy—"

"Myra, be *quiet*. If she wants to act like a two-year-old at a time like this, let her."

She whispered, "Look who's talking about two-year-olds."

"Listen, young lady. Your backtalk doesn't faze me one way or the other. There have always been smart-aleck teen-agers and there always will be, especially this generation. You just listen to me, that's all, and if you're too ashamed to look me right in the eye—"

"Ashamed!" she cried, but she did not move.

"Are you or are you not going to visit Cousin Vera?"

"I don't even *know* Cousin Vera."

"That isn't what I'm asking."

"I can't go off alone to someone I don't even know—and what? Make up filthy lies for the neighbors—?"

"But they wouldn't be lies," said her mother.

"What would they be, Mother? The truth?"

"They would be *stories,*" her father said. "That you have a husband overseas, say, in the Army."

"Oh, you know all about stories, I'm sure. But I tell the truth!"

"Then," he said, "just what do you intend to do about getting in trouble with somebody who you say you can't even stand?"

She turned violently from the wall, as though she intended to hurl herself at him. "Don't you take such a tone with me. Don't you dare!"

"I am not taking any tone!"

"Because I am not ashamed—not in front of you I'm not."

"Now watch it, you, just watch it. Because I can still give you a licking, smart as you think you are."

"Oh," she said bitterly, "can you?"

"Yes!"

"Go ahead, then."

"Oh, wonderful," he said, and walked to the window where he stood as though looking outside. "Just wonderful."

"Lucy," said her mother, "if you don't want to go to Cousin Vera's, then what do you want to do? Just tell us."

"You're the parents. You were always dying to be the parents—"

"Now look," said her father, turning to face her once again. "First, Myra, you sit down. And stay down. And you," he said, waving a finger at his daughter, "you give me your attention, do you hear? Now there is a crisis here, do you understand that? There is a crisis here involving my daughter, and I am going to deal with it, and it's going to be dealt with."

"Fine," said Lucy. "Deal."

"Then be still," her mother pleaded, "and let him talk, Lucy." But when she made a move to sit on the bed, her husband looked at her and she retreated.

"Now either I'm going to do it," he said to his wife, speaking between his teeth, "or I'm not. Now which is it?"

She lowered her eyes.

"Unless of course you want to call your Daddy in," he said.

"I'm sorry."

"Now," said her father, "if you wanted to marry that Roy Bassart—such as we understood you did, Lucy, till just today, and backed you up on all the way—that would be one thing. But this is something else entirely. Who he is I see pretty clear now, and the less said about him the better. I understand the whole picture, so there is just no need for raising voices. He was older, back from service, and just thought to himself he could come back here and take advantage of a young seventeen-year-old high school girl. And that's what he did. But he is his father's business, Lucy, and we will have to leave it to his high and mighty father, the big schoolteacher, to teach something into that boy's hide. Oh, his father thinks he is very superior and all in his ways, but I guess he is going to have another guess coming now. But my concern is with you, Lucy, and what is uppermost to you. Do you understand that? My concern is your going to college, which has always been your dream, right? Now, the question is this, do you still want your dream, or don't you?"

She did not favor him with a reply.

"Okay," he said, "I am going to go ahead on my assumption that you do, just as you always did. Now, next—to give you your dream I am going to do anything I can . . . Are you listening to me? Anything that is going to give it to you, do you follow me? Because what that so-called ex-G.I. has done to you, which I would like to put my hands around his throat for, well, that is not going to just take away your dream, lock, stock and barrel . . . Now, anything," he went on. "Even something that isn't usual and ordinary, and that might to some folks seem very—out of the question." He came closer to the bed so that he could speak without being heard outside the room. "Now do you know what *anything* means, before I go to the next step?"

"Giving up whiskey?"

"I want you to go to college, it means! I have given up whiskey, for your information!"

"Really?" she asked. "Again?"

"Lucy, since Thanksgiving," her mother began.

"Myra, you be still."

"I was only telling her—"

"But *I* will tell her," he said. "*I* will do the telling."

"Yes," his wife said softly.

"Now," he said, turning back to Lucy. "Drink is neither here nor there. Drink is not the issue."

"Oh no?"

"No! A baby is!"

And that made her look away.

"An illegitimate baby is," he said again. "And if you don't *want* that illegitimate baby"—his voice had fallen almost to a whisper now—"then maybe we will have to arrange that you don't have it. If Cousin Vera's is still something you are going to consider out of the question—"

"It absolutely is. I will not spend nine months lying. I will not get big and pregnant and lie!"

"Shhh!"

"Well, I won't," she muttered.

"Okay." He wiped his mouth with his hand. "Okay." She could see where the perspiration had formed above his lip and on his forehead. "Then let's do this in order. And without voice-raising, as there are other people who live in this house."

"We're the other people who live here."

"Be still!" he said. "Everybody knows that without your backtalk!"

"Then just what are you proposing to me? Say it!"

Her mother rushed to the bed at last. "Lucy," she said, taking hold of her hand, "Lucy, it's only to help *you*—"

And then her father took hold of the other hand, and it was as though some current were about to pass through the three of them. She closed her eyes, waited— and her father spoke. And she let him. And she saw the future. She saw herself seated between her two parents as her father drove them across the bridge to Winnisaw. It would be early morning. The doctor would only just have finished his breakfast. He would come to the door to greet them; her father would shake his hand. In his office the doctor would seat himself behind a big dark desk, and she would sit in a chair, and her parents would be together on a sofa, while the doctor explained to them exactly what he was going to do. He would have all his medical degrees right up on the wall, in frames. When she went off with him into the little white operating room, her mother and father would smile at her from the sofa. And they would wait right there until it was time to bundle her up and take her home.

When her father had finished, she said, "It must cost a fortune."

"The object isn't money, honey," he said.

"The object is you," said her mother.

How nice that sounded. Like a poem. She was just beginning to study poetry, too. Her last English composition had been an interpretation of "Ozymandias." She had only received the paper back on Monday morning—a B-plus for the first interpretation she had ever written of a poem in college. Only on Monday she had thought it was going to be her last. Before Roy had finally returned to Fort Kean that night, her recurring thought had been to run away. And now she didn't have to, and she didn't have to marry him either. Now she could concentrate on one thing and one thing only— on school, on her French, her history, her poetry . . .

> The object isn't money,
> The object is you.

"But where," she asked softly, "will you get it all?"

"Let me do the worrying about that," her father said. "Okay?"

"Will you work?"

"Wow," he said to Myra. "She sure don't pull her

punches, your daughter here." The red that had risen into his cheeks remained, even as he tried to maintain a soft and joking tone. "Come on, Goosie, what do you say? Give me a break, huh? Where do you think I've been all day today, anyway? Taking a stroll on the boulevard? Playing a tennis game? What do you think I've been doing all my life since I was eighteen years old, and part-time before that? Work, Lucy, just plain old work, day in and day out."

"Not at one job," she said.

"Well . . . I move around . . . that's true . . ."

She was going to cry: they were talking!

"Look," he said, "why don't you think of it this way. You have a father who is a jack of all trades. You should be proud. Come on, Goosie-Pie, how about a smile like I used to get back in prehistoric times? Back when you used to take those 'yumps.' Huh, little Goose?"

She felt her mother squeeze her hand.

"Look," he said, "why do you think people always hire Duane Nelson, no matter what? Because he sits around twiddling his thumbs, or because he knows every kind of machine there is, inside and out? Now which? That's not a hard question, is it, for a smart college girl?"

. . . Afterward she would read in bed. She would have her assignments mailed up to her while she recuperated in her bed. Yes, a college girl. And without Roy. He wasn't so bad; he wasn't for her, that was all. He would just disappear, and she could begin to make friends at school, friends to bring home with her when she came to visit on the weekend. For things would have changed.

Could that be? At long last those terrible days of hatred and solitude, over? To think, she could begin again to talk to her family, to tell them about all the things she was studying, to show them the books she used in her courses, to show them her papers. Stuck into her English book, right there on the floor, was the essay she had written on "Ozymandias." B-plus and across the front the professor had written, "Excellent paragraph development; good understanding of meaning; good use of quotations; but please don't stuff your sentences so." And maybe she *had* overdone the main topic sentence somewhat, but her intention had been to state at the outset all those ideas that she would later take up in the body of the essay. "Even a great king," her paper began, "such as Ozymandias apparently had been, could not predict or control what the future, or Fate, held in store for him and his kingdom; that, I think, is the message that Percy Bysshe Shelley, the poet, means for us to come away with from his romantic poem 'Ozymandias,' which not only reveals the theme of the vanity of human wishes—even a king's—but deals also with the concept of the immensity of 'boundless and bare' life and the inevitability of the 'colossal wreck' of everything, as compared to the 'sneer of cold command,' which is all many mere mortals have at their command, unfortunately."

"But is he clean?" she asked.

"A hundred percent," her father said. "Spotless, Lucy. Like a hospital."

"And how old?" she asked. "How old is he?"

"Oh," her father said, "middle-aged, I'd say."

A moment passed. Then, "That's the catch, isn't it?"

"What kind of catch?"

"He's too old."

"Now what do you mean 'too old'? If anything, he's real experienced."

"But is this all he does?"

"Lucy, he's a regular doctor . . . who does this as a special favor, that's all."

"But he charges, you said."

"Well, sure he charges."

"Then it's not a special favor. He does it for money."

"Well, everybody has got bills to meet. Everybody has got to be paid for what they do."

But she saw herself dead. The doctor would be no good, and she would die.

"How do you know about him?"

"Because—" and here he stood, and hitched up his trousers. "Through a friend," he finally said.

"Who?"

"Lucy, I'm afraid maybe that's got to be a secret."

"But where did you hear about him?" Where *would* he hear about such a doctor? "At Earl's famous Dugout of Buddies?"

"Lucy, that's not necessary," said her mother.

Her father walked to the window again. He cleared a pane with the palm of his hand. "Well," he said, "it's stopped snowing. It's stopped snowing, if anybody cares."

"All I meant—" Lucy began.

"Is *what?*" He had turned back to her.

"—is ... do you know anybody who he's ever done it to, that's all."

"Yes, I happen to, for your information."

"And they're alive?"

"For your information, yes!"

"Well, it's my life. I have a right to know."

"Why don't you just trust me! I'm not going to kill you!"

"Oh, Duane," her mother said, "she *does.*"

"Don't speak for me, Mother!"

"Hear that?" he cried to his wife.

"Well, he might just be some quack drinking friend who says he's a doctor or something. Well, how do I know, Mother? Maybe it's even Earl himself in his red suspenders!"

"Yeah, that's who it is," her father shouted. "Earl DuVal! sure! What's the *matter* with you? You think I don't mean it when I say I want you to finish college?"

"Dear, he does. You're his daughter."

"That doesn't mean he knows whether a doctor is good or not, Mother. Suppose I die!"

"But I told you," he cried, shaking a fist at her, "you won't!"

"But how do *you* know?"

"Because she didn't, did she!"

"Who?"

No one had to speak for her to understand.

"Oh, no." She dropped slowly back against the head-board.

Her mother, at the side of the bed, covered her face with her hands.

"When?" said Lucy.

"But she's alive, isn't she?" He was pulling at his shirt with his hands. "Answer the point I'm making! I am speaking! She did not die! She did not get hurt in any way at all!"

"Mother," she said, turning to her, "when?"

But her mother only shook her head. Lucy got up out of the bed. "Mother, when did he make you do that?"

"He didn't make me."

"Oh, Mother," she said, standing before her. "You're my mother."

"Lucy, it was the Depression times. You were a little girl. It was so long ago. Oh, Lucy, it's all forgotten. Daddy Will, Grandma, they don't know," she whispered, "—don't have to—"

"But the Depression was over when I was three, when I was four."

"What?" her father cried. "Are you kidding?" To his wife he said, "Is she kidding?"

"Lucy," her mother said, "we did it for you."

"Oh yes," she said, moving backward onto her bed, "for me, everything was for me."

"Lucy, we couldn't have another baby," said her mother. "Not when we were so behind, trying so to fight back—"

"But if only he did his job! If he only stopped being a coward!"

"Look," he said, coming angrily at her, "you don't even know when the Depression was, or what it was, either—*so watch what you say!*"

"I do too know!"

"The whole country was behind the eightball. Not just me! If you want to call names, you, call the whole United States of America names!"

"Sure, the whole *world*."

"Don't you know history?" he cried. "Don't you know anything?" he demanded.

"I know what you made her do, you!"

"But," her mother cried, "I *wanted* to."

"Did you hear that?" he shouted. "Did you hear what your mother just said to you?"

"But you're the man!"

"I am also a human being!"

"*That's no excuse!*"

"Oh, what am I arguing with *you* for? You don't know *a* from *z* as far as life is concerned, and you never will! You wouldn't know a man's job if I did it!"

Silence.

"Hear, Mother? Hear your husband?" said Lucy. "Did you hear what he just said, right out in the open?"

"Oh, hear what I *mean*," he cried.

"But what you *said*—"

"I don't care! Stop trapping me! I came in here to solve a crisis, but how can I do it when nobody lets me even begin? Or end! You'd rather trap me—throw me in jail! That's what you'd rather do. You'd rather humiliate me in this whole town, and make me looked down on as the town joke."

"Town *drunk!*"

"Town drunk?" he said. "Town *drunk?* You ought to *see* the town drunk. You think *I'm* the town drunk? Well, you ought to just see a town drunk, and then think what you're saying twice before you say it. You don't know what a town drunk is. You don't know what anything is! You—you just want me behind bars— that's your big wish in life, and always has been!"

"It's not."

"It is!"

"But that's *over*," cried Myra.

"Oh, sure it's over," said Whitey. "Sure, people just forget how a daughter threw her own father in jail. Sure, people don't talk about that behind your back. People don't like to tell stories on a person, oh no. People are always giving other people a chance to change and get their strength back. Sure, that's what this little scene is all about too. You bet it is. Oh, she's got me fixed, boy—and that's the way it's going to be. That's how brilliant she is, your so-called college girl scholarship daughter. Well, go ahead, so-called daughter who knows all the answers—solve your own life. Because I'm not good enough for a person like you, and never have been. What am I anyway? The town drunk to her."

He pulled open the door and went loudly down the stairs. They could hear him bellowing in the parlor. "Go ahead, Mr. Carroll. You're the only one can solve things around here. Go ahead, it's Daddy Will everyone wants around here anyway. I'm just extra anyway. I'm just along for the ride, we all know that."

"Shouting won't help anything, Duane—"

"Right, right you are, Berta. Nothing will help anything around here."

"Willard," said Berta, "tell this man—"

"What's the trouble, Duane? What's the fuss?"

"Oh, nothing you can fix, Willard. Because you're the Big Daddy, and me, I'm just along for the ride."

"Willard, where is he going? Dinner is all ready."

"Duane, where are you going?"

"I don't know. Maybe I'll go down and see old Tom Whipper."

"Who's he?"

"The town drunk, Willard! That's who the town drunk is, damn it—Tom Whipper!"

The door slammed, and then the house was silent except for the whispering that began downstairs.

Lucy lay without moving on the bed.

Her mother was crying.

"Mother, why, *why* did you let him make you do that?"

"I did what I had to," said her mother mournfully.

"You didn't! You let him trample on your dignity, Mother! You were his doormat! His slave!"

"Lucy, I did what was necessary," she said, sobbing.

"That's not always right, though. You have to do what's *right!*"

"It was." She spoke as in a trance. "It was, it was—"

"It wasn't! Not for you! He degrades you, Mother, and you let him! Always! All our lives!"

"Oh, Lucy, whatever we say, our suggestions, you refuse."

"I refuse—I refuse to live your life again, Mother, that's what I refuse!"

Roy's best man was Joe Whetstone, home from the University of Alabama, where he had kicked nine field goals and twenty-three consecutive extra points for the freshman football team. The maid of honor was Eleanor Sowerby. Unbeknownst to Joe, Ellie had fallen in love at Northwestern. She simply had to tell Lucy, though she made her promise to speak of it to no one, not even Roy. She would shortly be having to write Joe a letter, and she would just as soon not have to think about that during her vacation; it would be difficult enough at the time.

Either Ellie had forgiven Lucy for calling her a dope at Thanksgiving, or else she was willing to forget it during the wedding. All through the ceremony tears coursed down her lovely face, and her own lips moved when Lucy said, "I do."

After the ceremony Daddy Will told Lucy that she was the most beautiful bride he had seen since her mother. "A real bride," he kept saying, "isn't that so, Berta?" "Congratulations," her grandmother said. "You were a real bride." That was as far as she would go; she knew now that it was not the grippe that had caused Lucy to be sick in the kitchen sink.

Julian Sowerby kissed her again. "Well," he said, "I suppose now I get to do this all the time." "Now *I* do," said Roy. Julian said, "Lucky you, boy, she's a cutie-pie, all right," in no way indicating that he had once lectured Roy for four solid hours in the taproom of the Hotel Kean on the evils of becoming her husband.

Nor did Irene Sowerby indicate that secretly she believed Lucy had unusual emotions. "Good luck to you," she said to the bride, and touched her lips to Lucy's cheek. She took Roy's hand and held it for a very long time before she was ready to speak. And then she was unable to.

Then her own parents. "Daughter," was all she heard in her ear; so stiff was she in his embrace that perhaps it was all he said. "Oh, Lucy," her mother said, her wet lashes against Lucy's face, "be happy. You can be if only you'll try. You were the happiest little girl . . ."

Then both Roy's parents stepped forward, and after a moment in which each seemed to be deferring to the other, the two Bassarts lunged at the bride simultaneously. The mixup of arms and faces that ensued at long last gave everyone present something to laugh about.

Lloyd Bassart was the adult who had finally gotten behind the young couple and supported them in their desire to be married at Christmas—sooner than Christmas if it could be managed. This sharp change of attitude had occurred one night early in December when Roy broke down over the phone and in tears told *his* parents- who had been pouring it on, once again— to stop. "I can't take any more!" he had cried. "Stop! Stop! Lucy's pregnant!"

Well. Well. It had required only the two "wells." If what Roy had just confessed was the actual situation as it existed, then his father did not see that Roy had any choice but to take the responsibility for what he had done. Between a man doing the right thing and a man doing the wrong thing, there was really no choice, as far as Mr. Bassart could see. Weeping, Roy said it was more or less what he had been thinking to himself all along. "I should certainly hope so," said his father, and so that, finally, was that.

III

1

※━○━※━○━※━○━※━○━※━○━※━○━※━○━※━○━※━○━※

She moved into his room at Mrs. Blodgett's. Mrs. Blodgett, who had called her a hussy. Mrs. Blodgett, who had called Roy crooked. Mrs. Blodgett, with her thousand little rules and regulations.

But Lucy said nothing. In the weeks and months following the wedding she found herself trying with all her might to do what she was told. You could not question someone's every word and deed and expect to be happy with them, or expect them to be happy either. They were married. She must trust him; what kind of life would it be otherwise?

Mrs. Blodgett and Roy had worked out the arrangement beforehand: only another five dollars a month for the room. Surely Lucy had to admit that was a bargain, especially since Roy had gotten Mrs. Blodgett to throw in kitchen privileges for the hour between seven and eight in the evening. Of course, they would have to leave the kitchen exactly as they had found it. It was not, after all, the kitchen of a hotel, it was the kitchen of a dwelling place; but apparently Roy had assured Mrs. Blodgett that Lucy was neat as a pin, and knew her way around a kitchen, having worked for three years after school and summers in the Dairy Bar up in Liberty Center. "But that, Mr. Bassart, is my very point, it is not some dairy bar, it is not some—" He assured her then that he would work in the kitchen right along with Lucy. How would that be? In fact, if Mrs. Blodgett had any dishes left over from her own dinner, they could easily wash hers while washing up their own. In the Army he had once had to wash pots and pans for seventeen hours straight on K.P.; as a result, one dish more or less wouldn't faze him too much, she could be sure.

Mrs. Blodgett said she would extend them the privilege, on a trial basis, and only for so long as they didn't abuse it.

During the next few months Roy several times went out after dinner and knocked on the parlor door to ask the landlady if she would like to join them in the kitchen for dessert. Privately he said to Lucy that the extra chocolate pudding or fruit cup cost no more than a few pennies, and with someone of Mrs. Blodgett's changeable disposition, it was worth building up points on your side. Their getting married had more or less restored Mrs. Blodgett's faith in him, but still and all, where three people were living together under one roof, there was no sense looking for trouble, especially if you could just as easily avoid it by using your head in advance.

She said nothing. They must not squabble over issues that were of no real consequence. She must not criticize him for what—she told herself—was really nothing more than a desire to please. Some people did things one way, and Roy did them another. Weren't they married? Hadn't he acted as she had wanted?

TRUST HIM.

To her surprise, hardly a Sunday passed when they did not travel up to Liberty Center to visit his family. Roy said that under ordinary circumstances it wouldn't be necessary, but what with all the strain of the past months and the hard feelings that had developed, it seemed to him a good idea to try to smooth things over before the baby was born and life *really* began to get hectic. The fact was that she was a stranger to his family, as he was a stranger to hers. Now that they were married, what sense did that make? They would all be seeing a lot of one another in the years to come, and it seemed to him ridiculous to start off on the wrong foot. It was an easy two-hour ride up, and aside from the gas, what would it cost them?

So she went—to Sunday dinner at the Bassarts', and on the way out of town, over to say hello to her own family. Silently she sat in the parlor she had hoped never to set foot in again, while Roy engaged her family in fifteen minutes of small talk, most of it for the benefit of her father and Daddy Will. They talked a lot about prefab houses. Her father was supposed to be thinking about building a prefab house, and Daddy Will was supposed to be thinking that it was something her father was capable of doing. Roy said he had buddies down at Britannia who could probably help them draw up plans, when they got to that stage. Contractors were throwing up whole communities of prefabs overnight, Roy said. Oh, it's a real building revolution, her father said. It sure is, Mr. Nelson. Yep, looks like the coming thing, said Daddy Will. It sure does, Mr. Carroll, they're throwing up whole communities overnight.

One Sunday evening, while driving back down to Fort Kean, Roy said, "Well, it looks as though your old man is really on the wagon this time."

"I hate him, Roy. And I will always hate him. I told you long ago, and I meant it: *I don't want to talk about him, ever!*"

"Okay," said Roy lightly, "okay," and so no quarrel resulted. He seemed willing to forget that he had even brought up the subject—as willing as he was to forget that hatred of which Lucy had sought to remind him.

So they set off, Sunday after Sunday, like any young married couple visiting the in-laws. But why? *Why?*

Because that's what they were: she was his wife. And her mother his mother-in-law. And her father, with the thick new mustache and the bright new plans, was Roy's father-in-law. "But I'd really rather not, Roy, not today." "Come on, we're up here, aren't we? I mean, how would it look if we went away without even saying hello? What's the big deal? Come on, honey, don't act like a kid, get in the car—careful, watch the old belly."

And she did not argue. Could it be she had actually argued her last? She had fought and fought to get him to do his duty, but in the end he had done it. So what more was there to fight about? She simply could not find the strength to raise her voice.

And she must respect him anyway. She must not pick at what he said, or challenge his opinions, or take issue with him, especially on matters where his knowledge was superior to her own. Or was supposed to be. She was his wife; she must be sympathetic to his point of view, even if she didn't always agree with it, as she surely didn't when he began to tell her how much more he knew than the teachers at Britannia.

Unfortunately, Britannia hadn't turned out to be the place it was cracked up to be in all those fancy brochures. For one thing, it hadn't been established in 1910, at least not as a photography school. They had only decided to branch out into photography after the war, so as to catch a bigger hunk of the G.I. Bill trade. For the first thirty-five years of its existence it had been a drafting school called the Britannia Technical Institute, and two thirds of the students still were guys interested in getting into the building business—which was how Roy came to know so much about the prefab boom. The drafting students, as a matter of fact, weren't too bad; it was the photography students who were a scandal. Though you had to fill out a long entrance application, and with it send samples of your work, it turned out that there weren't any real entrance requirements at all. The procedure for photography applicants was just a ruse to make you think that the new department had some sort of standards. And the quality of the faculty, he said, was even more appalling than the quality of the students—particularly one H. Harold LaVoy, who somewhere along the line had got the idea that he was some sort of expert on photographic technique. Some expert. There was more to be learned about composition by flipping through an issue of *Look* than spending a lifetime listening to a pompous

idiot like LaVoy (who some of the guys said might be a
fairy, besides. A real queer. For Lucy's edification, he
imitated LaVoy walking down the halls. A bit la-dee-da,
didn't she agree? But even a homo could teach you
something if he knew something. But a dumb homo—
well, that was just about the end).

LaVoy's class was at eight in the morning, Roy's
first of the day. He got up and went off to it faithfully
every single morning of the first month of the second
semester, every morning went off to listen to that nasal-
voiced know-it-all going on and on about absolutely
nothing that a ten-year-old kid couldn't figure out if he
had a pair of twenty-twenty eyes. "Shadows are pro-
duced, gentlemen, by placing object A between the
sun and object B." Bro*ther*. One stormy morning they
got as far as the front porch, when Roy turned around,
came back into the room, and Army boots, field jacket
and all, threw himself back on the bed, moaning, "Oh, I
don't mind a homo, really, but a *dumb* homo!" He said
he could find better uses to make of that hour right
here in their room, he was sure. And since his next
class wasn't until eleven, by staying home he would be
saving not only the hour LaVoy shot for him, but the
two hours following, which he usually spent down in
the lounge, watching one of the endless blackjack games
that was always in session. It was so smoky and
noisy down there that that's about all you could do.
Having a conversation about photography was practically impossible—not that any of his fellow students
seemed to be disposed in that direction anyway. Sometimes with those guys it actually seemed to him that he
was back in the day room up in the Aleutians.

And what did Lucy do? She went down to the
corner and caught the crosstown bus to school for her
eight o'clock. Roy said he would drive her over if she
wanted; now that she was getting bigger he didn't like
the idea of her taking public transportation, or walking
around on slippery streets. But she declined that first
morning, and on those snowy mornings thereafter. It
was all right, she said, there was nothing to worry
about, she preferred not to inconvenience him by tak-

ing him away from his studying *if that's what studying was to him, sitting up in bed with a scissors and the magazines his mother saved for him every week, eating handfuls of those Hydrox cookies!* But maybe he knew what he was doing. Maybe the school *was* a fraud. Maybe his colleagues *were* dopes. Maybe LaVoy *was* pompous and an idiot, and a homosexual too. Maybe everything he said was true and everything he did was right.

That was what she told herself, walking through the snow to the bus, and then in class, and in the library, and in the coffee shop, where she went by herself for her lunch, after her one-thirty. Most of the girls ate in the cafeteria at noon, as she had when she lived in the dorm, and she preferred now to avoid them whenever she could manage it. Eventually one of them would take a sidelong glance at her belly, and why did she have to put up with that? There was no reason for any of those little freshman twerps to look down their noses at her. To them she might only be the kid who'd had to get married over Christmas, somebody to whisper about and make fun of, but to herself she was Mrs. Roy Bassart, and she didn't intend to go around feeling ashamed of herself all day long. She had nothing whatsoever to be ashamed of or to regret. So she ate her lunch alone, at two-thirty, in the last booth of The Old Campus Coffee Shop.

On the first Sunday of June, while they were driving up to Liberty Center, Roy decided he wasn't going to take his finals the following week. Frankly, he could go in and pass things like camera repair and negative retouching without too much sweat, to use an Army expression. So it wasn't a matter of chickening out, or of being too lazy to do the studying. There really wasn't very much studying that he could see to do. What made it senseless to go in and take the final exams—which, by the way, no one had flunked in the history of the photography department, except in La-Voy's class, where it wasn't a matter of whether you knew the material anyway but whether you agreed with Hot Shot LaVoy and his big ideas—but what made it senseless was that he had decided not to return to Britannia in the fall. At least that, at any rate, was what he wanted to talk over with her.

But they had already talked it over. To support her and the baby, he was going to have to give up school during the day; but the plan had been for him to enroll in the night program. It would take two years more that way instead of only one, but this was the solution they had agreed upon months before.

Well, that's why he was bringing it up again. He didn't see any sense hanging on at that place days *or* nights. What good did she think that Master of Photographic Arts degree was going to do him anyway? Anybody who knew anything about photography knew that a Britannia degree wasn't worth the paper it was printed on. "And given the day teachers, you can just imagine the geniuses they have teaching there at night. You know who the head of the whole night program is, don't you?"

"Who?"

"H. Pansy LaVoy. So you can imagine."

Then he told her his surprise. Yesterday morning he and Mrs. Blodgett had got into a conversation, and the upshot was that he was on the brink of his first commercial job. So who needed Peaches LaVoy? On Monday morning he was to do a portrait sitting of Mrs. Blodgett for a week's rent, provided she liked the pictures when they came out.

Up in Liberty Center, Alice Bassart took Roy aside early in the afternoon and told him about Lucy's father blackening her mother's eye. After dinner Roy got Lucy alone upstairs and as gently as he could broke the news. She immediately put on her coat, and against Roy's wishes, went over to the house to see the black eye for herself. And it was not vicious gossip; it was real.

For three days Whitey had been off doing penance for his misdeed—the afternoon he chose to return was the afternoon of his daughter's visit. He never got through the door.

The baby was born four days later. The labor began

in the middle of her English exam, and continued for twelve long, arduous hours. She was awake throughout, swearing to herself every minute of the time that if she survived, her child would never know what life was like in a fatherless house. She would not repeat her mother's life, nor would her offspring repeat her own.

And so for Roy (and, in a sense, for Whitey Nelson too, who after that Sunday had simply disappeared from the town), the honeymoon came to an end.

His first suggestion to be met with opposition was the one he made while she was still in the hospital. Why didn't they move back to Liberty Center for the summer? His family would sleep on the screened-in back porch, which they liked to do anyway in the hot weather, and the two of them and Baby Edward could have the upstairs all to themselves. It seemed to him that it would really be a wonderful change for Lucy. As for himself, he could endure living with his parents for a few months, what with all it would mean for Lucy to be able to relax and take it easy for a while. And think what it would mean to the baby, who would surely feel the heat less up in Liberty Center. All in all, it sounded like such a good idea that the previous night, when his parents came to visit at the hospital, he had taken them aside and broached it to them. He hadn't wanted to tell Lucy beforehand for fear that she would be disappointed if his family had any objections. But actually it had suited them just fine; his mother was absolutely tickled pink by the idea. It was a long while since she had been able to go full steam ahead with her specialty— Pampering with a capital P. Furthermore, the presence of Edward would probably mean the end of that last little bit of tension still existing between themselves and his parents—the unfortunate result of the particular circumstances of the wedding. Moreover, they'd now had six months of marriage, and a really harmonious marriage at that. Roy said he couldn't get over how compatible they had turned out to be, once all that premarital uncertainty had ended; had he known it was going to be like this, he said, taking her hand in his, he would have proposed from the car that first night he followed her down Broadway. He had to admit that it would give him a certain secret pleasure to go back for a while to Liberty Center and show his doubting Thomas of a father just how fantastically compatible his son's marriage had turned out to be.

And how, Lucy asked, would Roy support them when they were living in his father's house?

He assured her that if ever there was a place he could pick up jobs as a free-lance photographer, it was in his own hometown.

No.

No? What did she mean, no?

No.

He couldn't believe his ears. Why not?

No!

How could he argue with somebody in a hospital bed? For a while he tried, but all he got was no.

Fortunately, in the month after Edward's birth, Mrs. Blodgett let them bring into the room the crib the Sowerbys had given them, and allowed them even more expanded use of the kitchen facilities, all for only another dollar a week. Moreover, she had accepted the portrait Roy had done of her in exchange for a week's rent. She thought it made her features look too small, particularly her eyes and mouth, but she said herself that if she expected a professional job she should have gone to a professional; she was an honest person and would not welsh on her end of the bargain. Certainly, said Roy, Lucy had to agree that the landlady was doing the best she could to be considerate. A man and his wife and a tiny infant wasn't at all what she had bargained for the year before, and so he wished that Lucy would be a little more cordial—or else just say okay, and even if only half the summer was left, agree to go up to his parents' for a month or so, and live for a while in an environment more suited to their present needs . . . Well, would she?

Would she what? Which question did he want answered?

Would she go up to Liberty Center?

No.

Just for the month of August?

No.

Well then, at least would she be more pleasant to Mrs. Blodgett when she passed her in the corridor? What did it cost to smile?

She was being as pleasant as was necessary.

But the woman was surely going out of her way—

The woman was being paid the money she asked for her room and her kitchen. If she didn't like the arrangement, or them, she could ask them to move.

Move? *Where?*

To an apartment of their own.

But how could they afford an apartment of their own?

How did he think?

"Well, I'm *looking* for a job. Every day! It's summer, Lucy! And that's the truth! The bosses are all on vacation. Every place I go—sorry, the boss is on vacation! And our savings are dwindling like crazy too. If we were up in Liberty Center, we wouldn't have had to spend a penny all summer long. Instead we're down here, accomplishing nothing, and the baby is hot, and our money is just dribbling away, and all I do is waste time sitting in offices waiting and waiting for people who aren't even there. We could all of us have had a little vacation—a vacation all of us need, too, whether you know it or not. Because now do you see what's happening? We're arguing. Right this minute we're having an argument. And why? We're just as compatible now as we were six months ago, Lucy, but we're arguing because of living in this one room in all this hot weather, while up in Liberty Center that whole upstairs is just sitting there going to waste."

No.

Just before Labor Day, Lucy said that since there did not seem to be any jobs for a photographer available, perhaps he should start to look for some other kind of work, but Roy said he was not going to get stuck in a job he hated, because the job he liked and was equipped to do hadn't yet come along.

But their savings *were* rapidly dwindling, and this money, she reminded him, consisted not only of what he had saved in the Army, but what she had saved during all those years at the Dairy Bar.

Well, he happened to know that. That's what he had been telling her all summer long. That was exactly what could have been avoided—and then he slammed the door and left the house before she could deliver the speech he saw coming, or before Mrs. Blodgett, who had already hammered on the floor above them with her shoe, could make it down the stairs to deliver hers.

Only an hour later there was a phone call for Roy from Mr. H. Harold LaVoy of the Britannia Institute. He said he understood that Mr. Bassart was looking for a job. He wished to inform him that Wendell Hopkins was in need of an assistant, his previous assistant having just enrolled as a full-time student in Britannia's television department, which would be getting under way in the fall.

When Roy came home at lunchtime he was flabbergasted at the message. From *LaVoy?* Hopkins, the society photographer? He was shaved and dressed and out of the house in a matter of minutes; within the hour he had called Lucy to say that he wanted her to put Edward on.

Put Edward on? Edward was sleeping. What was he even saying?

Well then, she had better tell the baby herself: his father was now the assistant to Wendell Hopkins in his studio in the Platt Building in downtown Fort Kean. Well, was it or was it not worth waiting for?

What he couldn't get over that night at dinner was that LaVoy had thought to call *him*—even after those disagreements they used to have almost daily in class, during the month that Roy had even bothered to show up. Apparently, however, LaVoy wasn't really as touchy as he had appeared to be in the classroom. True, the old fruitcake couldn't take criticism in public, but privately it appeared that he had developed a certain grudging respect for Roy's knowledge of composition, and light and shadow. Well, you had to give him credit, he was a bigger man than Roy had thought. Who knows, maybe he wasn't even a fruit; maybe that just happened, unfortunately for him, to be the way he walked and the way he talked. Who knows, if they had ever gotten beyond the arguing stage, LaVoy might even have turned out to be a pretty sharp guy. They might even have become friends. Anyway, what difference did it make now? At the age of twenty-two he was the sole assistant to Wendell Hopkins, who, it turned out, only a few years back had done a portrait of the whole Donald Brunn family of Liberty Center. Oh, what a pleasure it would be to telephone his father directly after dinner and tell him about his new job—not to mention the fact that Mr. Hopkins was the family photographer for his father's well-known boss.

Before the month was over they had found their first apartment; it was on the top floor of an old house at the north end of Pendleton Park, practically on the outskirts of Fort Kean. The rent was reasonable, the furniture wasn't bad, and the big trees and quiet street reminded Roy of Liberty Center. There was a bedroom for the baby, and a large living room in which they could also sleep, and a kitchen and bath of their very own. There was also a dank and musty cellar back of the furnace that the renting agent said Roy was welcome to turn into a darkroom, so long as he realized that he would have to leave behind him any improvements he made in the building. The apartment was a twenty-minute drive to downtown, but the prospect of the darkroom clinched the deal.

The thirtieth of September was a Saturday, brisk and cloudy. They spent the morning driving their belongings over to their new home. Late in the day, when the moving was over and they had washed the last of the plates used for their last meal, Roy sat tapping lightly and sporadically on the horn of the car, while Lucy stood up on the porch, the baby in her arms, and told Mrs. Blodgett what she thought of her.

In the next year Roy drove in his car all over Kean

County, photographing church socials, Rotary dinners, ladies'-club meetings, Little League games—and, most frequently, grade and high school graduation classes; the biggest share of Hopkins' business, it turned out, was not out of the Fort Kean social register, but from the Board of Education, of which his brother was a member. Hopkins himself stayed in the studio all day to do the serious sittings—the brides, the babies and the businessmen. His first week Roy had carried around a small spiral notebook in which he had planned to jot down the tips and advice that might pass from the lips of the seasoned old professional during a day's work. Shortly he came to use it to record the cost of the gas pumped each day into the car.

Edward. A pale little baby with blue eyes and white hair, who for so long had the sweetest, mildest, most serene disposition. He smiled benevolently up at everyone who looked admiringly down into his carriage when Lucy wheeled him through the park; he slept and ate when he was supposed to, and in between times just smiled away. The elderly couple who lived in the apartment below said they had never known a baby to be so quiet and well behaved; they had been prepared for the worst when they heard that a child was going to be living over their heads, but they had to tell young Mr. and Mrs. Bassart that they had no complaint so far.

Just before Edward's first birthday, Uncle Julian hired Roy to come up to the house to take the pictures at Ellie's pinning party. The next day Roy began to talk about leaving his job and opening a studio of his own. How much longer could he go on doing the D.A.R. in the afternoon and the high school prom at night? How much longer could he go on getting peanuts for doing the dreary dirty work, the weekend work, the night work, while Hopkins raked in the money and did all the creative jobs besides (if you could call anything Hopkins did "creative")? Exactly how long was he supposed to let Hopkins get away with paying only for the gas, while Roy himself absorbed the depreciation on the automobile?

"LaVoy!" said Roy one night, after a gruesome afternoon photographing the boys and girls of the 4H Club. "I really ought to go down to the Britannia and punch that pansy one right in the mouth. Because, you know something, *he* knew what this job was all along. A glorified errand boy. The photographic technique involved—well, Eddie could do it, for God's sake. And I'm telling you something, LaVoy knew it. Well, just think about it. Remember how surprised I was? Well, it was actually a piece of vengeance against me—can you imagine?—and I'm so dumb it never dawned on me till today, right in the midst of shooting all those kids going 'cheese, cheese.' Well, I'll show him, and I'll show Hopkins too. If I started my own place, I'd have half of Hopkins' portrait trade within a year. And that's a fact. That I know for a *fact*. All he needs is a little competition, then he'd be crying Mamma, all right."

"But where would you run this studio, Roy?"

"Where would I run it? To begin with? Where would I *have* it? Is that what you mean?"

"Where will you run it? How much will it cost? What will you do to support us until the customers begin to leave Hopkins and come running to you?"

"Oh, damn," he said, banging a fist on the table, *"damn* that LaVoy. He really couldn't take criticism, not the slightest bit of it. And the thing is, I knew it all the time. But that he'd stoop to this—"

"Roy, where do you intend to start a studio?"

"Well—if you want to talk seriously about it . . ."

"Where, Roy?"

"Well—to start off, there'd have to be another rent, see."

"Another rent?"

"But that's what we can rule out. Because we have to, I know. We couldn't afford it. So, to start off, well . . . I thought, here."

"Here?"

"Well, the darkroom I'd have in the basement, of course."

"And your studio itself would be in our living room?"

"Just during the day, of course."

"And Edward and myself during the day?"

"Well, as I say, Lucy, it's open to question, needless to say. I'm certainly willing to talk over the pros and cons, and peacefully too—"

"And the customers?"

"I *told* you, that would take time."

"And what darkroom are you even talking about? You haven't even begun a darkroom. You've talked about beginning a darkroom; oh, you've talked about it, all right—"

"Well, I work all day long, it so happens, you know. I come home at night bushed, frankly. And half the time on weekends he's got me going out to some wedding somewhere out in the sticks—oh, forget it. You can't understand anything about my career. Or my ambitions! I have a kid growing up, Lucy. And I happen to have ambitions that I haven't given up, you know, just because I'm married. I'm sure not going to be the victim of that LaVoy's vengeance for the rest of my life, I'll tell you that. He tricked me right into this job, which is really for a grind, you know—and Hopkins pays me peanuts, compared to what photographers *can* make, and because I say I want a studio of my own to you, to my own *wife*—oh, you won't understand anything! You won't even try!" And he ran out the door.

It was nearly midnight when he returned.

"Where have you been, Roy? I have been sitting here waiting up for you, not knowing were you were. Where have you been? To some bar?"

"Some what?" he said sourly. "I went to a movie, Lucy, if you have to know. I went into town and saw a movie."

He went off to the bathroom to brush his teeth.

When the light were off he said, "Well, I tell you one thing. I don't know about all the suckers before me, but as far as I'm concerned, Old Tightwad is at least going to split the car insurance starting when it gets renewed. I'm not working my you-know-what off to make him the richest guy in town."

The months passed. No further mention was made of the studio, though from time to time Roy would mutter about LaVoy. "I wonder if the administration of that so-called school knows about that guy. A real honest to God homemade fruitcake, just like you hear about. Old la-dee-da LaVoy. H. Harold. Boy, would I love to run into him downtown some day, would I love to confront him some day face to face."

One Sunday in the spring when they were visiting Liberty Center, Lucy overheard Roy's mother saying that a package had arrived for him and was up in his bedroom on the dresser. Driving home that night she asked him what was in the package.

"What package?" said Roy.

The next day, after cleaning up from breakfast and making Edward's bed, she began to search the apartment. Not until after lunch, when Edward was napping, did she find a small box jammed down into the top of one of Roy's old Army boots, way at the back of the hall closet. The box was from a printing firm in Cleveland, Ohio; inside were hundreds and hundreds of business cards reading

BASSART PHOTOGRAPHIC STUDIO
Finest Photographic Portraiture
in all Fort Kean

When Roy came home in the evenings, he usually played this game with his little boy (bushed as he might be). "Ed?" Roy would say as he came through the door. "Hey, has anybody here seen Edward Bassart?" whereupon Edward would pop up from behind the sofa, and aiming himself for the front door, go running full tilt into his father's arms. Roy would sweep him up off the floor and twirl him around overhead, crying out in mock amazement, "Well, I'll be darned. I will be absolutely be darned. It's the original Edward Q. Bassart himself."

The evening of the day Lucy had discovered his secret, Roy came through the door, Edward ran wildly to him, Roy swung him up over his head, and Lucy thought, "No! No!"—for suppose the tiny, innocent, laughing child were to take his father for a man, and grow up in his image?

She controlled herself throughout the dinner and while Edward was read to by Roy, but after he had put his son to bed she was waiting for him in the living room with the package from Cleveland, Ohio, sitting on the coffee table. "When are you going to grow up? When are you going to do the job you have without looking for every single way there is to get out of it? *When?*"

His eyes filled with tears and he rushed out of the apartment.

Again it was midnight before he returned. He'd had a hamburger, and gone to another movie. He took off his coat and hung it in the closet. He went into Edward's room; when he came out—still refusing to engage her eye—he said, "Did he wake up?"

"When?"

He picked up a magazine and spoke while flipping through it. "While I was gone."

"Fortunately, no."

"Look," he said.

"Look what?"

"Oh," he said, plunging into a chair, "I'm sorry. Well, I am," he said, throwing up his arms. "Well, look, am I forgiven or what?"

He explained that he had seen the ad for the business cards in the back of a trade magazine down at Hopkins. A thousand cards—

"Why not ten thousand, Roy? Why not a hundred thousand?"

"Let me finish, *will you?*" he cried.

A thousand cards was the smallest amount you could order. That was the bargain, a thousand for five ninety-eight. Okay, he was sorry he had done it without talking first to her; that way they could have argued out the sense of ordering the cards before some of the other things were planned. He knew that as far as she was concerned it wasn't the money but the principle of the thing.

"It's both, Roy."

Well, maybe both, according to her, but really and truly he didn't know how much longer he could stand

the way Hopkins was exploiting him for sixty-five lousy
dollars a week. At this point the resale value on the
Hudson was practically nil. If she was so concerned
about five ninety-eight for business cards, what about
that, the depreciation on the car? And what about a
little thing called his career? Last week, two whole
evenings photographing practically every single Brown-
ie and Cub Scout in the county! By now he would
have been a graduate of Britannia, if he hadn't had to
go out and get a stupid job like this one so as to
support a family.

"But you didn't *want* to graduate from Britannia."

"I'm talking about the time that's passed, Lucy,
while I do Hopkins' dirty work!"

Well, if he wanted to talk about time, she would
have been a junior now, and a senior in the fall; in a
year she would be graduating from college. Well, said
Roy, don't act as though it's my fault. But it *was* his
fault, she said; whose idea was that "interruption" business but his? Look, he said, they'd been over all that a
hundred times already. Over what, Roy? Over that the
interruption had worked all summer, for one—and for
another, she had let him do it. She had let him do it,
she said, because he had forced it on her, because he
had insisted and insisted—*Okay!* he cried. Then you
have to take the consequences, she told him, you have
to pay the price for what you do! All my *life?* he asked.
A whole life long pay the price for *that?* God damn it,
just because he'd had to marry her didn't mean that he
had to be the slave of Hopkins for the rest of his life, or
the patsy of some no-good rotten pansy fruit!

"LaVoy has nothing to do with this!" she cried.

"Oh, and I suppose Hopkins doesn't either, according to you?"

"He doesn't!"

"Oh, no? Oh, you don't happen to think so, do you?
Who does then, Lucy, just me? Just me and no one
else?"

The tears flowed from his eyes, and once again he
ran for the door. He drove straight up to Liberty

Center and did not return until the following afternoon.

Looking very determined. He wanted to have a serious talk, he said, like adults. About what? she asked. She happened to have a two-year-old child to take care of while he went off downtown to a movie, or running home to his Mommy. She happened to have a bright, alert little boy, who got up in the morning and found his father missing and didn't know what to make of it at all.

Roy followed her around the living room, trying to make himself heard over the sounds of the vacuum cleaner. Finally he pulled out the plug and refused to surrender it until she heard him out. What he wanted to talk about was a separation.

A what? Please, she told him, Edward was in his bedroom taking his nap. "What are you even saying, Roy?"

"Well, a sort of temporary separation. So we can both sort of calm down. So we can think things through, and probably afterward be all the better for it ... An armistice, sort of."

"Who have you been talking to, Roy, about our private life?"

"No one," he said. "I just did some thinking. Is that unheard of, that a person should do some thinking about his own private life?"

"You are repeating someone else's idea. Well, is that or is that not true?"

He threw the plug to the floor and once again was out of the house.

Edward, it turned out, had not been napping; at the start of the argument he had run from his bedroom to the bathroom and fastened the little hook that locked the door. Lucy knocked and knocked. She promised him all kinds of treats if only he would just lift the little hook out of the eye of the little screw. She said Daddy was upset about something that had happened at his work, but that nobody was angry at anybody. Daddy had gone off to work, and would be home for dinner, just like every other night. Didn't he want to play his game with Daddy? She begged him to open up. Meanwhile she pressed and pressed against the door, thinking that the screw might ease free of the old boards of the house. In the end she had to bang the door sharply with her shoulder for the thing to pull out of the wall.

Edward was sitting under the washbasin, holding a washcloth over his face. He sobbed hysterically when he heard her approaching, and only after half an hour of holding and rocking him in her arms was she able to persuade him that everything was all right.

She was in bed when Roy came home that night and began to undress in the dark. She turned on the light and as softly as she could, fearing for Edward's sleep, she asked him to sit down and listen to her. They had to talk. He had to be made to understand what his behavior was doing to Edward's peace of mind. She told him about Edward's locking himself in the bathroom—a two-year-old child, Roy. She told him what it had been like to see him sitting there under the basin, hiding behind a washcloth. She told him that he could not keep running off and expect that their child, tiny as he was, was not going to understand that something was going on between his mother and his father. She told him that he could not come home from work and be all lovey-dovey to a little two-year-old, and play with him, and read to him, and kiss him good night, and then just not be there in the morning. Because the child was able to put two and two together, whether Roy knew it or not.

Several times Roy tried to speak in his defense, but she went right on, refusing to be interrupted until the truth was heard, and after a while Roy just sat there on the edge of the sofa bed, his head in his hands, saying he was sorry. Had Eddie really locked himself in the bathroom?

She told him how she'd had to force herself inside.

Oh God. He felt awful. He didn't know what was happening to him. He was just so emotionally wrought up. Nothing like this had ever happened to him in his life. How could she possibly think that he wanted to harm Edward? He loved him. He adored him. All afternoon long he looked forward to that moment when he would throw open the door and Edward would come racing at him from across the living room. He loved him so. And he loved her, he really did, even if he hadn't been acting like it. That's what made it all so confusing. She was the most important person in his life, now as always. She was so strong, so good. She was probably one of the most incredible girls for her age there had ever been. Look at Ellie—at twenty she had already dumped Joe Whetstone to get pinned to this guy Clark, and within six months was already depinned from Clark and going steady with this guy Roger. Look at the average twenty-year-old girl, then look at Lucy, and all she'd had to suffer. He knew what her father had put her family through. He knew all the things she'd had to do to save her family from him when they wouldn't save themselves. He knew what it must be like for her, to have to remember that it was she who finally had to lock the door on him, to send him away so that he never came back to ruin her mother's life.

She said that she never thought about it. Where he was, was not her concern.

Well, *he* thought about it. He knew she did not like to talk about her father, but the point was, he wanted her to know that it was her courage in the face of her father's behavior that he had always admired, and always would. She had courage. She had strength. She knew right from wrong. There was no one in the world like her. He felt privileged and honored to be her husband, did she know that? Oh, why was he crying? He didn't seem able to help it. He hadn't meant to do little Eddie any harm, she must know that. He didn't mean to do her any harm, to cause anybody in the world the least little harm or hardship. Didn't she know that? Because it was the truth. He wanted to be good, really he did. Oh, please, oh, please, she had to understand.

He was kneeling on the floor, his head in her lap, weeping uncontrollably. Oh, God, my God, he said. Oh, he had something to tell her. And she had to hear him out, she had to understand and to forgive. She had to let it be over, once he told her, and never bring it up again, but she had to know the truth.

What truth?

It was just that he had been so mixed up. He hadn't even known what he was thinking about or what he was doing. She had to understand that.

Understand what?

Well, in Liberty Center he had not gone to stay with his family; he had stayed with the Sowerbys. He admitted that the idea of a separation was not his but his uncle's.

Not even a week passed. At dinner one evening he began to grumble again about being shoved around by Hopkins. Before she even had a chance to reply, Edward had gotten up off the kitchen floor, where he had been playing, and rushed away.

She threw down her napkin. "Must you whine! Must you complain! Must you be a baby in front of your own child!"

"But what did I *say?*"

This time he stayed away two full days. On the second morning Hopkins telephoned to inform her that he didn't know how much longer he could put up with this disappearing act of young Roy's. She said that there was illness again in Liberty Center. Hopkins said he sympathized, if that was the truth, but he had a business to run. Lucy said she understood that, and so did Roy; she was expecting him back momentarily. Hopkins said so was he. And he hoped that when he did return he'd be better able to keep his mind on his work. Apparently two weeks back Roy had shot the Kiwanis luncheon down in Butler without any film in the camera.

That afternoon Julian Sowerby's lawyer telephoned from Winnisaw. He said that he was representing Roy. He wanted to suggest to her that she have her own lawyer get in touch with him. "Please," she replied, "I haven't time for nonsense."

He said that either she should get somebody to represent her or else they would serve the divorce papers on her personally.

"Oh, you will? And on what grounds, may I ask? Is it me who runs off? Is it me who doesn't show up for his job, who doesn't concentrate on it even when he's there? Is it me who breaks into tears and tantrums in front of a little tiny child? Is it me who dreams up business cards for a business I couldn't even begin to run? Don't tell me to get a lawyer, sir. Tell your client Mr. Sowerby to tell his nephew to grow up. I have an apartment to look after, and a confused little boy whose father keeps running out the door to get the advice of a disreputable and irresponsible person. Good*bye!*"

Roy returned a new man. All that crying business was over, finished, couldn't even understand it. Must have been off his nut, honestly. He had sat down with his father and talked the whole thing out. Till then Lloyd Bassart had known nothing about his son's secret visits up to Liberty Center. Roy had asked the Sowerbys not to speak of it, and though the first time they had agreed, when it happened again Irene Sowerby said she felt she had no choice but to tell her own sister what was going on.

The experience with his father hadn't been any picnic either. They had sat up together in the kitchen one whole night, clear through to dawn, hammering out their differences of opinion. Don't think voices weren't raised and tempers short. But they had stuck with it anyway, till daylight actually began to come through the back windows of the house. He by no means, even now, agreed with everything his father had said; and he could hardly bear the thought of the way he said it. Half of it was out of Bartlett's quotation book, to begin with. Nevertheless, arguing out all he had been brooding over for a long time—some of which she herself didn't even know about—well, it had given him the chance he needed to get a lot off his chest. It hadn't been easy, she could imagine, but he had gotten his father to admit that Hopkins was most definitely exploiting him, and exploiting the Hudson too. Secondly, he had gotten him to agree that if Roy had the financial backing (so that it wouldn't be a slap-dash operation right off the bat) a studio of his own was certainly not beyond his capabilities. If it hadn't been beyond Hopkins all these years, it surely wasn't beyond him, that Roy could guarantee. In the end he had made it clear to his father that it was a sacrifice, and a hard one too, but that he was willing temporarily to give up his professional ambitions for the welfare of his wife and child. He had only wanted his father to recognize that sacrifice was exactly the word to describe what it was.

And once his father would—around five in the morning—everything else sort of fell into place. The decision to come back to Lucy was Roy's own, however, and he wanted her to know that. All the pissing and moaning of the previous weeks (if she could pardon him using a crude but accurate old Army phrase), well, it was as much a mystery to him as it must be to her. But it was over, that was for damn sure. God damn sure. There was a decision to face and he had faced it. He had come back. And why? Because that's what he wanted to do. And if there was anything he ought to be forgiven, then he wanted to ask to be forgiven, too. Not down on bended knee either, but standing up and looking her right in the eye. He wanted her to know that he was a big enough person to admit to a mistake, if he had made one. And in a way he supposed he had—though it was actually more complicated than that.

But enough explaining. Because explaining was just a way of begging, and he wasn't begging for anything. No pity, no sympathy, no nothing. He was willing to let bygones be bygones, and to start in clean and fresh, and be a lot better off for the experience—if she was.

She said she would not forgive him unless he promised never to speak to Julian Sowerby again as long as he lived.

As long as he lived?

Yes, as long as they *all* lived.

But the thing was, he had really sort of led Julian down the wrong path, in terms of what he wanted.

She did not care.

"But as long as I live—well, that's sort of ridiculous, Lucy. I mean, that might be a very long time."

"Oh, Roy—!"

"I only mean I don't want to start off making a promise I'm not going to *keep,* that's all. I mean, a year from now, who knows? Well, look, either bygones *are* bygones, or they're not. A year from now—heck, a month from now, it's all going to be so much water under the bridge. Well, I sure hope it will be. It will be at my end, I know that. I mean, it is now, really."

She had no choice. How else prevent him from ever again seeking the counsel of that man? It was wrong to break a confidence, but if she failed now to tell him the truth, what would prevent him from rushing back to Julian Sowerby the very next time he wanted to find the easy way out of his responsibilities and obligations? How else could she make him see that the uncle who pretended to be so nice and kind and easygoing, all jokes and laughs and free cigars, was at bottom a cruel, corrupt, deceitful human being?

And so she told Roy what Ellie had overheard on the telephone. At first he was unbelieving, and then he was appalled, he said.

By the fourth summer of their marriage Roy found he had to tune the car up practically every month. It was now seven years old and you couldn't expect it to hold up forever without an awful lot of care. Not that he was complaining, just stating a fact. More than one Sunday morning a month Lucy looked down into the driveway to see Roy's feet sticking out from under the car, as she used to see them from Ellie's bedroom window. And once she saw him holding Edward up over the hood, explaining to him how the engine worked.

If Roy didn't have a wedding to photograph on Sundays, the three of them would go out for a ride, or else up to Liberty Center to visit Roy's family. To make the traveling time pass more rapidly, Roy would often amuse Edward by telling him about his Army days up near the North Pole. They were simple little stories about how Daddy had done this and Daddy had done that—stories involving penguins and igloos and dogs that pulled sleds over the snow—and what sometimes made her anger rise was not so much that the child naturally took them for the truth, but that Roy seemed to want him to.

She might no longer even have consented to those Sunday trips if it hadn't been for Edward, who loved so the idea that he had grandparents he had to travel to see. They kissed him, they hugged him, they gave him presents, they made him laugh, they told him what a beautiful, brilliant little boy was he . . . And why shouldn't he enjoy that? Why should he be denied anything that came as a matter of course to other children in other families? Visiting grandparents was a part of childhood, and whatever was a part of childhood he was going to have.

It pleased her far less to see how willingly her husband made the trip. He pretended, of course, that it was more or less a bore to him at this point, that he did it out of filial obligation, a sense of duty and decency, but then he had been pretending that from the start.

She saw him pretending now nearly all the time, so as to avoid the clashes that had taken place almost weekly after the first six months of the marriage. Every time he opened his mouth she could hear that he did not mean a single word, but was trying only to disarm her by saying what he thought she wanted him to say. He would do anything now to avoid a battle, anything but really change.

He pretended, for instance, that he was more or less happy working for Hopkins. Wendell had his limitations, but-then-who-didn't? he quickly added. Yeah, good old Wendell, when all the time she knew that secretly he hated Hopkins' guts.

And he pretended that he believed she had been right to discourage him from opening a studio of his own. There was still an awful lot he had to learn, and he was only twenty-four, so what was the hurry? Meanwhile, at least once a month she would find lettered in the margin of the newspaper, or doodled on the scratch pad by the phone, the words "Bassart Portrait Studio," or "Portraits by Bassart."

Worst of all, he pretended to continue to feel outrage toward Julian Sowerby. After her disclosure of Julian's secret, Roy had agreed that henceforth they must have nothing whatsoever to do with such a person. Yet as the months passed, he began to wonder if they weren't being somewhat unfair to his aunt. *She* might care to see Edward once in a while . . .

Lucy said that if Irene Sowerby wanted to see Edward badly enough she could come to visit any Sunday afternoon they were at the Bassarts'. Roy said that was true, of course, only his understanding was that Aunt Irene believed that they were as angry at her for interfering in their marriage as they were with Uncle Julian. The deeper cause of the split with Julian was something she didn't know about, and that they couldn't reveal to her, or to his family either. It was horrible to think of Aunt Irene living in ignorance of her husband's real nature, but they had problems enough of their own, Roy had decided, without trying to extricate Aunt Irene from hers. Furthermore, wasn't she better off *not* knowing? And that wasn't the issue anyway. The issue was this: Irene believed Lucy and Roy to be angry with *her*—

Lucy wished to inform Roy that Irene Sowerby wasn't altogether wrong.

What? *Were* they as angry with her? Really? A year later?

Lucy went on. She knew what his mother whispered to him on Sundays. Perhaps next time Roy should take the opportunity to whisper back to his mother that her sister Irene might have considered the welfare of this little nephew she so missed seeing when Julian Sowerby started arranging for Roy's divorce!

What?

Unless, of course, Roy didn't see in Julian's scheme

anything that might endanger Edward's development as a healthy, happy child. Maybe Roy even agreed with his uncle that the well-being of one's family did not matter nearly so much as the satisfaction of one's own selfish desires.

Well, no. Well, of course not. Look, was she kidding? He had been appalled, hadn't he, practically sickened to hear about Uncle Julian and his women? And didn't she think he still was? Sometimes when he began to think about Julian's playing around like that all those years, it made him so disgusted and angry he didn't even know what to do. Was she kidding, to associate him with Julian Sowerby? Had he not said no to the whole idea of a divorce, once he gave it five minutes' thought? Look, marriage isn't something you just throw out of the window, like an old shoe. Marriage isn't something that you enter into idly, or that you dissolve idly either. The more he thought about it the more he realized that marriage was probably the most serious thing you did in your whole life. After all, the family was the backbone of society. Take away the family, and what do you have? People just running around, that's all. Total anarchy. Just try to imagine the world with no families. You actually can't do it. Oh, sure, some people of course run off to a divorce lawyer at the drop of a hat. First sign of anything that doesn't sit right with them, boom, off to the divorce court—and the heck with the children, the heck with the other person. However, if a couple has any maturity at all they sit down and talk out their differences, they voice their grievances, and then when everybody has had a chance to make his accusations—and also to admit where he might have been in the wrong (because it's never so simple as one being all in the right, of course, and the other all in the wrong)—then, instead of running off to Reno, Nevada, two people who have any maturity stop being kids, buckle down and really decide to *work* at the marriage. Because that's the key word, all right—work—which you don't know, of course, when you go waltzing merrily into holy matrimony, thinking it is going to be more or less a continuation of your easygoing pre-marital good times. No, marriage is work, and hard work too, and pretty darn important work when there happens to be a little child involved, who needs you the way nobody has ever needed you before in your life.

She could not stand the pretense; so she tried with all her might to believe that it was not pretense, that he actually believed what he was saying, and found she could not stand that either.

After dinner and a visit with the Bassarts, they would drive Edward around to Daddy Will's house. First Great-Grandmother brought out the cookies that had been baked especially for him; then Great-Grandfather did tricks that he said he had used to do for Edward's mother when she was a little girl. He would make Edward close his eyes while he wrapped his fist and two projecting fingers into a white handkerchief. Then, well, well, he'd say, open your eyes, Edward Bassart, there's a little bunny here that would like to make your acquaintance. And there was a bunny, with two long ears and a little mouth, and an endless number of questions about Edward and his Mommy and Daddy. At the end of the conversation, Edward was allowed to whisper a wish into the bunny's ear. Once, to the delight of all assembled—except Daddy Will, who believed he had some small ability to throw his voice— Edward announced that what he wished most was that the bunny was real.

"What do you mean, real?" asked the great-grandfather.

"Real. Not a hankie."

Best of all Edward liked to climb up onto the piano bench, either beside Grandma Myra, while she played for him, or right in her lap so that he could "play." She would take his fingers in hers, and haltingly out of the piano would come "Frère Jacques" and "Mary Had a Little Lamb," and a song called "Michael Finnegan," to which Daddy Will had taught him the words. At every visit Edward and Grandma Myra and Daddy Will would sing it together, while the child's great-grandmother sat with the cookie plate in her lap, and his father, his long frame stretched out in a chair, kept time by tapping the toe of one shoe against the toe of the other.

> I know a man named Michael Finnegan,
> He grew whiskers on his chin-negan,
> Along came the wind and blew them in-negan,
> Poor old Michael Finnegan—begin-negan.

And so again they would begin, while silently Lucy watched. These were all the songs, said Grandma Myra, that Edward's mother used to like to sing when she was a little child no older than he was. Lucy saw that her son did not understand what that meant at all. His mother had been a little child? He couldn't believe it, no more than she could.

Then there was the famous story of her "yumping" from the window seat in the dining room, of which she had no recollection either. The first day that Daddy Will introduced Edward to the sport, Grandma Myra disappeared into the bathroom and did not come out until the visitors had left for home.

In the years since the disappearance of her husband, Myra had come to look her age, and more; there were Sundays when she seemed less a woman in her early forties than a woman into her sixties. Deep creases ran to the corners of her mouth, a purple hue had seeped into the skin beneath the eyes, the lovely throat had lost its smoothness and its glow. Yet the coarsening, the darkening, the wearing away, did nothing to diminish her air of delicacy. Certainly it was easier, even for those who believed they had known her intimately, to understand how deeply rooted in her nature was that characteristic softness of appearance. The years passed, the woman aged, and soon it became more and more difficult, even for her daughter, to remember that the reason Myra Nelson had suffered such abuse in her marriage was because essentially she was no more than her Daddy's little girl. Time passed, and very slowly, sitting silently in that living room, observing now as she had never been able to while the battle raged, while she herself raged—very slowly it began to dawn on Lucy that her aging mother actually had a character. "Weak" and "insipid" no longer seemed adequate to an understanding of the whole person. It began to dawn on her that why the mouth had always looked so gentle, and the eyes so merciful, and the body so yielding was not simply because her mother had been born dumb and beautiful.

Time passed, and men began to appear in the parlor on Sundays. They were invited for dinner, and to spend the afternoon. At first it was young Hank Wirges, who wasn't exactly what you could call a man, of course. He was a nice-looking, dark-haired boy who had taken journalism at Northwestern, where he had used to date a girl who was a sorority sister of Ellie Sowerby. Hank had come to Winnisaw to work as a cub reporter on the *Leader,* and had looked up the Carrolls because his grandmother and Berta had been childhood friends years and years ago.

Once a week Hank took Myra to the movie, Dutch treat, and every Sunday he was invited to the house for dinner. It pleased them all to be kind to him and make him feel that he had a home away from home, but of course no one was surprised when after a year the movie dates became less frequent. Eventually he asked if he might bring to Sunday dinner a girl named Carol-Jean, whom it turned out he had been seeing on the side.

It was actually just as well that Hank got himself involved with this Carol-Jean, said Willard, for it had begun to seem that he was developing a full-scale crush on Myra; though he never called her anything but Mrs. Nelson, he looked up to her like some sort of goddess. He came twice to dinner with his young lady friend, and then Myra went through a bad siege of migraines and Hank sort of passed out of their lives. But at least he had been a kind of gradual start back into the world for her, as Daddy Will phrased it, in that year after "Whitey's picking up, going off, and finally showing his true colors." That was a time when Myra hardly had it in her to be seen on Broadway; if she hadn't had young Hank's homesickness to pay attention to, she might have done nothing but give her lessons in the afternoon, and then retire back to her bed to weep for all those years thrown away on somebody who had 'turned out to be hardly the person we all originally expected of him."

Lucy herself never gave her father a moment's thought, not if she could help it; when his name was mentioned, she simply tuned out. His welfare was of no more concern to her than hers had been to him; where he was now, what he was now, that was his business— and his doing too. She might have been the one to lock that door, but what had sent him running was his own shame and cowardice. When Edward was still an infant and they had just moved into the new apartment, the phone had rung one night while she was home alone, and to her "Hello," the other party had made no response. "Hello?" she had said again, and then she knew that it was her father, that he was in Fort Kean, that he was planning to take his vengeance against her, through Edward. "Listen, you, if this is you, I advise you very strongly—" and then she had hung up. What could *he* possibly do to her? She had nothing to fear, nor to regret, either. She had locked him out—what of it? It was not *she* who had robbed *him* of a proper home and a proper family; hardly. There was a debt that would never fully be paid, but it was not hers to him; hardly . . . Then one afternoon she was pushing Edward through Pendleton Park in his stroller, when a bum rose up off a bench and came lurching toward them. Quickly she had turned the stroller around and walked away, only to realize again in a matter of minutes that even if it was her father lying in wait for her, she had nothing to fear, nothing to regret. If he was a bum, begging and sleeping in the streets, it was not she who had put him there. He was not worth a moment of her thought, or of her pity.

In the summer after Edward's third birthday Blanshard Muller began to become a regular caller at the house. Mullers had lived over on Hardy Terrace, back of the Bassarts', in fact, for as long as Willard could remember. Blanshard lived alone there now, for his wife had died a tragic death three years back— Parkinson's disease—and his children were all grown and away. The older son, Blanshard, Jr., was married and had a family of his own in Des Moines, Iowa, where he was already a junior executive in the purchasing department of the Rock Island Railroad; and Connie Muller, whom Lucy remembered as a big, beefy boy two years behind her in school, was finishing up in veterinary medicine at Michigan State.

Thirty years back Blanshard Muller had started out in business with a kit of tools and his two strong legs— Daddy Will's description—and had gone around to offices all over the county, repairing typewriters. Today he rented, sold and serviced just about every kind of office machine in existence, and was sole owner of the Alpha Business Machine Company, located right back of the courthouse in Winnisaw. In his early fifties, he was a tall man with iron-gray hair that he combed very flat, a ski nose and a manly jaw. When he removed his square rimless spectacles, which he did whenever he sat down to eat, he bore a strong resemblance to none other than Bob Hope. Which was a little ironical, Daddy Will said, because Mr. Muller himself did not have much of a sense of humor. But there was no doubt that he was a respectable, dependable and hard-working person; you only had to look at the record to know that. Berta had taken to him immediately, and even Willard was heard to say, as the months went by, that there was cerainly a lot to admire in a fellow who didn't just ramble on or talk your ear off, but said what he had to say and left it at that. Certainly when he did express himself on a subject—such as the modernization of mail-sorting through automation, which Willard had brought into the conversation one Sunday after dinner—his thinking was clear and to the point.

Christmas Eve, with Whitey gone now more than

three years, Blanshard Muller asked Myra to divorce her husband on the grounds of desertion, and become his wife.

Lucy learned of the proposal the next morning when Roy called his family, and then hers, to say that they would not be able to get up to Liberty Center for Christmas. That morning Edward had awakened with a high fever and a bad cough; that he was too sick to go up and celebrate the holiday with his adoring grandparents caused the child to cry and cry with disappointment—and this saddened her. But it was all that saddened her. She had every reason to suspect that on that day someone would have suggested that they all go on over to the Sowerbys' after dinner, or that the Sowerbys come to the Bassarts'; and given the spirit of the holiday, what could she have said or done to prevent the reunion? Of course she knew that she could not keep Roy from his aunt and his uncle forever, but she also knew that once such a meeting took place, he would once again be open to the most pernicious kinds of advice, and she and Edward would again be in danger of being abused, or even abandoned. If only she could arm him against his uncle's influence once and for all! But how?

When they finally got up to Liberty Center late in January—Edward's bronchitis had lingered nearly three weeks—they found that Lucy's mother hadn't yet given Mr. Muller a definite answer to his proposal. By the New Year, Berta had about lost patience with her daughter, but Daddy Will had made it clear to her that Myra was forty-three years old and in no way to be pushed or pressured into an important decision such as remarriage. She would make it official when she was ready to. Anybody who had eyes could see she was edging up on saying yes with every day that passed. Twice a week now she drove over to Winnisaw to have lunch with Blanshard at the inn; and even on weekday nights she either went off with him to a movie, or to a social evening among his own circle of friends. In the middle of the month she had even helped him pick out new linoleum for his kitchen floor. The kitchen and bathroom had begun to be modernized years ago, but the job had never been completed because of Mrs. Muller's illness and death. Myra told her family that helping him choose his linoleum was a favor she would have done for anyone who asked; they were not to interpret it as any kind of decision on her part to become his wife.

However, the very next night, when Blanshard had to be at home interviewing a new salesman, she had paced and paced the living room, and after an hour of anguish, gone off into the kitchen and telephoned his house. It was really none of her business, she did not want him to think that she was in any way criticizing the woman who had been his wife, but she could not keep it inside her any more. She had to tell him how much she disapproved of the color scheme that had been chosen for the upstairs bathroom; if it was not too late to cancel the cabinets and fixtures he had gone ahead and ordered, she hoped very much that he would. She would understand, of course, if he didn't wish to, for reasons of sentiment, but of course that wasn't what he said.

So the cat appeared to be in the bag, so to speak. Except that if Berta kept on endlessly chronicling Blanshard's accomplishments and virtues, she might find that single-handed she had gained just the opposite effect of what she had intended. Maybe the best thing was to let Blanshard Muller argue his own case, and let Myra herself decide whether she wanted to start out on a new life with such a man. It was surely no solution to anything to hold a shotgun to someone's head until the person said "I do"; you cannot force people to be what it simply is not within their power to be, or to feel feelings that they just do not have in their repertoire of tricks. "Ain't that so, Lucy?" he asked, figuring probably that she would ally herself with him as against Berta, but she pretended not to have been following the discussion.

It was a most dismal afternoon. Not only because she had to listen to her grandmother spouting the weak-kneed philosophy that had brought them practically to the point of ruin—the philosophy that encouraged people to believe that they couldn't be more than they were, no matter how inferior and inadequate that happened to be; it was dismal not only because what her grandfather seemed to want was to keep his daughter living in his house as long as he possibly could, and what her grandmother seemed to want was to shove her out into the street, man or no man, within the hour; it was dismal because she discovered that she herself did not really seem to care whether her mother married Blanshard Muller or not. And yet it was what she had prayed for all her life—that a man stern, serious, strong and prudent would be the husband of her mother, and the father to herself.

They drove to Fort Kean through a blizzard that evening. Roy was silent as he navigated slowly along the highway, and Edward fell asleep against her. Bundled in her coat, she watched the snow blowing across the hood and thought, yes, her mother was on the brink of marrying that good man her daughter had always dreamed of, and her own husband had stopped trying to evade his every duty and obligation. He had settled at last into the daily business, whether he liked it or not, of being a father and a husband and a man: her child had two parents to protect him, two parents each doing his job, and it was she alone who had made all this come about. This battle, too, she had fought and this battle, too, she had won, and yet it seemed that she had never in her life been miserable in the way that she was miserable now. Yes, all that she had wanted had come to be, but the illusion she had, as they drove home through the storm, was that she was never going to die—she was going to live forever in this new world she had made, and never die, and never have the chance not just to be right, but to be happy.

It snowed and snowed that winter, but almost always after dark. The days were sharp with cold and brilliant with white light. Edward had a blue snowsuit with a hood, and little red mittens, and new red galoshes, and when she had finished straightening up the apartment, she would dress him in his bright winter clothes and take him with her as she pulled the shopping cart to the market. He would walk along beside her, planting each red galosh into the fresh snow and then pulling it out, always with great care and concentration. After lunch and his nap, they would go around to Pendleton Park with his sled. She would draw him around the paths and down a gentle little slope on the empty golf course. More and more they took the long way home, around by the pond where the schoolchildren were dashing about on skates, and out of the park by the women's college.

Her classmates had graduated the previous June. Probably that explained why she could now walk casually around by the campus that she had purposely avoided all these years. As for her teachers, she doubted if any of them would even remember her; she had come and gone too fast. Oh, but it was strange, very strange, to be pulling Edward on his sled past The Bastille. She wanted to tell him about the months that she had lived there. She wanted to tell him that he had lived there too. "The two of us—in that building. And no one would help, no one at all."

Since her student days, the barracks had been torn down and replaced by a long modernistic brick building that housed the classrooms, and now a new library was being built back of The Bastille. She wondered where the student health service was located these days; she wondered if that same cowardly doctor was still employed by the college. She would not have minded if he were to cross her path some afternoon and recognize her with her child. She believed there might be some satisfaction for her in that.

Some afternoons she and Edward warmed themselves over a hot chocolate in the very same booth at the back of The Old Campus Coffee Shop where she had used to eat her lunch during the last months of her pregnancy. In the mirror beside the booth she saw the two of them, their noses red, their pale strawlike hair hanging into their eyes, and the eyes themselves, exact-

ly the same. How far the two of them had come since
those horrible days in The Bastille! Here, at her side,
was the little boy she had refused to destroy—the little
boy she now refused to see deprived! "Thank you,
Mamma," he said, as he solemnly watched her spoon the
marshmallow from the top of her hot chocolate onto
his, and she thought, "Here he is. I saved his life. I did
it—all alone. Oh, why should I feel such misery? Why
is my life like this?"

The icicles they had passed when they had come
out into the sunshine earlier on had lengthened by dusk.
Every day Edward broke off the longest icicle he could
find and held it carefully in his mitten until, at home,
he would put it into the refrigerator for his Daddy to
see when he returned from work. He was truly an
adorable child, and he was hers, indisputably hers,
brought into the world by her and protected in it by her
too: nevertheless she felt herself doomed forever to a
cruel and miserable life.

For Valentine's Day, Roy brought home two heart-
shaped boxes of candy, a big one from him, a smaller
one "from Edward." After the little boy's bath, Roy
took a picture of him, with his hair combed, and in his
bathrobe and slippers, presenting Lucy with her gift a
second time.

"Smile, kiddies."

"Take the picture, Roy, please."

"But if you're not even smiling—"

"Roy, I'm tired. Please take it."

After Edward was in bed, Roy sat down at the
kitchen table with a glass of milk and some Hydrox
cookies and one of his manila folders. He began to
look through all the pictures he had taken of Edward
since he was born. "You want to hear an idea I had
today?" He came into the living room, wiping his
mouth. "It's just an idea, you now. I mean I'm not
serious about it, really."

"About what?"

"Well, sort of getting all the pictures of Eddie, putting them in chronological order according to his age,

and giving it a name. You know, it's probably just a silly idea, but I've got the pictures for it, I can tell you that much."

"What is *it*, Roy?"

"Well, a book. Kind of a story in photographs. Don't you think that could be a good idea, if somebody wanted to do it? Call it 'The Growth of a Child.' Or 'The Miracle of a Child.' I wrote out a whole list of possible titles."

"Did you?"

"Well, during lunch. They sort of started coming at me . . . so I wrote them down. Want to hear?"

She got up and went into the bathroom. Into the mirror she said, "Twenty-two. I am only twenty-two."

When she came back into the living room the radio was playing.

"How you feeling?" he asked.

"Fine."

"Aren't you all right, Lucy?"

"I'm feeling *fine*."

"Look, I didn't mean I'm going to *publish* a book even if I could."

"If you want to publish a book, Roy, publish a book!"

"Well, I won't! I was just having some fun. Jee— zuz." He picked up one of his family's old copies of *Life* and began leafing through it. He slumped into his chair, threw back his head and said, "Wow."

"What?"

"The radio. Hear that? 'It Might As Well Be Spring.' You know who that was my song with? Bev Collison. Boy. Skinny Bev. I wonder whatever happened to her."

"How would I know?"

"Who said you'd know? I was only reminded of her by the song. Well, what's wrong with that?" he asked. "Boy, this is really some Valentine's Day night!"

A little later he pulled open the sofa, and they laid out the blanket and pillows. When the lights were off and they were in bed, he said that she had been looking tired, and probably she would feel better in the morning. He said he understood.

Understood what? Feel better why?

From the bed they could see the snow falling past the street lamp outside. Roy lay with his hands behind his head. After a while he asked if she was awake too. It was so calm and beautiful outside that he couldn't even sleep. Was she all right? Yes. Was she feeling better? Yes. Was there anything the matter? *No.*

He got up and stood for a while looking outside. He carefully drew a big letter B in the frost on the window. Then he came and stood over the bed.

"Feel," he said, putting his fingertips to her forehead. "What a winter. I'm telling you, this is just what it was like up there."

"Where?"

"The Aleutians. But at four in the afternoon. Can you imagine?"

He sat beside her and put one hand on her hair. "You're not angry at me about the book, are you?"

"No."

"Because of course I'm not even going to do it, Lucy. I mean, how could I?"

He got back under the blankets. Half an hour must have passed. "I can't sleep. Can you?"

"What?"

"Can you sleep?"

"Apparently not."

"Well, is anything the matter?"

She did not answer.

"You want something? You want a glass of milk?"

"No."

He made his way across the dark living room into the kitchen.

When he returned he sat in the chair near the bed. "Want a Hydrox?" he asked.

"No."

A car went ticking through the snowy street.

"Wow," he said.

She said nothing.

He asked if she was still awake.

She did not answer. "Twenty-two," she was thinking, "and this will be my whole life. This. This. This. This."

He went into Edward's room. When he came back, he said that Edward was sleeping like a charm. That was the great thing about kids. Lights out, and they're off in dreamland before you can count to three.

Silence.

Boy, wouldn't it be something if some day they had a little girl of their own.

A what?

"A little girl," he said.

He got up and went into the kitchen and came back with the milk carton in his hand. He poured all that remained into his glass and drank it down.

As long as he could remember, he said, he had dreamed of having a little daughter. Did she know that? And he had always known what he would call her, too. Linda. He assured Lucy that he had come upon the name long before the song "Linda" had gotten popular. Still, whenever he used to hear Buddy Clark singing it on the jukebox, back in the PX up in the Aleutians, he used to think about being married and having a family, and about this little daughter he would have some day who would be called Linda Bassart. Linda Sue. "Isn't that pretty? I mean, forget the song. Isn't it, just for itself? And it goes with Bassart. Try it . . . You awake?"

"Yes."

"Linda—Sue—Bassart," he said. "I mean, it's not too fancy, on the one hand, and yet it's not too plain either. Edward, too, is sort of right in the middle there, which is what I like."

Another car. Silence.

He got up and looked out of the window. "Miss Linda . . . Sue . . . Bassart. Pretty good, 'eh what?"

. . . Till that moment, to make him a proper father to his little boy had been so great a struggle that she had never once thought of a second child. But in that deep winter silence, listening to what he had said, and to the tone in which he said it, she thought that maybe at long last he wasn't mouthing words for the sole purpose of pleasing her. He seemed not to be pretending; she could hear it in his voice, that he was expressing a real feeling, a real desire. Maybe he really did want a daughter. Maybe he always had.

The whole next day she could not put out of her mind what Roy had said to her the previous night. It was all she could think of.

When he came home in the evening, when, as usual, he swung Edward up over his head, she thought, "He wants a daughter. He wants a second child. Can it be? Has he actually changed? Has he finally turned into a man?"

And so it was that in the early hours of the following morning, when Roy came rolling over on top of her, Lucy decided it was no longer necessary to continue to use protection. After Edward was born, the obstetrician had suggested that she might want to be fitted for a contraceptive device, if she did not already have one. Instantly she had said yes, when she understood that henceforth their fate would no longer be in Roy's hands; never again would she be the victim of his incompetence and stupidity. But now he had told her that to have a daughter was one of his oldest desires. And though it had not sounded as though he had simply been trying to please her with his words, how would she ever know unless she gave him the chance to prove himself sincere and truthful?

In the next few weeks Roy did not mention Linda Sue again, nor did she. In the dead of the night, however, she would be awakened by a hand or a leg falling upon her; and then his long body working against her small frame—or, if he was not wholly conscious, against her nightgown. This was how their love was made that February, and there was nothing extraordinary about it; it was how it had been made for years. Only now, while he pushed and thrust against her in the dark, she looked beyond his shoulder at the snow steadily blowing down, knowing that very shortly she was going to be pregnant for the second time in her life. And it would be different this time; there would be no one they would have to plead with, or argue with, nor would they have to argue with each other. They were married now, and there were no families upon whom either of them was dependent in any way. This time it would be something that Roy himself had said he wanted. And this time, she just knew, the child would be a girl.

Suddenly her illusion of an endlessly unhappy life just disappeared. All the heaviness and sadness and melancholy seemed to have been drawn out of her overnight. Could it be? A new Lucy? A new Roy? A new life? One afternoon, walking home with Edward's mittened hand in hers, and the sled rasping behind them over the cleared walks, she began to sing the silly song that Daddy Will had taught her little boy.

" 'Poor old Michael Finnegan,' " he said cautiously, as though nonplused she should even know it.

"But Daddy Will told you, I used to sing when I was a child. I was a child once too. You know that."

"Yes?"

"Of course. Everyone was a child once. Even Daddy Will!"

He shrugged.

"He grew whiskers on his chin-negan . . ."

He looked at her out of the corner of his eye, and then he began to smirk, and by the time they got to the house, he was singing with his Mamma—

"Along came the wind and blew them in-negan,
Poor old Michael Finnegan—begin-negan."

Really, she could not remember ever having been as happy as this in her entire life. The sensation she began to have was that the awful past had finally fallen away, and that she was living suddenly in her own future. It seemed to her that great spans of time were passing as the month wore down to Washington's Birthday, and then to that final Sunday when they drove Edward up to visit the grandparents and great-grandparents in Liberty Center.

After dinner Roy went outside to take pictures of Edward helping his grandfather break up a slick patch of ice in front of the garage doors. Lucy could see the three of them in the driveway, Roy telling Lloyd where to stand so that the light and the shadows fell right, and Lloyd telling Roy that he was standing where he had to in order to get the job done, and Edward plunging his red galoshes into the drifts at the side of the drive. She stood at the sink watching the scene outside and intermittently listening to Alice Bassart's stream of chatter; they were finishing the dinner dishes, Alice washing and Lucy drying.

Ellie Sowerby was home for the weekend, and all Alice could seem to talk about was the trouble Irene was having with her daughter. Lucy wondered if the conversation was primarily intended to irritate her. She and her mother-in-law hardly had what could be called a warm and loving relationship; no girl who had taken Alice Bassart's big boy out of the house could have been her pal to begin with, but recently there had come to be another grievance. Whatever the resentment felt toward Lucy because of the marriage itself, her refusal to have anything to do with Alice's sister and brother-in-law had only made things worse. Not that Alice ever came right out with it; that was not her little way.

But what difference did Alice Bassart make to her today? Or even the Sowerbys? They were all a part of that past that seemed to have dissolved away to nothing. That past and these people had no power over her any longer. She had made it through the month without her period. There was only the future to think about now.

So, with no real discomfort and even with a certain remote curiosity, she listened to the Eleanor Sowerby story, bits and pieces of which she had been hearing since Ellie had graduated from Northwestern in June. With three friends Ellie had spent the summer at a dude ranch in Wyoming, where one of the girls' families lived. Now she was down in Chicago, with the same three girls, crammed into what was, according to Ellie, a "crazy" apartment on the Near North Side—

just off Rush Street, or "Lush" Street, as Skippy Skelton, a roommate of Ellie's, called it. Of course Lucy already knew that "this Roger" (the second young man at Northwestern to give Ellie a fraternity pin) "this Roger," to whom she was to have been engaged following their graduation, had suddenly decided in the last semester of their senior year that he really didn't like Ellie as much as he thought he had. One day, out of the blue, he dropped her; and so unexpectedly, so cruelly, that Irene had had to rush all the way down to Evanston and stay for a whole week while Ellie got her bearings again. The family had only given their consent to the idea of a dude ranch way off in Wyoming in the hope that it would help get her mind off what had happened. As for this Roger, said Alice Bassart, he must have been quite a person. Do you know when he asked to have his precious pin back? A week to the day after having spent a perfectly lovely Easter vacation in Liberty Center as Ellie's house guest!

But despite his cruelty toward her, Ellie was beginning to bounce back at last; beginning to understand how much better off she was with a person such as this Roger out of her life entirely. And she wasn't having the crying sieges any more, which was a relief to them all. It was the crying that had almost made it necessary for Irene to get on a plane and fly out to Wyoming. But Skippy Skelton had apparently turned out to be a very strong young lady, and had given Ellie some kind of talking-to that made her stop feeling so sorry for herself; and now Ellie was so busy down in Chicago that she just didn't have the time any longer to spend whole days on her bed, weeping into her pillow. She was working as a receptionist at some kind of advertising research firm; and the people there were "fabulous"—she had never met so many "brainy" men before in her life. She hadn't even known that they existed. What she meant by that, they weren't quite sure as yet. Irene, frankly, was nervous, knowing how important it was for Ellie to get through the coming year without any kind of shock that would cause her another emotional setback. And Julian didn't at all like the sound of who it was she might be hanging around with down there. As he understood it, they had a university down there full of so-called brainy men, half of them Commies.

And to make matters even worse, Ellie just kept blooming and blossoming: each time you saw her she was more beautiful than the last. She had filled out so very nicely, and though she now saw some reason to wear her hair down into her face so that you could hardly even see those wonderful dimples, she was still the kind of girl who unfortunately attracted boys to her just by walking down a street minding her own business. But boys wouldn't be so bad; it was these brainy men they were worried about. She was even more of a fashion plate than she had been as a child—to walk around in Chicago a person apparently needed twenty-four pairs of shoes, said Alice—and what worried the Sowerbys was that a man without scruples would see her, make up to her, and then take advantage of her, with no regard for her feelings whatsoever. Ellie was still on the rebound from this Roger, and what with her sweet, generous, trusting nature, she might easily fall head over heels in love with somebody who would break her heart a second time in a row. The Sowerbys were particularly upset now because it turned out that Skippy, who had seemed to be such a good influence on Ellie, was going out with a thirty-seven-year-old man who wasn't living with his wife—and who was thinking of taking Skippy (age twenty-two) and going off with her to hide away in Spain for about ten years; maybe even forever. Why Ellie was home for the weekend was to talk over with her parents the kind of a girl this Skippy Skelton had turned out to be.

A few minutes later they were all in the living room when Ellie drove up in her mother's car.

Lucy didn't even have time to turn to Roy to ask if this visit had been planned: her old friend was up the walk, up the steps, and into the house.

In the first instant Ellie seemed somehow taller than Lucy remembered her. But that was an illusion, created partly by her hair—she had let it grow long and thick, like a kind of mane—and partly by her coat, which was made of some honey-colored fur and had a belt pulled tight around the middle. How dramatic. She stepped into the living room as onto a stage. Nothing Lucy could see indicated that Eleanor was a person recovering from a disaster; she did not look as though she even lived in a world where disaster was possible.

Lloyd Bassart had opened the door and so was the first to be embraced. "Uncle Lloyd! Hi!" and Ellie got him directly on the lips. Lucy could not recall ever having seen anyone kiss Lloyd Bassart on the lips before. Then Ellie's hair, cold and crackling, was against her own cheek. "Hi!" and then, Ellie was looking down at Edward: "Hey! Hi! Remember me? No? I'm your cousin, do you know that? Aren't I his cousin? I'm your second cousin Eleanor, and you're my second cousin Edward. Hi, second cousin!"

The child stood by Roy's chair, his head pressed against his father's knee. In only a few minutes, however, she had coaxed him onto her lap, where she let him cuddle up on the fur coat—which Ellie said was only otter, though the collar was mink. Edward slid his hands into her fur-lined leather gloves and everybody laughed; they fit him clear up to the elbow.

When Lucy reminded Roy that it was time to visit her family, he said that Ellie wanted to know if they would all come over to her house first. He had followed Lucy into the kitchen, to which she had retreated, offering the excuse that she wanted a glass of water. If she had to hear the name Skippy Skelton one more time, she would go out of her mind. Skippy was somebody you didn't have to worry about. Skippy had been on the Dean's List every semester but her last at Northwestern, and then she had just stopped caring about grades. Skippy had no intention of running off to Spain with the kind of phony Greg had turned out to be. Spain, in fact, had been a slight exaggeration of Eleanor's. She didn't know why she had said it, except that speaking to your mother long distance once a week, you finally ran out of things to say. Greg was back now with his wife and children, so there was nothing to fret about, at least where Skippy was concerned. You didn't have to worry about Skippy, she could just joke herself out of a tight situation, that's the kind of person Skippy was. It was Skippy herself who had told Greg that he should scoot on back to his family, once she had found out there were three little kiddies involved. Now Skippy was dating a really "hip" guy who thought that Ellie was a jerk to be wasting her talents behind a receptionist's desk for fifty dollars a week . . . Which was why Ellie was home for the weekend. Her parents might think she had made the trip up to explain about Skippy, but actually why she was here was to tell them that through Skippy's friend she had gotten an introduction to Martita. They didn't know who Martita was? Well, she just happened to have been the most important model in America before the war. Now she was retired and ran the only *real* agency in Chicago. Ellie's news was that in a matter of a few weeks she would be leaving the receptionist job to plunge headlong into a new career. "Fashion model!" she said. "Me!"

"Well," said Lloyd; and "Great!" said Roy—"Don't forget who took your picture first, Ellie-o"; and Alice said, "Your parents didn't know this till today?" And here Lucy had gone off for her glass of water. She had closed the kitchen door behind her. When it opened, it was Roy, to say that Ellie's parents hoped they would all come over for coffee.

"Roy, was this all planned—and when?"

"What do you mean 'planned'?"

"Did you know Ellie was coming here?"

"Well, no, not really. Well, I knew she was in town. Look, they want to see Eddie, that's all. And they want to see us too, I think."

"Oh, do they?"

"That's what Ellie says. Well, obviously she's not lying. Lucy, look, we've been the ones who have been boycotting them—and with good reason too, I know, don't worry. But it hasn't been that they haven't wanted to see us, not that I know. And anyway, it's over. Well, it is. The mistake they made was a bad mistake, and the mistake I made was a bad mistake, but it's over. Isn't it?"

"Is it?"

"Well ... sure. You know, another thing is that maybe this really isn't that fair to Edward any more— if you want to talk about his welfare in this thing."

"It was his welfare in this thing, Roy, that I had to bring to your attention—"

"Okay, *okay*—and you did! And so now I'm doing it to you, that's all. Whatever you think about Uncle Julian, or even Aunt Irene, whatever the two of us may think, well, they're still Eddie's aunt and uncle too, and he doesn't know anything about this, needless to say ... Oh come, on, Lucy, Ellie's waiting."

"She can wait."

"Lucy, very honestly—" he began.

"What?"

"Do you want me to talk very honestly with you?"

"Please do, Roy."

"Why are you being so sar*cas*tic all of a sudden?"

"I'm not being 'sar*cas*tic.' If I am, I can't help it. Talk to me honestly. *Do.*"

"Well, honestly, I really think that at this point, given all that's happened, and all that hasn't happened too, and this isn't a criticism, to begin with, but I think that at this point you might actually be being a little silly about this. I mean, without knowing it. Well, that's what I think, and I said it. And to be honest, it's sort of what I think my parents think too. It's over a year already that everything happened, about the way I behaved and so on, and now it's over, and maybe where the Sowerbys are concerned enough is enough, and we just sort of all ought to go on, and so forth ... Well, what do *you* think?"

"The opinion of your parents is important to you? That's a surprise."

"I'm not saying *opinion!* I'm not saying *important!* Stop being so *sarcastic!* I'm just saying about what it looks like to a neutral party. Don't confuse me, will

you, please? This is important. It's just not sensible any
more, Lucy. Well, I'm sorry if that sounds like a criticism of my own wife, but it's not."

"What's not?"

"To keep up with a war, when the war is over, when
nobody is even fighting any more, at least that I can
see."

Ellie called from the living room, "You coming?
Roy?"

"Roy," said Lucy, "if you want to go and take
Edward, you go ahead."

". . . You mean it?"

"Yes."

His smile dimmed. "But what about you?"

"I'll stay here. I'll walk over to Daddy Will's."

"But I don't want you just walking around, Lucy."
He reached out and flipped her bangs with his fingers.
"Hey, Lucy." He spoke softly. "Come on. Why not?
It's over. Let's make it really over. Lucy, come on, you
look so pretty lately. Did you know that? I mean, you
always look pretty to me, but lately, even more. So
come on, huh, what do you say?"

She felt herself weakening. *Let's make it really over.*
"Maybe I ought to go down to Chicago and be introduced to Martita, the most famous model in the history
of America. Martita and Skippy Skelton—"

"Oh, come on, Lucy, you *are* pretty. To me you are,
and plenty prettier than Ellie, too. Because you have
character and you're you. You don't have to be a
glamour puss, you don't have to have mink coats,
believe me, to be pretty. That's just a material thing,
you know that. You're the best person there is, Lucy.
You are. Please, you come too. Why not?"

"Roy, if you want to go, you can."

"Well, I know I *can,*" he said sourly.

"Pick me up at Daddy Will's at four."

"Oh, damn," he said, pushing one of the kitchen
chairs into the table. "You're going to be angry later. I
know it."

"What do you mean?"

". . . If I go."

"Why should I be? Are you planning to do something there that I might disapprove of?"

"I'm not planning *anything!* I'm going for a visit to a house! I'm going to have a cup of coffee!"

"All right, then."

"So just don't get angry when we get home . . . that's all I mean."

"Roy, you assured me a minute ago that the past is over, that I can rely on you. You have to admit that hasn't always been something I could do."

"*Okay.*"

"For six months now you have been assuring me that you no longer hold certain childish ideas—"

"I *don't.*"

"That you have decided to be responsible to me and to Edward."

"Yes!"

"Well, if that is really the case, if it's true that I have nothing to worry about when you are in the company of that man—if you haven't been fooling me, Roy, and just pretending—"

"I haven't been fooling anybody about anything!"

"Hey!" Ellie was calling them again. "Lovers! You coming out of hiding, or what's going on in there?"

In the living room, Alice was sitting in a chair, already in her coat and galoshes. Whenever Roy and Lucy quarreled, it was Alice's assumption that the fault lay solely with her daughter-in-law; it was something Lucy had had to accustom herself to long ago. She ignored the face that Alice turned to her, the compressed lips and the clenched jowls.

Ellie was kneeling down in front of Edward, zipping up his snowsuit; her skirt and coat had ridden up above her knee.

"Hey, let's go," said Ellie, "before we all catch puhneumonia."

"Lucy can't," said Roy.

—while Lucy was thinking, "Don't you dare dress him to go without my permission. It is up to me whether he sets foot in that house of yours, and sees those parents of yours, and not up to you at all. *I* am his mother."

She should never have weakened in the kitchen and said yes to Roy. The war over? The war was never over with people you could not trust or depend upon. Why, why had she relaxed her vigilance? Because this ninny was up for the weekend from Chicago? Because this *fashion model* was kneeling beside her child, playing Mommy while showing everybody her legs?

"Can't you?" said Ellie sadly. "Just for an *hour*? I haven't seen you in decades. And all I've done so far is talk about *me*. Oh, Lucy, come with us. I envy you so, married and out of the rat race. It's what I ought to do." Instantly her eyes became heavy with melancholy. "Please, Lucy, I'd actually like to talk to you. I'd just love to hear all about married life with that one."

"Oh, yeah?" said Roy, pulling on his coat. He smiled knowingly. "I'll bet you would."

"Wow," said Ellie, "how we used to sit up in that room."

"Sorry," said Lucy. She called Edward to her and hiked his snowsuit around. "You go with Daddy. I'm going to visit Grandma Myra." She kissed him.

He ran to his father, took his hand, and commenced staring at Ellie again as she pulled on her gloves. Roy laughed,

"He thinks they're his," he explained to Lucy. "The gloves."

"Gurrr," said Ellie, making one of her gloved hands into a claw. "Gurrr, Edward, here I come." The child broke into giggles, and when Ellie took a step toward him, drove his head into his father's side.

Roy looked at Lucy, then to Ellie. "Hey, El, Lucy's mother's getting married. Did you know?"

"Hey, that's terrific," said Ellie. "That's fabulous, Lucy."

Lucy took the enthusiasm coolly. "It's not definite yet."

"Well, I hope it comes off. That would be great."

Lucy neither agreed nor disagreed.

"Hey," said Ellie, "how's Daddy Will?"

"Fine."

"I really love him. I remember him at your wedding. Telling those stories about the north woods. They were really great."

No response.

To Edward, who was still staring, Ellie said, "Don't you, little Edward? Love Daddy Will?"

He nodded his head to whatever it was he thought Eleanor was asking him.

"I think it's Edward who has fallen in l-o-v-e with somebody," said Alice Bassart.

Ellie said to Lucy, "Give him a hug for me, will you? You do just want to hug him, don't you, when he starts telling those stories? He is really absolutely old-fashioned. He's just perfect. And that's what you miss in Chicago, all the fun aside—that kind of really genuine person, who really cares about people and isn't just a fake and a phony. When we were on this ranch down in Horse Creek, there was a man there, and he was the foreman, and he was just so polite and old-fashioned and easy-going, and you kept thinking that's probably exactly the way America used to be. But Skippy says that's all dying out, even out there, which is sort of the last outpost. Isn't that a shame? When you think about it, it's really awful. It sure has died out in Chicago, I'll tell you that much. Sometimes I wake up in the morning, and I hear all those cars starting up outside, and I wish I were right back here in Liberty Center, where at least you don't get all that hatred and violence. Here you leave your house unlocked, and your car unlocked, and you could go away for a week, for a month even, and not worry. But you ought to see the locks we have on our door alone. Three," she said, turning to Alice.

"My goodness," said Alice. "Lloyd, did you hear that? Ellie has to have three locks, because of the violence."

"*And* a chain," said Ellie.

"Eleanor, I don't know why you want to live in such a place," said Alice. "What about muggers? I certainly hope you don't walk on the streets."

"Sure, Mom," said Roy, "she walks on the air instead. What do you expect her to walk on, Mother?"

"It certainly doesn't seem to me," his mother answered, "that she should be out after dark in a place where you need three locks and a chain, Roy."

"Well," said Lloyd, "they've got a big colored problem down there, and I don't envy them."

"It isn't Negroes, Uncle Lloyd. You people think everything is Negroes—and how many Negroes do you actually know? Really know, to talk to?"

"Wait a minute," said Roy. "I knew one who I used to talk to a lot, Ellie, down at Britannia. He was a darn smart guy too. I had a lot of respect for him."

"Well," said Ellie, "I know a girl who dates a Negro."

"You do?" said Alice.

"Yes, I do, Aunt Alice. But you know what my father said? She's probably a Red. Well, the laugh is on him, actually. Because as a matter of fact she happened to have voted for President Eisenhower, which isn't exactly very communistic of her, do you think?"

"She goes out on dates with him, Eleanor? In public?" said Alice.

"Well, actually she met him at a party—and he took her home. But right on the street, and in a perfectly ordinary way, and color didn't make a bit of difference . . . That's what she said. And I believe her."

"But did she kiss him?" Roy asked.

"Roy!" said his mother.

"What are you getting excited about? I'm just asking a question. I'm just making a point."

"Well, that is some point," his mother said.

Roy went right on. "I'm only saying it's one thing to be friends and so on, which I am completely in favor of and have done myself, as I just mentioned. But to be very frank, Ellie, about this girl, well, I think very frankly intersex and so on is a whole other issue."

Ellie turned haughty. "Well, I didn't ask her about sex, Roy. That's her business, really."

"I believe," said Alice Bassart sternly, "that there is a child standing here with two very clean e-a-r-s."

"Well, all I'm saying is that every time something

terrible happens everybody blames the Negroes," said Ellie, "and I refuse to listen to that kind of prejudice any more. That's all. From anyone."

"But what about all that violence, Eleanor?" Lloyd Bassart asked. "There's an awful lot of violence down there, you said so yourself."

"But that's not the fault of Negroes!"

"Who then?" asked Alice. "They do most of it, don't they?"

"Actually," said Ellie, "more than anyone else, it's actually the dope addicts—who are really very sick people who need help. Jail is not the answer, I'll tell you that much."

"Dope addicts?" said Lloyd. "You mean dope fiends, Eleanor?"

"—are on the *street?*" asked Alice.

"Dopey!" Edward was grinning. "Dopey, Mommy!" he said to Lucy.

Ellie threw her head back, and the mane of hair shimmered. "Dopey! Wait'll I tell Skip. Oh, how delicious. *Dopey!*" she said, rushing to Edward and lifting him up. "And Grumpy. Right?"

"Uh-huh," he said. He put a hand out to touch the collar of her coat.

"And who else?" asked Ellie, jiggling him in her arms. "Sneezy?"

"Sneezy!" he cried.

"Lucy," said Ellie, "he's wonderful. He's fab, really. Hey, let's go!" She lowered Edward to the floor, but he kept hold of one of her hands.

"Let's go," the child said.

Roy said, "You want to come later, Lucy? After you see them? I could pick you up."

She said, "I'll be at my grandparents'."

Alice said, "You're coming later, Lloyd?"

"Right, right."

Out the door they went, Edward tugging on the coat of his newly discovered relative. "And Bashful."

"Bashful! Little Bashful! How could I forget Little Bashful? He's just like you."

"And Doc too."

"Doc too!" said Ellie. "Oh, Edward what a little fellow you are. I can't even believe you exist, and here you are!"

"And the bad stepmother."

"Oh, yes, her. 'Mirror, mirror, on the wall'—" and the door closed.

Lucy watched through the window as her husband and his cousin decided which car to use, the Hudson or the new Plymouth convertible that belonged to Ellie's mother. While the debate went on, Alice Bassart stood on the front walk, holding Edward's hand and stepping first in one direction, then in the other. Roy said, "You want to get there alive, Mother, or not?" Ellie pointed at the Hudson and said something Lucy couldn't hear, but that made Roy laugh. "Oh, yeah? That's what you think," he called. "Come on, Roy," said Ellie, standing with the door of the Plymouth ajar, "live a little." "Live? In a product of Chrysler Motors?" cried Roy. "Are you kidding?" "Come on, Aunt Alice, come on, Ed," called Ellie, and Roy said, "Hey, it's not just your life, Mother—that there is the heir to my estate," and Alice said, "Roy, now stop this minute being silly!" "Well, okay," he said, "here goes nothing," and all finally piled into the Sowerby car. Edward climbed in back with his grandmother, and Roy slid in beside Ellie.

Lucy was about to move from the window when the front curb-side door opened and Roy ran around back of the car to the driver's door. At the rear of the car he slipped and fell. "Ow!" He got up, and was brushing the snow from his trouser cuffs, when he looked up and saw Lucy in the window. He waved a hand at her; she did not wave back. He cupped both hands to his mouth: "Want to come . . . in half an hour?"

Inside the car Ellie was sliding away from the steering wheel.

"Lucy? Want me to—?"

She shook her head.

Then he did not seem to know what to do. She did not move. Would he decide not to go, after all? Would he remember what his uncle was? Would he take Edward from the car and come back with him into the house—of his own free will?

Ellie's window rolled down. "Roy! We're all freezing to death in here."

Roy shrugged his shoulders—then suddenly he threw Lucy a kiss and climbed in behind the wheel.

Instantly the horn went off. Ellie put her hands up over her ears. Two tries, and the motor turned over; puff after puff of fumes blackened the snow back of the car. Alice Bassart rolled the window up on her side, then rolled it down so that Edward could shove his little red mitten through. Lucy raised her hand. The horn went off again, and then the car jerked away from the curb and started up toward The Grove. The last thing she saw was a red flash as Roy, for some reason of his own, hit the brakes.

Ellie apparently was pleading with her father to give her the car to take back to Chicago; it was supposedly her mother's, only Irene had driven it less than two hundred miles in four months, which Ellie said was ridiculous. "And he'll probably give it to her, too," said Lloyd, as Lucy came away from the window. "Not that I begrudge him that he can. I didn't go into education so as to own a fleet of automobiles in my old age. I went in for the satisfactions of training young people to meet the challenges of life, and I think you will understand, Lucy, that cars have nothing whatsoever to do with it. However, very frankly, my opinion is that Julian ought not to indulge that girl any more than he has already. I have nothing against any race, creed or color, but between the two of us, I'll tell you who I think it was who was out with a Negro. I think it was Eleanor."

"I thought it was her friend," she said, pulling on her galoshes; Ellie had shown up in heels, as though it were July.

"Well, that may well be, Lucy. I don't like the sound of that person, for such a young person. Not at all. But it was one of them who that colored boy walked home, you can be sure of that. I know young people when they talk. I have been around them all my life. It is always 'a friend of mine' when the one they are speaking of is themselves. Eleanor was always over-pampered because of her beauty, and now Julian is going to have to reap the harvest of that beautiful daughter he was always going on about. Letting a girl of twenty-two live off in the middle of a city like Chicago, without proper supervision, with wild influences all around her, that is something of which I am heartily skeptical, to say the least. Especially someone as boy-crazy as Eleanor has always been. I will tell you my personal opinion, Lucy, for whatever it is worth. Eleanor is riding for a fall, and a bad one too, given the kind of things I heard her saying here this afternoon. *But,*" he said, showing her the palms of his hands, "I am keeping my nose out of it, and I have advised Alice—"

She was no longer listening. She had done a stupid thing; she saw that now. To let Roy go off by himself, to let him confront his uncle this first time without her at his side—how foolish, how dangerous!

It occurred to her to tell her father-in-law, then and there, that she was pregnant.

No, tell them all.

So the solution came to her, and it was perfect: *she would tell them all.* She would join them at the Sowerbys', and to Julian, Irene, Ellie, Alice, Lloyd, Roy and Edward, she would make her announcement. To the news of a new child, the family, all gathered together, would have no choice but to be enthusiastic ... Yes, yes. She could see Eleanor, clapping her hands together, calling for champagne. And everyone raising his glass in a toast, as everyone had four years before at the party for Roy's future—"To Linda Sue!" and so, whatever uncertainty Roy might feel if she were to make the announcement to him alone, whatever his defiance if it seemed to him that she and his father were ganging up—well, any such response would be swept away in the general mood of celebration.

Yes, yes, this was what she would have to do:

First she would go to Daddy Will's. Wait fifteen

minutes, then telephone the Sowerbys—and, yes, ask Ellie to pick her up. In the car, oh, of course, confide first in Ellie. "Ellie?" "What?" "Roy and I are going to have another baby. You're the first to know." "Oh, Lucy, fab!" Then she would tell them all—with Ellie at her side saying all the while, "Isn't that marvelous? Isn't that just divine?" In honor of the occasion, Irene Sowerby would doubtless ask them all to stay on for supper. Then she would telephone Daddy Will. She would ask her mother and Mr. Muller, and her grandparents too, to come to the Sowerbys' after supper; she had wonderful news to tell them. And then everyone would know. There would be chatter and high spirits, fun and noise, and Roy's anxiety upon hearing that he was to be a father again would be nothing to the sense he would have of pride and hope and expectation.

And she would tell them, too, that they were hoping for a girl—that that was Roy's preference—that he himself had already settled on a name—that it was the name he had always wanted, for the little girl he had always wanted. If all toasted Linda Sue together, then there would be no confusion afterward as to whose idea it was to have the little girl in the first place. Afterward there could be no accusations, no recriminations . . . The Sowerbys had a tape recorder in their new stereo unit; if only she could somehow get them to turn it on—to tape-record the festivities. Then it would forever be on record, how everyone had been absolutely thrilled by the prospect of Linda Sue. "To our daughter, I hope," Roy would say, *and it would be on record*.

But maybe that was going too far . . . though maybe it wasn't at all. Had she not seen the limits to which people would go to deny the truth? Had she not seen how people would tell lies, make accusations, do *anything* to avoid their duties and obligations? If only she'd had a tape recorder with her the night Roy spoke of his desire to have a little girl . . . But surely he would not deny *that?* How could he? Why should he? He was perhaps slower than she in coming to maturity, but he really wasn't a liar by nature. Nor was he a cheat, or a scoundrel, or a gambler, or a philanderer, or a drunk.

He was, under everything, a sweet and kind soul . . . and she loved him.

She loved Roy? She could not deceive herself into thinking that she always had—or ever had, really. But that Sunday afternoon, with four harrowing years of marriage behind them, she believed that she might actually be in love. Not with the Roy he had been, of course, but with the new Roy he had become. Because that was who had been addressing her in the kitchen: a Roy no longer childish and irresponsible, a Roy no longer pretending. Could that be? Had he changed? Had he become a good man?

Her husband was a good man?

She was married to a good man?

The father of Edward, the father-to-be of Linda Sue, was a good man?

Oh, she could love him, at last: she had made him a good man.

It was over! He was no longer fighting the marriage, and no one else was fighting it either. That was the meaning of Ellie's visit—the Sowerbys had capitulated! Sending Ellie around to invite everybody to the house was nothing less than their admission that Lucy had been right, and they had been wrong. Julian Sowerby was admitting to defeat. With all his money and lawyers and treacherous, deceitful ways, Julian was waving the white flag!

The misery she had undergone that previous spring, the misery she had undergone when she had been pregnant with Edward, all the heartache and humiliation—it was over. This time she would be pregnant as a woman is supposed to be. Her belly would grow round, and her breasts full, and her skin would become smooth and shiny, and none of this would cause her to feel fear and disgust and dismay. She would delight this time in what was happening. It would be spring, then summer . . . and the picture she had was of a woman in a white lace nightgown, and long hair—it was herself—and she is in bed, and her little daughter is in the bed beside her, and a man sits in a chair, smiling at the two of them. He holds in his one hand flowers he has brought for the infant, and in the other, flowers he has brought for her. The man is Roy. He watches the child feeding, and it fills him with tenderness and pride. He is a good man.

Such were her thoughts as she left the Bassarts' and walked toward Daddy Will's. Her husband was a good man . . . and Julian Sowerby had been defeated . . . and when she was in the hospital there would be flowers . . . and she would let her hair grow to her waist . . . and if in her life she had been stone, if in her life she had been iron, well, that was all over. She could now become—herself!

> Along came the wind and blew them in-negan,
> Poor poor Michael Finnegan . . .

Herself! But what would that be like? What was she even like?—that real Lucy, who had never had a chance to be—

Singing, smiling, wondering to herself—who would she be? what ever would she be like?—she climbed the stairs to her grandfather's house, and without even ringing the bell, pushed open the door upon disaster.

"Sit back down, Blanshard." Daddy Will was speaking. "Please, Blanshard."

Mr. Muller shook his head. He finished buttoning his coat and reached for the hat Willard was holding.

Upright, her arms crossed on her chest, Grandma Berta was sitting in the armchair by the fireplace. Lucy looked at her angry face, then back to the two men.

Daddy Will said, "Blanshard, tomorrow is another day," but he relinquished the visitor's hat.

Mr. Muller touched the older man's shoulder, and then he walked out of the house.

Lucy said, "What is it?"

Daddy Will shook his head.

"Daddy Will, what's happened?"

"Probably nothing, honey." He made a smile. "How are you? Where's Roy and Eddie?"

Grandma Berta began slowly to draw her fingers

down the loose flesh of her upper arm. "Probably nothing," she said.

"All right, Berta," said Willard.

"Probably nothing. Just that she has decided she doesn't feel like seeing him any more." In her fury, she rose and walked to the window. "And that's nothing!"

"Why won't she see him?" asked Lucy.

Her grandmother was silent now. She was watching Blanshard Muller's figure heading away from the house.

"Daddy Will, why did he go out like that? What's happening?"

"Well, tell her," said Grandma Berta.

"Nothing to tell," said Daddy Will. Berta snorted and went off to the kitchen.

"Daddy Will—"

"*There is nothing to tell!*" he said.

She moved after him, "Look," but he was up the stairs and into her mother's room; the door closed behind him.

She went into the kitchen. Now her grandmother was looking out the back window.

"I don't understand," said Lucy.

Grandma Berta did not speak.

"I said I don't understand what has happened. What is going *on* here?"

"He's back in jail," said her grandmother bitterly.

She sat alone in the parlor until Daddy Will came down the stairs. She said she wanted to know the whole story.

He said, "What story?"

She said again she wished to know the whole story. And from him, *now*, not later from some stranger.

She had her own life to worry about, Daddy Will said. "There is no story."

As he paced the room, she explained to him something that just possibly she had thought he might know by now: he could not spare people from the truth; he could not protect people from the ugliness of life by glossing over . . . She stopped. She wished to hear whatever there was to hear. If her father was in jail—

"Now who said that?"

"If he is, I want to hear it from *you,* Daddy Will. I don't want to have to piece the truth together from whispering and gossip—"

There wasn't going to be any gossip, not this time, he said. No one had been told, not even Blanshard, which was what had made it all so damn painful. Willard and Berta had decided last night that nothing was to be gained by advertising around what had happened, since, yes, something *had* happened. At dinner the previous evening Myra had lowered her head to the table and blurted out what she had been carrying around inside her for nearly a whole month. But why Lucy now had to be a party to it, he did not see. She had a life of her own to occupy her mind.

What was it?

"Lucy, what's the sense?"

"Daddy Will, where he is concerned I have no illusions. I took the realistic approach to him a long time ago, if you remember. Even before others did, Daddy Will—if they ever did."

"Well, sure they did—"

"Tell me the story."

"Well, it's a long one, Lucy. And I don't even know why you want to hear it."

"He is my father."

The remark seemed to confound him.

"He is my *father!* Tell the *story.*"

"You're going to start yourself crying now, Lucy."

"Don't worry about me, *please.*"

He walked to the foot of the stairs, then back. He would have to begin at the beginning, he said.

"Fine," she said, having brought herself under control. "Begin."

Well, first off, it seemed that Myra had more or less been in communication with him all this time. Almost since the day he left nearly four years before, he had been carrying on a kind of correspondence with her through a post-office box. Unfortunately, not one of Willard's old friends down at the post office had ever thought to tell him about Myra coming around some-

times to pick up her mail. On the other hand, he didn't
know what he would have done himself in such a
situation, given the rules of privacy that go hand in
glove with postal work. Anyway, maybe they didn't
even notice. Because it wasn't a matter of every day, or
every week, or even every month—or so Myra had
said, while weeping out her confession. He just sort of
kept her aware of his whereabouts and progress, particularly when something important happened to him.
And from time to time, depending upon her mood, how
blue she was, or how nostalgic she might get for the
long ago and far away, she answered.

... Well, to go on, if that's what Lucy wanted—in the
first months after his disappearance, he was living
downstate a ways, in Butler, working for an old chum
of his who owned a filling station there. But around the
time that Edward was born—

"He knows I have Edward."

"About most of the big things, such as Edward
would be, Lucy, he more or less knows, yes."

"Why?"

"Why? Well, I don't know why, Lucy. She thought
certain things, I guess, no matter what all had happened before, since he after all was still a human being
we all knew once, you know ... well, that certain
things he should know."

"Of course."

Anyway, sometime after Edward's birth, he got to
Florida. And down there it seems he tried to enlist in
the Navy again. For a while he was actually working
for them in Pensacola, and trying to get himself com-
missioned as a petty officer in electricity.

"An officer?"

"Lucy, I am just reporting what was reported to me.
If you want me to stop, I will, gladly."

"And after Pensacola? After he didn't get to be an
officer?"

After Pensacola, he went to Orlando.

"And what did he dream about there?"

He stayed for a while with his cousin Vera and her
family. It seems he got real close then to a lady in

Winter Park. Even got engaged. At least she believed they were engaged, until finally he told her the truth about himself.

"Oh, did he?"

"That he was married still," said Daddy Will.

"Oh, that truth."

"Lucy, I am not defending him to you. I am only telling a story that you have demanded to hear. I am telling you a story, actually, against my own better judgment. And I think, actually, that I am going to stop. 'Cause what good is the little details to you? It's done. It's over. So let's just forget it."

"Go on, please."

"Honey, you sure you got to hear all this? Because, you know, you may not be so strong on this subject—"

"Please! I am totally *indifferent* to this subject! This subject has nothing to do with me, outside of the fact that through some accident of nature that man impregnated my mother and I was the result! He is someone to whom I do not give a single moment's thought, if I can manage it. And I can. And I do! I am well aware this story has nothing to do with me, and that what has happened to him has nothing to do with me. Consequently, you have absolutely nothing to fear by telling me this story, in all its stupid little details too. I want the facts, no more and no less."

"But why?"

"So he told his fiancée 'the truth about himself.' And then how did he follow up a miracle like that, may I ask? Please go on, Daddy Will. Surely it is evident to you that I take no responsibility whatsoever for whatever idiotic things he has done since he decided to leave Liberty Center. I am not whoever it was in the Navy who told him that he was not exactly officer material—"

"Petty officer, honey."

"Petty officer. Fine. Nor did I tell him to get engaged and then unengaged."

"No one said you did, Lucy."

"Fine. So then where did he go?"

"Well, he wound up in Clearwater. That's where he stayed the longest, too. Got work in the maintenance department of The Clearwater Beach Arms, which is one of the biggest and swankiest hotels down there, apparently. And about four months back he was made chief engineer of the entire establishment."

"Really?"

"For the night shift."

"And then what happened?"

Well, apparently he had gotten on top of his drinking problem. What happened had nothing to do with that. He wouldn't touch a drop, and as he had always been a real workhorse when he was in control of himself, he most likely impressed the management with his abilities. They surely made no mistake when it came to estimating his knowledge of how to keep an establishment operating at full steam, day or night. Their mistake was to overestimate his strength of character, what with being so new to the job. Their mistake was to give him a key to just about every door in the place. But he was even managing the keys all right, or so it seemed; he was flourishing, responsibility and all, or so it seemed, until right after Christmas. It was then that Myra had sat down and written him a letter saying that she wanted him to know that after serious consideration she had decided to divorce him and marry Blanshard Muller.

Willard sank into the armchair, and with his eyes closed, rested his head in his hands. "And didn't tell any of us. All on her own, just made up her mind, all the way back then, to marry him ... I guess she thought it was her duty to tell Whitey first ... She didn't want him, see, to get the news first by one of his old cronies down at Earl's Dugout ... Oh, I don't know what she thought, more or less—but what's done is done ... And that's what she done."

"She was being a good wife, Daddy Will. She was being considerate of Whitey's feelings. She was being proper and respectable. She was being a good, subservient wife. Still!"

"Lucy, she was being herself, that's all she was being."

"And then he was *him*self, right? And what did himself do? *What?* Believe me, I can take it."

Well, when he received the news, it shook him up pretty bad. You might think that with his health back, and holding down a decent job, and living where he said he always wanted to live—you might think that having himself been more or less engaged to another person for practically a year, having stayed away for practically four years—you might think he would have been somewhat prepared for a shock such as this, and that after a day or two of getting used to the idea, he would go on with his new life and new job and new friends, and more or less adjust himself to something that was happening two thousand miles away to someone he hadn't seen in years and years. What he did do instead was absolutely stupid. And who knows, maybe he would have done it one day anyway, irregardless of Myra's letter. Maybe it had nothing at all to do with Myra, and was something he had been planning for a long time. Anyway, New Year's Eve he was in one of the offices of the hotel management, checking on some kind of trouble they were having with a window fan. Unfortunately, in that particular office some secretary had been sloppy or in a hurry or something, and had gone home for the night, leaving a whole bag of valuables sitting out on top of a filing cabinet next to the safe. "You know," said Willard, "what the guests check. Mostly jewels. Wristwatches. And some cash, too."

"So he was himself, and he took it."

"Well, a part of it."

"A part of it," she repeated, lowering her eyes.

"About a handful," said Willard sadly. "And then by the time he realized what all he had done—"

"It was too late."

"It was too late," said Daddy Will. "That's right."

"He drank it up."

"No, oh no," he said. "As for the drinking, that wasn't it. No, down there in Orlando he joined the AA again, like over in Winnisaw. But this time he stuck to it, see. That is even where he met the lady from Winter

Park. No, what he did is, he took it with him to where he lived, and then, well, he couldn't even sleep, you see, realizing what he had done, as any damn fool would. But by this time it was the next day already, and there was already somebody had come down to check out in the morning, and had asked for this lady's wristwatch, and well, it just wasn't there. And so then the checking around started, and even before he could even get back to the hotel, the scandal was all over the place. And then he didn't know what to do. He knew he couldn't return it right then, not with the mood that his boss was in and the detectives swarming all around. So he figured for the time being it was smartest to say nothing and just go home. He figured he would just sort of slip the stuff all back somehow, maybe that night. But it was only a few hours, and the finger of suspicion had already pointed around to him, and they came to this room where he lived, and he didn't see where there was any choice, and since it seemed the right thing to do anyway, and what he had planned on doing practically an hour after he had done it to begin with, he made a clean breast of it; turned over every single item; said he would pay out of earnings any damages. But by this time the boss had already fired the secretary who had left the stuff out, and since he had to reassure his guests and all, there was somebody had to be made a strong example of. Every single thing was insured, and returned to boot, but he didn't show no mercy. I suppose he figured he had his interests to watch out for, too. So instead of just firing Whitey, like he did the girl, he turned on him and hard. And so did the judge. That's big hotel country down there, and I guess they all know which side their bread is buttered on, and so they really slapped it on him. As an example for others. That's what it seems, anyway. Eighteen months. In the Florida State Prison."

He was finished. She said, "And you believe that story. You actually believe it."

He shrugged his shoulders. "Lucy, he is in the State Prison in Raiford, Florida."

She was on her feet. "But it's not his responsibility, right?"

"No, I didn't say—"

"You never say! Never!"

"Honey, never say *what?*"

"He was forced to steal from being so sad, right? He didn't know what he was doing, even! He didn't *mean* what he was doing! He wanted to take it back once he did it! But he was framed!"

"Lucy—"

"But that's what you *believe!* The sloppy secretary! The bad boss! And people can't help it! They just have their faults and weaknesses that they were born with— Oh, you!" She was on the stairs before he could stop her.

Her mother was lying with her face in the pillow.

"Mother," she began, "Mr. Muller has just left the house. Do you know that, Mother? Do you hear me, Mother? You have just sent out of the house your one chance of having a decent human life. And why? Mother, I am asking you why."

"Leave me . . ." The voice was barely audible.

"Why? To throw twenty more years away? To be humiliated again? Abused again? To be deprived? Mother, what do you think you are doing? Who do you think you are saving? Mother, what does it possibly do or mean to tell Mr. Muller to go, when that idiot, that moron, that useless, hopeless—"

"But you should be happy!"

"What?" Suddenly she was without force.

Her mother was sitting up in the bed. Her face was swollen, her eyes sunk deep in black. She shrieked, "Because he's where you always wanted him to be!"

"I . . . No!"

"Yes! Where he never, never . . ." The rest was lost in her sobbing as she rolled back on the bed.

An hour later she was down the stairs and out the door before Roy could even step from the car. Her mother had a migraine and it would be too much for

her to have Edward, or any of them visiting; even Mr.
Muller had gone home early. And heavy snow was
predicted by the radio for the evening. They must
go.

Daddy Will had followed her onto the porch. Earlier
he had knocked lightly on the door of her old room,
but she forbid him to enter. "I can manage alone, thank
you," she had said.

"Lucy, you are acting like I'm in favor of all this.
You act like I want it."

"What did you do to prevent it? What have you ever
done?"

"Lucy, I am not God—"

"Leave me to myself, please! I am not the one who
needs you. Go to your darling daughter!"

Now Daddy Will followed her down the driveway.
She was already seated in the car, Edward beside her,
when her grandfather leaned his elbows on the door.

"How's Prince Edward here doing?" He reached into
the car to pull the child's hood down over his eyes.

"Don't," said Edward, giggling.

"How you, Roy?" asked Daddy Will.

"Oh, surviving," Roy said. "Tell Mom I hope she's
better."

Mom was what he called Lucy's mother. *Mom!* That
weak, stupid, blind . . . It was the police who had put
him there. It was he himself who put him there!

"Take care, Lucy," Daddy Will said. He patted her
arm.

"Yes," she said, busily adjusting Edward's hood.

"Well," said Daddy Will, as Roy started up the
motor, "see you next month—"

"Yeah, see you, Willard," said Roy.

"Bye," called Edward. "Bye, Daddy-Grandpa."

Oh no, she thought, oh no you don't . . . *I will not be
accused, I will not be held responsible* . . .

Dusk. Snow. Night. As they drove, Edward made
little popping noises with the saliva in his mouth, and
Roy chattered away. Guess who Ellie had seen down in
Chicago at Christmastime? Joe the Toe. Bumped into

him down there in the Loop. Turns out he's a med student now, still down in Alabama. But the same old Joe the Toe, Ellie said. Hey, guess what Eddie said. Out of nowhere, he asked Ellie if Skippy was the name of her dog. Oh, the Sowerbys asked after her, of course. Julian had some business over at the golf club, so he'd only had a chance really to say hello. That's all he'd said to him, practically. Oh, and the big news—Ellie had invited them to spend a weekend with her this spring. They could leave Eddie with the family . . .

She closed her eyes and pretended to be asleep . . . Perhaps she did sleep, because for a while she was able to drive out of her mind any recollection of what had been said to her that afternoon.

They were almost into Fort Kean. To Edward, who had remained awake all the way down, watching the wipers beat the heavy snow off the window, Roy was saying, ". . . so the captain came in and asked, 'Who here is willing to go off and help this Eskimo find his dog?' And so I thought to myself, 'Sounds like there might be some fun in it—' " and it was here that Lucy screamed.

Roy maneuvered the car over to the side of the road. When he leaned across Edward to touch her, she pulled her shoulder away and huddled against the door.

"Lucy!"

She pressed her mouth into the cold window. *The whole thing is not worth a moment's consideration.*

"Lucy—"

And she screamed again.

Bewildered, Roy said, "Lucy, is it a pain? Where? Lucy, did I say something—?"

He sat a moment longer, waiting to hear if it was something he had said or done. Then he edged the car back onto the road and headed into the city. "Lucy, you all right now? You better? . . . Honey, I'll go fast as I can. It's slippery, you'll just have to hang on . . ."

Edward sat frozen between them. From time to time Roy reached over and patted the little boy's leg. "Everything's okay, Eddie. Mommy just has a little pain."

At the house the child followed behind, clutching to the back of his father's trousers, as Roy helped her up the three flights of stairs and into the apartment.

In the living room, Roy turned on a lamp. She dropped onto the sofa. Edward stood in the doorway in his snowsuit and red galoshes. His nose was running. When she extended a hand toward him, he ran past her into his room.

Roy's hands dangled at his side. His hair was wet and hanging onto his forehead. "Do you want a doctor?" he asked softly. "Or are you all right now? Lucy, did you hear me? Do you feel better?"

"Oh, you," she said. "You hero."

"Do you want me to open it out?" he asked, pointing to the sofa. "Do you want to rest? Just tell me."

She pulled the cushion from behind her and threw it wildly at him. "You big war hero!"

The cushion struck his leg. He picked it up. "I was only keeping him entertained. Look, I always tell him—"

"I *know* you always tell him! Oh, I know, Roy— every Sunday of our lives you tell him! Because that's all you can do! God knows you can't *show* him!"

"Lucy, what did I do wrong now?"

"You idiot! You dolt! All *you* can show him is that carburetor in the car—and probably you get that wrong too! I saw you, Roy, in that brand-new Plymouth. To drive a new Plymouth—that was your biggest thrill of the year!"

"Well, no!"

"To sit behind the wheel of a new Sowerby car!"

"Jee-*zuz*, Lucy, Ellie asked if I wanted to drive, so I said yes. I mean, that's no reason ... Look, if you're angry because I went over there ... Look, we talked that over, Lucy—"

"You worm! Don't you have any guts at all? Can't you stand on your own two feet, *ever*? You sponge! You leech! You weak, hopeless, spineless, coward! You'll never change—you don't even *want* to change! You don't even know what I *mean* by change! You stand there with your dumb mouth open! Because you have no backbone! None!" She grabbed the other cushion from behind her and heaved it toward his head. "Since the day we met!"

He batted down the cushion with his hands. "Look, now look—Eddie is right be—"

She charged off the sofa. "And no courage!" she cried. "And no determination! And no will of your own! If I didn't tell you what to do, if I were to turn my back—if I didn't every single rotten day of this rotten life . . . Oh, you're not a man, and you never will be, and you don't even *care!*" She was trying to hammer at his chest; first he pushed her hands down, then he protected himself with his forearms and elbows; then he just moved back a step at a time.

"Lucy, come on, now, please. We're not alone—"

But she pursued him. "You're nothing! Less than nothing! Worse than nothing!"

He grabbed her two fists. "Lucy. Get control. Stop, please."

"Get your hands off of me, Roy! Release me, Roy! Don't you dare try to use your strength against me! Don't you dare attempt violence!"

"I'm not attempting *anything!*"

"*I am a woman! Release my hands!*"

He did. He was crying.

"Oh," she said, breathing hard, "how I despise you, Roy. Every word you speak, everything you do, or try to do, it's awful. You're nothing, and I will never forgive you—"

He put his hands over his eyes and wept.

"Never, never," she said, "because you are beyond hope. Beyond endurance. You are beyond everything. You can't be saved. You don't even want to be."

"Lucy, Lucy, no, that's not true."

"LaVoy," she said disgustedly.

"—What?"

"LaVoy's not the pansy, Roy. You are."

"No, oh no."

"Yes! You! Oh, go!" She dropped back onto the sofa. "Disappear. Leave me, leave me, just get out of my sight!"

She cried then, with such intensity that she felt her organs would be torn loose. Sounds that seemed to originate not in her body but in the corners of her skull emerged from her nostrils and her mouth. She pressed her eyes so tightly shut that between her cheekbones and her brow there was just a thin slit through which the hot tears ran. It began to seem she would be unable to stop crying. And she didn't care. What else was there to do?

When she awoke the apartment was without light. She turned on the lamp. Who had turned it off?

"Roy?"

He had gone out.

She rushed to Edward's room.

In the next moment she lost all sense of where she was. She could not get her mind to give her any information. *I am a freshman.*

No!

"Edward!"

She ran to the kitchen and turned on the light; then she was in his bedroom again. She opened the closet, but he was not hiding there. She opened his dresser to see ... to see what?

He has taken him to a movie. But it was nine o'clock at night.

He has taken him for something to eat.

Back in the living room, she ran her hand over every surface: no note, no nothing. In Edward's bedroom she dropped to her knees. "Boo!" But he was not beneath the bed.

Of course! In the kitchen she dialed Hopkins' studio. *He is showing him where he works, showing him what a big strong man he is. Showing him the kind of studio he could have in his own house if only Mommy wasn't such a terrible person.* Well, she hoped—while the phone rang and rang—she hoped that he was also showing him where they were all supposed to live while their living and bed room became a business office, showing him what they were supposed to live on, too, while he waited for the customers to—

There was no one at the studio.

She searched the apartment again. *What am I look-ing for?* Then she telephoned Liberty Center. But the Bassarts were still at the Sowerbys'. The operator asked if she wished to place the call later, but she hung up without giving the Sowerbys' number. Suppose it was a false alarm? Suppose he had only taken Edward for a hamburger, and the two of them returned just as Julian Sowerby picked up the phone?

She would just wait for him to come back and ex-plain himself. To disappear without leaving a note! To take an exhausted little child out into a snowstorm at nine o'clock at night! There were cold things in the refrigerator; there was soup on the shelves. Don't tell me it was to get him something to eat, Roy. It was to frighten him. It was to . . .

At ten-thirty Roy phoned to say that he had just arrived back in Liberty Center. She did not even wait for him to finish. She told him what he was to do. He said that Edward was fine—fine now, at any rate, but it had been one ghastly, horrible experience for him, and she ought to know it. She had to raise her voice to interrupt; once again, she made clear to him what he was to do, and instantly. But he just said she shouldn't worry. He'd take care of everything at his end; maybe she ought to just worry about getting everything under control at her own. It was necessary now to shout at him to make him understand. He was to do what she told him. He said he knew all about that, but the point was what she had done in the car, and what she had done afterward, what she had screamed at him, all in earshot of a small defenseless child. When she shouted again, he said that it would take the U.S. Marines to get him to return any child to a place where, to be honest about it, he really couldn't stand it one day longer, as long as she kept on being the way she was. He was, to repeat, not returning any three-and-a-half-year-old to live one day more with a person who—he was sorry, but he was going to have to say it—

"Say what!"

"Who he hates like poison, that's what!"

"Who hates who like poison, Roy?"

No answer.

"*Who* hates *who* like poison, Roy? You will not get away with that insinuation, I don't care where you're hiding! I demand you clarify what you just had the audacity to say to me—what you would never dare to say to my face, you crybaby! You coward! *Who* hates—"

"Hates *you!*"

"What? He loves me, you liar! You are lying! He loves me, and you return that child! Roy, do you hear me? *Return my child!*"

"I told you, Lucy, what he told me—*and I will not!*"

"I don't believe you! Not for a single second do I believe—"

"Well, you better! All the way up here, he cried his little heart out—"

"I don't believe you!"

" 'I hate Mommy, her face was all black.' That's how he cried to me, Lucy!"

"*You're lying, Roy!*"

"Then why does he lock himself in the toilet? Why does he run away from his dinner every other night—"

"*He doesn't!*"

"He did!"

"Because of you!" she shouted. "Not doing your job!"

"No, Lucy, because of *you!* Because of your screaming, hateful, bossy, hateful, heartless guts! Because he never wants to see your ugly, heartless face again, and neither do I! Never!"

"Roy, you are my husband! You have responsibilities! You get into that car this instant—you start out right *now*—and whether you drive all night—"

But at the other end, there was a click; the connection was broken. Either Roy had hung up, or someone had taken the phone away and hung up for him.

2

The last bus out of Fort Kean got her to Liberty Center just before one in the morning. The snow was barely drifting down, and there was no one to be seen on Broadway. She had to wait at the back of Van Harn's for a taxi to take her up to The Grove.

She used the time as she had used the hour of the dark trip north: rehearsing once again what she would say. What was demanded of her was now clear enough; the scene to be enacted became vague only when she had to imagine what she would do if Roy refused to drive her and Edward back to Fort Kean. To stay at Daddy Will's till morning was out of the question. That assistance she could live without. When hadn't she? Nor would she stay overnight with the Bassarts, though the chance that she would even be invited to was very slight indeed. Had her in-laws had even a grain of loyalty to her, the instant Roy arrived back in town they would have demanded some explanation of him; they were at the Sowerbys', they could have gotten on the phone with her themselves, they could have intervened in behalf of a mother and a child, even if the husband happened in this instance to be a son. There were principles to be honored, values to respect, that went beyond blood relationships; but apparently they had no more knowledge of what it meant to be human than did her own family. None of them had so much as raised a finger to stop Roy in this reckless, ridiculous adventure, not even the high-minded high school teacher himself. No, she could not be innocent, not where people like this were concerned: she knew perfectly well that when Roy pronounced himself unable to undertake a second trip to Fort Kean at one in the morning, his parents would join with the Sowerbys in supporting him. And she knew too, that if she allowed him to stay behind while she and Edward returned alone to Fort Kean, then he would never return to live with them again.

And how she wished that she could permit that to be. Had he not proved to her that his soul was an abyss, not just of selfishness, of mindlessness, but of heartless cruelty too? Try as she would to believe him capable of a deeper devotion, deceive herself as she might by believing him to be "sweet" and "kind," a good and gentle man, the truth about his character was now glaringly apparent. There was a point beyond which one could not go in believing in the potential for good in another human being, and after four nightmarish years she had finally reached it. With all her heart she wished that she and Edward might return to Fort Kean, leaving Roy behind. Let him return to Mommy and Daddy and Auntie and Uncle, to his milk and his cookies and his endless, hopeless, childish dreaming. If only it were a month ago—if only there were just herself and Edward, then Roy, for all she cared, could disappear forever. She was young and strong; she knew what work was, she knew the meaning of sacrifice and struggle, and was not afraid of either. In only a few months Edward could begin nursery school; she could get work then, in a store, in a restaurant, in a factory—wherever the pay was highest, it did not matter to her how strenuous was the labor itself. She would support herself and Edward, and Roy could go off and live in his parents' house, sleeping till noon, opening "a studio" in the garage, clipping pictures from magazines, pasting them up in scrapbooks—he could flounder and fail however he liked, but without her and Edward suffering the ugly consequences. Yes, she would get work, she would earn what they needed, and cut that monster—for who but a monster could have said on the phone those terrible things he had said to her?—cut him out of their lives, forever.

All this she would have done, and gladly too, had he revealed the depths of his viciousness as briefly as a month ago. But now such a severing was out of the question—for very shortly her job would be not to earn a living for a family, but to be a mother to a second child. There was not just herself and Edward to protect: there was a third life to consider too. Whatever her own feelings and desires, she saw no gain, but only endless hardship, in permitting this man to run out on a child in its infancy . . . So, though she had now been given every cause to loathe him; though she understood now the horrid extremes to which he would go to defend himself and humiliate her; though she would as soon open the door of the Sowerby house to learn that he was dead, for him to desert his family was out of the question. He had duties and obligations, and he was going to perform them, whether he liked them or not. He was not staying behind in that house, or anywhere in this town, and thereby unburdening himself of the pain there just happened to be in life. Who, after all, was Roy Bassart that he should feel no pain? Who was Roy Bassart that he should live a privileged existence? Who was Roy Bassart to be without responsibilities? This was not heaven. This was the world!

There were no lights on in any of the houses at The Grove. The plow had been through already, and the taxi was able to make its way easily up the street. When they stopped in front of the Sowerbys', she thought of telling the driver to wait; in a moment she would be out with her child . . . But that could not be. Hateful as he was to her, there were facts and circumstances she must not be blind to: she would never, never save herself at the expense of an unborn child.

But there was no sign of the Hudson. Either he had pulled it in the Sowerby garage—or he was no longer there. He had fled further north! To Canada! Beyond the reaches of the law! He had stolen Edward! He had abandoned her!

No! She closed her eyes to shut out the worst until the worst was known; she pressed the doorbell, heard its ring, and saw her father sitting in a cell in the Florida State Prison. He is sitting on a three-legged stool wearing a striped uniform. There is a number on his chest. His mouth is open and on his teeth, in lipstick, is written INNOCENT.

The door was opened by Julian Sowerby.

Instantly she remembered where she was and what exactly had to be done.

"Julian, I am here for Roy and Edward. Where are they?"

He was wearing a shiny blue robe over his pajamas. "Well. Lucy. Long time no see."

"I am here for a purpose, Julian. Is Roy hiding out with you or not? If he is with his parents, tell me please, and—"

He placed a finger over his lips. "Shhh," he whispered. "People are sleeping."

"I want to know, Julian—"

"Shhh, shhh; it's after one. Come on in, why don't you?" He motioned for her to hurry through the door. "Brrrr. Must be ten below."

Was she to be let in without resistance? On the bus coming north she had prepared herself for the possibility of a scene right out on the doorstep. Instead she was following Julian quietly through the hall and into the living room. And why? Of course—because what Roy had done was so obviously outrageous that even the Sowerbys could no longer take his side. In her isolation she had exaggerated—not the seriousness of Roy's act, but the seriousness with which even her enemies would accept his story. The person who had slammed down the phone earlier was only Roy himself; the chances were he hadn't even had the nerve to make the call in the presence of a rational human being.

To understand this came as a tremendous relief. In her entire life she had never retreated from a struggle that had to be, and she would not have retreated here;

she would, if necessary, actually have hurled herself against Julian Sowerby in order to enter his house and reclaim her husband and her child. But how grateful she was to be able to follow calmly and quietly behind. It was the scene with her family earlier in the day that had caused her imagination to become so extreme, that had led her to prepare herself for the fiercest struggle of her life. But as it turned out, Roy had now been revealed in such a way that even the most hard-hearted and unthinking of his supporters had lost all sympathy.

And was that not bound to happen? Eventually, must not the truth prevail? Oh, it had not been in vain then that she had sacrificed and struggled! Oh yes, of course! If you know you are in the right, if you do not weaken or falter, if despite everything thrown up against you, despite every hardship, every pain, you oppose what you know in your heart is wrong; if you harden yourself against the opinions of others, if you are willing to endure the loneliness of pursuing what is good in a world indifferent to good; if you struggle with every fiber of your body, even as others scorn you, hate you and fear you; if you push on and on and on, no matter how great the agony, how terrible the strain—then one day the truth will finally be known—

"Sit down," said Julian.

"Julian," she said evenly, "I don't think I will. I think, without delay, really—"

"Sit down, Lucy." He was smiling, and pointing to a chair.

"I'd rather not." She spoke firmly.

"But I don't care what you would rather do. I am telling you what you are going to do. First thing is sit."

"I don't need to rest, thank you."

"But you do, Cutie-Pie. You need a long, long rest."

She felt anger shoot through her. "I don't know what you think you're saying, Julian, and I don't care. I did not come here at this hour, at the end of a grueling day, to sit—"

"Oh, no?"

"—and talk with you."

She stopped. Of what use *was* talk? How she had deluded herself only the second before—how pathetic, how foolish, how innocent of her, to have a generous thought about a person such as this. They were no better than she'd thought; they were worse.

"I've been sitting up for you, Lucy," said Julian. "What do you think of that? I've been looking forward to this, actually, for a long time. I figured you'd be on that bus."

"There is no reason why you shouldn't have expected me," she said. "It's what any mother would have done."

"Yes, sir, that's you, all right. Well, sit down, Any Mother."

She did not move.

"Well," he said, "then I'll sit." He settled into a chair, all the time keeping an eye on her.

She was suddenly confused. There were the stairs— why didn't she just walk up them, and wake Roy? "Julian," she said, "I would appreciate it if you would go upstairs and tell my husband that I am here and I want to see him. I have come all the way from Fort Kean, Julian, in the middle of the night, because of what he has done. But I am willing to be reasonable about this, if you are."

Julian took a loose cigarette out of the pocket of his robe and straightened it between two fingers. "You are, huh?" he said, and lit it.

What a disgusting little man! Why did she say "if you are"—what had he to do with it? And why *was* he waiting up for her in his pajamas and robe? Was this all preparatory to making some indecent offer? Was he going to try to seduce her while his own wife, his own daughter—?

But at the top of the stairs Irene appeared—and it was then that Lucy understood fully the monstrousness of what these people were planning to do.

"Irene—" She had the sensation that she might fall backward. "Irene," she said, and had to take a deep breath to go on, "will you please, since you are up there, awaken Roy? Please tell him that I have come all the way from Fort Kean. That I am here, please, for him and for Edward."

She did not have to look over at Julian to know his gaze was fixed upon her. "The snow has stopped," she said, still to the woman at the top of the stairs, who was wearing a quilted robe over her nightgown. "So we will drive home. If he is too tired, then we will take a room somewhere for the night. But he is not staying here. Nor is Edward."

Instead of heading back along the corridor to awaken Roy, Irene started down the stairs. Her hair had gone nearly white in the last few years, and she seemed heavier; or else, without a corset the thickness of her body was more easily discernible. Altogether her appearance was that of an elderly matron, thoroughly composed, and of all things, sympathetic.

"Irene, I want to tell you that your letting Roy think he could get away with this—"

"Yes?" said Julian, from where he sat, smoking.

"—will make it altogether impossible for us ever to see you again. And that means all of us, including Edward. And I hope you will all realize, once again, that this is something you have absolutely brought upon yourselves."

"We realize everything, kiddo," said Julian.

Irene moved toward her, with one hand extended. "Lucy, why don't you sit down? Why don't we try to talk and see what's happened?"

"Look," she said, stepping back, "I do not choose to stay in this house, or even in this town, one second longer than is necessary. You are not my friend, Irene, and don't suddenly pretend that you are. I am not that stupid, and you should know that. From the very first day that Roy began to take me out, you have behaved as though I were some kind of inferior thing. As though *I* weren't worthy of *him*. I know what your true feelings are, so don't think you can trick me by taking hold of my hand. You may deceive yourself however you like, but your actions have spoken louder than your words. This is plain idiocy on Roy's part, and he and Edward are to leave here this instant, and return with me—"

"I think," said Julian, standing now, "that, first thing, you better calm yourself down."

"Don't you tell me what to do, Julian!" She turned to face him, to look right into those dishonest eyes. Oh, she would wipe that little smirk off his face. How superior they thought they were, these people with the morals of animals! "You have no authority over me whatsoever. I think you had better be reminded of that, Julian. I don't happen to be one of the people dependent upon your millions."

"Billions," he said, grinning.

Irene said, "Lucy, if I make some coffee—"

"I don't want coffee! I want my child! And my husband—such as he is! They are to be returned to me immediately. This instant."

"But, Lucy dear—" Irene began.

"Don't you 'dear' me! I do not trust you, Mrs. Sowerby—any more than I do him!"

Julian's figure had suddenly moved between Lucy and his wife. "Now," he said, "rule number one—either you calm down with that bossy little voice, missy, or you get out."

"But suppose I will *not* get out."

"Then you are a trespasser, and I will heave you out—on your butt."

"Don't you *dare* speak to me—" And she broke for the stairs. An arm, however, fell instantly upon her back; she pulled away, but he had caught hold of her coat.

"No! Let *me*—"

But his other hand fell upon her shoulder, and she was driven down so forcefully that she felt herself become ill. He had seated her; and was over her, his face purple with fury. His bathrobe had fallen open, and she had a glimpse of his stomach between the buttons of his pajamas.

She did not move or speak. He straightened up and

pulled his robe closed, but remained directly before her.

Precise and exact in her diction, Lucy began. "You have no right—"

"Don't you tell me rights, you little twenty-year-old twerp. It is you who is going to learn rights."

"Well," said Lucy, her mind racing, "well, Irene"— trying to look past him to his wife—"you must be very proud of having as a husband a brute, who beats someone half his—"

"Who you are dealing with, Lucy, is me. So it's me you talk to. Not Irene."

Now Ellie came out onto the landing. She stood there in her white wrapper, both hands on the banister, looking down.

Lucy turned her face up to Julian's, and spoke so only he could hear. "I know about you, Julian. So just you be careful."

"Oh, do you?" He pushed right up against her knees. She drew her head back from his belly. "And what is it you know?" he asked, his voice gruff and low. "You trying to threaten me? Speak up!"

She could not see beyond his bulk. She could not even think now, *and she must.* "Since I did not come here to discuss your character," she began, addressing the belt of his robe, "I'm not going to, Julian."

"Good idea," he said, and stepped back.

Eleanor had disappeared.

Lucy folded her hands in the lap of her coat; she had to wait until she was sure that her voice would not falter. "So long as I can do what I came here to do, and then leave, there is no need to enter into any kind of discussion . . . That is fine with me." Then she looked up at Irene. "Now will someone please awaken my husband—*please.*"

"Maybe he is sleeping," said Julian. "Ever think of that? Maybe he has had one hell of a day from you, sister."

He remained standing so that she could not get up out of her chair; she hammered on the arms. "We have all had one hell of a day, Julian! I have had a *horror* of a day. Now, I demand that he be told—"

"But your demanding days are over. That, twerp, is the point of all this."

"Please ..." she said, breathing deeply, "I would much prefer to deal with your wife, who has a civil tongue at least, if you don't mind."

"But my civil wife isn't dealing with you."

"Excuse me," said Lucy, "perhaps she has a mind of her own, sir—"

"My wife *dealt* with you, kiddo. Back when she told me there was still some evidence you were a human being. But it turns out that I should never have taken her advice four years ago, back when you started *out* sinking your fangs into that boy."

"That boy seduced me, Julian! It became that boy's duty to me—"

He turned away and looked at his wife. "Duty," he said, snorting.

She jumped up from the chair. "You may not like the word, Julian, but I repeat—it was his duty to me—"

"Oh," he said, shaking his head, "everybody has got that there duty to you. But who is it you got the sacred duty to, Lucy? Seems to me I forget."

"To my child!" she answered. "To the offspring of my husband and myself! To someone starting out in life, that's who! To see that he is given a home and a family and proper upbringing! To see he is not misused by all the beasts in this filthy world!"

"Oh," said Julian, "you are a real saint, you are."

"Compared to you, I most certainly am. Yes!"

"Well, Saint Lucy," he said, running a hand over his stubble, "don't worry so much about your offspring any more. Because he hates your guts."

She brought her hands up over her face. "That's not true. That's Roy's terrible, terrible lie. That's . . . no. No, that isn't—"

She felt Irene's hand on her arm.

"No, no," she wept, and fell back again into the chair. "What . . . what are you planning to do to me?

You can't steal my child. This is kidnaping, Irene. Irene, this is against every law there is."

Julian spoke. "Leave her alone."

Irene answered something that Lucy could not hear.

"We are settling something here, Irene. Get away from her. Let her alone. She has done her last—"

Suddenly Lucy came charging up at him, shaking her fists. "You won't get away with this! Whatever it is you think you are going to do to me!"

Julian only jammed his hands down into the pockets of his robe.

"This is kidnaping, Julian, if that's what you have on your mind! Kidnaping—and abandonment! He can't run out on me and take my child! There are laws, Julian, laws against people like you!"

"Fine. You go out and get yourself a lawyer. Nothing would make me happier."

"But I don't *need* a lawyer! Because I intend to solve this right here and now!"

"Oh, but you do need one, Lucy. Let me tell you something. You are going to need the best damn lawyer money can buy."

Irene said, "Julian, the child is in no condition—"

He shook off his wife's hand. "Neither is Roy, Irene! Neither is Eddie! Neither is any of us! We have all taken enough orders and insults from this little bitch here—"

"Julian—"

But here he turned angrily back to Lucy. "Because that's all you are, you know. A little ball-breaker of a bitch. That's the saint you are, kiddo—Saint Ball-Breaker. And the world is going to know it, too, before I'm through with you."

"Don't," said Irene.

"Irene, enough don't! I already have heard your don'ts a long time ago."

Lucy was shaking her head. "Let him go on, Irene. I don't care. He is only showing himself for what he is."

"Right you are, Saintie. That's what I am. And that is how come the busting of the balls stops with these. That's right, you smile through your tears, you smile how smart you are and what a terrible mouth old Julian has. Oh, I have got a terrible mouth. I am an old no-good beast, besides. But I'm going to tell you something, Lucy—you busted his balls, and you were starting in on little Eddie's, but that is *all* over. And if that strikes you funny now, let us see how funny it is going to strike you in the courtroom, because that is where I am dragging your ass, little girl. Little twerp. Little nothing. You are going to be one bloody little mess when I get through with you, Saint Lucy."

"You're taking *me* to a courtroom?"

"Dirty language and all. Uh-huh."

"You?" she asked, still with a strange smile on her face.

"That's right. Me."

"Well, that's marvelous." In her purse she found a handkerchief. She blew her nose. "That's wonderful, really. Because you, Julian, are a wicked man, and to get you in a courtroom—" At the top of the stairs, at last, Roy appeared, Eleanor behind him. So here they all were, those who only a few hours earlier had conspired against her . . . Well, she would not weep, she would not plead; she did not have to. She would speak the truth.

She looked from one to the other of them, and with that unshakable knowledge that she was right and they were wrong, a great calm came over her. It was not necessary to raise her voice, or to shake a fist; only to speak the truth.

"You are a wicked man, Julian. And you know it."

"Know *what?*" His shoulders seemed to have thickened as he hunched forward to hear her words. "Know what, did you say?"

"We won't need lawyers, Julian. We won't have to go any further than this living room. Because it is not for you to tell me, or to tell anyone here, what is right and what is wrong. And you know that, I'm sure. Shall I go on, Julian? Or do you wish to apologize now before your family?"

"Listen, little loudmouth," he said, and started for her.

"You are a whoremonger," she said—and it stopped him. "You pay women to sleep with you. You have had a series of mistresses. You cheat on your wife."

"Lucy!" Ellie cried.

"But isn't it the truth, Eleanor?"

"No!"

She turned to Irene Sowerby. "I would rather not have had to say what I just did—"

Irene dropped onto the couch. "You didn't have to."

"But I did," said Lucy. "You saw how he was treating me. You heard his intentions. Have I any choice, Irene, but to speak the truth?"

Irene was shaking her head.

"He had a sexual affair with the woman who was the manager of the laundromat in Selkirk. I have forgotten her name. I'm sure he can tell you, however."

The glare Julian had fastened on her was murderous. Well, let him try. Let him lay one finger on her, just let him try, and then he'll see who it is who will be appearing before a judge. Then his marvelous dream would come true all right—only the defendant would not be her, but himself.

"And," she said, returning his gaze directly, "there was another woman, who he was either supporting, or keeping, or paying for her services. I would imagine there is now someone else, somewhere. Am I wrong, 'Uncle' Julian?"

It was Irene who spoke. "Be still."

"I am only giving you the truth."

The woman stood. "You have spoken enough."

"But it is *the truth!*" said Lucy. "And it will not go away, Irene, because you refuse to believe it. He is a whoremonger! A philanderer! An adulterer! He schemes behind your back! He degrades you! He despises you, Irene! Don't you realize that? That is what it means when a man does what he is doing to you!"

Ellie was holding the banister with her two hands, her hair half covering her face. Whatever she was sobbing, Lucy could not understand.

"I'm sorry, Eleanor. This is not my idea of how to behave either. But there is only so much bullying, so much filth and treachery and hatred I can willingly stand here and take. I did not come here, I assure you, for the purpose of attacking your father. What I said I said in self-defense. He is a heartless man—"

"But she knows," wept Ellie. "She knew, she always knew."

"Eleanor!" said Irene Sowerby.

"You know?" cried Lucy. "You mean," she said to Irene, "you *know* what he is—" She was incredulous. "All of you in this room *know* what he is and what he has done and still you were going to allow . . ." Momentarily she could not even speak. "I don't believe it," she said at last. "That you can be so utterly unscrupulous and deceitful, so thoroughly corrupt and—"

"Oh, Roy," said Ellie, turning to her cousin. "She's crazy." And she put her face into his chest and wept.

Roy was wearing a plaid robe of Julian's that was sizes too small for him. With one arm he began to pat Ellie's back.

"Oh," said Lucy, looking up at the two of them, "is that the story, Roy? Not that your uncle is crazy, not that your aunt is crazy—but that I am? And what else, Roy? I'm crazy, and what else? Oh, yes, Edward hates me. And what else? Surely there must be more? What other lies have you invented to justify what you have done to me?"

"But what has he done to you!" Ellie screamed. "You are crazy, you *are!* You're insane!"

She waited until Ellie had regained enough control over herself to listen. Irene Sowerby was now standing by her husband, preventing him from making any move toward Lucy; she had her face half hidden in his chest—in the chest of that man who cared nothing at all for her honor.

To Eleanor, Lucy said, "I am not Skippy Skelton,

Ellie, if that's what you mean. Nor am I you. Nor am I your mother, though probably that is clear by now."

"Nothing is clear! Nothing you *say* is clear!" cried Ellie, even as her mother raised a hand to tell her to be quiet.

But Ellie cried, "I want to know what she even means!"

Lucy said, "I mean, Eleanor, that I am not promiscuous—I don't run around with married men. I mean that I am not a vain and idiotic child. I don't spend half my waking hours, and probably more, thinking about my hair and my clothes and my shoes—"

"What are you?" wailed Ellie. "The Virgin Mary?"

Julian stepped forward, freeing himself from his wife, who had begun to cry now too. "Enough, Eleanor."

"Daddy," Ellie wept.

"Daddy," repeated Lucy. "Wonderful Daddy."

"You get on the phone, Lucy," said Julian, breathing thickly. "You call your grandfather. You tell him to get over here and take you home . . . Now either you do it, or I will."

"But my home happens not to be here, Julian. My home is in Fort Kean, with my husband and my child." She looked up toward her husband. "Roy, we are going home. I want you to get ready."

All that moved were his eyes; they darted from one to the other of the people in the living room.

"Roy, did you hear me? We're returning to our own home."

He remained motionless and silent.

"Of course," she said, "the choice is yours, Roy. You can either be a man about it, and return with me and Edward, or you can follow the advice of this most worthy—"

"Lucy!" Roy threw his hands over his head. "For God's sake, cut it out!"

"But I can't, Roy!" Cut it out, indeed! "Nor can you! Oh, you can cut out, all of you, the fact that this uncle, this Daddy, this husband here, happens to be a filthy beast. You can fool yourselves about this cheat, and tell yourselves I'm insane—oh, live with him, sleep with him, who cares! But cut it *out?* Oh, no, Roy—because there happens to be one more important fact to consider. I'll tell you why it so happens you can't take your uncle's advice, Roy—and I'll tell your uncle too. It so happens, Roy, and Julian, and Eleanor, and Irene, it so happens that I am pregnant."

"You are what?" whispered Julian.

Roy said, "Lucy . . . what do you mean?"

There was no need to raise her voice now to be heard. "I am going to have a baby."

Roy said, "I don't understand you."

"The daughter that you wanted, Roy, is alive inside me. Alive and growing."

Julian was saying, "What daughter? *Now* what in hell are you—?"

"Roy is going to be the father of a second child. It is our hope that it will be a girl."

Julian was looking up at Roy.

"Roy," she said, "go ahead. Tell them."

"Tell them *what?*"

"What you told me. Roy, tell them what you told me you wanted."

"Lucy," he answered, "I don't under*stand* you."

"Roy, are you actually now going to deny—"

"Pregnant?" said Julian. "Oh, not that old song and dance—"

"Ahh, but I *am,* Julian! I know you yourself happen not to like them, but facts are facts! I am pregnant with Roy Bassart's child. The child he wanted. The child he has been dreaming of all his life. Linda, Roy. Well, tell them!"

"Oh, no," Roy said.

"Roy, you *tell* them."

"But, Lucy—"

"Roy Bassart, that snowy night—did you or did you not—I can't believe you will actually lie about this now too! Did you or did you not get out of bed—? Did you or did you not tell me—? Linda, Roy—Linda Sue!"

"But, Lucy; oh my God—we were just talking."

"*Talking!*"

He sank onto a step at the top of the landing, his head cradled in his hands. "Yes," he moaned.

"Just *talking!* Roy, do you seriously mean—"

"Daddy," cried Eleanor, "*do* something!"

But Julian had already started after Lucy, who was advancing toward the stairs.

Swiftly she turned on him. "Don't you dare lay a finger on me. Not if you know what is good for you, you whoremonger."

"You get your ass down here," he said fiercely.

"I am a woman, Mr. Sowerby. You may think I'm a twerp like your daughter, but I am not! You will not treat me like nothing. No one will! I am pregnant, whether it suits you or not. I have a family to protect, whether that pleases you or not. Now, Roy," she said, turning once again and making for the stairs.

"Oh, no," said her husband, still with his head in his hands. "I can't take any more. I really can't."

"Oh, but you can, Roy. Because you have made me pregnant again, Roy!"

"Roy," called Julian as Lucy broke for upstairs, "stop her!"

"Roy," she cried, "we are getting Edward! We are going!"

He raised his face, which was wet with tears. "But he's *asleep.*"

"Roy—move—" Then Julian's hand fell upon her once again. She kicked backward—the hand grasped and caught her ankle. Meanwhile Roy's face was moving up—to block her way! Her husband, who should be protecting her! defending her! shielding her! guarding her! instead stood between herself and her child, herself and her home, between herself and the life of a woman!

"Get her!" said Julian. "*Roy!*"

"No!" cried Lucy, and with no choice left, brought her hand up from behind her, and closing her eyes, swung it with all her might.

And had the vision once again.

INNOCENT

When she opened her eyes, she saw Roy standing over her; he was holding his mouth. She herself was stretched across the stairway.

Then above her on the landing, in his undershorts and shirt, a blanket dragging in one hand, she saw little Edward looking down.

He began to shriek, either at the blood on his mother's hand or the blood on his father's face. Eleanor, who had been hovering over Lucy, swept up the stairs, lifted the screaming child and carried him away.

They could not get her to let go of the banister, so she remained across the stairs while Julian stood on the step below her, holding firmly to the back of her coat, and Irene telephoned to Daddy Will.

He came, and moved her down the stairway, and through the hall to the door. Every light was on in the Sowerby house when Willard backed the car out of the driveway and drove her home from The Grove.

Father Damrosch.

Where was a window? Where was a wall? She was under a blanket. She reached out into the dark. *I am only a freshman.*

She was in a bed. In her own bedroom. She was in Liberty Center.

How long had she been sleeping?

She had let him lead her up the stairs and cover her with a blanket ... She had been crying ... He had been sitting in the chair beside the bed ... And then she must have slept.

But every minute that passed was a minute lost to those who would destroy her. She must act!

Father Damrosch!

But what can he do? Father Damrosch, why can't you *do* something? She could see him—black hair that he combed with his fingers, and a great swinging jaw, and that long beautiful stride that even the Protestant girls swooned over when they spotted him in his collar rounding a corner downtown. "Father *Dam*rosch!" calls one of the girls who knows him. "Father *Dam*rosch!" He waves—"Hi"—and disappears, while they all fall moaning into one another's arms . . .

And there, bouncing, swaying, soaring from her seat, there is Lucy, off to her first retreat. And Father Damrosch, swaying too, over the enormous wheel of the bus. And the other girls, rising in their seats, then crashing down, and gazing off at the black and flashing woods like condemned prisoners being driven to the place of execution; as though shackled together, they hang together arm in arm. Someone in the back begins the singing—"Pack up your troubles in your old kit bag—" but only a voice or two joins in, and then there is just the racket again of the old parish bus. It leaps forward and lands hard, and with winter overhead, aching to move down, and the horizon pushing up a last crust of light, the mood is of a race against disaster. A bird shoots past the window, its underside illumined red; it is swinging away, behind her head, and as she twists in her seat to follow its flight, the words go plunging through her, the words of Saint Teresa: God! Lamb! Astray!

"Whoa!" bellows Father Damrosch, his Army boots pumping down on the brake pedal. "Whoa," and they swerve, so that legs spring up and skulls go rocking together. "Whoa there, Nelly," and the girls giggle.

Clinging tightly to the belt of Kitty's coat, she shuffles in her unclasped galoshes down the dark aisle of the bus. As though falling from a cliff, she drops through the open door onto the convent grounds, expecting to see fires burning.

She waits alone by the side of the bus, holding tight to Daddy Will's hunting satchel. She hears Kitty calling for her and ducks around to the back. No one can see her there. She bites into the cold dark air—to hear it snap like a hard apple, to take between her teeth a pure hard clear thing, to devour . . . Oh, she cannot wait for her first Communion! Only, she must not bite down. No, no, it will melt down into the grooves of her mouth, and stream into her body, His body, His blood . . . *and then something will happen.*

But suppose it was what secretly she prayed for? "No!" She stands alone behind the bus, her two watering eyes taking in the dark shapes, the looming figures—the priests, the nuns, the girls lining up and marching into the dark; the pickup trucks, the buses, the cars, flashing lights and rumbling away . . . She hears the tires crackling over the gravel—what would it sound like, bone beneath wheels? Inside, that is all they are, just skeletons; inside, all of them are the same. She has learned the names of every human bone in her biology class—the tibia, the scapula, the femur . . . Oh, why can't people be good? Inside, they are only bones and strings and blood, kidneys and brains and glands and teeth and arteries and veins. Why, why can't they just be good?

"Father Damrosch!"

"Who is it back there?"

". . . Lucy."

He makes his way along the side of the bus. "You all right? Lucy Nelson?"

"Yes."

"What's the trouble? You bus-sick, Lucy? You go up there and get your room. Well, what's the matter?"

Her hand reaches out and finds a motionless tire.

"Father Damrosch . . ." But can she tell him? She has not even told Kitty. She has not even told Saint Teresa. No one knows the horrible thing she really wants. "Father Damrosch . . ." She wedges her mitten down between the ridges of the tire, and into the side of her mackinaw hood, mumbles what she can no longer keep a secret— ". . . to kill my father."

"Speak up, Lucy, so I can hear you. *You* want to—"

"No! No! I want Jesus to! In a car crash! In a fall! When he's drunk and stinks and is drunk!" She is weeping. "Oh, Father Damrosch," she says, "I think I'm committing a terrible sin. I *know* I am, but I can't help it."

She presses her face against him. She feels him waiting. "Oh, Father, tell me, tell me, is it a sin? He's so bad. He's so wicked."

"Lucy, you know not of what spirit you are."

". . . No? Please, then, please—what spirit am I?"

Then she is with the sisters. Between the swishing cloaks she moves to the chapel. The candles waver all around—and above, the suffering Lord. O God! Lamb! Astray! O Jesus, who does not kill! Who comforts! Who saves! Who redeemeth us all! O Holy Glorious Gleaming Loving Healing Jesus who does not kill—*make my father a father!*

By Sunday night she is so run-down from praying that she hardly has the strength to speak. The other girls are jabbering on the side steps of St. Mary's, waiting to be picked up and taken home; in her pocket she clutches the black veil given her by Sister Angelica of the Passion. "Patience. Faith. Suffering. The little way, remember," said Sister Angelica. "I know, I will," said Lucy. "To destroy takes no patience," said Sister Angelica. "I know," said Lucy, "I know that." "Anybody can destroy. A hoodlum can destroy." "I know, I know." "To save—" "Yes, yes. Oh, thank you, Sister . . ."

"Hey, Lucy Nelson." Her father is waving at her from the car. All around her the other girls are running and shouting—horns are blowing, car doors opening and slamming shut. Everyone seems so proud! so happy! so alive! It is cold and black, clear and glittery, a Sunday night, and they are all stepping into warm cars to be driven to warm houses, to warm baths, to warm milk, to warm beds. "Please!" she prays. And so, with the others, like the others, she rushes to the door her father has pushed open.

Father Damrosch looks like something black burning as he stands directing traffic in the headlights of the cars. "Good night, Lucy."

"Yes, good night."

Her father tips his cap to the priest. Father Damrosch waves. "Hi, there. Good evening."

Lucy pulls shut the door. To Father Damrosch she calls out the window, "Bye," and out the drive they go.

"Welcome back to civilization," he says.

Let him be redeemed! Make him good! O Jesus, he is only someone gone astray! That's all!

"That's not funny," she says.

"Well, I just can't be funny right off the bat, you know." Silence. "How'd the revival meeting go?"

"Retreat."

They drive. "You didn't catch cold, I hope. You sound like you caught cold."

"They took very good care of us, Father. It's a convent. It's very beautiful, and they have plenty of heat, thank you."

But she does not want to fight. O Jesus, I don't want to be sarcastic ever again. *Help me!* "Daddy—Sunday, come with me."

"Come with you where, Goosie?"

"Please. You must. To Mass."

He cannot help himself; he smiles.

"Don't laugh at me," she cries. "It's serious."

"Well, Lucy, I am just an old-fashioned Lutheran—"

"But you don't *go*."

"Well, when I was a boy I did. When I was your age I surely did go."

"Daddy, you know not of what spirit you are!"

He takes his eyes from the road. "And who said that, Goosie? Your priest friend?"

"Jesus!"

"Well," he says, shrugging, "nobody knows everything, of course." But he is smiling again.

"But tomorrow—don't joke with me! Don't tease! Tomorrow you'll be sick again, you know you will."

"You let me worry about tomorrow."

"You'll be drunk again."

"Hold it now, young lady—"

"But you won't be saved! You will not be redeemed!"

"Now listen, you, you may be a big religious person over in that church, but to me, you know, you are who you are."

"You're a sinner!"

"Now *enough!*" he says. "You hear me? That is enough," and he pulls the car into the driveway. "And

I'll tell you something else too. If this is how you come home after going away on your so-called religious weekend, then maybe going away is something we are going to have to think twice about giving permission for, freedom of religion or not."

"But if you don't change, I swear to you, I'll become a nun."

"You will, will you?"

"Yes!"

"Well, one, I never heard of them having nuns who were only in their first year of high school——"

"When I'm eighteen I can do anything! And legally too!"

"When you are eighteen, my little friend, and if you still want to dress up like Halloween, and have a prune face, and be afraid of regular life, which is what a nun happens to be, in my estimation——"

"But you don't know! Sister Angelica is not afraid of regular life! None of the sisters are! I'll become a nun, and there is nothing you can do to stop me!"

He pulls the key from the ignition. "Well, they have sure wasted no time turning you into a real Catholic, I'll say that for them. You have got all the answers in about a month's time, don't you? You have got your own way of believing, and that's the only way anybody else in the world can believe. And that's your idea of religious freedom, that you said you were entitled to. Brother," he said, and opened the door.

"I'll become a nun. I swear it."

"Well, if you want to run away from life, you go right ahead."

She watches as he cuts across the lawn, and up the porch stairs. He pounds the snow from his boots, and enters the house.

"Jesus! Saint Teresa! Somebody!"

One month of winter passes; then another. She tells Father Damrosch everything. "The world is imperfect," he says. "But why?" "We cannot expect it to be other than it is." "But—why not?" "Because we are weak, we are corrupt. Because we are sinners. Evil is the nature of mankind." "Everyone? Every person in mankind?"

"Everyone does evil, yes." "But, Father Damrosch—you don't." "I sin. Of course I sin." What does he do? How can she ask? "But when will it stop being evil?" she asks; "when will the world be not evil?" "When Our Lord comes again." "But by then . . ." "What, Lucy?" "Well, I don't mean to sound selfish, Father . . . but not just me, but everybody alive now . . . well, they'll all be dead. Won't they?" "This is not our life, Lucy. This is the prelude to our life." "I know that, Father, it's not that I don't believe that . . ." But she cannot go on. She lives too much in the here and now. Sister Angelica is right. That is her sin.

Sunday after Sunday she stays with Kitty through Mass, twice. And prays: *Make him a father!* then home to see what has happened. But Sunday after Sunday there is waiting for her only leg of lamb, lima beans, baked potato, mint jelly, Parker House rolls, pie and milk. Nothing changes, nothing ever changes. When, *when* will it happen? And what will it look like? His Spirit will enter . . . But who? and how?

Then the Friday night. She is at the dining table with her homework; her mother is in the parlor, reading a magazine and soaking her feet; the door opens. He pulls at the shade and it slips down off its fixture. She jumps to her feet, but her mother sits without moving. And her father is saying such terrible, horrible things! What should she *do*? She lives too much in the here and the now as it is. This is only the prelude to our life. The nature of mankind is evil. Christ will come again, she thinks, as her father pulls the pan from beneath her mother's feet and pours the water out onto the rug. *The nature of mankind is evil. Christ will come again*— but she can't wait! In the meantime this man is ruining their life! In the meantime they are being destroyed! Oh, Jesus, come! Now! You must! Saint Teresa! Then she rushes to the phone. "I want the police. At my house." And within minutes they arrive. I want the police, she says, and they come. Wearing pistols, it turns out. She watches while they take him away to a place where he can no longer do them any harm.

As she dialed the Bassarts', Daddy Will stepped into the kitchen.

"Lucy," he said. "Honey, it is three-thirty in the morning. Why are you up? What are you doing?"

"Leave me alone."

"Lucy, you cannot telephone people—"

"I know what I am doing."

At the other end her father-in-law said, "Hello?"

"Lloyd, this is Lucy."

Willard sat down at the kitchen table. "Lucy," he pleaded.

"Lloyd, your son Roy has kidnaped Edward and abandoned me. He is hiding out at the Sowerbys'. He has refused to return to Fort Kean. He has put himself into the hands of Julian Sowerby, and something must be done to stop that man immediately. They have constructed a network of lies, and they are planning to go into a courtroom with it. They are planning to go to a judge and tell him that I am an incompetent mother and Roy is a wonderful father—and he is going to try to divorce me, your son, and get custody of my child. They have made all this perfectly clear, and they must be stopped before they take a single step. They have already begun to lie to Edward, that is perfectly clear—and unless someone intervenes over there, and instantly, they are going to brainwash and brainwash that little defenseless three-and-a-half-year-old child until they can get him, a baby, to go before a judge and say he hates his own mother. But you know, Lloyd, even if they don't—you know full well that if it weren't for me he would never have been allowed into this world in the first place. Everybody else would have scraped him down a sewer, or put him into an orphanage, or given him away, or left him to roam the world alone, I suppose, without a family, without a name, and now they are going to try to establish in the courtroom that my own child would rather live with his father than with me, and that is absurd and ridiculous, and it can't be, and it isn't true, and you must step into this, Lloyd, and immediately. You are Roy's father—"

Daddy Will's hand was on her back. "Leave me alone!" she said. *"Lloyd?"*

He had hung up.

"Please," she said to her grandfather, *"please do not interfere.* You are not capable of understanding what is going on. You are an impotent and helpless man. You always were and you still are, and if it weren't for you, none of this might have begun in the first place. So please, leave this to *me!"*

She was dialing the Bassarts' once again as her grandmother came to the kitchen door. "What is that child doing, Willard? It is the middle of the night."

He looked at her, unable to speak.

"Lloyd," said Lucy into the phone, "this is Lucy again. We were cut off."

"Look," said her father-in-law, "go to sleep."

"Didn't you hear a word of what I have been telling you?"

"I heard it, Lucy. You better go to sleep."

"Don't tell me to go to sleep, Lloyd! Sleep is not the issue at a time like this! Tell me what you intend to do about your son, and your brother-in-law Julian, and their plan!"

"I am telling you nothing," Lloyd Bassart said. "I believe it is you who is going to have to do the telling, Lucy. I am not very happy about what I have heard, Lucy. Not one bit," he said ominously.

"Tell what? Tell who? I am pregnant! Do you know that? That's what I have to tell—I am pregnant!"

"I am afraid I am not going to choose to talk to you any longer in this condition."

"But have you heard what I just said? My condition is that I am pregnant with a second child!"

"As I said, I have heard an earful. I have heard plenty."

"Lies! If it's from them it is lies! I am speaking the truth, Lloyd, the only truth. I am pregnant! He cannot leave me at a time like this!"

"Good night, Lucy."

"Lloyd, you can't hang up! You're supposed to be so good, so honest—so respectable! You better not hang up

on me! Lloyd, four years ago—it is exactly what he
wanted to do then. I was eighteen years old, and he
wanted to run then too. Exactly what you would not let
him do *yourself*. Lloyd, it is the same thing—exactly
the same as then!"

"Oh, is it?" he said.

"Yes!"

"Yes is right!" It was Alice Bassart.

"Alice, get off," said Lloyd.

"You cheat, you no-good cheat—you tricked our
son! And now again!"

"Alice, I will take care of this."

"I tricked *him?*" said Lucy.

"Took our son, with a scheming trick! Miss Tom-
boy! Miss Sarcastic! Miss Sneerface!"

"Alice!"

"But he tricked *me,* Alice! Tricked me to think he
was a man, when he's a mouse, a monster! A moron!
He's a pansy, that's what your son is, the worst and
weakest pansy there ever was!"

"Willard!" said Berta.

Daddy Will was standing over the phone, right behind her. "Don't you—" she said, over her shoulder,
"—dare—"

But he brought his hand down upon the phone and
held it there, breaking the connection.

"What do you think you are doing?" she cried. "The
world is caving in! The world is on fire!"

"Honey, Lucy, it is four A.M."

"But haven't you heard a word I've said? Don't you
hear what they are trying to do to me? Don't you
understand what all these good, respectable people really
are? I am pregnant! Does that mean nothing to anyone?
*I am pregnant and my husband refuses to be responsi-
ble!*"

"Lucy," he said softly, "in the morning, honey, if
that is really so—"

"I am not waiting for any morning. By morning—"
She tried to yank the phone from his hands.

"No, honey, no. That's got to be enough right
now."

"But the lies are growing *every minute!* They are saying I tricked him into marrying me. When *he* seduced *me!* He made me do it in the back of that car, insisted and insisted and insisted, and wouldn't stop, ever, and finally against my will, to show him—to let him—I was seventeen years old—and now they're saying *I* tricked *him!* As though I wanted him. Wanted a *him* like that, ever! I wish he were dead, that's what I wish. I wish he had never been born." She glared at Willard. "Give me that phone."

"No."

"If you do not give me that phone, Daddy Will, then I shall have to take measures of my own. Either you give me that phone and let me call his father ... because I want to tell that Lloyd Bassart that he is not going to be such a pillar in the community, if he doesn't stop this thing, and stop it now. Either you give me that phone—"

"No, Lucy."

"But *he* seduced *me!* Don't you see that? And now they are saying that I seduced him! Because there is nothing they won't say against me. Nothing they won't stoop to, to destroy me. Julian Sowerby will stop at nothing—don't you understand? He hates women! He hates me! He's trying to crush my life because I know the truth! And I will not let that happen!"

"Call the doctor, Willard. Dial the doctor," Berta said.

"Call a *what?*" cried Lucy.

"Berta, in the morning."

"Willard, now."

"Oh yes, oh sure," said Lucy to her grandmother. "Oh, wouldn't you like that? You've been waiting all these years to do me in—because I see through you too, you—you selfish-hearted bitch. Call a *doctor?*" She shook her fists at the two of them. *"I am pregnant!* I need a husband, not a doctor—a husband for myself and a father for my child—"

"Dial the doctor," said Berta.

But he continued to hold the phone. "Lucy," he said, "won't you just go to bed now?"

"But can you not get it into your *head*—Julian Sowerby is stealing Edward! A man who is a whoremonger! And they all know it. And they don't care! He buys women with money, and nobody cares! Do you understand what I am *saying* to you?"

"Yes, honey."

"Then what are you going to do about it? The world is full of fiends and monsters, and you do absolutely nothing, and you never did! You listen to *her*," she said, pointing to her grandmother. "But I don't! And I won't!"

She started from the kitchen, but Berta stood in the doorway.

"Let me through, please."

Her grandmother said, "Where are you going?"

"To the police station."

"No," said Daddy Will. "No, Lucy."

"Let me by, Grandmother dear. Daddy Will, tell her to let me by, if you have any power over your own wife. I am going upstairs to get my coat and my shoes, and then I am going to the police station. Because they are not getting away with this, none of them. And if they have to come and arrest them all, Roy and Julian and that famous good man, Lloyd Bassart, then that is what they will have to do. Because you cannot steal a child! You cannot ruin a life! You cannot walk out on a marriage and a family! Let me through, please, Grandmother, I am going upstairs for my coat."

"Berta," said Daddy Will, "let her go."

"And if you call a doctor once I turn my back, Daddy Will, then you are as bad as they are. I want you to know that."

"Let her go, Berta."

"Willard—"

"I'll call," he said, nodding.

"Well," said Lucy, "the truth will out, won't it, Daddy Will? I always held out some hope for you, if you care to know. But I was sadly mistaken. Too bad," she said as she stepped through the doorway and proceeded up the stairs. The door to her mother's room was closed; she must be awake in there, but as always, too timid and frightened to confront what was happening in her own family.

When she was dressed for the outdoors she came into the hall, and before heading down the stairs and off to the police station, she stopped at her mother's door. Should she leave this instant and let the words spoken by her mother that afternoon be the last ever to pass between them? Because once Edward had been returned and disaster averted, she would never again set foot in this house.

In the parlor below she could hear her grandparents talking, but what they were saying she could not make out. Did it matter? It was clear enough which side they had chosen. She had wept the whole story to Daddy Will as he drove her through the dark town to the house—and he had comforted her. In her exhaustion he had helped her onto her bed, covered her to the chin with a blanket, told her she must rest now, told her that in the morning he would take care of everything—and like one who did not understand what she had understood so long ago, like a fool, like an innocent, she had let his words and her despair drag her down into dreams of another world, another here, another now, dreams of sweet Jesus and Father Damrosch and Sister Angelica of the Passion. And now she had wakened to discover that he too had turned against her.

Oh, how absurd this all was! How unnecessary! Why must they force her always to the extreme? Why must they bring this down upon themselves when the simple and honorable solution was always and forever at hand? If only they did their duty! If only they would be men!

A doctor. That was who they were waiting for down in the parlor. Dr. Eglund! To give her a pill to make life rosy by morning! To give her a good old-fashioned talking-to! Or was Dr. Eglund a blind? At long last was she to be the benefactor of an abortion designed to get everybody else off the hook? Yes, anything, *anything*, no matter how it might debase and mortify her—so long as it spared all those respectable people from personal burden and public shame. Oh, but shame was surely going to fall upon them all, once it became known that she had had to be driven up to The Grove in a squad car, in order to recover what they would steal, and shatter, and destroy.

For that was the choice they had left her. Surely she was not going to return alone to Fort Kean, and leave Edward behind to be assaulted with lies, to be readied by her enemies and his to be a witness against his own mother. She was certainly not going to oblige them by being idiot enough to step into a court of law with Mr. Sowerby and his lawyer, either—to oppose her pennies to Julian's millions, oppose her scruples to the unprincipled techniques of his attorney, as they pressed their case from one court to another, and the costs mounted, and the lies were piled one atop the other. Oh, just imagine them telling the court how she—a seventeen-year-old high school girl, hopelessly innocent of all sexual experience—had seduced and deceived into marriage a man who happened to have been three years her senior and a veteran of the United States Army. Oh no, she was not about to wait patiently for that—or to wait for Ellie Sowerby, that noted authority on mental illness, to break into tears and testify in a courtroom that in her professional opinion Lucy Bassart was insane, and always had been. Nor did she intend to be a silent witness to that pathetic moment when her own grandfather was called to the stand, and proceeded to tell the judge how he himself figured that maybe the best thing for Lucy was a heart-to-heart chat with the family doctor . . . No, she did not intend to be frightened of what they themselves had given her no choice now but to do to save the lives of herself, and her children, born and unborn.

She opened her mother's door. It was almost dawn.

"I am going now, Mother."

The form beneath the blanket did not move. Her mother lay huddled on the half of the bed nearest the window, her face hidden behind one hand. Lucy pulled on her gloves. On the back of her left hand there was a scratch, where Roy's tooth had dragged over her flesh.

"I know you're awake, Mother. I know you heard what was going on downstairs."

She remained motionless under the blanket.

"I came in here to say something to you, Mother. I'm going to speak whether you respond or not. It would be easier if you could bring yourself to sit up and face me. It would certainly be more dignified, Mother."

But there was no dignity; that was her mother's decision, again and again and again. She only turned her face into the pillow, showing her daughter the back of her head.

"Mother, what I heard earlier in the day—yesterday, it was—about my father—I allowed it to upset me. That's what I want to tell you. After we left here I thought about what you had said to me. You said, if you remember, Mother, that he was where I always wanted him. You said you hoped that I was happy now. And so I went back to Fort Kean, thinking, 'Oh, what a terrible person I am.' I began to think, if it weren't for me, he could have been spared whatever he is now going through. I thought, 'He has stayed away almost four years now—and why? He has been afraid even to show his face here. He has had to write to her through a post-office box—all because of me.' Then I tried to tell myself, no, no, I wasn't the reason ... But do you know something, Mother? I am! Because of his fear of me he is not here—that's true. Because he is terrified of my judgment. And do you know? That is the only human response that man has ever had, Mother. Staying away—that is the only thing he has been able to do successfully in his entire life."

She heard her mother weeping. All at once the sunlight came into the room, and she saw a letter on the blanket. It was cradled in a fold where it must have fallen from her mother's hand. She had taken it with her into her bed. *My God, there is no limit, there is no end.*

As she charged toward the bed, her mother turned to

see what was about to happen. And the fright in the woman's eyes, the grief in her face—oh, her utter hopelessness! "Mother, *he* is who destroyed our lives." She grabbed the letter from the bed. *"Him!"* she cried, shaking it over her head. *"This!"*

And then she ran. For Daddy Will burst into the doorway of the bedroom, dressed now in trousers and a shirt.

"Lucy—" He caught her by the coat, and she heard a tearing sound as she broke away from him and ran wildly down the stairs. Now Grandma Berta was moving toward her through the parlor, but she screamed, "No! You selfish, selfish—" and when her grandmother jumped back, she was able to fling open the door and rush out onto the porch.

"You stop," Berta called. "Stop her!"

But there was no one on the street, no one between herself and downtown.

Then her legs were shooting out from under her. Her elbows struck the icy ground a second before her chin; a sick sensation went through her, but she was instantly to her feet and across the street, heading toward Broadway. There was an inch of fresh snow over the cleared walks, and patches of ice underfoot, and she knew that if she fell again she would be overtaken, but she ran as fast as she was able to in coat and galoshes, for she had to get to the police station before they could stop her. Daddy Will was already out on the porch; she saw him there in the moment she took to look back. Then a car was pulling up before the house, and Daddy Will was headed down the stairs in his shirtsleeves. Dr. Eglund! They were going to come after her in the car! The car would be alongside her in seconds! Then people would be at their windows, doors would fly open, others would come running out of their houses to give aid to the two old men—to prevent her from ever getting justice done!

Quickly she turned up a driveway, slid between a car and a house, and plunged across the thick white crust of someone's yard. A dog barked, and she went sprawling, her foot caught upon a low wire fence buried in a drift. Then she was up, running again. There was a bluish light over everything, and the only noise was the packing sound that rose as her galoshes hammered into the snow and she ran, ran for the ravine.

But they would be waiting when she arrived! Once they had lost sight of her, they would go directly to the station house. Two old men, thoroughly confused about what actually was going on, without the slightest sense of all that was at stake, would tell the police that she was on her way. And what would the police do? Telephone Roy! By the time she had made her way across town to the ravine, and then up to Broadway by way of the river, her husband would be at the station house, waiting. And Julian! And Lloyd Bassart! And she would arrive last, her coat thick with snow, her face red and wet, breathless and exhausted, looking like some runaway child—*which was how she would be treated.* Of course! They would have so distorted the facts that instead of the police instantly coming to her aid, they would turn her over to her grandfather, to the doctor . . .

But would those others settle for that now? A man like Julian Sowerby knew only one thing—to have his ugly way. His own wife knew, his daughter knew, what he was *everybody* knew, but as long as he continued to pay everybody off, what did they care? She could hear him, hear them all, promising this, promising that, begging forgiveness, and then going right on being just what they always had been. Because they simply will not reform! They simply will not change! All they will do is get worse and worse! Why were they against a mother and a child? Why were they against a family, and a home, and love? Why were they against a beautiful life, and for an ugly one? Why did they fight her and mistreat her and deny her, when all she wanted was what was right!

But where to now? Because she knew what it would mean to continue on to the police station, she knew what Julian Sowerby would try to do; she knew the use to which such a man would put this opportunity, how he would seize it to destroy her, once and for all. Yes, because she knew right from wrong, because she saw her duty and did it, because she knew the truth and spoke it, because she would not sit by and endure treachery and betrayal, because she would not let them steal her little boy, and coddle a grown-up man, and scrape out of her body the new life beginning to grow there—they would try to make it seem that *she* was the guilty party, that *she* was the criminal!

. . . Where then? To turn back made no sense at all; there was no *back*. But to run straight into the arms of her enemies—straight into their lies and treachery! She turned and rushed back up the driveway from which she had emerged; she turned this way, the other way, toward Broadway, away from Broadway, and back out to the street again. She scuttled around corners; she withdrew against walls; she stepped deep into drifts. Powder came down into her face. She pressed her head to a drainpipe encased in ice. She fell. Her skin burned. A window flew up; she ran. The blue light became gray. She began to come upon the footprints she had left in the snow minutes earlier.

Then she was looking up into the kitchen window at the rear of Blanshard Muller's house. With one shoulder she pushed open the garage door, slipped inside and closed the door behind her. Gripping her side, she leaned across the trunk of the car, lowered her head and closed her eyes. Colors swam. She tried not to think. *Why should he hate me like poison? He doesn't! He can't! That's Roy's lie!*

With tremulous breaths she filled her lungs, and the sensation that all sound was being pushed outward from the inside of her head diminished. She began to be swept with chills, then grew strangely calm at the sight of the objects arranged against the side wall of the garage: a coil of garden hose, a shovel, half a bag of cement, a deflated tire tube, a pair of hip boots.

She tried the door of the car. If she could just have a moment to rest, to think; no, not to think . . .

The noise was sharp and clattering. She jumped around; there was nothing. Through the garage window she could see into the kitchen; she was able to discern on the walls the cabinets her mother had chosen for Mr. Muller. Again she heard a crash, and this time saw the ice sliding down off the roof into the yard. She stepped into the car.

And now what? Morning had come ... If a light went on in the kitchen, how quickly could she be out of the garage? Suppose he had seen her already and was sneaking around by way of the front door? How could she explain herself? What story would he believe? What would she be able to tell him, other than the truth?

And then? She would tell him everything, what they had already done, what they planned to do; and then? He would push open the garage door, back the car out the driveway, he would take her to The Grove himself. He would ring the Sowerby bell and wait beside her on the front porch, and then he would make it clear to Irene Sowerby why he and Lucy were there ... But if he were to come upon her unexpectedly, discover her kneeling, hiding, in the back seat of his car—he would jump to the conclusion that she was in the wrong! She must go immediately around to the back door then— no, the front door—and ring, say that she was sorry to be bothering him so early in the morning, that she understood this was totally out of the ordinary, but that she was in desperate need of ... But would he even believe her? It was so monstrous, what they were doing, would he even believe that it could be? Might he not listen, thinking to himself all the while, "Of course, that's only her side of the story." Or suppose he listened, and then telephoned her mother to check on the story. What was Lucy Bassart to him, anyway? Nothing! Her mother and her father had seen to that. "Sorry," he would say, "but don't see that it's my affair." Of course! Why would he come to her aid, when even those closest to her had turned against her? No, there was only one person she would rely upon; it was now as it had always been—the one to save her was herself.

She must hide; she must find some hideaway nearby, and then when the moment was right, she would swoop down, make off with Edward, and the two of them would disappear.

To *where?* Oh, to some place where they would never be found! Some place where she would have her second child, and where the three of them could begin a new life. And then never again would she be so foolish and gullible and dreamy as to place the welfare of herself or of her offspring in any hands but her own. She would be mother and father to them both, and so the three of them—herself, her little boy, and soon her little girl too—would live without cruelty, without treachery, without betrayal; yes, without men.

But if Edward would not come? If she called and he ran the other way? "*Your face is all black! Go away!*"

In her glove she was still carrying the letter she had taken from her mother's bed. She had sunk to her waist in drifts of snow; she had tripped and fallen over backyard fences; she had pushed open the door of the garage, climbed into the back seat of the car—and still the letter addressed to her mother was clutched in her glove.

She should be on her way now. The moment was right. By now they were all at the police station. Soon they would disperse and begin the search. There was not a second to waste, not on something so ridiculous as a letter from him. She had barely permitted him to enter her thoughts since the day of Edward's birth; she had driven him from their lives, then from her mind. There was clearly nothing to do with this letter but destroy it. And how appropriate that would be. To burn this letter, to scatter the ashes to the wind—that would be a most fitting ceremony indeed. Yes, goodbye, goodbye, brave and stalwart men. Goodbye, protectors and defenders, heroes and saviors. You are no longer needed, you are no longer wanted—alas, you have been revealed for what you are. Farewell, farewell, philanderers and frauds, cowards and weaklings, cheaters and liars. Fathers and husbands, farewell!

The letter consisted of one long sheet of writing paper. There were spaces to be filled out at the top, and then his message below. The page was closely covered with writing on both sides, and lined in blue, so that the prisoner's handwriting ran evenly from one end to the other.

She forced it back into its envelope. At any minute Blanshard Muller would be out of bed, down the stairs, out of the house—she would be discovered! And turned over to them—her enemies! So go!

But where? To a place where no one will think to look . . . to some place close enough for her to descend quickly upon the Sowerby house . . . in the afternoon, when he is at play in the yard . . . no, at night, when they are asleep . . . yes, in the night, while he sleeps too, bundle him off—*"Your face is poison! Your face is black! Put me down!"*

No! No! She must not weaken now. She must not weaken before their filthy lies. Whatever strength was required, she must find. Whatever daring, whatever boldness . . .

She removed the letter from the envelope once again. She would read it, and destroy it—and then be off. Of course, she would read what he had written, and in his words find that which would harden her against the trials to come . . . the lying in wait . . . the kidnap . . . the flight . . . Oh, she did not know *what* was to come, but she must not be afraid! Against the cold and the dark, in her solitude, while she waited to free her child from his captors—*"Mamma, where have you been?"*—while she waited to rescue him—*"Oh, Mamma, take me away!"*—to flee with him to a better world, to a better life, all she would have to sustain her would be the power of her hatred, her loathing, her abhorrence of those monsters who so cruelly destroy the lives of innocent women and innocent children. Oh yes, read then, and remember the horror inflicted upon you and yours, the cruelty and the meanness inflicted willingly and without end. Yes, read what he has written, and in the face of hardship you will have the courage. Whatever the wretchedness, the desolation, you will be implacable. Because you must be! Because there is only you to

save your son from just such men as this—to save your
helpless, innocent daughter-to-be. Oh, yes, draw them
down, these words of his, inscribe them on your heart,
and then fearlessly set forth. Fearlessly, Lucy! Against
all odds, but fearlessly nonetheless! For they are wrong,
and you are right, and there is no choice: the good must
triumph in the end! The good and the just and the true
must—

NAME: D. Nelson   NO: 70561   DATE: Feb. 14.
TO WHOM: Mrs. Myra Nelson (WIFE)

Dearest Myra:

I guess I read your letter over about twenty times.
There is no question about all the things you say. I was
all that and probably more. As I've said before, I am so
sorry and will be as long as I live that I have caused you
so much embarrassment and pain. But now there is no
doubt you are really forever free of trouble from me again.
I presume the State of Florida will see to that. For me, it
doesn't matter. All my life has been a more or less rough
deal. No plans, no matter how good they were, ever seemed
to work out. But it shouldn't be arranged to hurt the one
who is closer to you than anything in the world. That is
what is wrong.

One thing I feel better about is that you say there is no
one else. That was more than I could stand to hear. I just
couldn't stand to hear it. Remember just one thing, that I
had nineteen years of happiness. That the only fly in the
ointment was the inability to give you the things I wanted
you to have. Maybe when I get out, if I last, I will be
able to be some help to you financially, even if from a
distance, if that's the way you still want it. But you must
have a sponsor and a job to get out of here on your
minimum and though I shouldn't be bothering you I
wonder if you can think of anyone at all.

Of course it will depend upon how vindictive the "al-
leged Justice" is inclined to be anyway. There is a point
where punishment becomes corrective. Beyond that, it
becomes destructive. I've seen cases just since I have been
here where Justice depended upon how you spelled it.
Whether as Webster spelled and defined it or by spelling it
with either a dollar sign or influence. Many times already
I have seen cases where Justice was not "served" but
purchased. I see how fellows become hard and bitter who
there was a chance of helping.

But I will not dwell on these issues. Especially not today.
Myra, Myra, the growing years seem to make the mem-

ories of the past more and more poignant. I miss you so much that it is worse than hunger. I said years ago that without you I would slide to hell in a hurry. I guess it was a prediction that came all too true. There are some names I could mention who I could have lived without all right, but Myra, Myra, Myra, never you.

O Myra, I had always hoped by this time in my life I could express this wish to you much more materially, but if you can forgive me, this will have to do until the State of Florida decrees otherwise:

As years go by—with accelerated speed,
We find with us, an ever growing need
To recall to mind, and a wish to live,
In that glorious past—to re-have and re-give.

We bring to mind—the mistakes we made,
The aches and hurts—that we've caused, I'm afraid
Are brought in distinctly—with increasing pain
Till we wish, with all heart—to re-do it again.

Only to do it better—so that the pain is gone,
And make them all the good things, all along.
At least the great wish that would be really mine,
That I could just once more—be your Valentine.

Your Faithful,
Duane

On the third night after Lucy's disappearance two kids from the high school drove out to Passion Paradise to be alone. Near midnight, at which hour the girl had to be home, they tried to start back to town and found that the tires of the car had sunk into the snow. At first the boy pushed from behind while his companion sat at the wheel pumping on the accelerator. Then he took a shovel from the trunk, and in the dark, while the girl held her gloves against her ears and begged him to hurry, he started to dig his way out.

In this way the body was found. It was fully clothed; in fact, the undergarments were frozen to the skin. Also, a sheet of lined paper was frozen to her cheek, and her hand was frozen to the paper. An early hypothesis, that the hand might have been raised to ward off a blow, was rejected when the coroner reported that aside from a small abrasion on the knuckle of the right hand, the body bore no wounds, bruises, or punctures, no marks of violence at all. Nor was there any indication that she had been sexually molested. Of pregnancy nothing was said, either because the medical examiner found no evidence, or because the investigation included only routine laboratory tests. The cause of death was exposure.

As to how long she had been lying there undiscovered, the medical examiner could only guess: the freezing temperatures had preserved the body intact, but judging from the depths of snow above and below the body, it was surmised that the young woman had probably been dead about thirty-six hours when she was found. If that was so, she had managed to survive up in Passion Paradise through a day and a night and on, somehow, into the following morning.

It was some months after the funeral, during one of those cold, fresh, wet springs such as they have in the middle of America, that the letters from the prison began to come directly to the house.

Another Important Book By
Philip Roth
Author of PORTNOY'S COMPLAINT

LETTING GO

Philip Roth really lets himself go in this wry, sad, and somehow amusing first novel—a remarkable performance that shows his enormous energy, his wide range of characterization, and his gift for totally engaging the reader.

He has brought his wit and insight to bear on a contemporary scene of love and responsibility. This is the story of a young teacher's ill-fated love for a lusty woman. The fabric of the novel is hilarious, compassionate, even wicked.

"The sharply observant qualities of his first book GOOD-BYE, COLUMBUS have been expanded and enriched; he has become more probing, tentative, complex . . ." Comments **Atlantic**.

A Bantam Book / Available Where Paperbacks Are Sold.

PR2-2/70